The Fury

APPLAUSE FOR
THE FURY

"Tension and turmoil add up to high-stakes suspense as the characters are skillfully played across a global chessboard. Written like a born bard of old, you won't be disappointed. But be warned, treachery comes from all directions, even those that cannot be seen."
—Bestselling author STEVE BERRY

"*The Fury* is one of the most remarkable thrillers I've read in a long time. Shane Gericke's twenty-five years in the newspaper world make every scene resonate with a you-are-there authenticity, as if I'm reading fact, not fiction. His characters feel remarkably real also: vivid, likeable, and compelling. I want to spend more and more time with them. Every scene has an intensity that made me turn the pages faster. The action is state-of-the art. Pay attention—this one's a winner."
—Bestselling author DAVID MORRELL, creator of *Rambo*

"A fireball of awesome!" —Bestselling author JOSHUA CORIN

PREVIOUS NOVELS BY SHANE GERICKE

Blown Away

Cut to the Bone

Torn Apart

THREE CHEERS FOR
TORN APART

"This is an A-grade thriller." —Bestselling author LEE CHILD

"A high-rev, page-turning thriller that offers a searing look at the very thin blue line separating good and evil. Set in a sharply observed Midwest, *Torn Apart* features one of the best heroines to come along in years, whose dedication to her job throws her into a deadly cat-and-mouse game against complex, fleshed-out villains, some driven by good, some by evil, but all intent on leaving plenty of carnage in their wake."
—Bestselling author JEFFERY DEAVER

"Beautifully drawn characters, sharply observed detail, and exceptional writing. Has the impact of a large-caliber handgun fired at point-blank range."
—Bestselling author DOUGLAS PRESTON

"*Torn Apart* will keep you turning the pages so fast, you won't even notice that half the night's already gone. Shane Gericke knows how to tighten the screws and keep the fear and tension building."
—Bestselling author TESS GERRITSEN

"One of those scary rides through criminality that can melt away a fifteen-hour flight. The scenarios (trust me on this!) will haunt you for weeks."
—Bestselling author JOHN J. NANCE

"A no-nonsense thriller, action-packed and explosive. A real page-turner!"
—Bestselling author ERICA SPINDLER

continued...

"A roller coaster ride of a suspense thriller, and not for the faint of heart. There is a dark underlying humor in the book, and of course, plenty of bloody mayhem. The characters are well defined, the dialogue is dead-on realistic, and the action is nonstop. The intertwining of subplots is expertly orchestrated, and the action scenes are so well-choreographed that you're right there in the middle of the violence, dodging bullets and body parts." —*Suspense Magazine*

KUDOS FOR
CUT TO THE BONE

"Shane Gericke is the real deal." —Bestselling author LEE CHILD

"Crackles from the opening page!" —Bestselling author ZOE SHARP

"Cross James Patterson with Joseph Wambaugh and you get Shane Gericke." —ROY HUNTINGTON, *American Cop* magazine

"Gericke's writing is a blistering rush of sheer artistry."
—Award-winning author KEN BRUEN

"A deadly game of cat and mouse." —Bestselling author ALEX KAVA

"CSI meets Law & Order!"
—Bestselling author KATHLEEN ANTRIM

"In a word: Wow!" —Bestselling author JULIE HYZY

RAVES FOR
BLOWN AWAY

"Shane Gericke writes with the clear eye of a hard-nosed reporter and the sweet soul of an artist. His power is visceral and unforgettable."
—Bestselling author GAYLE LYNDS

"A rambunctious, devious novel full of chutzpah, high energy, and surprises. Forget roller-coaster; this one reads like a rocket."
—Bestselling author JOHN LUTZ

"A first-rate cops-and-psychos novelist. . . . His plucky heroine evokes the spirit of Thomas Harris's Clarice Starling." —*Publishers Weekly*

"A shotgun start, an Indy 500 wild ride, and an explosive finish."
—*RT Book Reviews*

"Gericke is an expert in providing suspense with horror, surpassing that of a Stephen King or Dean Koontz." —*Who Dunnit Mystery Reviews*

THE FURY

A THRILLER

SHANE GERICKE

Tantor
media

This is the work of fiction. All characters, organizations, and events portrayed in this novel are either products of the author's imagination or used fictitiously.

Tantor Media, Inc.
6 Business Park Road
Old Saybrook, CT 06475

tantor.com
tantorpublishing.com

The Fury

Copyright © 2014 Shane Gericke
Author photo © Abbey Miller
Design and Illustrations by Jessica Daigle

All rights reserved. No part of this book may be used or reproduced in any manner without written permission except in the case of brief quotations for reviews or critical articles.

ISBN: 9781630150037
Printed in the United States of America
First Tantor Media Printing, September 4, 2015

To Jerrle, forever walking on sunshine.

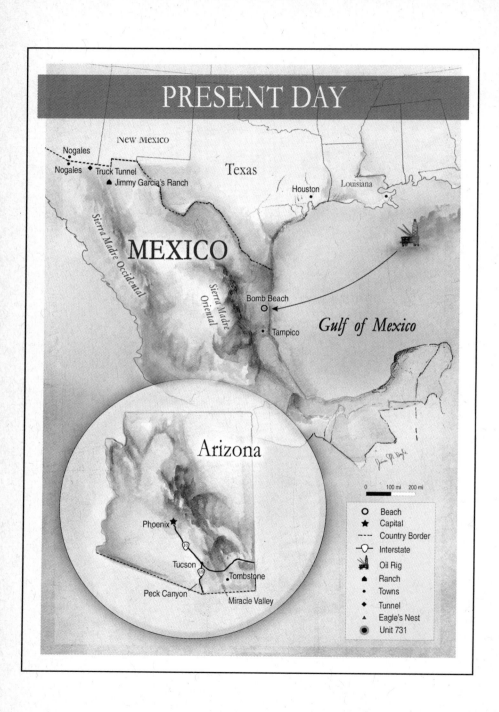

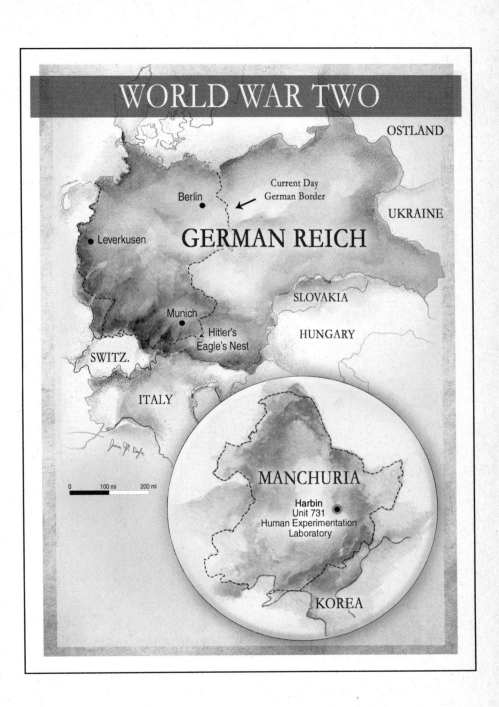

fu•ry

[fyoo•ree] Noun, plural furies. 1. Unrestrained or violent anger, rage, passion, or the like: The gods unleashed their fury on the offending mortal. 2. Violence; vehemence; fierceness: the fury of a hurricane; a fury of creative energy. 3. The Furies. [Greek and Roman mythology.] A spirit of punishment, often represented as one of the three goddesses—Alecto, Megaera, and Tisiphone—who executed the curses pronounced upon criminals, tortured the guilty with stings of conscience, and inflicted famines and pestilences. 4. A fierce and violent person, especially a woman: She became a fury when she felt she was unjustly accused.

Five Years Earlier

ABOARD THE *DEEPWATER HORIZON*
GULF OF MEXICO
APRIL 10, 9:44 P.M.

The rig began trembling like caffeine withdrawal.

Kemper, panicked, spun to warn his crewmates but saw them stampeding for the lifeboats, having felt the deadly vibrations too. Relief washed his sunburned body, and he broke into a run. Then remembered his best friend was perched in the superstructure, fixing antennas.

"Blowout!" he screamed at the blue-black sky. "Blowout! Hit the line, Pie!"

Pieton jerked around, wild-eyed at the dooming word. He leapt for the "Geronimo line," the emergency escape cable, that would zip-line him to the sleek orange lifeboats squatting in their launchers, ready to spit desperate men into the sea.

Instead, he caught the leading edge of the shock wave as the first cloud of methane gas exploded, turning a hundred million pounds of oil rig into a fiery chainsaw of shrapnel.

"Help me!" Pieton's head bleated as his body detached from his neck.

Kemper froze as rivets, brains, and elbows rained down on the drilling deck, which the BP recruiter had bragged was bigger than an NFL football field. The superheated deck made his boot soles smoke, jerking him back into action. He picked up a wailing, blinded toolpusher and staggered toward the nearest lifeboat, the abandon-ship Klaxon driving needles through his ears.

"Thirty . . . feet . . . to go," Kemper wheezed, coughing lung and burnt petroleum onto the blind man's face. The man writhed frantically. Kemper gripped tighter, shoved one boot forward and then the next, slipping on flesh and seaweed. "Down to twenty . . . now ten . . . and guess what, man, there's plenty of seats!" He cackled like a lifer set free. "We made it! We're gonna sail off this hell-beast as soon as I pull the ripcord—"

He was knocked off his feet as methane and crude oil roared out of the well-hole in the bottom of the Gulf, past the ruined blowout preventers, up a vertical mile of pipe, and into the oceangoing behemoth, belching like too much Schlitz, catching a spark and going supernova, the fireball disemboweling riggers, roasting crane operators, gobbling wrenches and life rings and blueprints and overalls and cell phones and gimme-hats, Cat and Bud and Deere. The blind man exploded into pink confetti, I-beams flew like drinking-straw wrappers. Fuel barrels lit off, bashing the superstructure like cannonballs. "Oof!" Kemper blatted as Pie's scorched torso pile-drove him into the deck. He faded to black.

Came back.

He blinked a dozen times at the stadium roar in his ears, then frantically patted himself tip to toe. Nothing broken, no parts missing. His survival was a miracle, plain and simple . . .

At once remembered where he was.

Kemper struggled to his feet, reeling like he'd mainlined a quart of Scotch. He watched Pie's head skitter along the deck and drop off the edge. He cried out as a flying snake of drilling chain wrapped him like a straitjacket, fracturing his jaw with the slam of its hot, whippy tail.

He staggered to the edge of the quaking rig, spitting broken teeth, the night sky boiled yellow and sulfurous from oil- and gas-fed flames. He peered over the edge and considered the astronomic odds of surviving the seven-story leap to the foaming green seas. He shook his head and backed away, thinking maybe there was just enough time to find another lifeboat . . .

The curly black hairs on his neck ignited, and he knew he was out of options.

He whimpered, afraid, then snugged up his charred Levis and faced the water. He stared at the half-moon brightening the waves that pounded the Godzilla legs of the platform. He prayed he'd see his children again. He pinched his nose and closed his eyes.

And he jumped.

As the metal bones of the *Horizon*, the pride of British Petroleum, crashed noisily into the sea.

Chapter 1

PRESENT DAY
CHICAGO

The duct-taped Buick swam north on Rush Street, hunting whores like a lesser white shark.

Superstition Davis pushed out her chest and waved. The driver flashed high beams in response. He clicked on his turn signal and angled for the curb. She licked her lip and kicked out a hip, sealing the deal.

He immediately straightened out and shot past.

She pouted, stamped her feet, and made a motion, *come back*. When he didn't, she hiked her skirt from micro to vanishing, tossing her chocolate tresses and widening her violet eyes.

He screeched to a halt, then back-whipped the Buick into an empty slot, scattering pedestrians like ten-pins.

Superstition hurried as fast as her towering stilettos allowed. She peered through the windows as she moved around the car, noticed his hands were already below his waist, moving furiously. *Hey, buddy, wait for me,* she thought, amused. *There's a penalty for early withdrawal—*

But he was shaking Tic-Tacs into his hand.

"Aw," she murmured. "You're new at this."

She leaned into his window as his round, hopeful face appeared over the descending glass line. The streetlights and humidity gave her cleavage a damp orange shadow.

"Wow, you look like a Creamsicle," he murmured.

She ran a hand over her scanty clothes. Her figure-hugging microdress was the blinding neon of Orange Crush. Likewise the five-inch stilettos accenting her long, lean legs. Her skin was the white of pastry cream, and her smile, moonglow on piano keys. "A Creamsicle, huh?" she teased. "Does that mean you'll lick me?"

He wiggled in his upholstered seat. "Uh, yeah, I'd like . . . um . . . where . . ."

"My place is around the corner," Superstition said, scouting for clues the driver was what he appeared. Like fortune-tellers and con artists, she had to read clients accurately if she wanted to avoid fatal mistakes.

He was middle-aged and clean-shaven. Bald on top, styled on the graying fringes. He smelled like Drakkar Noir, lightly applied. He wore pleated tan chinos, a parrot shirt from Tommy Bahama, and beef-roll loafers without socks. His Buddy Holly glasses had silver insets at the temples, and there was a pale indent on his ring finger, where a wedding band used to gleam. He was freshly divorced, or stepping out. She guessed the former. Players didn't waste breath mints on street hookers. They also spray-tanned their telltale divots . . .

"I'm, uh, John," he said, his anxiety thickening his voice.

"Fantasi," she lied back as she slid into the passenger seat. "With a heart-thingy over the *i*. It's a pleasure to meet you, John."

"Likewise." He glanced at the rearview, then back at her. "Is your place, um . . ."

"I'm at the Wainwright Hotel," she said. "There's free HBO if you don't like me."

John looked her over again. "That's not remotely possible," he murmured. He caressed her knee with trembling fingertips, but didn't move higher.

Horny, but polite. She decided he'd been dumped for Higher Earning Potential. He hadn't seen it coming, got shellacked by wifey's law-shark, was forced into an efficiency under an O'Hare flight path. He paid for her golf lessons and tooth bleaching, saw his kids Saturday afternoons at the Woodfield Mall food court, and lay awake nights wondering how his carefully charted life had gone so completely to hell. After months of Internet porn because all the women he knew were *her* friends, he showered, groomed, hopped into the only car he could afford after alimony and child support, and headed into the Viagra Triangle—the Near North Side club district prowled by Important Men, the tanned and bejeweled divorcées who adored them (or at least their investment portfolios), and the upmarket hookers who serviced the rest.

She kissed his downy cheek. "Gonna rock your world, Johnnycakes," she murmured into his ear, making sure he felt the tip of her tongue. "As soon as we get to my room. Does that sound all right?"

John nodded like a puppy and put the Buick in gear.

NOGALES, ARIZONA

The mosquito landed on the *narco's* sun-crisped arm, preparing to sink its blood-fang.

It died in a crushing splatter.

"The courier is late," Ortega said, scratching the bloody pieces. "Should I call?"

"Road construction in South Phoenix," Garcia reminded, calculating the circuitous route the man had to take to this remote desert canyon, fifteen miles north of the Mexican border. "Give him another thirty."

Ortega nodded, went back to sweeping the canyon with binoculars. "Makes me nervous, sitting this long exposed."

"Eleven million in drugs will do that," Garcia agreed.

"This, my friend, is your work cubicle," said Brian Charvat, waving his bony hand at the cactus and boulders lining Peck Canyon Road, a potholed rattletrap that reminded his passenger of the Dan Ryan Expressway back home. "And this bad boy," he continued with a knuckle-thump of the dashboard, "is your company car."

"Impressive," Derek Davis said over the engine whine of the Border Patrol Jeep. He surveyed the dusk-bitten landscape. They were only a few minutes west of Interstate 19, which connected Nogales—the nation's busiest border crossing—with Tucson an hour north. Yet, they were deep inside smuggler country. He heard the *whissssh* of speeding cars—and the random *pop* . . . *pop-pop* of gunfire. Since it was too dark for hunting, the shots were most likely from smugglers, the hard cases who plied their deadly trade in the big lonesome of Arizona's border with Mexico. He tingled with excitement. His job in Chicago was hazardous, no question. But this was bad to the bone.

They drained their water bottles, then headed into Peck Canyon. "Smugglers hide in these rocks," Charvat explained as they bounced along the hard pack. "Waiting for the drivers who'll haul the drugs up to Phoenix and Tucson. You want to hunt bad boys, you start here." He gave Davis a long look. "I know, vacation postcard, right?"

"It's dangerous," Davis agreed, hearing the warning underneath. "But I'm used to that."

Charvat grinned. " 'Course you are, tough guy—Chicago SWAT's no picnic," he said. "But this isn't the big city, with backups just seconds away. It's . . . Mars." His lips pursed with long-held frustration. "Your department has, what, ten thousand cops?"

"More or less."

"I've got two hundred for a wilderness the size of Rhode Island." He bit into the half-a-burrito left over from their supper at a lime-green cantina on the Mexican side of the fence. Made a face. "Not as good cold as I'd hoped," he said, throwing the rest out the window. It splattered on a cactus, beans flying one way, tortilla and jalapeños the other.

Davis stared at the passing scenery. The tangerine-infused sunset had dissolved, replaced by a velvet-Elvis starscape and a full yellow moon that shimmered through crevices in the canyon wall. A wild dog howled, setting off an orchestra of beasts. A lively wind brought scents of juniper, mesquite, and grasses, spiced with animal spoor and road dust. Hawks swooped and soared on the heat eddies. It was achingly beautiful.

And dangerous as a rabid wolf, he reminded himself. The borderlands were awash in desperation: Illegals who'd do anything for a job to feed their children. Coyotes who guided them across in exchange for their life savings—and sometimes their lives, if the water ran out. Bandits who robbed everyone except the apex predators: the traffickers, the *narcos*, who hauled billions of dollars' worth of drugs, weapons, and human beings across the invisible border that separated Venus from Mars.

"Out here, you're on your own," Charvat expanded. "Put out an SOS and you might get help in an hour."

"Or, never."

"If the radios don't work, sure," Charvat said, skirting a beagle-sized lizard moving sluggishly across the road. "You know, I get lots of cops asking for ride-alongs. I'm happy to oblige because it's good for both of us to see how the other half lives." He shook his head. "But you're the only fella ever asked to work a week for free just to see if you liked it enough to take your job and shove it."

Davis shrugged. "I'm a moron."

"Good. You'll fit right in with the Killer Bees."

Davis arched an eyebrow.

"*B* for Brian. *BP* for Border Patrol," Charvat explained, flicking the toy bumblebee hanging from his rearview. Its zigzag grin glowed coppery in the moonlight. "Which makes me the Killer Bee."

Davis laughed. "I'm going to work in your hive?"

"Yep. We'll even issue you a government stinger."

"Don't need it," Davis said, spreading his hands. "Mine's a mile long."

"Mine's a mile, too," Charvat said. "Wide."

"Rock breaks scissors," Davis laughed, holding out his fist for a bump.

Ortega stiffened as if electrified. "Quick, *Jefe*. Top of the ridge," he grunted, blading his hand to the south-southwest. "Behind those dead saguaros."

Garcia peered through his night-vision scope. Saw the Jeep with the forest-green stripe. It was the Border Patrol, kicking up dust on the road into the canyon that hid Garcia, his crew, and carefully bundled sacks of profit.

He studied the jouncing vehicle for clues to its destination. One agent sat shotgun, elbow out the window. The other was behind the wheel, hands at ten and two, head on an easy swivel, reading the landscape. Both appeared relaxed. Not on the radio and not clutching weapons.

Not scanning the sky for tactical teams in helicopters. Not looking for anything in particular. Just seeing what they could see.

"Routine patrol," he decided.

"And if it isn't?" Ortega challenged. "If someone ratted us out and they're coming to check?"

Garcia patted the backpacks stuffed with enough Taliban heroin and Colombian cocaine to ease the withdrawal pains of Godzilla. He stroked the ammunition belts crossing his chest, the cartridge at the top of each curved magazine winking brassy in the moonlight.

"Ten of us. Two of them. Do the math," he said.

"My boss has juice in D.C.," Charvat said. "She'll get you assigned you to my sector." He wagged a crooked finger. "Assuming, of course, we accept your application, you graduate with distinction from the Border Patrol academy, and you don't kill your dumb ass training."

"You will, no problem, and har-de-bleepin'-har."

"That's the spirit," Charvat said, slapping the dash. Dust scattered like fruit flies.

A long, comfortable silence ensued as they bounced along the ridge. Another good sign, Charvat thought. Nothing worse than a partner who never shut up.

"You married, Derek?" he said.

"High school sweetheart," Davis said.

"Nice when that happens. What's her name?"

"Superstition." He smiled at Charvat's arched eyebrow. "It's a long story."

Charvat laughed. "Best ones are. You have kids?"

A long silence.

"No. We don't have children."

The flatness implied a touchy subject, so Charvat changed the subject. "What's she think about picking up and moving?" he said.

"She's psyched," Davis said, rebrightening. "Sue loves Chicago, but the winters get her down. She's a sunshine kinda gal."

"We got even more sunshine than we do illegals," Charvat said. "Though some days it's a toss-up. She'll like it just fine. Wanna call her with the good news?"

Davis scratched his head. "Well, sure, I'll try, Chief," he said, pulling out his phone. "But she sees it's me, she might not answer."

"Why's that?"

"She's trying to get laid."

He let Charvat stew in that while he speed-dialed her cell. Not surprisingly, he got: *At the tone, please leave a message . . .*

He did, and Charvat goosed the accelerator over a hill. Davis felt like a kid again as they both went weightless.

"I trust there's a story behind that little statement?" Charvat said.

Davis heaved a sigh as he pinked with discomfort. "Yeah. And to tell the truth, I wouldn't mind talking about it," he said. "But I hardly know you."

"Easier, sometimes, with strangers."

"I guess. Hell, Bee, I gotta tell someone. About what Sue does when I'm out of town. Sometimes, when I'm home, even." He clenched and unclenched his fists.

Charvat nodded encouragement.

"She puts on this neon dress," Davis said in a voice just above a whisper. "It's cut up to here and down to there. She paints on lipstick and slips into do-me heels. She gets in her car and drives to known pickup spots in the city. Then she parks and starts looking for men. Women too, sometimes." He cleared his thickening throat. "My wife is a . . . she's a . . ." He waved his hands as if batting flies. "Ah, shit, man, I can't believe I'm telling you this . . ."

"Say what you mean, Derek, it's all right."

Davis took a deep breath.

CHICAGO

They crossed under a neon sign that pulsed WI-FI/HBO/BEST RATES IN TOWN. John centered the Buick between two faded stripes, turned off the engine, pocketed the keys, and glanced at the hotel entrance.

He turned white as ricotta.

"Are you all right?" Superstition said, alarmed.

"Yeah . . . yeah . . . fine," he muttered. Sweat poured off his bald spot, soaking his banana-colored collar. "Just a little . . . nervous, I think."

"Being here with me?" Superstition said.

He nodded. She squeezed his arm.

"Aw, that's sweet," she said. The cell in her pocket vibrated. She ignored it. "But I'm a nice girl, honest. I wouldn't hurt a fly. We'll talk, get to know each other a little." Her smile turned naughty. "Then we'll have to do something about your handsome clothes."

He touched a green parrot dampened by his flop-sweat. "You like, Fantasi?" he said, clearly pleased.

"Very chic. So, are you ready?" She watched him closely for signs of a heart attack. The last thing she needed was a dead john named, ironically, John . . .

"I'm sorry," he said, dabbing sweat with a monogrammed handkerchief. "I mean, for being such a doofus. It's just that you're the first."

I knew it, I just knew it. "Since she left you?" she said.

He nodded. Removed his glasses and dabbed at his eyes. "Yeah. My wife. Tabitha. Tabby. I thought we were doing great."

"She thought otherwise."

John shrugged. "She had me served at work. You know, with the divorce papers. She wanted everyone to know."

"Wow, that's cold," Superstition said, meaning it.

"Yeah, I thought so." John made a face, then sat a little straighter. "Aw, listen to me," he said briskly, pulling the door handle. "You don't want to hear about my troubles. Let's go inside."

Superstition joined him at the front of the Buick. The engine ticked. The neon buzzed like horseflies. She slipped her hand into his. He caressed her fingers, and she squeezed back. They were warm and gentle. They belonged to a husband, a father, a son, a friend. They were no longer trembling. John was right, he was ready.

Suddenly, she wasn't.

"I'm sorry, I've changed my mind," she said, releasing his hand and stepping away, wishing her hair wasn't wired for sound. "Take me back."

He looked like he'd walked into a buzz saw. "Back?" he squeaked, an octave higher than before. "To Rush Street?"

"The corner you picked me up on, right."

He stared. "What the . . . I mean, why? Don't you like me?"

She patted his face. "That's the thing—I do like you. Which is why I want you to go back home. You shouldn't be doing this, John."

He stiffened, angry and embarrassed. She walked to her side of the car, motioning for him to use his remote opener. He planted his feet and crossed his arms. "Come on, John, it's for the best. You'd regret this later," she said, letting him down gently. "I don't want you thinking of me when you do."

"You're wrong, Fantasi," John said, hopping foot to foot to burn off his frustration. "I'm ready for action. Listen, I have cash in my pocket, a whole stinking pile—"

"Get this through your head, pal—I'm not going to date you," she snapped, needing to stop him before he dug in too deep. "Drive me back or I'll walk." She knew he'd do it, as he was too nice to refuse forever.

He sighed like the world was ending, then pulled out his keys and pushed UNLOCK. Ten silent minutes later he screeched into the curb. "If it's because you thought I was having a heart attack . . ." he muttered.

She touched his hand. "No. That's not it. It's exactly what I told you," she said. "I know men pretty well, wouldn't you agree?" she said.

His sullen shrug said, *So?*

"So, you're not cut out for this. You're a nice guy, you shouldn't be picking up whores. You'd lay awake nights feeling terrible from the guilt."

"Better than laying awake horny," he tried.

She smiled. "Find yourself a real woman," she said softly. "Not a rent-a-hole like me. There's tons of nice gals out there who'll fall for your good looks and personality."

He looked at her and started to snarl a curse. But he couldn't get it out of his mouth.

She patted his arm and hopped out to the sidewalk. He roared off, passing a knot of hotties not called "whores," because they slept with men for benefits, not cash. That he didn't even glance at them reinforced her feeling that John would be all right.

A minute later, a blue car desperately in need of washing pulled to the curb. Superstition walked over, bumping her hips for effect.

NOGALES, ARIZONA

"Superstition's a vice cop," Derek said calmly. "She trolls streets and hotels for johns, and her team's out working tonight."

Charvat stared, then burst out laughing at the gotcha. "I'm gonna deeply regret having you in my command, aren't I?" he said, punching Davis's arm.

"Probably."

"No probably about it. I take it she's the bodacious decoy?"

"Yup." Davis grinned slyly. "Really good at it, too."

Charvat groaned. "Peckerwood like you don't deserve anything that fine."

"Don't I know it."

"She been on the job awhile?"

Davis nodded. "More than a decade. Before vice she worked patrol, tactical, and robbery. She's a crack shot, and plans to compete in the Bianchi Cup next year."

Charvat whistled, knowing Bianchi was the Super Bowl of national pistol competitions. "My kinda woman. Let's drink to her health." He pointed at a track shooting east from the main drag. It was narrow, dusty, and humped as a camel's back.

"You want to toast her with . . . dirt?" Davis said doubtfully.

Charvat flung his hands like the devil had burped a blasphemy. "Imagine, if you will, a cantina. But not just any cantina, no sir. One with an old-fashioned jukebox, filled with Petty and Cash and Frank. Pretty waitresses who call you 'Hon.' All the beer you can drink, at only a buck a throw." He flicked the bee on the rearview. "Then imagine it sits at the other end of that yellow brick road you so dismissively call 'dirt,' and that only the Killer Bee knows the password to get you in."

Davis managed to look duly chastened, though it was hard through his choking laughter. "I stand corrected, O Kind and Worshipful Bee-ness," he said, salaaming as best he could in the cramped Jeep. "And I'm happy to give alms to your innkeeper. But are you allowed to drink on duty?"

Charvat looked at his Tag-Heuer, which his own wife, Deloris, had given him for his promotion to chief of Nogales Sector. "One of the perks of being the cheese is I decide when I'm on duty. As of this moment . . ."

"It's good to be king," Davis said.

"They are . . . turning our . . . way," Ortega said, his words coming in gasps as adrenaline flooded his body. "Accelerating . . . quickly."

Garcia glanced at the sky. No helicopters. He looked at the landscape. No other dust clouds. He reacquired the speeding Jeep on his night scope. The headlights were pointed his way, the dust wake billowing straight back. "It appears I was mistaken," he said. "Fortunately, they seem to be alone. Grenade, Manuel."

The *narco* shoved a rifle-propelled grenade into the AK's launcher.

"Don't shoot until my order," Garcia said as the rest of his men flipped fire selectors from SAFE to AUTO. "And for the love of God, don't miss. We must destroy them immediately so they cannot radio for their drones."

"We will not fail you, *Jefe*!" they shouted as one. Garcia grinned. They were good men who enjoyed the down-and-dirty. This was going to be fun . . .

"Fire!" he shouted.

The stubby grenade blasted from the launcher, propellant blooming like a fireworks display. The warhead accelerated to the speed of an Indy car. The *narcos* hugged the backs of their boulders.

The grenade corkscrewed into the Jeep's front bumper. And exploded as ten AKs opened up.

Chapter 2

Charvat and Davis clawed thin air as the Jeep flipped over, engine compartment roaring with flames and smoke. It slammed off a boulder, skidded into a gully, and crashed through a cactus-choked embankment, windows shattering, tires blowing. Bullets grazed the windshield. "Get outta here before she blows!" Charvat yelled.

Davis yanked at his belt, hardly able to hear over the *thwock-thwock-thwock* of bullet strikes. The buckle wouldn't unlock. He dug a Strider combat knife from his pocket, flicked it open. "You free, Chief?" he said, hacking through the restraint.

"I'm good," Charvat said, pumping out rounds with his Heckler & Koch, the forty-caliber pistol rounds deafening in the closed quarters. The front doors were jammed, so he turned around to scuttle over the broken driver's seat. "There's a cluster of tall boulders fifty yards back of us," he said, unlocking his rifle from the carrier. "We'll make our stand there. Hand me your rifle and I'll—*ahhhh*." Meat exploded from the backs of his legs as AK-47 rounds hit home. "Jesus, that hurts," Charvat wheezed as he flumped unceremoniously into the backseat.

Davis snatched up the radio mike. The cord dangled in pieces. The radio face spalled from the engine fire boiling behind it.

We're on our own.

He scooped up his own AR-15 and shoveled it to Charvat, who chucked both out the window, then squirmed through, ignoring the cactus punching needles into his face and the flames searing his arms medium rare. "C'mon, son, we got a war to fight," Charvat said, loosing rifle rounds as Davis squirmed free. They crabbed backwards toward the boulders, firing at what seemed like a billion muzzle flashes.

"Don't let them escape," Garcia said. Manuel nodded and stuffed in another round. The explosion shook the landscape like an earthquake.

"Goddammit," Davis groaned as rock shards peppered their flesh. "That's a grenade launcher."

"*Narcos* protecting a big shipment," Charvat wheezed, having abandoned the crawl for a full-out sprint. "Gotta be, carrying that kind of firepower."

"We need to even the odds, Chief," Davis said, vibrating like a guitar string as SWAT brain kicked in. "Once we're secure, you put out covering fire. Pistol and rifle both, make it sound like we're both there." He pointed at the saw-tooth hills overlooking the dirt path. "I'm gonna sneak up that ridge, pick them off from high ground. Sound like a plan?"

No answer.

"Brian? Bee?" Davis said, skidding and turning to see that Charvat had collapsed, blood spitting from the leg holes. He ran back, bullets pinging like hail stones around him. He slung Charvat's rifle around his neck, hefted the fallen Border Patrol supervisor like a sack of potatoes, and headed for the rocks, firing behind him as he ran, every step a Taser jolt of pain.

"I can't see them," Garcia said, crouching to avoid the *gringos'* return fire. That they had survived two grenade blasts was a very dark omen. "The flames from the Jeep makes the night scope useless."

"I think they're heading there," Ortega said, pointing at the boulders behind the disintegrating Jeep. "If their phones still work . . ."

Garcia snapped out orders. The men started toward the boulders, firing then dropping flat to the ground then firing again, moving from tree to cactus to rock.

Charvat's eyes flickered open as he coughed up blood.

"Welcome back, *Jefe*," Davis said between trigger bursts. "Thought you were gonna make me do all the work."

"Did I pass out?"

"A few minutes. You were bleeding like a stuck pig." He nodded at the shirts he'd knotted around the chief's thighs. "We're behind the boulders now."

Charvat sized up the terrain, nodded. "You saved my life. Thanks."

Davis answered with a rifle burst.

"Won't last, though. Them boys'll be coming over quick enough," Charvat said, struggling to sit up. "We gotta bring the fight to them."

"'We?'" Davis said.

Charvat looked at his legs, which were sticking out at odd angles. "Aw, hell. Just position me face-out so I can slow them down."

Davis moved the broken agent. Charvat blanched, then rallied. Davis handed him three spare magazines, ninety rounds in all. "All right, I'm heading out," he said.

"Screw this up, I won't hire you," Charvat said.

"*Now* you tell me?" Davis said.

Charvat grinned. The movement welled fresh blood over his lips. "Go get 'em, Capone." He pushed his AR through a crack between two boulders and launched a bullet stream. The killers responded in kind. It sounded like a machine gun festival.

Davis slapped Charvat's shoulder twice and charged up the goat path as *narcos* pockmarked the boulders with hundreds of high-powered bullets. The stocky desert fortress kept the American rifles from being silenced.

"Can you aim your grenades into the sky?" Garcia said, curving his hand to show the arc. "And drop one right behind those rocks?"

"*Sí, Jefe,*" Manuel said, working out the angles in his head.

Davis spotted a *narco* racing down the path from the other end. He slipped into a hollow in one of the high rock ridges and pulled out his knife, not wanting to tip his location with gunfire. He forced his breathing shallow, and waited, waited, waited . . .

He leaped from the hollow and wrapped his arm around the gunman's upper neck, squeezing like an anaconda. The *narco* kicked and gurgled, slamming them both against the sharp rocks. Davis, however, had size and leverage, and drove the blade into the side of the lower neck. A second later he ripped it straight out the front, the honed steel severing both windpipe and jugular. Blood spurted as if carbonated. The gunman's AK clattered to the rocks.

Davis shoved the corpse into the underbrush, then looked for a good sniping position. Heard the *whoomp* of the launcher pouring rockets at Killer Bee. He found a decent spot and dug in prone behind his gun, praying Brian's rock shields held.

Charvat's eardrums popped as rock knives carved new divots from his back. But he was still alive. He peered through the crack and saw several bandits creeping his way. He stayed silent, letting them draw closer. He slowly laid his sights on the closest man.

"Fill yer hand, you son of a bitch," he growled, channeling his best John Wayne.

"Get down!" Garcia barked as his compatriot's blood wetted the ground like a summer squall. The sharp crack of an AR-15 sounded a microsecond later. "They've got us in range!"

"This is the Border Patrol," he heard a hard voice bark. "Drop your weapons and put your hands in the air. If you do not, my men will kill you. This is your final warning."

Garcia laughed, impressed. "That one has balls the size of grapefruits," he said to Manuel. "Blast them off." Manuel nodded and reloaded. He'd spotted the rifle flash that killed his *amigo*, and knew exactly where to lay his next grenade—

The right side of his head exploded.

"*Vaya con dios,* asshole," Davis muttered as he moved to the next target.

"Sniper at three o'clock, *Jefe!*" Ortega shouted, whipping his bullet stream to his right. Rock chips flew as if chain-sawed. "They split up! One is in the hills to our—"

Davis watched his bullet rip out the mustached killer's throat. He moved the muzzle to the tall, rangy Mexican wearing crossed ammo belts, the one the dead man just called "Boss," and fired. Garcia darted sideways, escaping death by millimeters.

Davis scooted to a fresh location as bandit bullets thumped where he'd just been. He aimed carefully, put another gunman in the spin cycle, hunted for the next—

"Phone," he muttered, astonished he hadn't thought of it already. He reached for the cell strapped to his belt . . .

. . . and slapped shredded nylon.

He looked around frantically and spotted a small moonlit object on the goat path, halfway back to Charvat. *There's my cell,* he realized. *It ripped off my belt during the knife fight, when we scraped against that rock.*

He bit back his disappointment and got back to work.

"Ayyyy!" a *narco* bleated as he twisted into the ground. A compatriot joined him a moment later, brains splattering on a nearby cactus.

A battered Land Rover bounced into view. "The transport!" Garcia shouted. "Load the cargo!" The surviving gunmen fired as they retreated from rock to rock, hauling the narcotics backpacks to the SUV, trying their best to save the white powder draining from bullet holes.

"Faster, damn you, faster!" Garcia shouted, his voice a braided whip.

"Derek! Ground that Rover!" Charvat hollered.

"Working on it!" Davis yelled back.

The knob of a saguaro disintegrated inches from his elbow. He speed-crawled to the next protective outcrop and risked a quick peek. Gunmen were ignoring him momentarily to pitch overstuffed packs into the back of a vehicle bearing Texas plates. He memorized the number. Put his sights on the closest *narco*. Stroked the trigger.

Click.

Davis tossed the jammed rifle in disgust and grabbed the dead man's AK-47. A splintery piece of skull was wedged inside the trigger guard. He poked it clear, wiped the gore from his trigger finger, reinserted, aimed, and squeezed, praying the sights hadn't been knocked adrift . . .

A gunman spun screaming. The next one flopped atop him, forming a bloody cross.

"Rosito. Grenade that bastard or we're all dead," Garcia ordered, whirling and firing at the scorpion in the rocks. But his man was hugging the rear tire, whimpering. He'd never been in a firefight this extreme and was scared to death.

"Next time, wear a skirt," Garcia cursed, knocking Rosito aside. He picked up the launcher and swung it toward the rocks. Prayed the Yankee rifle stayed silent long enough . . .

The rocket grenade leapt like a bee-stung horse. It covered the distance in less than two seconds and exploded in a fiery *crump*.

"Uhnnnnhn," Davis grunted as a big hand bounced him off a tree. Disoriented, he staggered like a drunken ballerina into a clearing between the rocks.

Narco guns roared like lawn mowers. One AK bullet entered Davis's chest, below the right nipple. It deflected off a rib and exited through his armpit. Another ripped a deep, U-shaped groove across the left side of his head, creating the shock wave of a ball-peen hammer. Other bullets laid crimson his belly, feet, and legs.

"I got him! The bastard is down!" Garcia crowed when he saw the agent collapse.

"Guhh," Davis said.

Then faded to the pinpoint of grandpa's old TV.

Chapter 3

CHICAGO

"What are you, Dudley Do-Right?" Chicago Police Lieutenant Robert Hanrahan growled through the window of his unmarked car, his craggy Irish face pulled into a horseshoe of annoyance. "We don't do catch and release. We fry our fish."

"He was a nice guy," Superstition said.

"So was Ted Bundy."

"Tommy Bahama wasn't a serial killer," she said. "His wife dumped him. He was lonely, so he dolled up and came out here. He's human, Robbie, and he made a mistake."

"Yeah, by asking you for a 'date,'" Hanrahan said as the remainder of the vice team pulled to the curb. Four men with quarter-inch crew cuts scrambled out of their unmarked car and walked her way, limbs loose and jangly. "Just like he was supposed to, considering how glammed up you are."

She touched her Creamsicle skirt. "What, this old thing?"

Hanrahan cursed in Gaelic, then sighed. "All right, you felt sorry for the guy," he said. "No harm, no foul. But next time, remember your job isn't to judge these creeps, it's to arrest—"

"He wasn't a creep, and I'd let him go again," Superstition said, crossing her arms. She was the one wearing the Crayola-colored happy sack to reel in the men who hunted prostitutes. The rest of the team shadowed her on the street or waited in the adjoining hotel room, ready to pounce when the unlucky john said any approximation of *Here's plenty, let's party.* "I'm the girl on the griddle, so it's my decision."

"That's right, Loot," the tallest of the squad hooted as the others clapped and cheered. "Girl on the griddle makes the call, that's what you always say."

"My own people, using my very own words against me," Hanrahan said, shaking his head in mock sorrow. "What would poor Mother Hanrahan say if she wasn't already in the clouds rocking sweet baby Jesus?"

" 'Gonna kick yer hairy asses for making poor Robbie cry'?" the cop suggested.

"Amen," Hanrahan said, steepling his hands as if in prayer. "Now let's get on with the mope hunt."

Superstition winced theatrically. "I need to stop at Bubbles first."

"Why?"

"Icky girl stuff you don't want to hear about," she said.

"Oh, well, then, shoo," he said, motioning her away with both hands. "We'll set up down the block and await your tangerine presence."

She ran for the lounge as her team headed south.

NOGALES, ARIZONA

Derek Davis blinked.

Looked at his hands.

Saw twenty fingers.

Shook his head.

Saw thirty.

"Oh, man," he groaned.

He tried to stand, but his legs wouldn't work. His arms did, a little. He clawed out of the blast hole and onto the hard-packed flat, panting like hundred-meter gold.

Where am I?

He slapped himself a couple times to wake his memory. Examined his palms.

Slippery with blood.

He spit. More blood. He saw holes in his flesh, round and puckered and burning like arc welders. There was a constellation of cuts, scrapes, and gouges, plus a raw furrow on the side of his head. He slipped a finger into the trough. His nail tapped something hard.

Skull bone.

He blew out his breath. He wasn't dead, but it had been close. "World of hurt, cowboy," he muttered. The cobwebs cleared a little. He looked around. "Bee," he yelled in a phlegmy voice that sounded like nobody he knew. "You out there?"

"Damn tootin', son," the reply as sweet as apple cider. "They're gone. You drove 'em off."

"Good. That's good," Davis coughed. He wiped the dribble, took a look.

Frothy and pink.

Lung shot. Bullet or frag, he couldn't tell. It wasn't bad, since he was still breathing.

Not good, either.

"They banged me up some," he said.

"Me too," Charvat said. They traded explanations. "You gonna live?"

Davis shook his head. Then nodded, trying to be optimistic. "I'll try my best," he said. "Legs aren't working. Arms are all right."

"See if you can crawl," Charvat said.

Davis was sure he couldn't. Tried anyway. Made it a foot from the blast-hole. Strained real hard and made another foot.

"Slow as a constipated goat," he said.

"You're on a goat path, so that makes sense," Charvat said, trying to move away from the boulders. He got nowhere, a turtle flipped on its back. "I'm stuck. I can bandage your wounds if you can get to me."

"Deal," Davis said. Dynamite kept erupting in his head. His vision swam in and out. He throbbed in places he didn't know existed. "Does your cell phone work?"

"No. Shot up. Yours?"

"It's on the path between here and you."

"Can you get there?"

"Yeah, but you'd better pray that signal's good."

"Jesus, Mary, and Ma Bell," Charvat said, folding his hand over his heart.

Davis locked his eyes on the phone. Grunted like he was messing his pants. Moved a foot. Then another. Thought of Superstition. Made a yard.

"Any chance you saw the man in charge, Derek?"

"The *jefe*?" Davis said. He recalled a rangy Mexican with a perpetual scowl, wearing crossed ammo belts. "Yes. Caught a decent look from the ridge."

"Could you describe him?"

Davis did, added the license plate. Charvat whistled.

"What, you know this guy?" Davis said.

"Nope. Just pleasantly surprised at your good description. I'll hire you if you pass the physical."

Pass the physical. Davis began laughing. It turned into a hacking cough that brought up pieces of . . . well, he didn't want to know. Accompanied by a thick, black fog he feared wasn't actually in the air.

"Uh, Brian?"

"Right here."

"I'm finding it a little hard to see all of a sudden."

Silence.

" 'Course it's hard to see, son," Charvat said gently. "Sandstorm just moved in, doncha know."

Davis looked up. The Man in the Moon grinned bright.

"Yeah, that must be it," he said.

He coughed up more blood, kept crawling with his arms, which burned with effort and pain. Now the cell phone was within two yards. One yard. One foot. One inch. He wriggled his swollen hands from under his body and touched the lifesaving device . . .

Which snapped to attention with a silent blue glow.

"It works," Davis said, his voice cracking with awe. "The cell's got power."

"Cool beans, Derek. Does it look like it'll dial out?"

He hadn't actually considered that it wouldn't. He felt the rest of his dinner climb the stairs . . .

The phone bleated.

He jumped.

It bleated again. He looked at the display, hands trembling.

WIFE CELL.

"It's Sue," he breathed, wide-eyed. "She's returning my call."

"So, you gonna answer?" Charvat said. "Or make that poor gal leave a message?"

Derek poked CONNECT with a badly trembling finger—the pain from his wounds was starting to horse him around. He dropped his ear to the phone and heard his wife talking a mile a minute. It was the sound of an angel.

"Sue," he grunted as the black fog pulsed at his eyeballs.

Chapter 4

CHICAGO

Superstition felt an elbow smash her shoulder as she reached for Bubbles's door. The unstable orange stilettos launched her sideways, and she banged off a wrought iron fence, mashing her opposite arm so hard that she knew it would purple before she reached the bathroom.

"Hey, jerk," she snapped as she regained her balance. "You want a punching bag, go find a gym."

The tall, muscled black man who'd shoved her to get in first stared down with eyes as chilly as buckshot. "One more word from you, whitey," he said, his voice a November grave, "and I'll tear off your head and shit down your neck."

She bristled and started to snap, "Try it, see what happens," then held up her hands. Knocking him around would be fun, but she *really* had to pee. One more minute and she'd do it right here in the doorway, swear to God . . .

Mistaking her reaction for submission, he turned away and pushed through the door. The two men behind him shrugged. It was as close as she'd get to an apology, she figured, because hookers got respect from exactly nobody.

She watched the trio drift toward the back of the airy room, which wrapped around a thirty-foot mahogany bar. A tidal wave of bar-gabble engulfed her as she navigated the Moorish floor tiles. A hunky young man with three-day stubble smiled her way. The dirty blonde at his elbow shot her eye-daggers, then stepped closer to her prize. Superstition, amused, nodded at both, kept moving. Beautiful people were the norm at Bubbles. The place reflected its owner, one Bubbles Frankenberg, whose real name was Donna but preferred both *dramatis personae* and chilled Dom Pérignon. Superstition reached the bathroom door, her insides trembling from the strain—

Four fingers and a thumb grabbed her wrought iron bruise, making her yelp.

"Back the way you came, street meat," growled a man thick with drugstore cologne. "Don't want your kind pollutin' the decent folk."

Superstition turned to see a bullet-headed bouncer with a ruby in his left ear. "Wow. Did you think that up all by yourself?" she said. "Or read it in a comic book?"

His jaw twitched with annoyance. "Cracking wise is really bad for your health," he said, moving in so close that the cologne assaulted all her senses.

"Or yours," Superstition said, sneezing. "You're new here, right?"

He nodded, suddenly wary. "First night," he said.

"Tell Bubbles I said hi," she said, pushing into the bathroom with her butt.

He opened his mouth to say something, but decided against it. Instead, he lumbered away, adjusting his waistband and muttering under his breath.

She entered a stall, latched the door, did her business with a tabernacle choir of relief, then called her boss.

"Hanrahan," he said.

"It's me. I wanted to let you know I'm in position."

"Position?" he said, confused. "I thought you were using the—"

She held the phone next to the bowl and flushed.

"Har-de-frickin'-har," Hanrahan said.

"Frickin'?" she said.

"The captain says I shouldn't swear in front of the troops. Says it makes me suboptimal."

"Suboptimal?"

"I think it means 'big pecker,' " Hanrahan said. "So, you coming?"

"As soon as I get hold of Derek. He left a message, but I haven't had time to call back. Do you mind?"

"You? Asking for permission?"

"Thought I'd try something new."

A snort this time. "You're full of laughs tonight. Sure, go ahead. We're still setting up."

"Thanks, Loot," she said, using the diminutive for Lieutenant. Hanrahan was a tall, meaty man, born in Hegewisch, formed on the streets, polished by the Jesuits, and pipelined from junior college to the cops. He had no peer in commanding detectives, but his personal life was the very definition of *WTF, dude?* Movie-star handsome in a bulky, film noir way, he enjoyed walking on the wild side, which, among other things, meant dating a Chicago Bulls cheerleader, a runway model, and a CIA analyst, all at the same time—while he was married. Predictably, it ended in disaster and divorce court, but he remained cheerful about it, saying "Little Robbie" wanted what it wanted, so what could he do? He was the best boss she'd ever had, though, treating his cops, male or female, gay or straight, color or none, with great respect—and, if needed, some private ass-kicking, which became forgive-and-forget unless the kickee didn't get the point, in which case he or she found him or herself combing swere grates for important clues. She'd take a bullet for him, and most of her colleagues shared that assessment.

"G'wan, call your old man and talk dirty," Hanrahan elaborated. "Then hurry on down our way. A medical convention just let out, so the fishing looks excellent."

"Sir, yes, sir," Superstition said, saluting. Her shiny orange fingernails whipped up and back in Bubbles's vintage gilded mirrors.

"You said that respectfully. But I know better."

He disconnected.

Smiling, she hit speed dial ONE. Derek's phone rang. He picked up. She heard him say "Sue." She smiled and started to talk but then heard screams from the bar. She couldn't make out the words, but she knew the unmistakeable tone.

"Trouble," she said, her heart beginning to race with adrenaline. "I'll call you back, hon." She disconnected and hurried to the door, pulling it open and peering through the gap. One of the men from the doorstep encounter was holding a twelve-gauge pump. He noticed the movement and pointed it at her face. "Come join the fun, white eyes," he jeered, waving the slaughtergun. "We'd hate you to feel left out."

"Omigosh, is this a robbery?" Superstition wailed, praying the squad wasn't too far away to pick up the microphone under her hair, which Hanrahan used to document her conversations with johns. "What are you three guys doing with guns?"

Robbery . . . guys . . . guns?

"Shit," spat the driver, accelerating their heads into the rests. The shotgun rider called Hanrahan. "Robbery in progress at Bubbles," he reported. "Superstition's inside."

"Oh, shit," Hanrahan said.

"What we said," Shotgun said. "Three guys with guns. She's broadcasting live."

"Pedal to metal," Hanrahan said.

"This is a robbery! Get on the floor!" the man who'd elbowed Superstition shouted as he waved a Desert Eagle, a mammoth steel pistol whose forty-four-caliber bullets carved not holes but tunnels.

"Move it, whitey," Shotgun said, jabbing Superstition with the hard black muzzle. She hurried toward the bar as patrons began diving to the floor. Desert Eagle ordered the bartender to clean out the cash register, but the earringed hipster froze like a deer in headlights. Desert Eagle raked his face with the gun, misting the bar with blood and cartilage.

"Give him whatever he wants," Bubbles ordered.

"Smart move, mama," Desert Eagle said. "Give us the money and nobody gets hurt."

"Be advised, undercover officer is inside the bar," Hanrahan huffed as he sprinted down the service alley behind Bubbles, leaping over potholes and trash. "She's wearing an orange dress and high heels. Repeat, undercover officer is inside the bar."

"Wearing, orange dress," the emergency dispatcher confirmed. "What's your status?"

"Five in plainclothes, two minutes out. Tell responding units to run silent. Repeat, no lights and sirens, we don't want to spook them into opening fire . . ."

The bouncer flexed his fingers as he reached for his dangling shirttail. Superstition spotted the familiar imprint through his tight black jeans. She caught his eye and shook her head. *They only want money,* she tried to tell him telepathically. *Don't be a hero and you'll come out of this alive.*

He gave her a dirty look as he pulled up his shirt. He wrapped his fingers around the checkered brown grips of his pistol and pulled it free of the holster. The third robber spotted it and swung his nine- millimeter pistol.

"No, don't shoot!" Superstition yelled, lunging to shove the bouncer to safety as Shotgun and Desert Eagle joined Pistol for the kill.

"Shots fired!" Hanrahan barked as he ran. "ETA sixty seconds. We're going in."

"All units, active shooters, inside bar, plainclothes team entering in sixty seconds," the dispatcher told the blue tsunami. "Respond Code Three."

Sirens lit up across Chicago.

The crowd erupted as flesh plugs sprayed from the bouncer. "Stay on the floor!" the gunmen screamed. "Throw out your wallets and purses!"

Instead, the crowd bolted, billiard balls smacked by the white. The unexpected uprising startled the gunmen into directing fire. The man with the three-day beard stutter-stepped, then collapsed. A shrieking redhead tried frantically to reattach her blown-off ear. Superstition lowered her head, ran faster. She snatched up the fallen bouncer's pistol and pumped bullets into Shotgun, who'd turned his back to shoot women off bar stools. He collapsed, blood spraying from the four holes clustered between his shoulder blades.

Desert Eagle and Pistol swung her way, pulling triggers. She emptied the magazine at them as she leapt, forcing them to break off. She sailed over stools and black granite bar top and crashed into the back mirror, slicing herself from shoulder to elbow. She tumbled to the floor as the gunmen's bullets blasted wine and whiskey, the glass shelves shattering and falling. Her ears rang from the thunderstorm.

"Bitch shot Rancey, get her!" she heard Desert Eagle bellow.

She speed-crawled toward the cubbyhole where she knew Bubbles kept a gun. Glass exploded and booze rained, brown, blue, white, and clear. The shards deepened the ribbons in her knees and hands. She ignored it, kept crawling.

She reached Bubbles's well-worn Glock and checked that it was loaded. She quick-glanced between two shattered beer pumps. Saw waitresses gasping for air, dozens of patrons writhing in agony, and the two remaining predators who caused it.

"*Hasta la vista*, creeps," she hissed.

She rose to a combat crouch and laid the muzzle on Pistol, who was reaching for his dead buddy's shotgun. He spotted her, jerked back from the twelve with a curse, and whipped his barrel her way. She shredded his heart just as he fired. He corkscrewed to the floor, his final rounds splintering the dense red wood of the bar.

She swung her muzzle onto Desert Eagle and fired. He jerked out of range, lips in a feral snarl. She ducked as forty-four magnums sizzled back her way, thwacking the bar like steam hammers.

She crawled to the end. Peeked around. Saw him looking for her. Bad angle to take him down. Looked for options. Saw an overturned table with steel legs and a three inch granite top. Good cover, ideal firing angle.

Nine feet of air, here to there.

She coiled and sprang. He tracked and fired. She landed in a heap as his bullets carved chunks from the protective rock. She earthwormed across the tiles and stuck her head, hands, and gun out the right side of the table. His bullets sent tile chips into her face. She didn't flinch. Her Glock jumped. Flames spurted. Bullets flew.

And Desert Eagle collapsed, bleeding from forehead to belly.

She jumped to her feet and hustled over, ready to resume firing if he was playing possum.

"Go, go, go!" Hanrahan roared as the team raced into the bar, muzzles up, triggers straining for release.

"Don't, don't, don't!" Superstition shouted, waving wildly as her squad mates bulldozed through the doors. "They're down, they're down, they're down!"

Hanrahan jerked his gun front, back, side, side. No bullets. No explosions. Just cries from the wounded and silence from the dead. He called for paramedics, crime scene, crowd control, and the medical examiner. "Are you all right?" he said, racing to Superstition, who was slumping down a blood-streaked wall, looking dazed.

She blew out her breath. Felt a sticky wetness penetrate her gossamer dress. She patted herself, found no holes. Somebody's blood. Not hers. She grimaced, shifted away. Saw cell phone cameras waving like dandelions and tugged down the orange the best she could. Hanrahan handed her his raid jacket. He was so big that it fit her like a blue circus tent, but it kept the looky-loos from photographing her privates . . . "I was coming out of the bathroom when they announced the robbery," she said, voice squeaking from adrenaline. "The bouncer intervened, despite my warning him not to. They killed him, then started on the patrons. Gave me no choice but to open fire."

Hanrahan was nodding vigorously. "You did an outstanding job, Detective Davis." He said it loud for the benefit of the cell phone Tarantinos. "Your quick reaction saved a lot of people from dying tonight . . ."

She looked at the three gunmen as he continued in that vein. They'd been young and filled with energy. Now they were broken, a child's doll abused till the plastic disintegrated. Their limbs were loose and floppy, their eyes dull. Blood rivulets sparkled against their cooling, espresso-colored flesh.

It made her sad, those meandering rivulets. She'd shot people before, and she'd undoubtedly do it again—that was the nature of jobs with guns. Unlike some of her colleagues, who relished the thought of kill-or-be-killed gunfights, she preferred cajoling suspects into giving up, or, failing that, "convincing" them hand-to-hand. But these three called the play, not her, and she wouldn't lose any sleep over it. She hoped not, anyway. Logic didn't always fall in lockstep with emotion.

"Go call Derek," Hanrahan said gently. "Take all the time you need. I'll deal with the shoo-flies till you're ready."

Officer-involved shootings were investigated by the police department's internal affairs unit—the dreaded "shoo-flies"—then again by independent review teams. Superstition had no doubt she'd be cleared. There were a hundred witnesses led by Bubbles Frankenberg, plus the hair-radio recording. But it grated going through the drill at all. There were guns under the killers. Spatter on the walls. Bullets in the bouncer. Didn't *that* explain *what* the *hell* had *happened* . . .

"Bureaucracy," Hanrahan said, knowing what her heavy breathing meant. "I guarantee you'll be fine." He extended a hand and helped her to her feet. Her squad mates gathered and tapped her back and arms. "Ya done good," they said, the highest compliment in Cop Land. Bubbles ran up and hugged her so hard that she momentarily lost her breath.

Superstition thanked everyone with counter-taps but kept her face blank. The natural exhilaration of surviving a deadly shoot-out had been used against cops in the past, as "proof" of their "bloodthirsty nature." She excused herself and headed to the restroom, where there'd be a tiny bit of privacy. Several patrons stopped her to say thanks. She murmured, "You're welcome, glad I could help," but kept walking; the need for Derek's voice was beginning to overwhelm.

She pushed through the door then leaned against the wall tiles. She drank in the chilled calm—the bathroom was empty save for her—then pulled her cell and speed-dialed ONE. It rang twice, connected.

"Hi, baby," she said. "I'm sorry it took so long, but we just had a terrible—"

"Who's this?" an unfamiliar voice said.

"Uh, you first," Superstition said, taken by surprise—Derek guarded his cell like Fort Knox. "Why are you on my husband's phone?"

"Are you Detective Davis? Superstition Davis?"

"Yes," she said warily. Two women strolled in, chattering about the gunfight. She glared at them to curdle milk, and they immediately backed out, wordless.

"This is Commander Rivera with the Arizona Highway Patrol. Is it possible for you to get to Tucson right away?"

Panic clawed her insides. "Why?"

"You really need to get here, ma'am," the commander said. "Your husband was wounded tonight. There was a gunfight in one of our canyons and—"

"Is he dead?" she said, horrified.

Silence.

"I'm a cop, Commander, so just tell me, goddammit," she demanded, her heartbeat jacked back to middle-of-a-gunfight. "Is. Derek. Dead?"

"Yes, ma'am," River said with a genuinely mournful tone. "I'm afraid he—"

"Robbie!" she shrieked.

Ten seconds later Hanrahan was barreling through the door. "What's wrong?"

She held out the phone like it was radioactive. "He's gone," she gargled, tears carving gorges in her heavily rouged cheeks.

"Huh? Who's gone? What do you—"

"Derek. He's . . . he's . . .dead." She flashed on the three gunmen who'd kept her away from him in the final moments of his life. "Those dirty . . ."

"Sue, wait," Hanrahan said, reaching for her arm.

But she already out of the bathroom, bursting through a gob of medics, and running up to the corpses. "You black-eyed son of a bitch!" she screamed, drop-kneeing Pistol in the back, which snapped his spine like a dry stick. "My husband died alone and it's your fault, you motherless . . ." She mule-kicked her stiletto into Desert Eagle's face. The heel sank through his right eye like a golf putt, then snapped off at the base. "Tear off *my* head, huh, blackie?" she snarled as the heel vibrated like an orange tuning fork. "Shit down *my* neck, huh, black eyes?" She screamed and kicked and stomped, blood puffing from the dead men's wounds like air from a blacksmith's bellows. "He died without me, he died all alone—"

"Get hold of yourself," Hanrahan hissed as he wrestled her away from the corpses and the cell phone cameras. "The whole world is watching."

She squirmed out of his grasp and launched a molar-shattering kick at Shotgun. Her squad mates blocked her like the Bears' front line, pushing her away from the targets of her wrath. Her brain boiled over and her cursing grew multisyllabic.

Hanrahan moved in nose-to-nose.

"Shut the hell up, Detective," he snarled, squeezing her biceps so tightly that she yelped. "You don't, I'll put you in handcuffs."

The searing pain of the grab-hold plus the unexpected threat of arrest snapped her out of attack mode. Her energy leaked away, and she began to sag. Hanrahan held her steady. "I'm good, I'm good," she murmured.

"I know you are, I know," he replied.

The squad hustled her to the bathroom. Superstition slumped into a corner, trying to regain her composure. A cop wrapped a blanket around her, patted her arm. She nodded numbly. Hanrahan picked up her cell and dialed the last incoming number. Rivera picked up. Hanrahan asked questions but mostly listened. "Okay, thanks," he said, finally. "We'll get on the next flight." He told a detective to search O'Hare's outbound schedule and book a pair in business class. "I'll call when we hit your airspace, Commander. Thanks for offering to pick us up."

"Tucson?" Superstition croaked, vaguely remembering what the highway patrolman had mentioned before her brain turned into a road flare.

"Yeah. That's where the medevac took Derek after he was—"

She held up her hands.

If he didn't finish, it couldn't be true.

1937

JANUARY 17
IG FARBEN CHEMICAL LABORATORIES
LEVERKUSEN, GERMANY

"Be careful!" Dr. Gerhard Schrader chided as the dense, slippery poison splashed toward the top of the bottle. "Even sealed, that's a bottle of dynamite."

"Yes, *Herr Doktor*," his assistant said, firming his grip. "I'll treat her like a virgin, I swear." He placed the bottle on the polished steel table in the center of the test chamber. A German shepherd with a kinked tail smiled up at him, brown eyes glowing with adoration. Schrader, amused, tapped its solid glass crate with a precisely trimmed fingernail. The puppy, tail wagging, followed the taps with her nose, leaving smeary slug trails on the glass. The chimpanzees in neighboring crates flung poo as they howled. The cats across from them stretched languidly, looking bored, and a pair of chestnut-maned horses, one of each gender, whinnied between mouthfuls of hay.

Schrader nodded, satisfied. He'd come a long way since discovering last month that an experimental crop pesticide could be turned into a weapon of mass destruction. The memory of the remarkable find played in his head like a film reel, with the good doctor, brilliant and strong, taking front and center as the star . . .

The little white lab mouse stared at the blue-veined cheese. *Glanced at the exit.*

Back at the cheese.

Exit.

Cheese.

Exit.

Twitched its whiskers.

Wiggled its behind.

Decided.

It ran past the wide-open escape hatch in favor of the food, which wasn't a tough choice for the mouse, not really, having not been fed since yesterday. It skidded on all four paws as it reached nirvana, plunging nose-first into the soft triangle of Edelpilzkäse, the tiny blowholes of which pumped an aroma so rich that it flooded the glass cage with olfactory cries of Eat me! *The mouse happily obliged, stuffing its cherry-sized cheeks with breakfast.*

The handsome chemist observing this jotted a page of notes even as he cried toward the heavens: This has to work, Herr Doktor! The world depends on you! *His new pesticide looked fine on paper. All his formulas did. But he hadn't had a real-life success in months, and his bosses were grumbling that their star researcher couldn't seem to kill anything anymore.*

He sighed, then sealed up the exit, trapping the mouse. He squeezed a brick-red rubber bulb. A microscopic amount of chemical puffed into the airtight cage. The dirty mist rained down on the mouse, which jerked as if electrified. It spasmed uncontrollably and curled into a comma.

Then it died, head in a blow-hole, leaking cheese.

"Mein Gott," *Schrader breathed. as he trembled from the knowledge that he had just changed the world forever.* "Mein holy, holy Gott . . ."

Schrader waggled his head in self-amusement. Of course he wanted that feeling to continue forever! Who wouldn't? But it was time for bigger breakthroughs.

He walked to the crates and shook them as hard as his short arms could manage. Solid as rocks. The air hoses that fed them were properly gasketed. He lit a smudge pot to generate an oily black smoke. He waved it around each cage, checking the caulking for air leaks. None. The confinements were perfectly engineered.

"Sehr gut," he said.

They moved to the table holding the liquefied nerve gas. "You remove the lid. I'll place the hose in the bottle," Schrader ordered.

"*Ja, Doktor,*" his assistant said, handling the lid like a land mine. Schrader slid the pump hose into the urine-colored poison and sealed it with a stopper. The assistant transferred the lid to an airtight container. Neither noticed the pin-drop of solution dripping onto the tiled floor from the inside rim of the lid.

The assistant started the movie camera as Schrader switched on the pump. The liquid hummed as if alive, moving up the hose and into the misting devices, spraying poisoned perfume into each crate. The puppy's eyes bulged. It barked once, twice, and then flopped over dead, its coffee-and-white body curling into a comma, joined quickly by the cats, parakeets, monkeys, and jackals, their screeching fading to nothingness.

"Fourteen seconds," Schrader noted approvingly. "Twice as fast as last time. I wonder if the finer vaporization helped—" He clutched his throat as his lungs suddenly caught fire.

"*Dok . . . tor,*" the assistant belched.

"Eyes . . . let me see . . . your eyes," Schrader gasped.

The assistant peeled back his swollen lids as he reeled drunkenly. Schrader, laboring to breathe through the wool stuffed in his nose and mouth, saw the pupils had receded to pinpoints. "Poisoned. We've been poisoned," he gasped. "There is a leak inside the laboratory . . . out . . . get out . . ."

They stumbled for the exit. The assistant crumpled to the floor. Schrader grabbed his arm and clump-dragged him to safety as his vision faded to battleship gray. The room spun to the choking whinnies of horses.

Chapter 5

PRESENT DAY
ABOARD THE SUBMERSIBLE *SHAKEN*
GULF OF MEXICO

Raider peered through the observation port, shaking his head in wonder at the raw power of the crude blistering out of the gash in the earth. The pressurized boil reminded him of the space shuttle blasting off from the Cape. At this depth, a mile below the rainbow-slicked waves, the oil was tarry as a hot-mopped roof and shaped like the blobs in a Lava Lamp. The ocean floor was alive with the little spheres, which danced and jiggled from the power of the stream.

"We're gonna need a bigger boat," he said.

Denton laughed at the *Jaws* reference. "And with these strong currents, the surf's up in Mexico for sure. How do you want to approach?"

Raider thought it through. "Finesse is out," the owner and captain of the submersible decided. "We'll push the cap into the oil, inch by inch. Good old brute force should work."

Denton nodded and cut his forward speed to minimum. Raider readied the well cap—the multi-ton metal plug held tight by the hydraulic work arms bolted to the exterior of the submersible—and told *Stirred*, the mother ship at the surface, what they were planning.

"Ready," Denton said.

"Steady," Raider said.

"Go," they said together.

They crawled toward the hole like a ten-ton turtle.

Raider was a treasure hunter. Normally, he used his submersible—one of the few on the planet able to handle the immense pressures of deep ocean water—to scoop doubloons from ancient shipwrecks. But a couple of days ago, the CEO of British Petroleum had called in a panic. He said the oil well they'd capped after the *Deepwater Horizon* disaster had sprung a leak, and if the treasure hunter would dive down and replace the cap before Congress threw him in jail, he would personally fill Raider's swimming pool with hundred-dollar bills . . .

Raider felt unusually heavy vibrations in the hull. "Methane level?"

"Minimal," Denton said after scanning his gauges. "It's just the power of the oil stream."

Raider nodded. With every barrel of crude came tons of methane, which most people called "natural gas." They were trapped like Siamese twins in the oil-bearing rocks into which wells were drilled. Sometimes an overly large pocket of gas erupted from the hole, and when that happened, it tended to explode. That's what destroyed the *Deepwater Horizon*—pillows of natural gas shot up the drill pipe and into the rig, catching a spark and creating the shot heard 'round the world. "We're good."

"For now," Denton said.

Shaken inched into the blow zone. Raider felt the stream catch the outer lip of the cap, which was shaped like a teacup without a handle. He angled the mechanical arms—to compensate.

"Cap is ten percent into the stream," Denton said.

"Very good," Raider said, riding the constant shifts in pressure. Pushing a blunt object into an oil stream was not unlike sticking your hand out a car window at ninety miles per hour. If your angle was flat enough, your hand knifed effortlessly through the air. Turn your palm a quarter inch and the wind pressure swatted your hand into the window. "Keep 'er level, matey," he said. "I'm starting to lower the cap."

"Lowering, aye," Denton said, playing his communications keyboard like a piano. BP execs wanted real-time updates, and with the millions they were paying Raider to bottle this spilled ink, they'd get whatever they wanted. "We're thirty-nine percent inserted."

Raider felt sweat break out on his forehead. Fifty percent—half in, half out—was the most critical point because the cap was at its most unstable. One false move and the stream could wrench it sideways, tear out the work arms, breach the hull, and turn them into plankton—

Ah-oooga! Ah-oooga!

"Now what?" Raider muttered, turning off the digital Klaxon.

They watched a vast, tear-shaped bubble of methane erupt from the hole. It disrupted the oil stream, which kick-started a massive vibration that shook the submersible like a paint mixer, setting off the Klaxon. The vibrations turned the work arms into tuning forks, which weakened their hold on the well cap . . .

Which popped like a Champagne cork.

Denton enlarged his trackers to full sweep. They watched the multi-ton cap sail over their heads in a lazy, tumbling arc. "Giddyup," Raider drawled. Denton squirted go-juice into the propellers and drove toward the projected point of impact. Raider flipped on auxiliary searchlights. The gloom lit the sea like Friday night football.

"Oh, crap, it's in that graveyard," Denton said unhappily.

Raider nodded at the three-story shards stabbed into the seafloor like giant serving forks. Some resembled the burned-out skyscrapers from 9/11. Others formed shapeless hills of rubble. All had belonged to the wrecked *Horizon* . . . and each could play can opener to the thickest submarine hull. Denton drove slow and easy, picking his holes and threading the needles. Twenty minutes later they reached a pile of cylinders encased in steel netting. "What the heck are these things?" he wondered.

"Not part of the *Horizon*," Raider said.

"Nope. There's way too many barnacles. They've been down here for decades."

"Sea junk," Raider decided, turning his attention to the well cap. It had broken through the steel netting that prevented the strange metal cylinders from floating away. Fingers of broken netting clung to the cap like rusty fish hooks. "I don't see a problem," he said. "I'll cut away the net, then lift out the cap."

"Those cylinders will get loose," Denton warned, knowing how much his environmentalist boss hated adding to the trash piles wandering the Seven Seas.

"No choice," Raider sighed. "We can't let the shards scratch the cap any further."

He used the work arms to snip the heavy wire strands. Denton called out dips and rises as he maneuvered *Shaken* in a tight, neat circle. Iridescent bubbles clung to the submersible, then disappeared. A creature materialized in the viewing window. It was a bright reddish orange, with a bell-shaped dome sitting atop a round, thin undercarriage. It looked like the flying saucer from a bad sci-fi and wore oil globs like acne.

"*Benthocodon,*" Raider said.

"*Gesundheit,*" Denton said.

"It's Latin for—"

"A *pedunculata*, a jellyfish with fine red tentacles in the margin of the bell and gonads which run along its eight radial canals. Yeah, I know."

Raider whistled. "Someone's been reading Wikipedia on his days off."

"Only when I tire of Internet porn," Denton said.

Raider kept sawing, and finally, the hole was large enough. "Thar she blows, Cap'n," Denton announced as the first cylinder floated out and caught the current.

Raider pursed his lips as the rest joined the great escape. One cylinder bumped the viewing port. Eight feet long and two feet across, he estimated. Shaped like a cigar, with a flat bottom and gently pointed top. What metal wasn't studded with barnacles was painted a dull olive green. There were stenciled markings—letters mixed with numbers—but they were so faded that Raider couldn't make them out. One stenciled symbol looked like a hexagon. That rang a vague bell, something he'd seen on a Web site years ago. But he did tons of Internet research to find sunken treasure ships, and he just couldn't place it. Given the stencils, this could be military equipment. Depleted air tanks. Acetylene for welding. Something gassy, he assumed, given the shape. The military industrial complex heaved everything from bullets to baking sheets over the side—"Gee, we ran out, Admiral" was a fine excuse to buy more, keep those defense contractors whistlin' Dixie . . .

Denton made a wet gagging sound. Raider refocused and choked a little himself.

The skeleton was human. Its flesh had been picked clean by hungry sea creatures. Its bones were chalky and lightly barnacled, its eye sockets hollowed. Like every human skull, grinned without humor. It bobbed gently in the current, lashed to the netting by a scorched drilling chain loosely wrapped around its bones.

"One of the missing rig workers?" Denton said.

"Probably," Raider grunted. Two of his friends had been on the *Horizon* when it exploded. They'd escaped with "only" blistered burns. "Let's retrieve him."

"What about the leaking oil?"

"It'll be here when we're done." He pointed at the skeleton. "This is more important."

Denton maneuvered the submersible. Raider sawed away the drilling chain, scooped up the waterlogged bones, and deposited them into the collection tank bolted to the side. He mumbled a seafarer's prayer—*"Steer the ship of my life, good Lord, to the quiet harbor, where I can be safe from the storms of sin and conflict"*—but kept his eyes open for more surprises. None came, so he scooped up the well cap too and reversed course.

Two hours later, they made the final twist of the cap. The river of oil became a creek, then a dribble, then dry. Raider lit the underwater welding rig and melted the cap onto the well pipe. After it cooled, he shook the cap with the lobsters. It didn't budge. He made one more round of welds, and then nodded, satisfied. No more crude would escape this tomb. "Let's bring our sailor home," he said.

Denton pointed *Stirred* toward *Shaken*, as twelve mysterious cylinders drifted toward Mexico.

Chapter 6

NOGALES, MEXICO

Javier's pickax bit deep into rocks and dirt.

He paused to catch his breath, then pulled back for the next strike. The pick head wouldn't unstick. He spit on his hands and heaved with muscles corded by years of manual labor. Clumps flew. The men flanking him shoveled the debris into a barrow and wheeled off without a word.

"You work most hard," the supervising engineer said in Iranian-accented Spanish. The cartel's tunnel experts were on loan from Hezbollah, the Iranian-backed terror group that set up shop in Mexico after 9/11. The ayatollahs wanted terror teams close by if the Great Satan launched punitive attacks on Iran, and the terrorists' Middle Eastern coloration fit in better here than Canada. They were experts in holes, thanks to the thousands of tunnels they and Hamas had drilled into Israel and Egypt, so the narcotics cartels put them to work. "And you work quietly. That's best, the quiet. Do everything nice and silent, and the soldiers, they never catch you."

Javier nodded, swung the pick again. *Chunk*. His shoulders ached, and he was only feet into this new tunnel, which the cartel was carving from the basement of an old house a block south of the U.S. border. A jackhammer would make short work of this hard pack, but it would quickly alert the U.S. Border Patrol, which constantly swept its side of the fence for underground noises. So they'd dig this tunnel by hand, laying sound-absorbing mats onto the walls and ceiling and burrowing deep enough to ensure that ground-penetrating radars wouldn't notice the extra hole amidst the flood-control pipes that crisscrossed the border like the lattice of a blueberry pie.

Which reminded Javier that he hadn't finished lunch. He pulled an apple from his back pocket and bit hard. Felt the juice run down his chin. He lapped it with his tongue, not wanting to miss a drop of the energizing sugar. It tasted a little of dirt, but with his job, so did everything.

The cartel bought this house from a Mexican pensioner delighted to receive cash in a recession. It already owned dozens of buildings on the Arizona side of the fence, having scooped them up cheap in America's foreclosure tsunami. Connect the dots, and there was yet another way for the cartel to get its products to its customers. The engineer called it "the new underground railroad." Javier had no idea what that meant. He threw the browning core into the returning wheelbarrow and swung again. More muffled chunks. More quiet shoveling . . .

"Shhh!" the engineer hissed as his radio burbled. He spoke hurriedly with the man watching the house from the outside. "Trouble," he said, hurrying for the stairs.

Javier looked at the wheelbarrow men, who were sliding down the wall to sit on their dirt-crusted haunches. Their bored expressions said, *We're not paid to think, only to haul dirt.* Javier half-smiled. His ambitions were far bigger. But everyone started somewhere.

Hefting his pick, he climbed the rubble to the window facing the street. He parted the checkered curtains enough to peek out. A uniformed officer toting a small black submachine gun was striding to the front door.

"Policía federal," he whispered. Federal police.

He wondered if the engineer had remembered to lock the basement door. Just that tiny bit of roadblock might keep a lazy cop from discovering what was down here. He hustled up the stairs, hugging the wall to minimize creaks, and reached the half-opened door without a sound.

The cop was in the kitchen, facing away, lighting a cigarette. He took a deep drag and pinched out rings of hazy blue smoke. Then he flicked the Marlboro into the engineer's face. "I hear you're building a tunnel," the cop said.

"Me?" the engineer said, feigning innocence as he wiped tobacco ashes off his pockmarked cheek. "Who told you that dirty falsehood—"

The cop slapped him. The sound was loud as a gunshot. "Don't lie to me, you worm," he said. "I want money to look the other way."

The engineer sighed. "*Señor*, I have none here."

The cop touched his submachine gun and raised an eyebrow.

"Well, on second thought, perhaps there is a small amount here somewhere . . ."

The engineer walked to the cupboard under the sink and removed a stack of cash. Javier relaxed, figuring that would take care of it. Mexican policemen made less money than American busboys, so they hustled bribes to feed their families. This cop was a little more aggressive than most in soliciting *la mordida*—"the bite"—but certainly not out of the norm . . .

Till he pointed his gun at the engineer's heart.

"Every dime, *Señor*," he growled.

The engineer's eyes went wide. "This is cartel money," he protested. "Not mine. I'm not authorized to give you even what I did. But for the sake of getting along—"

"Put it all in this," the cop snapped, throwing a cloth bag on the table. "Or I'll shoot you and take it anyway." The engineer quivered with indecision. The cop flicked off the safety. "You have five seconds. Now four. Now three. Now—"

Thunk.

"Yi!" the cop shrieked as the pickax emerged from his chest, between his badge and his armpit. He sank to the floor, gurgling. The engineer staggered to the sink and threw up.

"Are you all right?" Javier said, hands on his knees as the adrenaline rush dizzied him. The charge from the half-opened door took less than a second, but it seemed forever.

"Yes . . . yes . . . I am fine," the engineer said, wiping his mouth with one hand and pulling his phone with the other. "Thanks to you."

"Who are you calling?" Javier said.

"*Jefe*. He'll know what to do with this dog."

Javier couldn't believe his luck. He'd always wanted to meet *Señor* Garcia, who was born in the industrial slums of Mexico City—same as Javier—but rose to a top September 27 cartel command thanks to brains, guts, and hard work. Only thirty-one, the man had a hundred confirmed kills and even more *narco* deliveries under his hand-tooled belt. Most of what he did now was management—outwitting rivals for turf, recruiting suppliers, mapping ever-creative ways of delivering the goods—but he still liked to lead mule trains into the Big Lonesome. With luck, get into bloody gunfights with any American who dared stand in his way! Javier hoped to be that kind of man. But until the day came, it was best to work hard. Garcia despised those who didn't pull their weight.

He walked to the cop, who was twitching as if hot-wired. Bent over and grabbed the pickax. It was as stuck as it'd been downstairs. Javier wrapped both hands around the scarred wooden handle and yanked. The blade came out with a sloppy *shhhhluck*. He walked down the stairs, and resumed digging, whistling softly.

Sixty-four wheelbarrows later, the engineer was calling his name. He buried the pickax in a wall and hustled up the stairs. Emerged to see a tall, rangy Mexican standing astraddle the dead policeman. The man had blue-black hair, bluer jowls, and sideburns trimmed at mid-ear. Dried mud dotted his jeans and T-shirt. His tattooed muscles were live wires, and the hazelnut eyes set deep in his darkly handsome face burned with an intensity Javier felt to his bones.

"You made this mess?" Garcia barked.

Javier was confused. He thought he'd be thanked for his initiative. "Yes, *Jefe*," he said, standing in the doorway. "I killed him."

"Why?"

"He was stealing our money."

Garcia's eyebrows flew up. " 'Our' money?" he growled, lips curling . off his teeth. "That is *my* money, cockroach. Not yours. Or his. Mine."

Javier shook his head. "Begging your pardon, *Jefe*, but we all work for your money. So all of us must protect it." He nodded at the corpse.

"The policeman wasn't going to take just his share. He demanded every penny. He was two seconds from machine-gunning the engineer for daring to refuse."

Garcia looked sideways at the Iranian. "You refused a policeman his bite? Brave."

"Not very. I would have acquiesced when he reached one," the engineer said, smiling faintly. "But Javier made it unnecessary."

Garcia nodded, redirected his piercing gaze. "Continue."

Javier's throat was sawdust. "I sneaked up the stairs to ensure the door was locked, so the policeman wouldn't discover the tunnel. He was aiming his gun at the engineer's heart. His back was to me. I had the pickax in my hand and . . . well . . ."

Garcia's glare grew darker. He touched his belt knife, whose mahogany handle was inlaid with elephant ivory. Sweat prickled Javier's head and back. Angering this man would shorten his life to the next blink of his eyes, but pride dictated he finish.

". . . that's why I killed him, *Jefe*. To . . . protect."

"So you say," Garcia said, each word a slap. "Tell me, cockroach. Would you do it again?"

Javier nodded, too frightened to form any more words. Garcia stared as a wolf regards a crippled fawn. Javier hoped his mother would select a nice coffin because he'd be spending eternity inside . . .

Instead, Garcia's face broke into a toothy grin. "Outstanding!" he said, clapping his hands. "Excellent!"

"Uh," Javier managed.

Garcia hitched up his jeans and kicked the cop in the head. Smiled at the flies buzzing out of the filmy eyes. "He held a machine gun, but you attacked. To save my money, tunnel, and most revered engineer. You didn't back down when I pushed you." He dug a mud clot from his ear, flicked it at the cop. It bounced off on his badge, which made Garcia laugh. "What you did takes courage, my friend. *Cojones*. I'm glad you have them. Many of my workers don't. They are content to be sheep, baaing for a paycheck."

Relief dripped down Javier's backbone. "I'm happy you think so."

"Where are you from, Javier? Who are your people?"

Javier told him, and Garcia seemed pleased. "Our life stories are not dissimilar, it seems. Are you interested in learning more of our ways?"

"Yes," Javier said, head bobbing like a dipping bird. "Very much."

"Then here is your first lesson," Garcia said, pulling the eight-inch blade from his belt. It gleamed like a steel tooth. "Cut off the head of this *puta*."

Javier gulped.

"Don't worry, you can do it," Garcia said.

Javier nodded, knelt, and began cutting, trying not to gag. When he got to the neck bone, he flipped the knife to use the saw teeth filed into the spine of the blade. The vibration made his wrist and forearm ache. Finally, the head was detached and Javier was soaked in cold blood. It was far harder to do than he'd assumed—the tendons were steel wires, and the spine like sawing through sunbaked adobe. He could have sworn the policeman's eyes were winking at him while he worked. That was crazy . . .

"What . . . what shall I do with him . . . this?" he breathed.

Garcia smiled. "This, and he, will warn them to quit screwing with us," he said, clapping Javier on his unbloodied back. "But first, go shower and change." He looked at himself, knocked off more dirt clumps. "I guess I should, too."

"Moonlight as a mud wrestler, *Jefe*?" the engineer said, dark eyes dancing with mischief.

Garcia snorted. "The Border Patrol crashed our party in Peck Canyon. We managed to escape, and the shortest route home was through one of our abandoned tunnels." He winced. "Narrow as a cat's ass, that tunnel was. But it sure saved mine."

He turned back to Javier.

"Go clean up. But don't dawdle. We need to display our policeman before he smells up my nice new car."

Chapter 7

FEDERAL BUREAU OF INVESTIGATION
WASHINGTON, D.C.

Special Agent Deb Williams groaned to wake the dead, which she was, halfway, anyway.

She'd just started the week of sleep she needed to recover from a bank-records examination so tedious that her eyeballs lapped themselves crossing. Then the Bat Phone trilled. It was her former boss, calling from his aerie in the J. Edgar Hoover Building. The man never slept, she swore. He'd have been a vampire, if vampires wore brogues with argyle socks . . .

"You realize I don't work for you anymore, right?" she said. He commanded the Bureau's elite counterterrorism division, and she was a lowly, if talented, special agent in the civil rights division he used to run.

"Things change, Grasshopper."

"So I'm back in your posse again?"

"For now."

"And nobody else in Hooverville can do whatever it is you have in mind?"

"Nobody with your grace, wit, and perspicaciousness."

Williams snorted. "Whenever you butter me up," she said, vertebra popping as she rolled into a cross-legged sitting position. "I know I'm gonna hate what's next."

"Did I mention how smart you are?"

She dug her fingers into her twitching eyes, trying to clear them. God, she wanted more sleep. "Okay, where am I going?"

"Chicago," the director said. "Where a white policewoman just killed three black men. One she shot in the back. The rest she kicked to flinders, screaming racial epithets. The video's gone viral, so I want you to check her out."

Williams shook out her hair. She'd watched the CNN bulletins before hitting the pillow. "Weren't the robbers shooting up a bar? Didn't she prevent a slaughter?"

"Yes and yes," he said. "Nonetheless—"

"You want me to bust the chops of a hero. Ensuring I'll get shit not only from ten thousand of Chicago's finest but from every broke-ass politician near a TV camera."

"Dramatic," he said. "But not inaccurate."

She sighed. "So what do you want me to find, exactly? Excessive force? Civil rights violations? Brutality? Racism?"

"Yes."

Williams nodded at the phone. Before being handed the crown jewel of the empire—hunting terrorists—he'd run the civil rights division. His hard-on for police brutality was the tomahawk with which he'd taken hundreds of blue scalps.

"What's her name again?" she said.

"Davis. First name Superstition."

"Super . . . uh, why?"

"Don't know. Find out."

Williams bounced off her Serta Sleeper, the other side of which was empty, like it had been, sadly, most of her life. She headed for the bathroom, exhaustion vanishing. Nothing like corpses to juice up a tired brain.

"Can I take the Gulfstream?" she tried. "I'd like to arrive while the memories are fresh." Also, she despised flying commercial, particularly when babies were crying and the smelly guy next to her "fell asleep" with his hand on her thigh . . .

"I already told the air boss you're coming."

"Really?" she said, incredulous. For agents at her level, the FBI normally pinched pennies till they turned back to ore.

"There's no time to waste. The Chicago Police Department has gotten away with corruption and brutality for much too long. Throwing Detective Davis into a federal dungeon will send a message that we're tired of it."

Williams couldn't disagree. In Chicago, police outrages blew stronger than its windbag politicians. A high-ranking commander ran a torture ring for two decades, then retired to the Sun Belt on a full pension. A drunken cop beat hell out of a bartender half his size for refusing him further drinks, then received probation because the judge said, in essence, *Hey, he didn't kill her, right?* There were dozens more examples, from nickle-and-dim to atomic-level WTF, and that was only off the top of her head.

"On it," she said, knowing her exhaustion didn't matter. When a Bureau Brahman said "jump," a smart agent said "how high?" It helped that she'd liked working for him. "Quick shower and I'm gone."

"Thank you, Deb," he said. "I appreciate your willingness to move so promptly. Particularly after frying out your brains on those neo-Nazi bank records."

"The little I have left, anyway," she said, appreciating that he still kept track. Most who entered the Promised Land forgot the serfs they left behind. "I'll call you when I get to the Chi."

The director cleared his throat delicately. "If you say that while you're there," he said, "the locals will pee on your government car. Nobody calls it 'the Chi' except ad guys in skinny jeans."

She laughed, and moved her finger over END. Then she heard her new-boss-same-as-the-old-boss say:

"Oh, did I mention that her husband, a decorated SWAT officer, was murdered tonight while helping the Border Patrol interdict Mexican traffickers?"

Williams nearly ran into the door. "Oh, and did I mention Elvis isn't really dead, he works at a mall in Fresno, so would you go find him?"

That brought a chuckle. "At least the Chi is closer."

Chapter 8

U.S. BORDER CROSSING WITH MEXICO
NOGALES, ARIZONA

"Big plans?" the border agent said, peeking over his Ray-Bans.

"Izzy's twenty-two today," Chantico explained, pointing to the woman driving the car. "We're heading up to Tucson to celebrate."

"Sounds good," the agent said, running his long-handled mirror underneath the Lexus, one side, then the next. No explosives or contraband. All parts were in place, and road dust was equally distributed. "Beautiful car."

"Muchas gracias, Señor," Isabel Garcia purred, flashing a mouthful of whites.

He was enchanted, not least by the tan lines wiggling seductively in her pink scoop top. But he ran the mirror one more time anyway—smugglers came in all shapes and sizes, from toddlers to grandfathers to babes in agent-distracting outfits. He nodded, satisfied he hadn't missed anything. "Okay, ladies, you're looking fine."

They giggled.

"The car, I meant the car," he said, winking. Mexicans were cool. A shame their brutal cartels made it so dangerous for Americans to hang out south of the border; it kept him from knowing them as well as he'd have liked. "Drive up to passport control, and you'll be in Tucson before you know it. You need directions to the bars?"

Isabel shook her head. "No, we're cool."

"Then happy birthday, *Señorita*," the agent said. "Maybe I'll see you up there sometime."

Isabel blew him a flirty kiss, then drove into the United States, holding up her papers, as did her three friends. They'd done this many times in search of the perfect margarita . . .

"Cute puppy alert!" Chantico piped.

Isabel stuck her head out the window. A sniffer dog was hard at work, big wet nose going a mile a minute. It searched an F-150, followed by Beetle, Beemer, and Barricuda, after which the dog would work her Lexus, sniffing for smuggled narcotics. Which didn't concern her. She wasn't her brother.

She turned her thoughts to tonight's celebration. Dancing, drinking, and a birthday cake would be great fun. But she hoped to blow more than candles. It had been six long months since she'd dumped her boyfriend, the louse, and she was so ready for love that she could hump a cactus. But a man who knew what he was doing would be better.

Chantico would drink only Bullshits—Mountain Dew mixed with Red Bull—so she could bring them home safely. Driving drunk was a serious offense in the States, and when Izzy enrolled in the *Instituto Tecnológico Regional de Nogales*, her brother drilled into her the importance of not breaking American laws. whenever she was across the border. "If you never do anything wrong, college girl," he'd explained, "they'll never have an excuse to do you dirt, even though you're related to me."

She heard the gentle panting of the German shepherd. "Hi, baby," she cooed. She loved dogs, and even though this was a police pooch, that wasn't his fault, was it? "Are you a good widdle boy?"

"Me?" the handler kidded. "Or Bosco?"

The shepherd wiggled his ears upon hearing his name.

"Oh, you're both so handsome, but . . ." she said. She looked down at Bosco. "You're the devil in disguise, oh yes you are," she sang in the mezzo-soprano she'd honed in countless karaoke bars. "The devil in disguise—"

Bosco stiffened, then dropped onto his haunches. American agents immediately fanned around the car. "What's wrong?" Isabel said, alarmed. "Why is he acting that way?"

"Step out of the car, ma'am," said a beefy agent with a ballcap tucked low on his eyes.

"But I didn't do anything—"

"Now, ma'am."

Uniformed agents yanked all four doors and dragged them out of their seats. "Do you own this vehicle?" Ballcap demanded. "Are there any narcotics inside?"

"No! Absolutely not!" Isabel said.

"No? You mean you don't own this car?" he barked, trying to trip her up.

"Yes, I own this car," she said, recognizing the game. "No, I don't carry drugs."

"Then you'll have nothing to worry about while we search, will you?" he said. "Follow that officer inside while—"

"Search?"

Ballcap nodded at the sun-bleached government building to their north. "Bosco picked up a scent in your vehicle. That gives me reasonable suspicion to conduct a search. Make it easier on yourself by showing us where you hid the bundles—"

"Oh, I get it. I'm Mexican, so I must mule dope, right?" she said, flushing with anger. "I tell you, there are no drugs."

Ballcap shrugged. "The dog says otherwise. We'll check it out. If he's wrong, you can go ahead with my apologies. If he's not . . ."

The flat tailing-off chilled her. This had to be a mistake. She'd never been involved in the narcotics business. She was earning a master's degree in digital engineering, with dreams of becoming the Mexican Bill Gates. She'd marry well and raise a handsome family with many *niños*. She'd make a splash in the legitimate business world, then run for legislative office and, after the appropriate length of time, the presidency, shedding a tear for the cameras as her official portrait was hung in the National Palace in Mexico City.

It wasn't that she disapproved of what her brother did—she wasn't a hypocrite. *Narco* had raised her family out of dirt-chewing poverty when nothing else would, and it paid for lots of nice things, including her college education and this Lexus, a present from her brother when she turned twenty-one. But narcotics wreaked so much havoc on the country she loved—beheadings, mass shootings, corruption so pervasive that even getting the trash collected required *la mordida*—that she wanted nothing to do with pills, plants, powders, or potions.

Bottom line, this car was clean. She would swear it on the graves of her parents, and so would her brother, whom she believed, without reservation, because they loved and respected each other, and neither had ever lied to the other about anything, not once, not even as children, and not when he became a *narco* kingpin and could do so without her ever knowing.

But if all that's true, why is Bosco so cranky?

"Come with me," a lady agent ordered.

They headed into the looming concrete bunker, fear dripping down Izzy's back.

Chapter 9

SEVEN HUNDRED MILES FROM MEXICO
GULF OF MEXICO

The first olive-drab cylinder bumped over a sand bar visited only by diarrheic seagulls. It was followed by the second, third, and twelfth. The pack slowed as sand and guano dragged at the barnacles that pocked the old steel like mumps.

Then, knocked loose by waves, resumed their westward drift . . .

"Hell are those things?" a mate on a fishing boat said, raking seaweed from his beard as they plowed the Gulf like a bean field.

"Prob'ly trash from that new oil leak," the skipper spat, feeling his blood pressure spike despite the cool wind in his face, which he'd been enjoying till he spotted the debris. Those Limey bastards were going to put him out of business for another couple years, and the courts still hadn't heard his lawsuit from the first time! "Haul up the nets before they foul."

The crew hurried to pull in what could be their final paycheck. Once the crude oil from the new leak arrived, the seafood would die, and they'd all be out of work.

Again.

As the crew dragged schools of madly flopping fish onto the deck, the captain ducked into his cabin. Grabbed the M1 Garand rifle clamped to his desk. It was his shark gun. He needed to blow off some steam or he'd stroke out, swear to God. And what better way than shooting the hell out of an oil company?

THE FURY

He clamored down the ladder and walked to the edge of the main deck, mentally noting paint that needed chipping—a boat was a continual remodeling project. He braced himself against the railing with well-scabbed knees and thighs. He shoved a clip of thirty-ought-six into the top and released the slide with a metallic *thang*. He thought of his father, who'd fought Nazis in France and Japs in China with this well-worn rifle. He'd visit the old man at the home when he got back on land, deliver the cheerful news that Old Bess still worked like a charm . . .

"Whaddaya shootin' at, Cap?" another mate piped up. "Jaws?"

"Nah. I'm putting some holes in BP's ass-sets," he said, taking careful aim.

Boom.

The bullet made a tiny splash in front of the first cylinder. A skipjack tuna flipped belly-up. "Who needs nets when you've got a Garand?" the mate hollered as the crew applauded. The captain bowed. Rewelded the nine-pound weapon to his shoulder. Corrected his lead, compensated for the waves, pulled firmly on the trigger.

BOOM!

"Whoa, nice shot!" everyone cheered as the metal fish exploded into confetti.

"Compressed air," the captain ventured. "Got stirred up from the bottom by the force of the new leak and—hey, what's that goofy looking cloud—"

The M1 Garand, hero of World War II, clattered to the deck as the captain started to violently retch, his crew falling down around him.

As eight hundred fish slowly ceased their writhing.

Chapter 10

PRESENT DAY
CHICAGO

Clop-clop.
 Clop-clop.
 Clop-clop.
 Clop-clop.
The dappled stallion halted abruptly and shuddered from nose to tail.
"I know what you mean," Superstition Davis said.
The horse dipped its head, as if it sympathized. Then it resumed its noble journey, pulling the waxed, black caisson through the turreted limestone gates of Rosehill Cemetery.
The caisson was trailed by a snake-line of Chicago Police cars, flashing blue, filling Ravenswood Avenue, spilling onto Peterson Avenue. It was followed by a second line, flashing red, blue, amber, and white, from cop shops nationwide, local to county, state to federal, FBI to ATF to CIA to DEA to ICE, filling Bryn Mawr Avenue, spilling onto Western Avenue, filling the city's largest graveyard with a squad-car honor guard.
All turning out to salute the fallen.
All turning out for the one who paid the price.
With them, skirl and thrum of bagpipe and drum, cops in kilts with naked knees, daggers gleaming, hobnails tramping.
In funereal beat.

THE FURY

Superstition's father squeezed her hand. She squeezed back, then glanced through her veil to the right. Mother stared straight ahead, shoulders back, chin up, thin hands folded. Her smile was faint but glowing. An expression of joy that Superstition both knew and hated.

"Try to look sad at least," she hissed.

Mother turned. "How can I be sad?" she whispered. "He's living with God now—"

"Fuck God." She glared at the passing caisson. "And the horse He rode in on."

Mother blanched, and Superstition turned away. Her father tightened his grip. Bagpipes soared with "Scotland the Brave," the fallen warrior's favorite.

Now the minister, dark and elegant, Bible flashing.

Now the honor guards, wheeling wide, swords and rifles by their sides, marching up the grassy knoll, halting at the clay hewn hole.

Now the caisson. Now the coffin. Now the bearers, blue hands in white gloves on brass rails. Preacher preaching. Singers singing. Reporters reporting. Superstition trembling, choking on rage and fire. Tearing away her veil, unwilling to hide anymore.

Cops, saluting.
Superstition, standing.
American flag, folding.
Hanrahan, delivering.
Superstition, accepting.
Trading funeral hugs.
Bearers leaving.
Brass departing.
Crowd retreating.
Families shuffling.
Bagpipes blowing.
"Amazing Grace."
"Flowers of the Forest."
"When the Battle Is Over."
"Going Home."

Haunting echoes.
Off the granite . . .
Off the marble . . .
Off the stone . . .

Superstition loved bagpipes. When she and Derek spent that month in Scotland, trying to escape the bone-deep sadness that haunted them even while asleep, they'd stopped at Kilberry's in Edinburgh to purchase a set of Great Highlands. Returning to the hotel, she shyly proposed a use for the chanter that the maker probably hadn't envisioned. Derek smiled—it was the first time either of them had felt this since laying their children to rest—and they tumbled into the duvet, chasing away the devil with their own form of heaven. Every day afterwards, in the limestone basement of their Northwest Side bungalow, that fondly remembered sound and fury brought a power to her soul that erupted through her lungs and lips as she practiced.

She got so good that she'd been recruited by the Emerald Society, impressing the pipe majors with her command of the long, mournful skirls that the bag o' banshees demanded of its acolytes. She loved the dedication of the pipe-and-drum cops—it proved a nice antidote to the tedium and aggravation that was the unfun part of police work—and they'd assured she'd quickstep next summer in the Chicago Highland Games.

But as soon as she got home today, she'd smash her chanter and splinter her drones, rip holes in her air bag, then burn the whole rotten thing in her Weber kettle.

Because today it was piping her husband to his grave.

"Hand salute," the commander of the honor guard barked. White gloves snapped to blue checkered hats. The bagpipes wept. So did she. The love of her life was going home.

Without her.

SUPERSTITION'S HOUSE, THAT NIGHT

"Not only no, but hell no!" Clayton Brooks thundered, thumping his leaf rake so hard that the metal fingers wiggled like vipers.

"But you saw the Facebook video—"

"It's a simple word, Agent Williams: *N* and *O*," Brooks said. "Superstition ain't no racist." He eased his weight off his right leg, suspicion clouding his broad face. "Unless you need to turn her into one for some reason I can't imagine."

Deb Williams shook her head. "I'm just trying to understand her, Mr. Brooks," she said. "You're one of her neighbors—"

"And a friend. Be sure to write that on your little pad."

"Friend, right," Williams said, scrawling the word, then sticking her notebook in her pocket. Her handwriting was illegible from shivering, as her black wool suit from this morning's funeral wasn't cutting it in tonight's October wind. "So how do you square who you say she is with what she called those black men?" Which was, in the shorthand of this morning's *Chicago Sun-Times*: SLAY IT AIN'T SO!

Brooks stabbed his rake at a fleeing leaf. "Three psychos open fire. She's forced to kill them. They're black. She calls 'em something inappropriate."

" 'Blackie' and 'black-eyed son of a bitch,' " Williams said, "are more than 'inappropriate.' "

He shrugged. "When I was in Vietnam, I sang 'chestnuts roasting on a gookish fire' while flame-throwing a squad of Victor Charlies. Did that make me a racist? No. Does 'blackie' make Sue a racist? Nope." He yanked up a coat sleeve to show a muscular forearm. "If you hadn't noticed, that verdict comes from the ace of spades."

"At least you're not a joker," Williams said.

Brooks softened a fraction. "You're judging her from a couple words on a video. Well, I know her a lot better." He patted his right leg, the one he kept favoring. "So does ol' Kilroy."

Williams raised an eyebrow. "You have pet names for your legs?"

He zipped his coat to his goatee. "A few years back, some cream-colored asswipes were driving down this street," he said, tapping the curb with the rake. "Hitler youth types."

"I'm familiar with the breed," she said, having grown up in South Boston.

"I was here, doing this." He raked a few leaves for illustration. "They started yelling the usual garbage—'Hey, jigaboo, swim on back to Africa,' all that."

"What'd you do?" Williams said.

Brooks made a face like she was ignorant. "Four of them and one of me? I didn't say a word. Just turned and kept raking." He put weight on the right leg, changed his mind. "Guess they didn't like I wasn't properly terrified. Figured I should have been wailing, 'Sorry, Bawse, jess doan beat me or nuffin.'"

Williams nodded her understanding. She'd done Klan investigations early in her career. The acid in those groups could strip the enamel off your teeth.

"They jumped out of the car. I took off for the house. Tripped on this damn rake." He glared like it was still responsible. "They were on me in a flash. One had an iron pipe." His voice grew stony. "Thirty seconds of beating and I was almost dead. Would have been all dead 'cept for Sue and Derek—"

"Her husband?"

"Man we buried today, right," Brooks said, nodding. "You go to the funeral?"

"I did."

"Showed your respect. Good for you," Brooks said. "Anyway, Derek and Sue ran out of their house ordering those boys to stop." He pointed to the yellow brick bungalow next to his Tudor, nestled under the tree canopy that blanketed this Edison Park neighborhood in the far northwest corner of Chicago. "White boys asked if they wanted some too. Superstition just laughed, then gave 'em this look."

"'Go ahead, make my day?'"

"Something like that." Brooks smiled with pride. "They were ready to wet their pants, those boys were. You should have seen that gal at that very moment. Her war face was so fierce it'd intimidate an H-bomb.. Asswipes hardly noticed Derek's shotgun."

"Hardly doesn't mean didn't," Williams said.

"You're right," Brooks conceded. "But puzzle me this, Agent Williams: If she's a racist, why would she help me at all? Why wouldn't she grab a beer, wander down to her rec room, and turn on *Law & Order*?"

Williams tried to suppress her shivering. A few more minutes and she'd have to retreat to her car and get her coat. "She's a police officer, Mr. Brooks," she pointed out. "That's her job. She would have rescued you even if she hated the color of your skin."

Brooks tapped his right leg. It rang like knuckles on a downspout.

"Not a racist in the world," he said, "who would have bought me this."

Superstition practically levitated, she was so angry. "How can you look so happy?" she hissed. "Derek is dead. Don't you care about that, even a little bit?"

Theresa Kallas sighed and folded her hands in prayer. "That's your pain talking, honey," she said, her voice soft and perfectly modulated. She wore the same faint smile as at the cemetery. "Let God take it from you. Just let Him into your heart and you'll feel so much—"

"Better? I'm never going to feel better," Superstition said. "Don't you get it? That bastard left Derek's brains on the desert floor. He's never coming back. I'm alone."

"You're never alone when you've got—"

Superstition stomped her foot so hard that her dishes rattled in the breakfront. "Don't you dare say it, Mother," she said. "If God is as all-powerful as you claim, then God killed him. And that, I don't forgive."

Theresa shook her tightly curled hair. "He is all-powerful, Superstition. So clearly He had His reasons to call your man home."

"Oh? And those reasons were?"

Theresa pressed her lips till they whitened, then blew out her breath. "Your babies were crying from loneliness. They needed their big strong father to take care of them. So they begged God to bring their daddy home, and He listened—"

"Leave my children out of this!" Superstition screamed, flinging her mug, the coffee just missing her mother's head, splashing instead across the front room's bay window.

For the first time since meeting her daughter's return flight from Tucson, Theresa's certainty cracked. "I think I'll take a walk," she said. "Allow you to cool off. Clearly, your emotions are getting the better of you."

"Clearly," Superstition hissed. Once upon a time they'd been so close. When did Theresa Kallas turn into this emotionless chainsaw? More important, why? Mom had always been a free spirit, warm and wise and knowing exactly what to say when her daughter was hurting. When did her heart become titanium —

"Honey, I'm home!" her father sang from the kitchen.

Superstition jumped, startled at the unexpected shout. Then she remembered he'd driven to the Jewel to pick up a case of Maxwell House, since uncles, aunts, cousins, friends, and a bazillion cops would be stopping by the house in a few hours to pay their respects.

"Let's set up the party urn, Dad," Superstition said as her mother punched her arms into her puffy blue coat. "Don't get mugged."

"Who's going to mug me in your kitchen?" he said, confused.

"I'm talking to your wife," she said.

"I'm going for a walk, dear," Theresa said.

"Bundle up, it's getting nippy."

"I will."

"Go with God," Superstition said.

"I always do," Theresa said.

Superstition ground her teeth. Her mother never did get sarcasm. The front door closed with a soft wooden *klump*. The American eagle knocker added a metallic clack.

Her father walked in with the steaming remains from the kitchen pot. "Want a refill?" he said, surveying the mess. "Or should I serve it to Mr. Window?"

"Very funny, Dad," Superstition said, grabbing an old T-shirt from a drawer. She walked to the plate glass, grateful her aim hadn't included the leather couch. The right side was worn into the shape of Derek's butt and shoulders, and she wouldn't want to desecrate it.

"I can do that," her father said.

"No, I'm fine," Superstition said, the shredded cotton slurping up all the brown liquid. Good to the last drop, indeed.

"What happened?" he said.

Superstition blew out her breath in a single sharp blast. "She jumped on my last nerve. With golf spikes." George Kallas smiled. Superstition adored that look. It was as full of warmth as her mother's used to be before she began slapping fives with The Man Upstairs—

"She means well," George said over the rag squeak on the glass.

She wiped the final drop with her thumb, absently licked it dry. *Yuck.* Dust bunnies had multiplied like, well, rabbits back here. She'd attack with Endust before everyone arrived. Maybe Derek could move the sofa, which was too heavy to manage by herself . . .

Jesus, what were you thinking? She bolted around the couch and hugged her father till her arms trembled. "I love you."

"I love you too, Skeeter," he whispered, using the nickname he'd bestowed the first time his little girl wrapped him around her little finger. "I miss Derek. Mom does too. He was a good man, and we loved him to pieces."

"Me too," she squeaked, her violet eyes growing hot. They held tight, swaying like boats in a gentle sea. Then George sat on the couch, balancing the mug on his knee.

"God is your mother's way of dealing with what would otherwise crush her," he said. "You know how bad it got after the twins—"

"I know," Superstition said. "But she needs to get over it."

George shook his head. "She will never get over it, and neither will I."

Deb Williams peered through the garage's double-hungs but saw nothing that pinged her sonar: cars, shovels, gas cans, a slumpy bag of Sakrete. The garage was on the alley at the rear of the property, separated from the house by a, neat, rectangular yard dotted with curled oak leaves. The bungalow was older but meticulously maintained, with fresh tuck-pointing, a new roof, and oversized windows that pushed away the darkness. She didn't know what compelled her to come here tonight; she had no intention of crashing the open house. Just doing reconnaissance, she supposed, seeing what might jump up to greet her—

"Peeping Toms go to Stateville," a voice growled. "Even if they wear federal badges."

Williams whirled, pawing her suit coat away from the Glock strapped to her hip. Then, recognizing the man in the shadow of the alley, eased off. "Nice to see you again, Lieutenant," she said drily. She'd interviewed Robert

"Robbie" Hanrahan the morning she'd arrived. He'd been aggressive, wary, and hostile, and his expression suggested that hadn't changed.

"What do you think you'll find in her garage, Williams?" he said, striding up and into her comfort zone. "Klan hoods?"

"I'm fact-finding. Poking around. Seeing what I can see."

Hanrahan looked angry enough to slug her, and she prepared to defend herself. Instead, he leaned against the garage and pulled out a pack of Camels. He put a cigarette between his lips, scraped the match against his fly, and sucked hard, staring at her pointedly. She folded her arms, refusing to take the bait. "Call me whatever you want, Hanrahan. I'm doing my job."

"Which is what, exactly?"

She decided to say it plain. "Deciding if Suzy's a racist who gets her jollies by gunning down people of color, and, therefore, deserves time in the federal can."

"And is she?"

"Yet to be determined. Not that it's any of your business. This is a Bureau matter."

"Uh-huh," Hanrahan said, dragging deep from the cigarette and blowing a stream of smoke at her. "Want to know what I think?"

"Not particularly."

"Too bad." Deeper puff, heavier smoke, forcing Williams to step out of the cloud. "Fine, yours is bigger," she said, coughing. "Happy?"

Hanrahan flicked the cigarette between her feet. The long ash broke away, an earthworm split by a hatchet. He immediately lit another. "You're a hotshot civil rights agent. You parachuted in from Washington instead of letting the Chicago field office handle the investigation," he said. "That means you're not here on the square but to make the evidence fit a conclusion somebody's already drawn for you."

"I don't work that way—"

"Sure you do. Feds need local scalps to justify your inflated budgets, and frankly, the dumbasses in my department have pitched you some mighty fat softballs."

"But going after Superstition Davis is a mistake, right?"

Hanrahan nodded. "She's one of the finest police officers I've met in twenty-two years of law enforcement. And she's as racist as Martin Luther King."

"Only Dr. King? Gee," Williams said, theatrically slapping her forehead. "I was hoping you'd say Gandhi. Or Jesus Christ. That would be so much better for my report."

A flicker of amusement crossed Hanrahan's lips. It would, she thought, be a terrific smile if it ever got wide enough, but the chances of that happening were as unlikely as her winning the Powerball. "She didn't shoot those assholes because they were black," he said. "She shot those assholes because they were assholes."

Williams crossed her arms. Every Chicago cop she'd interviewed, even the black ones, had sung a variation of that tune. They were closing ranks around their racist comrade . . . or they were telling the truth.

He finished the cigarette in a single drag and used the glowing ember to fire the next. "You want a sit-down with Sue? Here and now?"

Williams raised her eyebrows. "The day she buried her husband? That's too insensitive, even for a Feeb," she said, deliberately using the slur—short for "feeble"—that local cops hung on FBI agents like neon "kick me" signs. Part of the never-ending one-upmanship between local and federal law enforcers, who distrusted each another for reasons so tribal that she wondered sometimes how anything ever got done.

"She knows you're poking around," Hanrahan said. "You might as well get it over with."

Williams thought about it. "All right," she said with a deep shiver. "But first I'm getting my coat. I'm cold."

Hanrahan looked triumphant. Williams sighed and turned for her car. Even their weather had a bigger dick.

1941

SEPTEMBER 9
THE EAGLE'S NEST
BAVARIAN ALPS, SOUTHERN GERMANY

The gaunt man leaned close enough to the mirror to fog it with his breath. Frowned. Teased the gray hairs from the rest of his blunt-cut mustache and plucked the imperfections clean. He straightened, checked himself one more time—he was fastidious about his appearance—then nodded. He straightened his medals, shot his cuffs, and strode from his lavatory into his war room, accepting a chilled refreshment from his fawning chief of staff.

"*Seig heil!*" his cabinet thundered.

"Be seated," Adolf Hitler said.

They took their places at the conference table, which had been sawn from a single log of wood from the Black Forest. He greeted his intimates one by one: Goering and Goebbels, Himmler and Bormann, Eichmann and Heydrich, Jodl and Raeder, Keitel and von Ribbentrop. They, in turn, called him, affectionately, "Wolf." Two fresh-scrubbed aides served coffee and pastries, then hastily retreated, leaving their masters to their race.

"Four weeks into the invasion and Russia is not yet mine," Hitler said. "What do we do about that?"

Notebooks opened and arguments erupted: armor, aircraft, bullets, troops; Moscow, minesweepers, more, more—

"And what about the Jews?" Hitler interrupted. "We agreed on a final solution to this problem. Yet they continue to infest our homeland. How do you plan to exterminate this accursed race?"

"Carbon monoxide," Goering said.

"Too inefficient," Jodl said.

"Bullets," von Ribbentrop said.

"Too expensive," Himmler said.

"Hanging and burning take too long," Goebbels said. "The corpses pile up and there's no place to store them—"

"Enough!" Hitler shouted, banging the table till the coffee cups trembled. "I want solutions, not excuses!" The room went silent, and Hitler's rant turned thunderous. Spittle rained on Jodl. The general didn't move. Nobody did. Nobody dared. The most powerful military commanders on the planet feared his grotesque reactions to slights, real or perceived. Finally, a patrician-looking man raised his hand.

"*Herr* Eichmann!" Hitler sighed theatrically. "Can you save me from this ineptitude?"

Adolf Eichmann put on his silkiest smile. "Are you familiar with the work of Dr. Gerhard Schrader?"

Hitler sipped from his glass. "A chemist at IG Farben, I believe," he said. "Specializes in insecticide development." He waved his free hand. "So?"

"So," Eichmann said. "He's developed a new poison. You touch it, you die." He looked around the table, pleased to see all eyes on him. "He calls it 'nerve gas.' It's light-years ahead of our Zyklon-B poison because you don't have to inhale it. A drop—one tiny speck, mind you, anywhere on your body—kills instantly."

Hitler frowned.

"I know it sounds impossible," Eichmann said. "But I have proof. May I show you?"

Hitler nodded. The lights dimmed, and a film projector flickered on. His eyes widened as cats, horses, monkeys, and other test animals curled up dead. He whistled when Schrader stumbled out of the lab, tears and mucus flowing. "So we can exterminate our Jews with this . . . what did you call it again?"

"Nerve gas," Eichmann said as the lights came back up. "Unfortunately, no. Not yet. This poison is so corrosive there's no safe way to handle it in the field. It shows immense promise, but there is work to be done, taming it enough to put in the hands of our troops."

"But the Zyklon-B? That's ready to go?"

Eichmann nodded. Zyklon-B was a cyanide-based inhalation poison that the Reich heavily diluted to delouse prisoners. Its pure state was Thor's hammer. "Otto Ambros over at Farben swears he can produce Zyklon-B in enormous quantities. It doesn't kill as efficiently as nerve gas, but it will do the job." He reached for his coffee, drawing out the moment. "Imagine unloading boxcars of Jews at Auschwitz, Birkenau, and Majdanek. We escort them to the shower room, explaining that after their hard journey they deserve a nice, warm cleansing. They go along like the donkeys they are. We cram the room full, then open the nozzles."

"But instead of water, poison," Himmler said, catching on.

"We drop the Zyklon from hidden holes in the ceiling, right," Eichmann said, peeved that Himmler dared steal his thunder. The little *schiesse* was always doing that. "It fills the room with clouds of poison and kills whoever's there. We open the doors, carry the bodies to the crematoriums, pull out any valuables like gold teeth, and prepare the 'showers' for the next trainload. It's easy, efficient, and cheap."

The bunker fell silent in admiration.

"Better living through chemistry," Hitler said, stroking his perfectly black mustache.

His intimates burst out laughing. Hitler joined in. Then said, "Order Zyklon-B into full use. But keep developing that nerve gas. The war is going well, but if that changes, I want all options at my fingertips." He looked at Heydrich, who was Eichmann's superior in the Gestapo. "Think you might have room for another *obersturmbannführer* on your staff, Reinhard?"

"I can't think of a better man for the job," Heydrich said, meaning it. He liked people as ruthless as himself—not for nothing was he called the Man with the Iron Heart—and with the mass extermination camps opening soon, he'd need every industrial-grade killer he could get.

"Then effective immediately, *Herr* Eichmann, you are promoted," Hitler said, getting up to shake his hand. "Congratulations. I expect great things from you and your wonder gas."

Eichmann beamed as the cabinet applauded.

Chapter 11

PRESENT DAY
SAND DEVIL SOCIAL CLUB
FIVE MILES EAST OF NOGALES, ARIZONA

"Showtime," Brian Charvat said.

Two border agents raised their combat boots. The leg-powered explosion blew open the door, and curses from inside flew hard and fast. "Mailman!" Charvat bellowed as he limped into the stucco-and-block clubhouse. "Front and center!"

A wiry Italian with a Pancho Villa mustache looked up from his poker game. "Goddamn, Charvat," Joseph "Mailman" Stancato complained. "Can't you see I'm in the river?"

"Only river you get," Charvat said, "is the one I drown you in." He moved toward the card table covered with green felt, pork rinds, beer, and stacks of twenties, his cane clunking with each step.

Mailman's grin showed teeth so white they looked spray-painted. "That's right, dawg, I heard you got shot in the ass," he said.

Charvat grinned as if enjoying the gibe. Then he upended the table with his cane, sending money and pork rinds flying. His two agents shooed Mailman's complaining crew outside, leaving the two bosses to themselves. Charvat dragged over a chair. Mailman unrolled a soft pack from his Phoenix Suns T-shirt, smacked out a cigarette, and made a show of lighting it. " 'Chu want from me, dawg?" he drawled.

"The guy who did it," Charvat said. "Don't screw with me, 'dawg.' I want the name of the asshole that killed Derek Davis."

Mailman took another drag and blew it in Charvat's face. "I just tole you, man, I don't know nuttin' about no killers—"

Charvat knocked the marijuana dealer out of the chair. Picked him up and threw him over the bar, the crashing of bottles harmonizing with Mailman's nuclear cursing. Charvat limped around the bar, kicked him in the ribs. "Whatchu doin', man?" Mailman yelped, scrabbling to cover himself. "You never been no animal cop."

"I'm a Swiss fuckin' cheese with a dead friend keeping me awake nights," Charvat growled, wondering what was up. Mailman normally snitched without prompting because Charvat ignored his small-time dope deals in exchange for information that hooked bigger fish. His reluctance here was profoundly unusual.

"I let you bring your nickel bags across my border. I let you deliver them, and I let you keep the proceeds," Charvat reminded, nudging him with a steel toe. "All you need to do to keep me off your back is not hurt cops or citizens and tell me about those who do." He stared to vaporize concrete. "You failed me on both counts."

Mailman groaned. "It wasn't one of my people . . ."

"Meaning you know who it is," Charvat pointed out. "C'mon, who killed my man?"

Mailman's eyes darted like a squirrel dodging predators. In the drug business, getting a reputation as a rat got you disemboweled.

"Nobody will ever know we talked," Charvat assured. "Your guys, and mine, are outside, and that's what the beating's for, to cover you."

"I get it. But you gotta understand, this dude is *loco*."

"All druggies are *loco*."

Mailman shook his head. "Crazy for real. You hear about that head-less horseman?"

Charvat nodded. Nogales cops found the head of a *judicial federal* nailed to a tree, one steel spike through each eyeball. Witnesses said it looked surprised. "I heard."

"Word is, the dude did that. I don't know why. And I *don't* wanna know what he did with the rest of the body."

Charvat didn't care. That was Mexico's problem, not his. He only wanted the dirtbag that shot him and Davis. "Who is he, and where do I find him?"

"First, you swear it don't get tagged to me," Mailman said. His voice was shaky, and not from the beating. That interested Charvat even more. Mailman was a tough little shit and not afraid of much.

"Cross my heart and hope you die," Charvat said, making an *X* over his chest. Mailman still hesitated. Charvat sighed, wiggled his boots.

"Garcia," Mailman whispered. "The man who shot you is Jiménez Garcia."

Charvat had no idea who that was, but then again, his memory was still tattered from the shooting. He recalled some things with perfect clarity. Others were gone with the wind thanks to what the doctors called *traumatic amnesia*, which was a fancy term for *Fucked in the head, Fred.* "Refresh my recollection."

"*Narco* hotshot," Mailman said. "He's the chief enforcer for September 27."

"Those creeps, I know," Charvat said. The September 27 cartel was commanded by Vincente Delgado, who claimed to be a businessman from Acapulco. In reality, he was a global narcotics dealer, lethal as ten scorpions, and so volatile that even Los Zetas, runner-up on the *narco* crazy train, steered clear. To be Delgado's chief hard-ass, this Jiménez Garcia had to have smarts, stones, and not a little bit of crazy himself.

Mailman nodded. "He goes by Jimmy. Smuggles horse, coke, meth, weed, guns, pussy, children—you name it, he moves it. Smuggles the cash back into Mexico. He used to work the Texas border, but the Rangers been pouring on the heat, so he came to Arizona."

"Lucky us," Charvat said.

"Yeah, man, I don't like the competition, either," Mailman said, the sarcasm sailing way over his head.

Charvat bit back a smile. *At least he's a useful idiot.* "Where do I find Garcia?"

Mailman shrugged. "Mexico?" Charvat gave him a look. "Best I can do," Mailman insisted, holding up his hands. "Man keeps a fancy ranch in the mountains, but he lives here and there. Tries to make it hard for you guys to find him."

Charvat knew that all too well, as keeping track of the ant farm of creeps was the most vexing part of his job. "He got money? Ambition?"

"Up to his eyeballs," Mailman said. "He loves the *narco* business. And yeah, he wants it all. He'll run things sooner than later, mark my words."

Charvat thought about the policia's potato-shaped head, which had been plucked clean of its hair. Some sort of insult, he supposed, though he didn't know what. "Loves killing, too," he said.

Mailman tapped his right temple. "*Mi hombre* gets off on murder, *Jefe*," he intoned. *"Mi hombre* is *muy loco."*

Charvat rolled his eyes. "Cut the Spanglish, *mi amigo*," he said. "You're from Cleveland."

"Yeah, that Chief Wahoo is a gas, ain't he?" Mailman said, grinning but quickly regaining his seriousness. "Garcia muled a load of narcotics into Peck Canyon," he said. "On the same day you got shot. One of my guys seen him and his crew."

"Your guy reliable?"

"Pokes my sister, so yeah, I vouch for him."

"Well, the time and place fit," Charvat said, recalling what his agents reported after he came out of the anesthesia. "Where did the skag wind up?"

Mailman spread his arms wide. "The usual: Tucson, Phoenix, then everywhere." He tapped the side of his swollen nose. "Uncle Sam's children do love their candy canes."

Charvat sighed. Mailman was right. Without American demand for drugs, there'd be no Jimmy Garcias or Vincente Delgados. Or Brian Charvats to chase them. While he'd happily manage a Jiffy Lube if it meant eliminating the staggering violence of the narcotics trade, the *narcos* wouldn't. Frankly, neither would most American drug warriors. Too many budgets, careers, and adrenaline rushes relied on it.

"Yeah, yeah, all right," he said impatiently.

Mailman looked triumphant. "Something else to admit while you're at it, Bee," he said, easing from one butt cheek to the other. "That thing with the assault rifles. It was totally ironic, right?"

"What assault rifles?" Charvat said.

Mailman cocked his head. "You don't know?"

"They don't have TVs in intensive care," he said, deciding not to mention his recurring memory gaps. There was no upside in giving any mope an edge.

Mailman laughed. "Better sit up straight for this one, *mi amigo*," he said.

"It's kinda late for a house call, isn't it?" Agent Connor observed as he cleared traffic with the siren. Charvat looked out the window of the unmarked car, saw the Man in the Moon. Remembered the buttercream face smiling down at him moments before the shooting. Wished the glowing bastard had said something, maybe Derek would still be alive . . .

"Absolutely," Charvat said. "But this information can't wait."

Connor nodded. He would explain when he was ready. Charvat was always three steps ahead of everyone else, and, unlike most bosses, willing to get his hands dirty. The last thing he'd shouted at Mailman in front of his nickel-bag homies was, "All right, whipdick, don't talk to me. But one more cop gets shot around here, and I promise you'll never father children."

Connor would take a bullet for Charvat. But driving to Phoenix was easier. He put Interstate 19 in the rearview and joined Interstate 10, the direct route to the state capital. The yellow eyeballs of a coyote gleamed in the headlights. Connor honked to let it escape. The only predators he enjoyed hurting were human. "You want to go to his home or to his office?"

"This time of night?" Charvat said.

"Hell, you work this late all the time," Agent Otto said from the back.

Charvat grinned. "I don't have a life. He'll be at home."

He squinted like Eastwood, and his name was, ironically, Clint. But his voice was squeaky as Mighty Mouse. "Good kid, huh?"

"The best," Charvat said, sucking on Tecate while Clint digested the story. The CIA man ran spy networks in Mexico and Central America. He'd been nice enough to offer drinks to his old fly-fishing pal after getting over the surprise of the unannounced visit. They sat on Clint's shaded back patio, breathing the cool mist from the swamp cooler that made outdoor spaces habitable for anything more heat-sensitive than geckos. Charvat observed, and not for the first time, that for people professing to love the sun, Phoenicians actually spent little time in it.

"I knew that shit would come back to bite us," Clint said.

Charvat nodded. Several years ago, the U.S. Justice Department and the Bureau of Alcohol, Tobacco, Firearms and Explosives—ATF for short—got the bright idea that Mexican drug cartels should buy as many weapons as they wanted from American gun shops. "Operation Fast and Furious" secretly sold hundreds and hundreds to cartel buyers through firearms dealers in the Southwest, who didn't want to participate but figured they had little choice, considering ATF controlled their licenses. The idea was that tiger teams from the ATF would keep an eagle eye on the guns, document where they wound up, then swoop down like Batman and Wonder Woman, using the guns as evidence to stick those cartel boys where the sun don't shine. The problem was, the ATF lost track. As most everyone with a working brain knew they would.

Clint asked, "How'd you connect Peck Canyon with Fast and Furious?"

"We recovered AKs from the dead *narcos*," Charvat said. "We put the serials in the tracing computer, and an hour later my boss got a frantic call from Washington. Turns out they'd been sold to the cartels. Along with that effing grenade launcher." He cracked his still-scabbed knuckles, recalling the blast that turned his perfectly good Jeep into Burning Man. "But hold on to your knickers, Clint, it gets even better . . ."

The CIA officer drained his beer as he analyzed the information provided by Killer Bee's informant. "Interesting. Do you trust this Mailman jamoke?"

"Well, let's see," Charvat said. "He stores his weed in Priority Mail boxes. He figures if he gets caught, he'll claim he found the boxes in the street and was merely running them to the post office because he's a darn good citizen. What's not to trust?"

Clint rolled his eyes.

"I didn't say he was smart," Charvat said. "Just plugged in tight to the local asshole network." He took a little drink. Thought a little about Derek. Got a little sad. "One of his guys spotted Garcia in Peck Canyon that day. He told Mailman, who told me."

They fell quiet, opening fresh beers.

"You shoulda seen that kid, man," Charvat said after a while. "Knocking down those gomers like ducks at an arcade. That boy had a stout heart, and he was the best combat shooter I've ever seen. Without that grenade launcher, he'd have nailed the whole dirty dozen."

"Derek's Last Stand," Clint mused. "Damn shame, losing a man like that."

"I know what you mean," Charvat said, sighing theatrically as he got to the real point of the long drive north. "I only wish there was someone who could bring the alleged perpetrator to justice. The thin blue line of American law enforcement can't touch him now that he's back in Mexico."

The CIA officer drank more Tecate and then curled his lips into the resemblance of a smile. "Badges?" he said. "We don't need no stinking badges."

Charvat punched his fishing buddy's shoulder. "They never actually said that in the movies, you know."

"Yeah," Clint said. "But they shoulda."

Chapter 12

UNITED STATES PENITENTIARY
FARGO, NORTH DAKOTA

Isabel Garcia touched her forehead to the steel bar bisecting her window. It was as cold and unfeeling as the men who'd shipped her here. Razor wire glittered like thin strands of diamonds in the midnight sun of the floodlights. Dobermans trotted between inner and outer fences. Snipers roved in concrete towers shaped like Solo cups. The exercise yard was asphalt, not grass, the nets on the basketball hoops, chain link, and beyond it all, wheat and sorghum and scarecrows. It was a concrete tumor in a cold, barren sweep of a city named after a movie.

But yet, she wasn't in prison, they insisted.

This was a contract facility, investor-owned and -operated for profit, so her "intake counselor" explained that her steel cage wasn't a cell but "personal living space." She wasn't a prisoner but a "resident" living on a "campus." Her toilet sat in the open "to ensure your personal safety and hygiene," and the uniformed hulks roaming the halls were "staff," not guards. All of which made her, she supposed, intercoursed . . .

"Whachu in for, homes?" her sleepy new cellmate—*Roomie? BFF?*—drawled from the bottom bunk of the two-rack.

Izzy turned away from the window, which taunted her with promises of a world that, until the bumpy flight on "ConAir"—the federal air transport system that moved prisoners about the country; "Southwest with shackles," a U.S. Marshal cracked when she boarded—had been all hers. "They found cocaine in my car," she said. "In the engine compartment. Five pounds."

The cellie's wince said, *Gonna break rocks in the hot sun.*

"I didn't put it there," Izzy said, the explanation sounding pathetic, even to her. No wonder the judge said no bail. "I have no idea where it came from."

"I feel ya," the cellie said.

"You here for drugs too?"

"Ain't everyone? I was caught with heroin."

Izzy thought about her brother's business. "Where'd you hide yours?"

"Up my hoo-hah. But ah swear ah don't know how it got there!" She cackled wildly, her long fingernails waving like demented guitar picks.

"It's after curfew! Pipe down!" one of the guards shouted.

"Kiss my ass, screw!" the cellie shouted back.

Izzy shook her head, not needing this. Her first cellmate had been dragged out in chains for flinging feces at a guard. The extraction team flooded the cell with pepper gas so vile that Izzy vomited for an hour. "Don't rile them," she warned, telling the story.

"Quick on the gas here, huh?" the cellie said.

"And Tasers," Izzy said, remembering the blue crackle at her first meal, when one "guest" attacked another over a packet of Saltines. She wandered back to the window and breathed in the dank breeze, pretending she could see her family's mountain hacienda from here . . .

"Wanna eat my pussy?" the cellie said, snapping the waistband of her khaki uniform.

Stilettos of fear stabbed Izzy. The only thing she knew about being locked up came from prison shows on cable TV. "Hell no," she said, faking toughness, hoping the woman couldn't hear her madly pounding heart. "I'm no lesbian."

"Me neither," the cellie said.

"You aren't?" Izzy said, surprised.

"Nope. I like to gnaw on bones."

"Then why ask?"

The cellie shrugged. "Thought it'd take your mind off your problems."

It was so preposterous—and touching—that Izzy burst out laughing.

"I say something funny?" the cellie said, eyes narrowing.

Izzy shook her head. "No, what you offered was . . . well, it was sweet." She nodded at the blood-colored gelatin wiggling on her storage shelf. Leftovers from supper, which pretrials were allowed to take back to their personal living space. "You want something to eat?"

The cellie brightened. "Strawberry?"

"Cherry."

"Now you're talkin'." She hopped off the thin mattress and grabbed the paper bowl. "You've never jailed, have you?" she said, tipping it to her wide mouth.

Izzy sighed. She'd been trying so hard to appear hardened. "Is it that obvious?"

Sluuuuuuuurp. "Mm-hm. Bet you never even been arrested, either."

Izzy shook her head.

"Aw, don't worry none about it, you'll be fine. Couple months, you'll feel like you been here forever . . ."

Izzy had never felt so alone.

EIGHTY MILES EAST OF NOGALES, MEXICO

"I'll give you the weekend to make your arrangements, old man," Jimmy Garcia said, smacking his fist in his palm to emphasize his seriousness. "But Monday, you'd better be gone."

The parrot-beaked rancher gave him a frosty eye. "This land belonged to my grandfather," he snapped, his face a contour map of anger. "I have no intention of leaving."

Jimmy shook his head. Normally, they asked "how fast?" when a *narco* enforcer said "run." This one was a tough old beetle and not easily cowed. He admired that, but orders were orders.

"We need your property," he said. "I have no quarrel with you personally. I don't even know you. It's just business. You have to leave."

The rancher spat. It landed an inch from Garcia's boot. "Between our corrupt government and you drug *putas*, I have nothing but grief," he said. "I raise cattle. I need this land"—he swept his arm across the hundreds of acres sprawled along the U.S. border—"to do that."

"I understand," Jimmy said, growing impatient. He'd been heading for the mountains when Delgado called. The Taliban had just agreed to terms, he said, so a truck-sized tunnel needed digging right away. The exit on the Arizona side was in place—an abandoned factory in Miracle Valley, south of Tombstone. All that remained was securing the old man's land for the entrance, but the rancher had spurned cash, reason, and threats. The special skill set of Delgado's chief enforcer was needed.

Garcia pulled a nine-millimeter from his waistband. "Last chance."

The rancher's face hardened to limestone. "This is what it comes to? Killing a man for a few more dollars you do not need—"

The gun bucked. The rancher blinked, then slumped slowly to the ground.

"Yes, old man," Garcia said. "That's exactly what it comes to." He turned to his young associate. "Inform his cowboys they're staying on to run the cattle. It's good cover for what we're doing. Anyone argues, kill him as an example to the others." He pointed to the border-side factory in the distance. "That's your target. Round up the tunnelers and start digging. You're in charge till you get killed or I find somebody better."

"*Sí, Jefe,*" Javier said with a tingle in his spine. His own crew! The best thing he ever did in his entire life was sinking his pickax into that dirty cop.

He waved as Jimmy drove away, then turned to his assignment.

Chapter 13

GULF OF MEXICO

"This is the United States Coast Guard," the captain announced, his smoker's gravel scudding across the waves. "Do you require assistance?"

No reply from the fishing boat.

"*Redhawk*, this is the Coast Guard," he repeated. "Do you need our help?"

The helmsman closed the gap between the fast-response cutter and the aimlessly drifting tuna boat, which had been reported overdue by the owner's worried wife. The watch commander in New Orleans dispatched his closest vessel, the *Bernard C. Webber*, to its last known location.

"No activity. No people. No nothing," a binocular-equipped lookout reported.

"Do it," the captain said.

The chief of the boat barked out orders. The boarding party scrambled for rubber Zodiacs. Weapons crews dialed in the auto-cannon that could rip the *Redhawk* to shreds in a few bursts. If armed pirates were hunched belowdecks, hoping to spear one of Uncle Sam's sharks . . .

"Go ahead, make my day," the captain muttered.

"What's that, sir?" the helmsman said.

"Nothing," the captain said, biting back a smile. Helm was so damn young that he wouldn't get the reference even if he explained. "Move closer until I say otherwise."

"Aye, sir," Helm said, maneuvering the hundred-fifty-four-foot cutter like a Ferrari. Despite its gyroscopic stabilization, the ship bucked gently in the waves. The captain liked that. If he'd wanted terra firma, he would have joined the Army. "Commo, anything on I Spy?"

The communications mate operating the ship's mini-drone shook her head. "Just crossing the gunwales, sir . . . okay, I'm there, adjusting focus . . . oh." She shook her head. "Dear Jesus, they're dead. All . . . all of them . . . they're, they're, they're—"

"That's speculation, not a report," the captain barked. "Straighten up and give me a proper sit-rep." His crew was talented but green. His job was to teach the young'uns to act like warriors no matter how dire the circumstances.

"Uh, yes, sorry, Captain," she said, new fiber in her voice. "I see eleven, no, twelve bodies. They're sprawled across the deck. They're not moving. There are no visible injuries." She moved her joystick, sending the drone into a low-level deck sweep. "Bodies are fully intact. There are hundreds of fish spilled from their nets. They're also not moving."

"Put it on screen."

A moment later the drone feed appeared on the flat-screen monitors. The captain examined the casualties and shook his head—that weird shiny foam oozing from their mouths concerned him nearly as much as the fact that they were dead.

"Chief, send a flash alert to New Orleans," he ordered. "Mass casualties aboard fishing boat *Redhawk*. Tell them to send medical and forensic teams because we don't want to tow the boat and risk contaminating the port. Full encryption to keep away the news media." He dug at his chin cleft. "They look plenty dead to me, but let's make sure. Put the boarding party in NBCs," which was military shorthand for "nuclear, biological, and chemical protection suits."

"Aye, sir," the chief said, typing with one hand and mousing with another.

"Helm will approach from upwind," the captain said, laying out his plan for the crew. "Boarding party will determine if they're dead or just unconscious, then search the boat. Soon as that's squared away, boarding party will return for decontamination showers." If this were a floating meth lab with its highly toxic precursors, the NBCs would keep his sailors alive. If the suits proved overcautious, so what—it was a good drill anyway.

He felt the vibration of the twin diesels digging in and grinned, adjusting his cap. This queen-of-the-line battle cutter was more lethal than a World War II destroyer, and he controlled every bit of it. "Weapons, stay sharp, in case it's a zombie attack . . ."

Chapter 14

JIMMY GARCIA'S RANCH
SIERRA MADRE MOUNTAINS,
SOUTHEAST OF NOGALES

Chantico removed the blindfold and blinked from sunlight and fear.

"Mr. Garcia, I swear, I knew nothing about that cocaine," she babbled. "It was a shock to everyone, especially your sister—"

"I believe you," he reassured her. "And it's Jimmy. Please sit."

Chantico took the porch rocker. Jimmy offered *cerveza*. She drank greedily, then wiped her lips with her chipped manicure. "It was awful," she said, tears welling. "I was so scared. But Izzy stood up to those agents like she was queen of Mexico."

Garcia nodded, pleased at Izzy's guts. "Thanks for coming to see me, Chantico," he said. "If you like, I'll explain to your boss why you had to miss work today."

"That'd be great, Mr. Gar—uh, Jimmy," she said, looking relieved. "He's such a dick about time off." Garcia glanced at a henchman, who went to make the call. "Please relax," he said, noting that she was stiff as a broom handle. "You aren't in trouble, I promise."

"But . . . the blindfold . . ."

"That was only for your protection," he assured. "If the police were to ask where you went, you can truthfully say you have no idea."

She gulped more beer. "What do you want to know?"

"Everything," he said. "From the moment Izzy picked you up . . ."

Chantico was Izzy's best friend, and the one who called him with news of the arrest. As soon as he hung up, he put out the word through the prison gangs that Izzy was off-limits, then dispatched his American lawyer to see what could be worked out. That meeting was going on right now, with the lawyer promising to call as soon as it concluded. Garcia wasn't hopeful. Pounds of cocaine. Last name Garcia. Do the math.

"They ordered us out of the car," Chantico said, flipping her hair. "We didn't move fast enough, so they dragged us out." She touched her arm. "I still have scratch marks, the bastards . . ."

This hacienda, three hundred miles and a world away from Nogales, was 21,000 acres of paradise. It was timbered with oak and pine, aquiver with deer, bear, and quail. Every morning the evergreens swept the air with a piney broom as the sun poked over the mountains. It had its own river, the Bavispe, and even its own waterfall, which splashed into a natural basin pool, a soothing white noise for the random nights he stayed, which wasn't as often as he wished, because he slept place to place to avoid detection. He'd bought the spread when he was flush enough not to flinch at the price. Izzy lived here when she wasn't at school. Aunts, uncles, nieces, nephews, and grandparents were scattered across the slopes, each family in a home built to their chosen specifications, close enough for intimacy and apart enough for privacy, paid for by Jimmy and *narco*. No more slums for his family, not while he was breathing.

"They locked us in a holding cell. It was broiling 'cause the AC was broken, or so they said. Then they showed us this plastic bag. They insisted it was cocaine. Izzy said they were lying sacks of garbage. They put her in handcuffs and marched her away . . ."

Jimmy tapped out a Marlboro and flamed it with a Scripto Vu-Lighter. The iconic sixties' lighter with the fishing fly and hook in the transparent body had belonged to his father, a gentle man who'd died shoveling scrap metal. It was one of the many jobs he'd held trying to lift his family out of the industrial slums to which society had sentenced them. Mama was already gone, dying in childbirth with Izzy, in the shadow of a hospital they couldn't afford. Now Jimmy and the cartel owned the place, leaving strict orders that poor people were served before rich. It was such excellent PR for the cartel that Delgado happily approved the multimillion-dollar expenditure. Every day Jimmy lit the Scripto Vu in his parents' memory, preferring this personal candle to the cold wax in a cathedral.

"Izzy is innocent," Chantico said with a full-lipped pout. "She doesn't deserve this. Not after that nightmare with Peter."

Garcia burned half the cigarette in a single drag. "Who?"

"Uh," Chantico said, looking down.

"Tell me," he demanded.

"She didn't want you to know," she deflected. "She was . . . ashamed."

"It might have some bearing on her case, Chantico," Garcia said, alarmed that something bad had happened to his beloved little sister and he was unaware. "I need to know."

He burned as hot as the cigarette tip as she related the messy details of the breakup with a boyfriend Jimmy didn't know she'd had. Chortled at the outrageousness of the parting gift she delivered after catching him with a six-pack of whores. Fumed that the bastard beat her in revenge, so badly that she slept with Vicodin and ice packs. *I run a multimillion-dollar empire. Yet I'm not smart enough to know she's in danger!* Then again, women were clever, and if they didn't wish a man to know something . . .

"Mr. Lawrence and I will have a . . . conversation," Jimmy said, cigarette smoke pouring over his teeth like blue lava. "To make sure he isn't involved in this cocaine matter."

"And if he is?"

Jimmy smiled. Handed her a roll of money so fat it made her squeal. Motioned for his drivers to take her home. Then he made two calls.

HOUSTON, TEXAS

"Mr. Lawrence?"

The tall, blond American turned to see two Mexicans examining him with polite interest. They wore blue jeans and collared shirts. One carried a clipboard; the other, a canvas workbag.

"Finally, you're here," Peter Lawrence said, snapping his fingers. "Time is money, *amigos*, so let's get to work." The men looked at each other, and Lawrence pursed his lips. The project was behind schedule, and their unwillingness to ask "how high" when he said "jump" did not bode well for catching up. "You're my new electrical contractors, right?" he said, sweeping his arm at the half-built restaurant.

"Oh. Yes," the taller of the two said. "Electrical."

"Good," Lawrence said. "The first crew screwed things up, so I fired their asses. You do the same, I'll bounce your beans too. Savvy?"

"Absolutely, sir, sure thing," the shorter one said with utter politeness.

Better. Lawrence pulled out a handkerchief and dabbed his forehead. It wasn't the heat; it was the humidity. Well, yeah, it was the heat. And the crunchy air, belching refineries, southern accents, cowboy hats; it was goddamn Texas. First El Paso, then Laredo, Dallas, San Antonio, a yearlong diversion to Nogales and Tucson, Arizona—he'd wondered who he'd pissed off to earn that plum assignment—and now, Houston. But every executive ladder had its shitty rungs, and Mmm!Burger was no exception.

"Building inspectors rejected the wiring," he said. "Your job is to fix the mess. I don't care if you work till you collapse; it needs to be done by this weekend."

"Fine with us, Mr. Lawrence," the taller one said. "We're not the kind of Mexicans who need *siestas*."

That's what he wanted to hear. He'd had his fill of insolence in Nogales. He'd said he loved her, she'd welcomed him into her bed, she found out about all the others, she got even. With a bulldozer. It was a mess. He should have known better—ethnics didn't respect the rules of polite society—but God, she was a nice piece of refried ass. The blood he'd spilled knocking revenge into her gave him a chubby even now . . .

He spit out a text from his iPhone—"NOW, DAMMIT"—then turned into the scaffolding to goose the brick masons, who were moving slower than molasses in winter. "Mr. Lawrence," the taller one called, "you need to sign our paperwork."

"Can't it wait?" Lawrence snapped, impatience flaring anew. "I'm busy, in case you hadn't noticed."

"Won't take a minute," the taller one said. "Soon as you sign off, your electrical troubles are over. We'll take care of the work, the inspectors, the whole enchilada. You can concentrate on what's important." He dropped his voice. "Besides, we'd like to express our appreciation a little more, um, privately. You know, for hiring us."

These guys know how to play the game, Lawrence noted approvingly. They walked to the dusty cargo van idling in the alley. "Come on, the appreciation," he said, fingers snapping.

The taller one reached into his canvas bag. "Come behind the back doors, *Señor*, so your people don't see. Why should they get a taste if they did nothing to earn it?"

"Good point," Lawrence said, stepping around . . .

A lightning bolt crashed into his back. "Bwah," he moaned as his limbs turned to window putty. "Bwah shwar . . ."

"In truth, the only electric we know is stun guns," the taller one said, catching Lawrence as he collapsed. "If you cooperate you'll return here in no time, snapping your fingers at your lessers. If you don't, my associate will push an icepick into your spine. You'll drool into a sippy cup for the rest of your life."

"Entirely your choice, sir," the shorter one said, just as politely as before, as he pushed a sharpened point through Lawrence's shirt. Lawrence, feeling the prick in his lower back, managed to gargle. "What . . . who . . ."

The taller one leaned in. "Isabel Garcia sends regards."

Lawrence felt his eyelids flutter as he passed out.

The men duct-taped his arms and legs, chained him to U-bolts, and secured the blindfold and gag. They covered him with paint-spattered drop cloths, then took off with a squeal for a rural border crossing, where the only passport needed was an envelope stuffed with cash.

NOGALES, MEXICO

"I have to hear this from strangers? "What the hell were you thinking?" Vincente Delgado shouted, slamming his beer stein on the scarred wooden table. A waitress started over to clean up. The owner of the tavern held her back, knowing better than to interrupt the supreme commander of September 27.

Garcia was unfazed. "You are much too important," he said, leaning back in his chair, "for me to bother with personal problems." It wasn't sucking up. Garcia did not suck up. Delgado worked twenty hours a day running one of the world's most powerful narcotics cartels.

Delgado softened. "I'm never too busy," he said, sipping his *cerveza*, "to hear what's going on with my most valued associate."

Which also wasn't sucking up, Garcia knew. Delgado didn't have to, and Garcia was indeed his most important lieutenant, measured in any number of ways: enemies slain, product moved, dollars collected, business deals implemented—Garcia negotiated the routes that brought in heroin from the Taliban—and, most important, fealty. Garcia had personally slit the throats of six men who, when soaked to the gills with tequila one late night, were foolish enough to voice unkind thoughts about their leader. Word got around fast, and Delgado, pleased, made Garcia a blood brother, complete with sliced palms. Garcia hadn't killed the men for that reason, though it was a useful bonus. He was sending a message: *Don't ever mess with Jimmy Garcia.* He'd need that when he took over September 27. Something he intended to do when the time was right.

"I appreciate that, *Jefe*," Garcia said, signaling to the waitress that it was safe to approach. She wiped everything, replaced the mugs, and hurried away.

"She must be new," Delgado joked, letting his eyes linger on her soccer-balls backside. "Why, I'd never harm a fly."

"No, not a fly," Garcia said.

Delgado conceded the point and wolfed down a handful of nuts. Moist salt glistened on his fingers, which were permanently crabbed by a steel baton swung by *policía* who pulled him over for "speeding," demanded too big a bribe, and Delgado refused to pay. The baton was unlimbered, the hand forced onto a curb, the lesson delivered. Delgado had Garcia dynamite the police station as payback. "Anyway, you were saying about Isabel . . ."

Delgado was the second call Garcia made after Chantico departed. But his boss had already learned of the arrest from his watchers, who kept a close eye on border crossings. They agree to meet here. Garcia laid out details, and Delgado sighed.

"Families are such a burden," he said. "Yet what can we do? We love who we love." He crunched more nuts. "Her arrest isn't tied to us in any way?"

"No," Garcia said. "It's personal. Someone planted the cocaine, intending for her to get caught." He licked his fingers clean. "A boyfriend, I believe. Their affair ended badly." He gave her an edited version of his conversation with Chantico. "He'll tell me what he knows."

Delgado's eyes gleamed, and Garcia considered not for the first time that his boss's sadistic streak ran deeper than the Copper Canyon. He wouldn't wish to get on the wrong side of that streak. Those who did were dissolved in barrels of acid, soaked in honey, and staked to mounds of fire ants, or nailed, Jesus-like, to cactuses to die of sunstroke. "I'm sure he will," Delgado said, wiping his mouth on his sleeve. "Just make sure there was no pillow talk."

An alarm went off in Garcia's brainstem. "It doesn't matter if there was. She's clueless."

"You're sure?"

"Yes."

"She never overheard your plans? Ever? At the dinner table? During a family gathering? While you were out driving one day, dreaming about your futures?"

Garcia's gut tightened. Delgado named the cartel "September 27" for that glorious day in 1821 that Mexico gained independence from Spain. Delgado considered himself a blood brother of the native warlords who'd inflicted so much agony on the hated Spanish conquistadores who'd invaded Mexico's Aztec Empire three centuries earlier. He acted accordingly against whoever he considered an enemy, which was defined solely by how his lizard brain burped at any particular moment.

"I told you, *Jefe*. Since she was old enough to know what it meant, Isabel wanted no part of the narcotics business. We've kept ourselves separate on that ever since." He sipped more beer, deciding how far to push the defense. Repeat even the truth too many times and Delgado got paranoid, inventing problems that didn't exist. "As you know, she's a whiz with computer software. She wants to be the Mexican Bill Gates."

"She's much better looking, thank God," Delgado said with the boyish grin that made people who didn't know him think he was harmless. He leaned back in his chair, strummed the arm with his unmaimed fingers. "So the cocaine in her car doesn't represent a rival operation?"

"No." Garcia tapped his own heart. "I'd bet my life on that. I'd also bet yours."

Delgado nodded, satisfied. "Let me know how your meeting goes with this gonad of a boyfriend. If I can help spring your sister from prison . . ."

"They call it a campus," Garcia explained with a smirk. "But yes, thank you. I'll let you know what her lawyer says, and also the ex." They finished their beer and headed out.

"Where to, *Jefe*?" his driver said.

"Boyfriend," Garcia said.

He'd rattled in the van till his joints screamed, then was manhandled into this sagging adobe hut that stank of urine and fried meat. He told them he had to pee. They told him to go in his pants. He refused with a haughty stare, and they shrugged. He managed for an hour, then, abdomen spasming, he let go, humiliated. The taller captor made fun of the wet spot. The smaller one crushed a scorpion with his boot heel, studying its twitching poison-tail with the detachment of a chemist charting reactions. And now, after all that misery, here was brother dearest, looking for his pound of flesh. *Well, too bad for you,* amigo. *Peter Lawrence ain't nobody's bitch . . .*

"You don't know who you're dealing with, pal," Lawrence blustered, falling back on the brass balls that kicked rivals off the corporate ladder.

"They know i'm missing because i'm important. Police are on the way. Release me immediately or—"

"Exactly where do you think you are?" Garcia said. "France? You're in Mexico, my friend." *Meh-he-co*. "Nobody knows you're here. I can put a bullet in your brain"—he tapped Lawrence's forehead twice—"and nobody will find you. After a while even your mother won't remember what you looked like."

Lawrence's trembling was no longer just exhaustion.

"Fortunately for you, there's an alternative," Garcia said. He saw the spark of hope and blew it into a flame. "But first, explain why you set up my sister."

Lawrence began to protest that he hadn't. Garcia held up a finger. "If you lie," he said, "I'll know. And you will suffer."

"I didn't do it, Mr. Garcia, I swear—"

The taller one kicked him in the back. Lawrence shrieked. A second kick bruised the other kidney. "I can do this all night," Garcia said over the meaty thumps. "And tomorrow and the next day and the next. Did Isabel ever tell you about me?"

"N-n-no," Lawrence sobbed, his hardness flaking off like rust. "Just that she had a brother."

Garcia scooted his chair into Lawrence's sweat-beaded face. "I'm the chief enforcer of a Mexican drug cartel. The last man who crossed me was a cousin who worked for me as a driver. He tried to steal a nickel bag of my dope. If he'd asked, I would have given it to him for free." He pulled out his see-through lighter. Singed the long hairs in Lawrence's right ear. "Instead, I stuck ten feet of rebar up his asshole, tucked an apple between his teeth, and roasted him over a mesquite fire."

"He smelled like barbecue," the taller one offered.

"Roast pork, to be exact," the shorter one said. "Kinda like the smell in here . . ."

Lawrence's stomach turned inside out, and Garcia smiled faintly. "My sister is young and innocent. She suffers terribly in prison. So do I, knowing she's there," he said. "For our misery, I blame you."

"I swear on my mother I didn't set her up," Lawrence wheezed. "I didn't do a thing to Izzy—"

"Points for balls," the shorter one said.

"Cement for brains," the taller one said.

"I have you on video," Garcia said as Lawrence's lips formed an O. "If she'd driven more than a few hours, the engine would have stalled because the drugs were blocking the air intake. That gave me the timeline, and I started investigating, like one of your American private eyes. You know the rumpled one with the raincoat?"

"*Señor* Kojak?" the taller one offered.

"No, no, Kojak is bald and sucks the lollipop," the shorter one said. "I think it's Columbo."

"*Sí,*" Garcia said. He crooked his head and waved his finger in the air, mimicking the TV detective played by Peter Falk. "Oh, one more thing. Her condo association keeps security videos to defend against liability lawsuits. The guard who monitors the system at night was pleased to sell them to my associate." He cracked his knuckles one finger at a time, then lit the downy blond hairs in Lawrence's other ear. "You drove into the main garage, parked in a dark corner, went to her car, opened her door with a key, and popped her hood. A key I assume you kept after you broke up."

Lawrence opened his mouth to deny. Garcia pulled a saw-toothed knife from his belt. Crusted skin from the decapitated *policía* fluttered to the floor like cigar ash.

Lawrence sighed like the world was ending. "All right. I admit it. Your sister pissed me off when she dumped me. Did you know she . . ."

Garcia had to bite his tongue to not laugh. Izzy was such a sensible girl; he didn't know she had it in her to run a bulldozer through Lawrence's house, destroying it like a steel hurricane. "And then you beat her," he said, his amusement dying. "Like a donkey."

"It was an expensive house," Lawrence said.

No wonder she kicked this arrogant prick to the curb. He looked at the taller one, who pumped a carpentry nail into Lawrence's triceps. "God!" the contractor screamed as he bucked against the restraints. "God! God!"

"He won't help you, *Señor*," Garcia intoned. "Only I can do that." The taller one sank a few more from the nail gun to underline the point.

"Perhaps I should nail your balls to your fists, since you confuse the two whenever you see a woman—"

"All right, all right!" Lawrence howled. "Enough!"

Garcia let the nails burn awhile, then picked up a pair of pliers and slowly yanked them out, biceps-meat clinging to the shaft rings. Lawrence cried to rival Noah's flood. The shorter man cut away the duct tape and handed Lawrence an unlabeled bottle of amber liquid. Lawrence flinched like it was the squashed scorpion.

"It's tequila," Garcia said, amused. "Homemade. Dulls your pain very efficiently. Don't worry; it isn't poisoned. If I wanted to kill you, nail guns are more fun."

Lawrence drank a quarter of the bottle, hiccuped a full minute, then caught his breath. "Just tell me what I have to do," he wheezed. When he heard, his eyes turned to saucers. "They'll put me in jail!"

Garcia shrugged. "It's that or a hole in the desert," he said. "You're a businessman. Do a cost-benefit analysis and see if the math works for you."

Lawrence glared at him, then, finally, glanced down, defeated.

"Clean and bandage his wounds," Garcia ordered. "Then take him home. He has much work to do, and quickly."

1942

OCTOBER 22
UNIT 731 HUMAN EXPERIMENTATION LABORATORY
HARBIN, OCCUPIED MANCHURIA

It began as a whimper that ramped to a howl that turned to the screech of derailing trains.

"We don't use anesthetic on the logs," Ishii said, shrugging off the screams that reverberated along the long, brick-lined hallway of Ro Block. "It skews their reactions."

Sakamora glanced anxiously at the man-god to his right. He wasn't familiar with that term-, "logs.". But he didn't wish to show ignorance by asking. Ishii seemed to sense it and cleared his throat.

"The authorities here," he said, sweeping his arm toward the regional capital of Harbin, "believe this an epidemic prevention and water purification facility. Naturally enough, such a facility must contain a sawmill to turn trees into lumber and firewood. That's why we call our test subjects 'logs of wood.'" His brief smile showed two rows of square teeth sandwiched by a neat black goatee and a mustache the size of a small mammal. "I encourage such humor by my scientists. It makes their long hours more pleasant." He put his hand on Sakamora's shoulder. "The screaming bothers everyone at first," he said, quietly, so passersby wouldn't hear. "In a week you'll hardly notice."

His generosity warmed the young man. "I was startled only momentarily, General," he said. "I'll adjust immediately. I promise I won't let you down."

Ishii waved his hand dismissively. "Of course you won't, Sakamora. You come highly recommended from your engineering professors. And the weapon you've designed! It will alter war forever." He rubbed his hands with an expression both wistful and predatory. "Are you hungry?"

Sakamora nodded. His last meal was in Tokyo, before the long flight to Manchuria—occupied by the glorious forces of the Imperial Japanese Army in 1931—then the train ride to Japan's most secret human experimentation facility.

Ishii steered him into the cafeteria. The fleshy aromas made Sakamora's stomach growl so loudly that nearby diners chuckled. "You hide a tiger in your belly," Ishii said. "Let us feed it." He fired orders to the attendants, who bowed and hustled. They reappeared with vegetables and rice, a pot of tea, and meat on sizzling platters, delicacies that Sakamora hadn't seen in years in wartime Japan. He raised a questioning eyebrow.

"We eat well here," Ishii said as he stabbed a thick chop rimmed with singed fat. "The logs especially. If they aren't in excellent health, they wouldn't survive the experiments."

Sakamora bit into the lamb. It was the most delicious he'd ever tasted. "If they don't survive our medical experiments, we won't obtain useful data," he said slowly. "And brave Japanese soldiers will suffer because we failed to learn from the logs."

Ishii looked pleased. "You'll do well here." Sakamora lowered his eyes. "No false modesty, please," Ishii chided. "You're a brilliant young scientist. The emperor and I expect great things from you." Sakamora startled at hearing his name linked with God's. "He . . . he knows what we do here?"

"The emperor-," Ishii intoned, "knows all."

Sakamora lifted his eyes, nodding firmly. "My weapon is excellent, General," he declared. "I tested it on hundreds of animals. Each expired the moment the gas touched—"

"You tested on mere rats and monkeys," Ishii interrupted. "In an indoor laboratory with no wind or rain."

Sakamora felt like he'd been slapped. "Sir, I noted that in my reports—"

"It is not a criticism. Only an observation." Ishii cut into another chop, laying out its bloody interior. "That's why you're here, to test your weapons on targets that matter," he said, chewing noisily, a curl of masticated fat swinging from his mustache. He paused to avoid competing with the fresh screams reverberating through Ro Block, the main experimental lab that was constructed, like its hundred-plus satellite buildings, in the vast, windswept forests of central Manchuria.

Sakamora blinked but otherwise kept his face impassive. He fervently hoped he adapted quickly to life in Unit 731. Those howls were the stuff of nightmares . . .

"Where do you obtain these, um, logs, sir?" he said, just to be saying something.

"Many places. Some are thieves and pickpockets," Ishii said, motioning for sugar, which an attendant ran to the table. "Others are captured Allied soldiers. But most of our test subjects are Russians, Koreans, and . . . Chinese." He spit the last as rancid pork. "We round them up as needed from the conquered territories."

An attendant refilled their stone pot. Pearly steam rolled from the chipped spout. It reminded Sakamora of the prisoners he'd observed last night in the hot room. The doctors wanted to record how long it took soldiers to die of heatstroke in jungle conditions, so a dozen male logs were dressed in army uniforms and the temperature raised to one hundred and twenty degrees. Their humid breath-puffs resembled wet pearls in the harsh overhead lighting . . .

"Will we test my weapon here?" Sakamora said. "In the compound?"

"No," Ishii said, steepling his hands. "Logs tied to posts in the noonday sun will not do. I want to see what happens when an unsuspecting population is sprayed with your . . . what do you call your invention again? Nerve gas?"

Sakamora felt woozy even as he nodded. He hadn't expected a live test so soon—he thought he'd gas one prisoner, then maybe a dozen. After that, perhaps, tackle a hamlet. or small town. Would he wind up pumping his fist in glory, or would he wither from abject failure? General Shiro Ishii, chief medical officer of the Imperial Japanese Army and supreme commander of Unit 731, was a legend, and legends did not suffer fools gladly. "An entire living population, sir?" he ventured. "I've never worked on something that complex—"

"There's a city several hours away," Ishii said as if Sakamora hadn't spoken. "Chingcau. It contains thirty thousand Chinese, poor and stupid as Chinese are. We've occupied their city for a decade, so their lives are back to normal, and they won't be prepared. They'll provide a most excellent test." He waved at his driver. "Finish up and we'll go."

"Now?" Sakamora said, feeling twinges of panic. "What about my chemicals? All the spraying equipment?"

"I sent them ahead, so we'll be ready to launch when we arrive."

Sakamora jammed two strips of meat into his mouth and jumped to his feet. Ishii laughed. "Finish your meal, dear Sakamora," he said. "It takes time to pack the trucks."

Sakamora smiled sheepishly. He certainly didn't want to pass up the opportunity for more food, but the general was already walking. He stuffed in a third strip and followed. Darted back, grabbed a fourth, and caught up, marching toward the exit door at the end of the long hallway. He heard the muffled whump of explosions through the thick brown walls. They were from hand grenades, tested on chained prisoners in the outdoor corrals. Researchers set them off at thirty yards, then twenty-five, then twenty, all the way to point-blank, documenting the wound pattern from each detonation. He smelled burning flesh; heard sledgehammers crack bone. A soldier exited one room and entered another, waving an infant impaled on a bayonet. Men sobbed and women screeched in the guttural harshness that was the Chinese language. He cocked his head at an odd thumping sound. It was steady but faint, like a club on a melon. Puzzled, he asked what it was. Ishii pointed to a door. The driver opened it.

Sakamora saw thirty women lashed to heavy armchairs. They were middle-aged. Their coarse black hair was shorn to the stubble of grain harvest. They were naked. Their small breasts quivered from ceaseless shivering. Almond eyes that weren't already glazed with madness showed great terror. Soldiers in quilted coats and fur hats struck their biceps with wooden mallets. Right, then left, one strike per second, eerie in their metronomic precision. Each strike produced a hollow thump. The mallets were a yellowish wood, streaked with gray. The arms were a mottled black, streaked with green. A gray, milky liquid oozed from skin abscesses, ran down their arms. Glass jugs collected the drippings. Doctors recorded data, measured blood pressure, peered into logs' eyes. Imperial Army cameramen recorded every grimace and sigh.

"We froze their arms solid," Ishii explained. "Then we thawed them"

"Creating frostbite," Sakamora said, understanding.

"We wanted to see how long it takes for limbs to turn gangrenous," Ishii said. "And then how long for the gangrene to reach the internal organs."

A doctor's smile revealed steel teeth. "Just opening up the next, General," he said. "We froze and thawed her twenty-nine times."

"A record, I believe. Good work," Ishii said.

The doctor tightened the straps around a log writhing on a blood-scabbed table. Her dark eyes darted like ants. Her sharp yellow teeth clicked and ground. She looked feverish, and her torso was bloated. Her pubic region was hairless, her chest concave. Sakamora judged her at eight. Possibly ten.

The doctor picked a scalpel from a tray that was overflowing and walked toward the girl. Her kewpie lips sucked into a frightened O. Sakamora closed his eyes. He heard the howl and the derailing train. He trembled until the ensuing silence compelled him to open his eyes. The doctor was examining the girl's liver under a harsh light. He gave it to an assistant to weigh and measure, then turned to harvest her kidneys and heart. She struggled against the straps.

"The gangrene is deep in her organs, as I expected," the doctor said. "What I didn't expect is her astonishing level of resistance. As you can see, this girl was cut to ribbons. Every nerve screams for relief. Yet she still wants to live, and despite missing half her organs, fights desperately to hang on. That shows the resilience of human beings—no matter how horribly they're abused, they will keep on fighting. Her will to live is . . . magnificent."

"And that's why we don't use anesthetic," Ishii said.

"So we can accurately judge the reactions of the logs to any stimulus," Sakamora dutifully mumbled, unable to tear his eyes from the living autopsy. "And apply that knowledge to our soldiers in the field, so that we may save their lives under similar circumstances."

Ishii patted his arm as the little girl's struggle finally ceased. "The trucks are loaded and ready," he said. "Next stop, Chingcau. Where we will see what you are made of, my scientific genius."

THE FURY

Sakamora gulped.

A rollicking group of boys were playing outside when they heard a mechanical buzz. Glanced at each other, confused. Looked up. Saw a wide row of dark blips against the blinding sun. "Father! Mother!" one boy yelled, wheeling for home.

The father poked his head out the door. "Yes, what is it?"

"I hear noises in the air."

The family hurried outside. "Airplanes," the father said, shading his eyes. He counted. Gave up after twelve.

The boy's eyes glowed with excitement as the thrum grew loud as a sewing machine. He put out his thin arms and ran around the dusty yard, the long orange shirt sewn by his mother mirroring his swoops and jumps. Then he waved at the machines with both hands.

"Airplanes! Have you come to play with me?" he cried.

The lead plane waggled its wings.

Began to release a spray from its bowels. It was the color of dirty tears.

The boy started laughing.

"What's so funny?" the father said.

"The airplane is peeing on us!"

"Bomb doors open," the radio crackled. "Chemical disbursement begun."

Sakamora scribbled furiously as nerve gas rained on Chingcau.

"Timberrrrr," Ishii said.

The boy in the orange shirt felt fire in his lungs. His limbs jerked uncontrollably, and his throat began to close. "Father," he gasped, sinking into the dirt. "I can't . . . can't . . . breathe . . ."

The father couldn't answer because he was vomiting on the mother, who was reaching for the grandparents, who were trying to cover their grandson, while they all curled slowly into commas.

"Filthy . . . Japanese," the grandfather grunted, clutching his dead wife to his chest. Screeches filled the air as neighbors and friends and shopkeepers and animals collapsed. "Father," the boy croaked. "Help me . . ."

"My God," Ishii breathed. "I've never seen anything this destructive."

Sakamora couldn't believe it either. His nerve gas worked better than his most optimistic projections.

He swept his binoculars across the city. People were dropping like the piglets he'd tried in his gas chambers before graduating to dogs and horses. Vomiting. Twitching. Curling up like shrimp, or, more accurately, he decided, commas.

He noticed a boy in a bright orange shirt that hung past his knees, so long that it looked more like a girl's dress. Four adults were tented across his curlicued body, trying to shield him from the poisonous winds. It would do them no good. A single drop of nerve gas destroyed the central nervous system. There was no antidote.

"I've seen soldiers exposed to mustard gas," Ishii whispered. "They died but not this quickly or in these overwhelming numbers. How did you create this effect?"

Sakamora cleared his throat. "Mustard gas is caustic and burns the skin," he began. "Horrific burns, certainly, but nothing more than that. Nerve gas is totally different." The satisfaction of telling a legend something he didn't know was more delicious than the fatted lamb. "It's derived from insecticides. It was invented by a Doctor Schrader in Germany. I took his formula and improved it."

Ishii frowned. "How did you obtain German data? Isn't it top secret?"

"It is now," Sakamora said, nodding. "But Schrader discovered the poison before the war. The chemical company IG Farben, his employer, applied for a patent, and the formula appeared in public patent records. When the Nazis took power, they reclassified it as top secret, but the essentials were already out."

The general shook his head in disbelief. "Capitalists will sell us the rope we use to hang them, I swear," he murmured. "Go on."

Sakamora's leg was falling asleep, so he shifted his weight. "My alterations were successful, and the result is this improved nerve gas. Just one single drop"—he pinched fingers and thumbs together to show the pinhead size of the drop—"shuts down the chemical that orders muscles to relax. In essence, the body cramps itself to death. It is—"

"A miracle, is what it is. Those logs are smelling the devil's own breath," Ishii said, clapping the scientist on the back. "Seventeen minutes after the weapon's initial release, a city of thirty thousand is dead." He shook his head, then, unexpectedly, bowed to the scientist. "You've changed the world forever."

Sakamora was absurdly pleased at the high praise of the man-god but chose not to show how happy he was. It would be undignified. Instead, he studied the boy. Noted the density of the foam bubbling from his mouth, the wetness at his crotch. Marveled at the cessation of muscular twitching, indicating that the shutdown of the nervous system was complete.

"Can you load your gas into bombs?" Ishii asked.

Sakamora calculated, then nodded. "Theoretically, yes," he said cautiously. "Bombs, rockets, artillery shells. Anything, really, as long as the poison is insulated from the explosive element so the blast won't burn it up. I'm unfamiliar with the engineering requirements, but—"

"I'm giving you a dozen rocket men," Ishii said. "And twice as many engineers. I want the first working weapon in six weeks."

Sakamora gulped. Ishii's eyes grew cold.

"Failure is unacceptable, Sakamora," he said. "The Americans were crazed by our attack on Pearl Harbor. They will invade Japan to avenge their dead." He waved at the nerve gas–spewing airplanes circling back to base. The rising suns on their undersides glowed in the cloudless cobalt sky. "And when that happens, I'll turn every single one into that boy in the orange dress."

Chapter 15

PRESENT DAY
CHICAGO

Superstition glanced at the water-stained ceiling, wondering if the *bzzzzzz* was from the harsh yellow fluorescents or from the flies zipping in and out from the janitor closet next door. She shook her head in disbelief, then shifted uncomfortably in her broken chair, the padding of which was so worn that she'd be more comfortable on a pile of rocks. She'd been in crack houses more elegantly appointed than this "office" in the bowels of police headquarters.

"Welcome back," Hanrahan said as he squeezed between the sewer pipes flanking her doorway. Rust flaked off where his shoulders touched. He plopped into her "visitor seating," which consisted of the battered aluminum chair she'd stolen from an interrogation room. "We missed you." As proof, he tossed a sack of Dunkin' Donuts on her desk.

"They should put you on Mount Rushmore," she marveled, offering him first dibs. He selected a Boston cream and licked a trough through the frosting.

"That'd be cool," he said, wiping chocolate off his lip. "Put me next to Lincoln, I'll ask how he liked the play—" He winced. "I'm sorry. It's too soon for wisecracks."

Her little wave said, *No problem.* She turned the wave into a double arm sweep, which, when fully extended, nearly touched both walls. "This condo from hell is the department's way of sending me a message, right?" she said.

Hanrahan nodded. Officers involved in shootings were taken off the streets—i.e., assigned to "desk duty"—until they were officially cleared. Usually, that meant a windowed office with a coffee machine, answering minor-league calls from the public, then taking extended lunches with colleagues. This was not that. "Kicking and cussing those assholes reminded everyone of that mess down in Ferguson."

"I remember," she said, recalling the weeks of riots and looting in the St. Louis suburb after a white police officer shot and killed an unarmed black man.

"So does the Justice Department. It's been jonesing ever since to take down a police department. Any department'll do. Da Mayor wants to make sure it's not us."

"So they're making me invisible till the heat dies down," she said.

Hanrahan surveyed the room, which, at six feet by nine, was the size of a federal prison cell. "Could have been worse," he said. "Their first choice was a police garage on the West Side. They were going to have you inventory fan belts." He sucked cream from the doughnut and chased it with dark roast. "I called in some favors."

She nibbled at her vanilla-with-sprinkles. "Thanks," she said. "I think."

Hanrahan nodded at the paper piles. "What do they have you doing?"

"Proofreading arrest reports," she said.

He winced.

"Yeah," she said, pastel sprinkles littering her desk like autumn leaves. "It wouldn't be so bad if cops could spell 'perpetrator.' I'd even settle for 'subject' instead of 'subjek.'" She sighed. "Did any of them actually take English in high school?"

They batted that around awhile, then Hanrahan rose to leave. "You doing okay?" he said. "You came back awfully fast, you know."

She nodded. "Work's a good distraction. I was going crazy hanging around the house, seeing Derek everywhere but not. Does that make sense?" Hanrahan nodded. "I've been thinking about the kids a lot, too," she said. "What they'd be like now. How they were doing in school. Were girls icky or awesome? All that." She shook off a sudden chill. "I wish I could quit the woulda-coulda-shouldas."

"It's normal to look back on everything when your world has changed," he said. "So try not to worry about it. As for this reassignment, it's politics, not you. When the heat dies down, you're back in the orange dress with me."

She wriggled between her desk and the wall to walk him out, and banged her shin on a cast iron pipe fitting. Multi-syllable curses tumbled forth.

"You eat with that mouth?" he said, amused.

"Said the pot to the kettle," she said between gritted teeth.

"I cuss with elegance and class. You, on the other hand . . ."

"Want me to practice some more, sir?" she said, glaring as she rubbed her leg.

"Heavens no," Hanrahan said. "That would be suboptimal." He lumbered away, pleased that Sue's funny bone was intact, if understandably subdued. Cops sucked gun barrels when they lost their sense of humor, and no way he'd let that happen to her. "Get back to work, Officer. Those reports won't proof themselves."

Superstition limped toward her chair but only made it to the visitors'. She pulled up her trouser leg and examined the injury, which was already starting to swell. She remembered the last time something whacked that spot that hard—a rock launched by the cute boy who would become her handsome husband. She leaned back and closed her eyes, remembering . . .

They were in grade school on Chicago's Southwest Side. She'd seen him in the halls and thought he was awesome with his muscled frame, puppy-dog eyes, and long black hair that curled over his ears. Her girlfriends agreed when they talked on the phone. But she didn't know anything about him other than his name: Derek Davis. She intended to find out more.

Saturday mornings, a dozen neighborhood boys met in the parking lot of an abandoned warehouse to play hockey. Being that it was spring and there wasn't any ice, they got inventive, Chicago-style: They mounted bicycles, tipped a milk crate onto each end of the potholed asphalt, and dropped a rock in the center. The captain of each team met at the rock for the face-off.

"Your ass is mine, Lardo," Derek growled across the potato-shaped "puck."

"Don't bother pedaling; you'll just die tired," his counterpart growled back, shaking his handlebars in menace.

Territories properly marked, another kid shouted, "Go!"

Derek got the first kick in. The rock rimmed a pothole and spun away. Bikers pedaled furiously, kicking the rock and each other up and down the asphalt, yelling and laughing and cursing and falling and getting up again.

Superstition Kallas pulled up on her Sting Ray, which her father had found abandoned in a ditch along one of his mosquito routes, brought home, repaired, and painted a bright pink. She watched the game with fascination and envy—boys got to do all the cool stuff. She had nothing against Barbies, but she was athletic and would love to play this game too. Oh, well. At least she could see cutie-pie Derek in action . . .

"Yowww!" one of the other kids cried as he slammed through a pothole, flew sideways, and tore skin off knees and elbows skidding across the pavement. Everyone rushed over. As soon as they knew nothing was broken, they laughed and called him names. The kid tried to stand but fell again. Derek squatted and checked his ankle.

"I'm thinking sprain," he said.

"Yeh," the kid groaned. "I sprained my ankle sliding into third last summer. This feels the same."

"Head on home, then, cowpoke," Derek said, slapping the kid's butt. "Tell your mom and then put ice on it, so it doesn't swell. Good as new by next week."

The kid nodded, picked up his bike, and winced his way down the sidewalk.

Superstition saw her chance. "You're a man short," she hollered. "Can I play?"

Everyone turned, surprised.

"You're a girl," Derek said.

"No duh," Superstition said.

"Girls can't play rock hockey."

"Says who?" she said, crossing her arms and staring.

"Says me," he said. "Derek D."

Superstition tossed her long dark hair over her left shoulder. "Why? You afraid a girl will show you up?" she challenged.

Everyone laughed. Derek, too, but she noticed a glimmer of interest. He glanced at the rest of the team. They shrugged, willing to follow his lead.

"You're in," Derek said. "But don't go crying to mommy if you get hurt, Sis."

"The name's Superstition," she said.

"I know," Derek said.

Really? she thought with a flutter. *You know who I am?*

"I seen you around school," he said, as if reading her mind. "So let's go, we don't got all day."

She mounted her Sting Ray and took her place on the opposite team. She lowered her head, trying to look mean. It felt like Snoopy doing his vulture thing in the comics, so she abandoned the fakery—*let your playing do your talking.*

The same kid yelled, "Go," and the game continued. Superstition wheeled and dragged and dove and bounced, scoring one goal, then another. Derek got the rock and charged. She wheeled to block his thundering kick toward her milk crate . . .

The rock smashed her left shin. She felt the bone give way. She wanted to scream. She didn't. But she fell to the asphalt, unable to stay upright.

"Jesus!" Derek said, flinging his bike and running up to her. "You all right?"

"I'm fine," she said, trying not to cry.

"No, you're not," he said, pulling her jean leg up to her knee.

She looked down. The skin was shredded and blood flowed down her leg, pooling into her white cotton sock. A patch of bone was visible, surrounded by a large, irregular dent. He touched it. She paled.

"It's broken," he said.

"Wrap my sock around it," she said between gasping breaths. "I'm gonna finish what I started."

"Nope, you're done," Derek said, pulling off his T-shirt and draping it over the wound. He looked at the other captain. "Dukey, go call an ambulance, would ya?"

"Don't . . . need . . . ambulance," she said. "I'll walk it . . . off—"

"Why are you still here, man?" he spat at Dukey, who turned and ran for the pay phone in the store across the street. He turned back to Superstition. "Sorry, Sue, you're going to the hospital, and that's that."

"Says who?" Superstition said.

"Says me," Derek said. "Derek D." A distant siren cut the air. "And when you're healed up?"

"Yeah?" she said.

"Come on back. We play every Saturday at nine . . ."

A janitor, whistling a tune she didn't recognize, passed her door, pulling her from her reverie. She sighed, hobbled to her chair, and got back to proofreads, proud that even with memories of Derek and the kids pounding her 24/7, she was still holding it together.

Until she couldn't.

ONE WEEK LATER

"Are you sure you don't want us to stay?" Theresa Kallas said, the worry line deepening between her carefully plucked eyebrows. "You sounded . . . brittle at the restaurant tonight."

Superstition shook her head. "No, thanks, Mom. I just need some sleep."

"Sure you do, lone wolf," Theresa said, stroking her daughter's chocolate hair. "But call if you need anything."

"We're just down the road," said her father, George. They weren't, really—they lived in Mount Greenwood on the Far Southwest Side, and she was in Edison Park on the Far Northwest Side—but in the middle of the night, on a mostly deserted Cicero Avenue, the drive wouldn't take all that long. "We'll come right up."

Superstition hugged them, worrying about the quivering in their backs. They were exhausted. Little wonder—in the past seven days they'd marinated in Derek's savage murder, her triple homicide, fallout from the "blackie" video, Derek's funeral, and the open house afterwards. Family, friends, neighbors, cops, firefighters, and even a few John Q's, who'd seen it on Facebook, stopped by her house to pay their respects. Her parents learned names, made introductions, freshened food and drink, insisted everyone sign the memory book, and, key, rescued their daughter whenever they sensed her becoming overwhelmed. Her religious mother reveled in the call-and-response amen-ing when a coterie of Baptist ladies stopped by for hallelujahs and Crown Royal but otherwise limited God to prayers so silent that only Superstition realized she was asking direction. They'd stayed in her guest room that night and every night since, tending to her every need when she wasn't at work. She deeply appreciated their support and said so again and again. But now, finally, she needed to be alone with her thoughts.

Alone with Derek.

"Just remember what I said, honey," Theresa said, putting on her coat, "about letting Him take your burden."

Superstition bit her tongue, not wishing to prolong the good-byes.

Five minutes later, they were pulling away from the curb, Superstition watching through the window behind the couch, where Derek's butt had so nicely marked his territory. She eased into it now, clutching her denimed knees to her chest.

"Now what?" she murmured to the crinkled leather.

His ghost didn't answer.

She sighed, replaying Derek's funeral in her head. Killed-in-the-line-of-duty send-offs were as symbolic as papal installations. If it hadn't been for why she was there, she would have enjoyed it. She lost herself in reveries for a while, then padded for the kitchen. Family and friends had cleaned up the house, thank goodness, but she still had leftover liquor to pack, frozen casseroles to sort and label, thank-you notes to write, a future to plan. She found herself wandering into their bedroom.

My bedroom, she corrected. *Just . . . mine.*

She wiped her tears, annoyed at the weakness. She didn't break when the highway patrol called. She didn't break when the surgeons staggered from their antiseptic battleground to confirm her husband was dead—he'd coded twice on the flight from Peck Canyon but clawed back each time, and they'd been hopeful, but his heart finally gave from the shock and awe. She'd gotten so dizzy that she almost passed out—but she didn't break. She brought Derek home for burial, suffered through the funeral and open house, returned to work, and brushed off every click-bait reporter demanding she explain her "racist" video. But today, a week later, she was on and off, stoic, then weepy. *Suck it up, cowgirl,* she ordered herself. *You'll get through this. You'll keep getting through this—*

Then his scent crept into her nostrils. From his clothes. From the bedspread. The towels. The curtains, floors, and ceilings. The entire house smelled like Derek.

Which will fade to only me.

She whirled and punched the closest wall. Once. Twice. A flurry. Dents became jagged holes. Her rage deepened to fury, thick and unrelenting. Sheetrock exploded like the grenades that blew up her husband. Sweat soaked her shirt and jeans. She punched and kicked and hammered, screaming curses so unintelligible that she didn't understand them. Her knuckles bled, mixing with the wallboard dust to form a pink, gooey bandage.

Finally, spent, eyes burning and fists throbbing, she fumbled to the chair where Derek's workout clothes lay neatly draped. White cotton socks with faded orange stripes. Forest green sweatpants with holes in each knee. Gray UnderArmour. And his most treasured possession, a Chicago Bears game jersey signed by Walter Payton, No. 34, the greatest running back in the history of the game according to football-crazy Derek, so full of power and grace, then chopped down by a failed kidney, dead so traumatically, dead so young. Dead like Derek . . .

"What am I going to do?" she whimpered, mushing his jersey into her face. Derek was gone. Timmy was gone. Tommy was gone. Her man and their boys, her light and her soul, as critical to her well-being as oxygen and food and a beating heart . . .

Dead.

She threw herself across the bed, bridging her side to his, clutching his pillow as a life preserver, breathing in the maleness and warmth and kindness and ferocity that was Derek. She cried so hard that she began to hiccup. She bit her lip till she tasted blood, then tried to hold her breath. Sobs burst through. Her mind raced to the bottles on the kitchen table, the first piece of furniture they'd picked out as husband and wife.

"Boo-boo-booze," she finally gasped.

She stumbled toward the kitchen, stubbing her toes on furniture and doors. Gin, vodka, Scotch, bourbon, rum, brandy; name it, she had a bottle or twelve. Cops and firefighters drank after funerals—after anything—and a lot of them had showed at the open house, bearing alcoholic tribute.

She grabbed the Grey Goose from the chief of detectives, who'd delivered it along with regrets from the mayor and superintendent for not being able to attend tonight because of "pressing, uh, city business." He'd said it with a straight face. She'd pretended it was fine. She gulped two fingers. Felt the caustic burn in her throat. It belly-flopped a moment later and spread like a lava flow.

Two more fingers. Two more. Two more. Her ears began ringing, and she heard herself blinking. *Squish-squish. Squish-squish.* She burped, which bought up meaty fumes, which reminded her of Derek's famous bacon-wrapped baby backs, which sparked more tears. She abandoned the Grey Goose for the red-waxed bottle of Maker's Mark, which her boss had brought. Robbie stayed the entire evening, not giving "two shits and a fireman" about being seen with political toxic waste. "Cops are family," he'd said to more career-wary colleagues. "We do anything for family. Fuck a bunch of anything else." She peeled opened his bottle and drank till she gasped for breath, feeling this burn to the tips of her fading orange pedicure.

Dizzy, she scraped over one of the oak chairs they'd bought in Shipshewana, the Amish and Mennonite craft colony in northeastern Indiana. They'd made a weekend of it, shopping, eating, and fooling around. She aimed herself toward the dished seat.

Missed.

Didn't hurt, though.

Too anesthetized for that.

"Music," she breathed. "Gotta . . . gotta play our song . . ."

She stumbled toward the basement. Nailed the stairs without tripping—*kwell soo-prize,* as her high school French teacher might have quipped had she been the least bit fun or cool—and headed for her bagpipe cabinet. It was next to Derek's Fender Stratocaster, which had been autographed by Buddy Guy, the legendary blues guitarist they'd met working security at the Chicago Blues Festival several years ago. She thought about her vow at the funeral to burn her bagpipes.

Instead, she'd play her man a concert.

She touched their bar as she floated by. It was, she considered, her most precious possession other than her wedding ring. They'd been speeding down a country road in Scotland, looking for the castle ruins they'd seen on Google Earth. Derek spotted workers hauling lumber out of what looked like an old distillery. He skidded to a halt, leapt from their rental—"Right back, Sue!" he'd shouted—and disappeared into the building with a burr-headed muscle man. She shrugged and took pictures of sheep, wondering why they were spray-painted brown and green.

"I gave him a hundred bucks," Derek said ten minutes later. *Hunnert.*

"Why?" she said.

"To meet us at the freight office."

"I still don't get it."

He pointed at the planks piled in the driveway. "Meet the Littlemill distillery. They started making whiskey here in 1772, but now they're closing it. These guys are taking the malting floor to the dump." He tapped her forehead playfully. "We've always wanted a bar in our basement. Why not build one that goes with your new bagpipes?"

She thought about it.

"Hoot, mon," she said, kissing his stubbled cheek.

A month later, three hundred board feet of Scottish lumber, cut by the steam-powered sawmills of the Industrial Revolution, arrived at their Chicago bungalow, the freight driver wondering why his truck smelled like peat moss. Armed with Superstition's detailed sketches, Derek dove in with circular saw, mallet, and hardwood dowels. She planed, sanded, and de-splintered each plank, and before they knew it, they had a bar that blended beautifully with the limestone walls of their basement. They christened it the way they liked best—not for nothing had she sanded that wood till her shoulders cramped—and on Thanksgiving, the extended family trooped downstairs for drinks. Derek snickered when a relative exclaimed, "This is one bad bar, Cuz! Bet you come here a lot." Superstition greatly admired her husband's willingness to jump whole-hog into whatever intrigued either of them. The downside of that insatiable curiosity was canyons in Arizona . . .

"Music, maestro," she said, stifling another round of tears.

She blew into the mouthpiece, filling the drones with air, which filled the air with sound. She fingered the chanter holes and began to play . . .

"What the hell?" Deb Williams wondered as howls filled the crisp air.

Realized it was bagpipes.

After midnight, in Chicago.

She shook her head, confused. Then remembered a cop mentioning that Sue was a piper with the Emerald Society. "I guess she's awake," she said.

She debated with herself and voted to drop in unannounced. She might get more that way, and more important, avoid demands for lawyers; she didn't want a battle, just information. She also didn't want Lieutenant Hanrahan around to blow sunshine up her skirt, which is why she'd driven away after the open house instead of accepting his offer to take her to meet Sue. She'd interrogate gently, tweezing out facts as they worked their way to the surface. "I'm from the government and I'm here to help," she muttered, ringing the doorbell. No chime or eight-note; instead, a harsh *brrrring*, like summoning the butcher for meatier chops.

No answer.

She switched to good, old-fashioned pounding. More than one suspect had given up without a fight when she knocked, figuring a flock of gorillas was camped on his doorstep. By the time he figured out it was only a "lady cop," a term she despised as much as "male nurse," he was secure in her hot-pink handcuffs, a tongue-in-cheek gift from her FBI colleagues when she left bank robbery to join civil rights.

The door creaked open.
"Hello?" she hollered into the dark. "Is anybody home?"

Chapter 16

CHICAGO

Superstition blinked owlishly at the clock on the limestone wall, ticking her head with Kit-Cat's metronome eyes. She thought she heard the doorbell. No way, she decided. Nobody visits this late, particularly when the house is dark.

She went back to blowing her bagpipes, working through "Scotland the Brave" then "March of the Highlanders," interweaving the two, musical whiskeys in a barrel. Then, overwhelmed with the emotion of the haunting notes, she wailed too.

Williams blinked at the boil of raw pain and shouted again. No reply except gun-burst sobbing. She walked to the staircase and cautiously headed down. At the end, she peeked around the corner to see an astonishingly pretty woman splayed awkwardly on a lemon shag carpet, her back rounded against a wet bar, her legs akimbo, chocolate hair askew, violet eyes swollen, clothes wrinkled, shoes scattered, and knuckles smeared with a paste of blood and chalk. Her arms pumped a dead sheep with legs while she muttered, swore, cried, shuddered, and piped, all at the same time.

"Detective Davis, I presume?" Williams said.

Superstition startled like she'd been shot. "Who're you?" she screeched, scrambling to her feet. "What are you doing in my house at two in the—"

"Easy, take it easy," Williams said, flashing her badge. "I'm FBI. Special Agent Deb Williams. I'm sorry to barge in, but the front door was open and I heard you screaming."

"My door was . . . open?" Superstition said.

"Yes. Maybe it didn't latch. I thought something was wrong."

"Wrong?" Superstition said, wiping her face. "What could be wrong? Oh, wait. My husband was murdered last week. Does that count?"

"Yes, it does," Williams said. "I'm sorry for your loss." Dead cops weren't statistics but tragedies. "Everyone says he was a good man."

Superstition tapped her foot as she examined the invader. The agent was five-six but seemed taller due to her chin-up posture. Her tailored black suit accented her sturdy figure. Her plain-Jane face was an amalgam of wary, weary, and bright. She had sprays of freckles on her cheeks and nose. Her eyes were green or brown, depending on which way her head turned. Her shoes were polished and sensible, as they'd been when Superstition spotted her at the funeral, then later at the open house, talking with Clayton next door. The ribbon on the package was the Glock anchored to her right hip.

"So, Deb, do you enjoy crucifying cops?" Superstition said with a brittle smile. "Or is it good for your career, so what the hell?"

So much for gentle tweezing of information. "Crucifixions are a higher pay grade," Williams said. "I'm here to gather facts."

"You and Joe Friday," Superstition said. "You've been snooping around all week, so I figured you'd show up sometime. What do you want to know?"

Williams shrugged, deciding to abandon niceties. "Why you killed those three suspects instead of getting them to surrender. Why you shot one when his back was turned. Why you hate African Americans. You know, the usual stuff."

Superstition made a noise that resembled a laugh. "I don't hate black people. I like them as much or little as anybody else."

"Why'd you say 'blackie,' then? And 'black-eyed son of a bitch?' "

"Because they called me 'whitey' and 'white eyes.' I wish I hadn't said it."

"Because it was racist?"

Superstition rolled her eyes to show her disgust at that presumption. "Because I don't need this trumped-up bullshit with everything else I'm dealing with," she said. "They said 'white,' I said 'black.' It wasn't racism; it was simple tit-for-tat." She hiccuped. "Oh, wait, can I say 'tit' without getting charged with sexism?" Williams ignored the question, and Superstition crossed her arms. "By the way, they weren't 'suspects.' They were guilty as hell."

"So you executed them," Williams said.

"Wrong. I shot them in defense of self and others. That they died is their problem, not mine."

Williams leaned against the wall. The limestone was chilly but not as much as the atmosphere. "Where I come from, shooting someone in the back isn't self-defense; it's murder."

Superstition scowled. "The Shotgun man, right? Yes, his back was to me, and I took full advantage. I suppose you'd have given him a chance?" She crooked her pinkies and hung them in the air. "Oh, dear fellow, do be a good sport and face me with your double-oughts," she minced. "So we might stage a proper shootage in which the best chap shall prevail. Right? That's what Feebs do when a hundred lives are in your hands, and all you have is a gun you don't know will work?"

"Don't know will work?"

"I was working undercover that night," Superstition said. "In the skimpy orange dress I'm sure you've already seen. I can't carry a gun in that getup, so I had to use the bouncer's. When that ran dry, I grabbed the pistol the owner keeps under the bar."

Williams had no reply.

"Yeah, I thought so," Superstition said, sarcasm dripping. "I did what I needed to do, double-oh-Debbie, and under the same circumstance, I'd do it again."

The story matched what Hanrahan and his squad told Williams earlier.

"So, this has been blown out of proportion?" Williams pressed. "The 'blackie' remarks, shooting the man in the back, stomping your stiletto through the other one's eye, all of it is trumped-up media nonsense?"

"Yes."

"Maybe you're right. But wouldn't you think the worse of you, if you were me?"

Superstition thought about it. Nodded. "You want a drink?"

"I thought you'd never ask."

Superstition opened the fridge and pulled a Mondavi Pinot Noir.

"What, no rotgut?" Williams asked, pointing at the empty bottles of spirits.

"That was to get drunk," Superstition said. "This is because I like it."

She poured. They drank.

"I love two men in my life, Agent Williams," she announced when her glass was empty. "My dad and my husband."

"Fathers, I get. Why Derek?" Williams said.

" 'Cause he's hot. He's passionate, smart, and good at everything. And he wanted to marry me." She smiled till her eyes shut. "He really, really wanted to marry me . . ."

Williams blinked. *Of course he wanted to marry you! What guy in his right mind wouldn't?* Superstition Davis was beautiful, athletic, intelligent, courageous, and fun to be around, and every single person she'd interviewed confirmed that with such rousing enthusiasm that Deb found herself a little jealous. She'd always wanted to be the doe-eyed, heat-seeking missile that made romance-novel Highlanders fight over who'd take her to the cotillion. Unfortunately, that bus had long left the station, so she resigned herself to being a great FBI agent. It didn't make her less lonely, but it kept her internal pity parties at arm's length.

Which, she figured, she'd better start doing.

They traded war stories, talked about their lives, dissected the shootings and aftermath a second time, then a third, uncorked more wine, and slowly, but irrevocably, Deb decided what her recommendation was going to be.

Chapter 17

PRESENT DAY
UNITED STATES PENITENTIARY
FARGO, NORTH DAKOTA

Humidity dripped from the cement-block walls and ceiling, pooling into dirty rivulets that snaked into the welded drain. Pipes clanked and moaned as spray heads belched water greasy from dissolved minerals.

Here we go...

Isabel crept into the communal shower, tossing her uniform into the laundry cart. The room was empty except for an Amazon named Belinda, who faded in and out of the roiling steam. Isabel found herself entranced by the woman's Popeye muscles, which were covered with tattooed swords, guns, flames, Chinese characters, a topless blonde riding a Harley, and, incongruously, a hot-pink My Little Pony. There were gang markings, too, though which they represented, Isabel hadn't a clue. She drank it all in, having never seen a human comic book...

"Hell you lookin' at?" Belinda snarled.

"Nothing," Isabel said, instantly averting her eyes. Prison code demanded only glances at other inmates. Anything more was a direct challenge. She'd lingered too long on the neck-to-ankles dragon. A mistake. Perhaps fatal...

"Yeah, you was," Belinda said, slamming her soap bar off Izzy's ribs. She lunged, baring her square, yellow teeth. Izzy spun for the exit but couldn't get traction in the soapy streams. Vise-grip hands throttled her neck, and a knee with tattooed hearts slammed into her belly. Izzy vomited.

Fight or die...

Izzy snapped her head forward, a move she'd read about in the Jack Reacher novels she'd favored when she wasn't studying. The heavy bone ridge of her forehead slammed into the woman's hatchet nose. "Eeeeee!" Belinda screamed, tightening the chokehold as blood and soap foamed from the jaybird tattoos on her nostrils. "Gonna kill ya, bitch!"

Isabel dug her nails into the attacker's wrists. It had no effect. Her vision narrowed to the end of a tunnel, then a drinking straw. She felt herself turn blue . . .

"Break it up!" guards shouted as they splashed through soapy puddles. Rough, gloved hands yanked them apart. "Cunt was checking my titties!" Belinda screeched.

"They ain't all that nice, Belinda," the older guard said, tossing her a towel.

"You just jealous, Flatso," she said, wiggling her double-D's like Jell-O. "And she broke my nose."

"What you get, trying to choke her," the guard said. "Dry off and report to the infirmary. After that, you're going to the hole."

Belinda grinned, toweled, and walked away, accompanied by "Flatso." Isabel sank into the wall, legs turned to rubber. "Y'right, Garcia?" the guard asked.

I'll never be all right! Isabel wanted to scream. But she knew better than to show weakness. "I'll live," she grunted, wiping bits of Belinda off her face.

"Scrub-a-dub," the guard warned. "God knows where that blood's been."

Isabel picked up her own soap, which was the yellow of toe callus and filled with nubbins that rubbed the skin raw.

"I didn't do anything, CO," she said, knowing they liked "correctional officer," not "guard." Being naked in front of the CO didn't bother her, even though a week ago she'd have been mortified. Prison life hardened you fast. "Why did she attack me?"

"We stock painkillers in the infirmary," the guard said. "Belinda doesn't mind getting hurt to get some."

Isabel sighed. "I need to get out of here."

"Wouldn't hurry, I was you," the guard said, tossing her a towel. "This here's the Ritz compared to some cages I've worked."

Isabel smiled despite herself. "So why are you here, then?"

The guard shrugged.

"Wanted to marry a prince but Katy beat me to it. C'mon, let's go."

1943

DECEMBER 2
ALLIED SHIPPING DOCKS
BARI, EAST COAST OF ITALY

"Wish you'd say," Knowles repeated.

"Wish I could," Beckstrom replied.

U.S. Navy Captain Elwin Knowles flicked his cigar into the oil-slicked waves slapping the hull of the *John Harvey*. He'd driven the Liberty ship to Italy via Baltimore, Norfolk, Algeria, and Sicily, and as a naval commander, he was accustomed to instant obedience. "I outrank you," he tried.

U.S. Army Lieutenant Howard Beckstrom nodded in agreement. "And Roosevelt outranks us both."

Knowles considered that. He touched Beckstrom's collar insignia—two chemical retorts crossed over a hexagon. "You're a commander in the Chemical Warfare Service," he said. "With hush-hush orders from the White House. That tells me everything I need to know about those pretty little crates you stuffed in my cargo hold. Which, I'm guessing, ain't powdered eggs."

Beckstrom grinned. "And they said I'd never find one."

"Find one what?"

"Sailor who knows shit from Shinola."

Knowles's eyes crinkled. "Problem is, I don't know it officially. So I can't order the port authorities to rush us to the front of the line, can I?"

Beckstrom shook his head.

"This port's run by the Brits," Knowles objected. "They're allies, last I heard."

Beckstrom shrugged. "We have no friends with this cargo, Washington says."

"So everyone's pretending we're not moving chemical weapons into the European theater?"

"Who said anything about chemical weapons?" Beckstrom said, all innocence. "Far as I know, those powdered eggs are breakfast for General Patton."

"And I'm," Knowles said, "a monkey's uncle."

"Is the *Harvey* empty yet?" Franklin Delano Roosevelt asked.

Henry Stimson gazed through the White House window. The skies were as gray as his mood. "No, Mr. President," he said. "The bombs are still in the hold, awaiting stevedores."

Roosevelt unpinched his glasses and rubbed his red-streaked nose. "That ship's been docked for five damn days, Henry. How much longer will it take?"

The secretary of war stroked his graying mustache. "Bari's jammed with ships, Franklin," he said. "I'm trying to expedite things, but quietly. We can't risk making anyone suspicious. If old Adolf hears we're shipping in mustard gas, he'll fire every gun Krupp ever made."

Roosevelt stretched his arms over his head and waggled his fingers. He was tired. He'd been working around the clock since the Nazis invaded Poland in '39, making thousands of war decisions—including this one. Shipping two hundred thousand pounds of American poison gas through U-boat and bomber-infested waters—and then stabbing those gas bombs into the heart of civilized Europe—wasn't for the faint of heart.

"Ike understands, right?" Roosevelt said.

"I told General Eisenhower personally," Stimson said. "We don't use our gas munitions unless the Nazis do it first."

"If they even have gas," Roosevelt said.

"Japs got it," Stimson reminded him.

Roosevelt nodded. He'd been briefed about the poison-gas atrocities in Manchuria. Thousands of civilians were dying from a mystery chemical that didn't burn their flesh like mustard, just curled them into commas and left them dead. Allied scientists were poring over the reports, and the OSS had retrieved a few body parts, hoping to find enough residues to test. So far, no clues to what Roosevelt feared was the next plague to visit mankind.

"Then we can only pray," he said, "that Hitler's more civilized than Tojo."

Stimson touched his lips, then pointed at the heavens.

First Lieutenant Werner Hahn stifled another yawn. Patton, Montgomery, and the combined Allied armies had launched a massive invasion of Italy three months ago, and he was patrolling the top of the boot heel, looking for targets the Luftwaffe could bomb. It was his thirty-seventh patrol in nine days, and he was so tired that his bones ached. He gulped two days' worth of amphetamines, chased them with warm water, and confirmed the fuel tanks of his Messerschmitt Me 210 were at three-quarters. He leaned to the left to scratch his numbing butt—

He caught a metallic gleam from the sea below and wondered what it meant. He corkscrewed gently through the puffy winter clouds, checking the map on his knees.

Saw docks.

Saw ships.

Saw the legend on the unfolded map:

Bari.

It was a massive seaport that had, until the invasion, been safely in Axis hands, but now was unloading tons of Allied war materiel that would rip further holes in his quickly tattering Fatherland. He needed to confirm before bothering high command because false alarms drained resources. So he cut back his speed and flew as low as he dared. He shaded his eyes from the afternoon sun and grinned in triumph. More than thirty merchant ships were rocking in the greenish water, with ant-lines of stevedores unloading everything from bombs to beans. Ship masts fluttered with Union Jacks and Stars and Stripes.

Exhaustion disappearing, he circled back to base to deliver the stunning news. It would take Göring's bombers awhile to get here, but the port wasn't going anywhere, was it?

Captain Knowles rubbed his eyes. The wall of floodlights kept the unloading operations going around the clock but also gave him a pounding headache. Maybe one of those aspirin powders that Mrs. Manicotti, his landlady back home, gave him when he shipped out . . .

He cocked his head at the whispery tremolos in the sky. His vision was 20/10, but his hearing was even sharper, so he often heard things before anyone else.

"You hear that?" he asked Beckstrom, who'd stopped by to deliver a fresh cup of joe. Beckstrom cupped his ear. "Nope, sorry," he said, squinting like it might help.

Knowles whipped his head at his executive officer. "Air raid, air raid. Sound general quarters," he barked.

"Air raid, general quarters, aye sir," the XO said, thumbing the alert button. A harsh gong shattered the air, followed by *All hands man your battle stations*. Moments later, other ship captains took their cue and added to the cacophony. Sailors wheeled for machine guns and fire hoses. Gunners twisted elevation wheels on anti-aircraft cannons. Knowles hopped on the radio as dockside air raid sirens spooled up. "Bari command, this is *John Harvey*," he said. "German bombers approaching south-southwest."

"Radar just spotted them, *Harvey*," said Bari's defense commander. "Ack-ack spooling up."

"ETA on fighter cover?"

"We don't have any. Brits sent them away."

Knowles clenched his jaw, remembering. Arthur Coningham, the pooh-bah of the Royal Air Forces, had earlier that day assured wire-service reporters that the Luftwaffe was defeated in Italy and in fact would never attack Bari, the main resupply port for Montgomery's Eighth Army and headquarters for the U.S. Fifteenth Air Force. "I would regard it as a personal affront and insult," he'd declared, "if the Luftwaffe would attempt any significant action in this area." Apparently, he'd forgotten to inform the Germans they were licked . . .

"I'm going to try to get out of here," he told Bari.

"Are your boilers lit?" Bari said.

"Never turned them off," Knowles said.

"Remember Pearl Harbor, right," Bari said. With their engines shut down and cold, Pearl's mighty battlewagons were sitting ducks last

December, having no way to outrun the Japanese sneak attack. "If you can make open water, you might have a chance . . ."

Knowles turned to issue the command, but the engines were already at full speed. He smiled tightly. Damn fine men he commanded. He hoped to save a few . . .

As a hundred German bombers screamed out of the ink horizon.

A virus of joy infected First Lieutenant Gustav Teuber. Spread below his twin-engine Junkers Ju 88 were enemy ships fat with cargo. Massive floodlights on the docks made the dirty, gray targets so easy to spot, it was like bombing practice.

At which Teuber excelled.

"Bombs away," he sang as high explosives fell like diarrhea.

Beckstrom tackled Knowles as the ammunition ship to their left blew up, spinning hot razor shards across the deck. The aviation fueler to their right joined a moment later as Nazi incendiary bombs turned one ship after the next into volcanoes.

"Owe you!" Knowles shouted as he scrambled to his feet, directing gunfire at the diving steel birds while demanding reports on the fires breaking out over his ship.

"Captain! The poison gas bombs!" Beckstrom said, face ashen. "You gotta dump them in the sea the moment we clear the jetty. They gotta stay cool or they'll—"

He felt the rumble.

Heard the blast.

Saw the titanic fireball that used to be the *John Harvey* swallow the brave captain whole. Then it came for him.

So this is what it's like to die

Chemical Warfare Sergeant Leslie Carter ran toward the docks as a hell-beast of flames, smoke, and body parts rained down on the ancient coastal city. He'd been slugging shore-leave beer when the bombs began falling and thought maybe he could pull some of his friends off the *Harvey*. If any of them still existed . . .

He smelled garlic and skidded to a halt, eyes bulging. "Turn around!" he screamed at the sailors charging for their sinking ships. They didn't slow, so he shoved a burly Marine backwards. "Get out of here, Mac! Run for your life!"

"What the hell, mister?" the Marine swore, knotting his fists.

"Gas! There's mustard gas aboard the *Harvey*, and it's in the air. That garlic smell is poison—"

His skin began to blister, and his lungs started to burn. He turned toward the surrounding hills, blinded, his scalp peeling off in long bloody strips. The men around him screamed as they clutched their throats and fell to their knees.

Chapter 18

PRESTENT DAY
TWO MILES NORTH OF THE BORDER
NOGALES, ARIZONA

Mailman rubbed his eyes in disbelief. His ribs still hurt where Killer Bee had planted his steel-toes, and this dude, the cause of it all, had the stones to walk around Nogales like he was King of Shitonia! He picked up the six-pack of Mountain Dew from the checkout belt and pulled out his phone.

"What?" Charvat said.

"The guy I tole you about?" Mailman said. "I'm lookin' at him right now."

Charvat bolted from his office chair. "You see Jimmy Garcia?"

"Yep. He's at Walmart, a couple blocks north of your office." Mailman shook his head. "You guys couldn't find your dick with both hands, swear to Christ . . ."

Charvat charged into the radio room. "Garcia's been spotted," he said. "Walmart, White Park Drive. Light our guys up, tell the locals too."

"He's in the parking lot, near the main entrance," Mailman said. "He's walking to a car. He's not in a hurry, doesn't know I see him, the lousy mother—"

"I'm going after him, so tell my dispatcher the details," Charvat ordered, running for his body armor, huffing because he'd lost so much muscle tone.

"Better hurry, Swiss cheese," Mailman needled. "You lose him, you still owe me big-time snitch money."

"Quit flapping your gums and give her the tags and description," Charvat growled, thrusting the phone at the dispatcher, then running for the door.

"Hell you yellin' at me for? I'm on your side . . ."

Agents Earl and Connor ran from the break room, moon pies in hand. "I'll get the Jeep," Connor said, breaking left for the parking lot. "I'll grab rifles!" Earl squeaked, swerving right.

Charvat pounded out the main door. Doubled back to get his radio, cursing the maddening gaps in his memory. He saw Earl rush into the armory with his phone in his ear, his face pale, talking with an intensity unusual for the laid-back agent. He wondered why. Think about that later. He felt his lips pull away from his teeth.

Payback's a bitch, Jimmy.

Garcia dumped a sack of video games onto the backseat, then started the Charger with a silky *vroom*. His nieces and nephews at his mountain-top ranch would squeal over these presents from Uncle Jim-Jim . . .

He ran his mental checklist. The truck tunnel was well under way, so he needed to check the progress. The Taliban heroin had arrived in Ghana, so palms needed greasing to ensure safe transfer to South America. He needed to get his sister's lawyer more money. He needed to increase the pay of the gang chiefs protecting her in that godforsaken prison in . . . where again? Fargo? He needed to ensure the ex-boyfriend did what he was told. Need, need, need . . .

His phone chirped. He checked the number and quickly answered. His throat seized as the caller explained. He stomped the accelerator, sending the games flying.

Connor skidded to a halt, engine roaring. Charvat and Earl piled in. They slammed over the curb and raced north toward Walmart. "We got him, boys," Charvat crowed, touching all his wounds. "I'm gonna nail his pecker on my fireplace—"

"Runner, runner, runner," the dispatcher squawked.

"Son of a bitch," Charvat barked, slapping the dashboard in frustration. The loss of surprise would make Garcia's arrest that much more difficult. "What direction?"

"South on Morley, passing Frederick."

Only a mile to Mexico. Charvat glanced at Connor, who bootlegged the Jeep in a tight one-eighty and rocketed south.

Flashing lights swooped into Garcia's rearview. He whipped the Charger right, vectoring away, losing the cop. Fresh lights to his left. He went into a serpentine, left, right, left, cutting through a parking lot at a hundred miles an hour, scattering children playing soccer, barreling onto International, blowing stop signs and red lights, smashing cars, nailing pedestrians, chrome and blood and teeth and hair raining onto what was left of his windshield.

"There he is," Charvat said, seeing the Charger crash through the lot of the abandoned factory. "He's trapped like a rat," Earl said as Garcia disappeared inside. "Might be a tunnel," Connor worried, barreling out of the Jeep as Earl unhitched his gun. "I'll alert Mexico," Charvat huffed. "Get their cops to barricade the other end. No way we lose this guy."

Thighs burning with lactic acid, Garcia sprinted into the basement. He tripped on the last step and flew through the fetid air, tearing up his elbows on the rough flooring. He jumped up, cursing; split seconds were his only shot at freedom. He booted the plywood covering the tunnel entrance and heard shouts not nearly far enough away. He had to go now. Problem was, this particular tunnel was so fresh that its lumber and concrete reinforcements hadn't been knocked into place. It was a basically a sand castle that could collapse from the softest sneeze . . .

"Stop or I'll shoot!" he heard Earl shout. "Final warning, stop or I'll—"

He dove into the rabbit hole as bullets pinged inches above his heels.

"Shots fired, shots fired," Charvat broadcast as he limped down the stairs, his cell phone in one hand, his radio in the other.

"Earl did the shooting; we're all right, Boss!" Connor yelled. "Garcia's in a tunnel!"

"I've got Mexico on the phone," Charvat said, tossing Connor the radio to slow down the police response. "Yes, this is Chief Charvat," he said to the *policía federal* commander on the other end of the cell. "My murder suspect is running straight at you." He described where the tunnel likely ended. "Request you intercept and hold until we arrange extradition."

"A killer?" the commander said. "Who is he?"

"Name's Jimmy Garcia. Senior-level enforcer for one of your cartels—"

"We have many cartels, *Señor*," the commander said. "You'll have to be more specific."

"I don't have time for games," Charvat snarled, realizing what the commander intended not to do. "You know damn well who I'm talking about."

"What's the name again?"

Maddening. "Jiménez Garcia. Chief enforcer for September 27. He assassinated one of my agents in Peck Canyon and shot me full of holes. We spotted him in Nogales a few minutes ago and gave chase, but he jumped into a cross-border tunnel. If you don't grab him on your end, I'll come down there and kick your—"

"That incident was in your mountains, on your side of the border," the commander spat. "It was done by your own gangbangers, but you're trying to blame us."

"Are you insane? We're talking *Garcia*. He sawed off the head of one of your cops and nailed it to a tree for everyone to admire," Charvat shot back, all his wounds reigniting. "Hold him on that charge if nothing else, till our politicians work out a deal."

"I'd be happy to do that," the commander said icily. "If *Señor* Garcia were actually guilty of that terrible crime. Mexico City insists the dead officer was secretly a drug trafficker. He sold heroin and cocaine from his patrol car even as he went on his rounds upholding our laws. He was beheaded by a rival trafficker."

"Really? What's this rival's name?" Charvat said.

"That is confidential. But I can assure you it wasn't this Johnny Garcia you mentioned, and Mexico City will confirm that if you wish to ask."

Johnny Garcia. Charvat stared at the phone.

"It's a tragedy," the commander said to fill the empty air.

"The only tragedy," Charvat said, "is your astounding lack of balls."

"There's no reason to use such language—"

Charvat disconnected.

"I tried to get in there, Boss," Earl said, stalking the basement as he wiped mud off his shoulders. "But the hole's too small. I fired at him, don't think I hit him, though—"

"I know that, don't worry, you done good," Charvat said. "Both of you, fine job." He saw Earl relax and remembered the phone mashed to his ear at the station. He recalled that Garcia took off running just moments later. Also, Border Patrol agents weren't allowed to fire at fleeing subjects unless they were fired upon first, which hadn't happened here. Was Earl shooting in self-defense? Or shutting someone's pie hole?

He moved his hand to his gun butt, feeling sick.

"Earl, can I borrow your phone?" he said casually. "Mine's run out of juice and I need to let Tucson Sector know what's happening."

Earl's eyes darted up and left, the classic body language of lying and evasion. "Uh, sorry, Boss. Mine's low, too—"

"You drained it in the armory, right?" Charvat said, drawing and pointing his H&K at Earl's heart.

"Bee!" Connor sputtered. "What are you doing?"

"Jimmy Garcia escaped," Charvat said, his own heart breaking. Earl had been with him for a decade. Had been to the house. Had played with his kids. "Because someone called to warn him. Earl, you wanna explain? Or do I let the techs tear your phone apart?"

Earl broke for the stairs. Connor wrapped him in an immobilization hug so brutal that even Charvat winced. "One more twitch, man," Connor growled. "And I'll tear off your arms." His voice was equal parts fury and sorrow. "You were on Jimmy's pad? Christ, I woulda given you money."

"I want a lawyer," Earl mumbled.

"You'll need one," Charvat said, handcuffing his agent as uniforms flooded the basement.

"Garcia went down the rabbit hole," Charvat announced. "Border agents, tear this building apart and see if he dropped anything useful."

Rest of you, figure out where the tunnel goes. A Caterpillar's on its way, maybe we can dig him out." He shook hands all around. "I appreciate your quick response. You're real po-lice, and I'm proud of you." He glared at Earl.

Who at least had the decency to look ashamed.

Garcia speed-crawled through the sphincter of a tunnel, blinded by the swirling fog of dirt. He broke two fingers slamming into a rock and bit his lip to keep from screaming his pain—the BPs might have listening devices. He heard muffled shouts above his head, then the roar of an earthmover. His gut tightened in fear; his pursuers wanted to pluck him out of the ground like a tree root. Whole or in parts made no difference to these blood-frenzied men.

He advanced another yard, choking and coughing as the earth shook around him, rocks clonking him on head and back. Another yard. Another. His head popped clear of the rubble. He wiped dirt from his eyes to see where he was . . . .

Mexico.

"*Ay . . . dios mío,*" he wheezed as he wormed into the clear. "That was close."

Thank God he'd lured that Border Patrol agent onto his payroll. Thanks to his massive gambling losses, Earl was loan-sharked up to his eyeballs and thus tailor-made for Garcia's pitch: *Warn me about drug raids, and I'll pay your debts.*

Prompting Earl's frantic call today.

If it had come just one minute later, Garcia reflected, it would have resulted not in an escape worthy of Hollywood but in a needle filled with poison on death row . . .

One. Minute.

He crawled out the tunnel entrance and rested on the cold basement floor. He climbed the stairs into the kitchen, where Javier had saved the day with his pickax. He spit dirt chunks from his mouth, sneezing until his chin ran muddy with snot. He pulled the cell and wiped it clean, then punched in a number from memory.

"*Sí, Jefe,*" Javier said.

"Pick me up," Garcia said, naming a nearby intersection. "Is our friend making his pitch?"

"As we speak," Javier said. "I should hear from the keepers any minute."

Garcia disconnected, then laughed out loud. Another bullet dodged! One of hundreds in his long *narco* career. He really wished he'd killed that Border Patrol chief back in Peck Canyon. The man was proving incredibly smart and tenacious. Not as much as him, of course, but still . . .

His laughter changed to derision. In his mad dash to escape, he'd left the Christmas presents back in America!

"Not as smart as you think, *estúpido*," he moaned, slapping his forehead.

Chapter 19

U.S. FEDERAL COURTHOUSE
PHOENIX, ARIZONA

The assistant U.S. attorney raised a shaggy eyebrow. "Is this some kind of media stunt?" he said, fixing his visitor with a gimlet eye. "If so, I really don't have the time—"

Peter Lawrence's blond locks shook violently. "It's no joke," he said. "Isabel Garcia is completely innocent."

"Because you framed her."

"Yes, sir, I did." He slid the DVD across the desk. "This video shows how."

The AUSA jotted down some notes and sighed. "So let me get this straight. You put the lime in the coconut, mix it all up—"

"Huh?" Lawrence said.

No sense of humor, this one. "Sorry," the AUSA said. "To summarize, you were cheating on Miss Garcia. She found out. Being hot-blooded like the rest of 'those people,' to use your term, she obtained a bulldozer and ran it through your house. You were furious at this appalling disrespect from a 'lesser'—again, your term—so after beating her, you purchased the cocaine. Knowing Miss Garcia was attending a birthday party in Tucson, you stashed it in her engine compartment—"

"Air cleaner, sir. Specifically."

"All right, air cleaner. You knew drug dogs sniff cars entering the United States, so the odds were high she'd be caught, and you'd have your revenge." The AUSA tapped the DVD. "This video from her parking garage confirms your role in planting said cocaine."

"Right."

More notes. "And you're confessing to this crime because . . ."

"It's the right thing to do," Lawrence said. "And I feel ashamed."

As he'd rehearsed with the *banditos* on the ride north. When he walked into the federal building, he seriously considered ratting out his handlers and demanding witness protection. But he remembered the nail gun—his punctured arm still burned like holy hell—and stuck with the script. Better to peel potatoes in an American jail than to die in a spider hole in *Me-he-co*.

The AUSA nodded. "Well, sir," he said, getting to his feet. "Thanks for stopping by today."

Lawrence stared. "That's it?"

"As you can imagine, we need to investigate your claims before making any decision or decisions on what, or what not, to do with what you told me, and with the evidence you provided." It was, the AUSA thought, a masterful way to say nothing.

"Oh. Well, okay, then."

"My secretary will show you out . . ."

Lawrence left. The U.S. attorney for the district of Arizona came in from the adjacent office, rolling his eyes. "If they insist on lying, I wish they'd be more creative."

"I dunno, Max. The bulldozer part, that was cool."

"True dat."

They took their seats and mulled over the implications of the interview.

"Jimmy's a *narco* badass," the U.S. attorney said. "Who wants baby sister out of jail. So he grabs a dupe he's got something on—drugs, kiddie porn, whatever—fills said dupe with a story, and sends him our way. Figuring because Lawrence belongs to the white guy club . . ."

"We'd be gullible enough to believe him," the AUSA completed. "Yeah, sure, I think he's a put-up, too."

"I hear a 'but' in there, Clement."

The AUSA sighed. "Mr. Lawrence is a flaming douche but not unintelligent. That makes him capable of framing her. Plus, there's the video."

THE FURY

"Which can be confirmed with the condo board," the U.S. attorney said.

"Yes. So I'd like to check this out before committing us to a trial. I think she might indeed have been framed by Blondie there." He slid the case file across the desk.

The U.S. attorney read it, then flipped to the booking photos. Even in the harsh light of the prison camera, Isabel Garcia was stunning. "Dayum," he said, fanning himself.

"What I said," the AUSA said. "We wrongly convict someone that gorgeous, the press will crucify us."

The U.S. attorney smoothed his hair into place. "Worse, Washington sends you to North Dakota to investigate sheep fucking."

"Me? Why me?" the AUSA said, shivering at the thought. North Dakota was where they sent screwups. People without teeth lived there. And drunken Indians. He'd rather have dysentery. "You're the one with the sign on the door."

"Why God made assistants, to take the blame. It's right there in the Bible, next to plagues and walking on water." He considered his options. "All right, check out the story. But take your time. We sent her to Fargo for a reason."

"To piss off Jimmy for killing our guy?" the AUSA said.

The U.S. attorney grinned. "War is hell."

Chapter 20

J. EDGAR HOOVER BUILDING
WASHINGTON, D.C.

"Good flight?" the director of counterterrorism said as she settled in a chair.

"Screaming Baby Airlines," Deb Williams said. The FBI jet wasn't available, so she flew coach back to D.C. "But at least a drunk spilled bourbon on my laptop."

They talked about flying for a minute and agreed it mostly sucked.

"So what should I do about Superstition Davis?" he said.

Williams took a deep breath. "Nothing."

"Care to elaborate?"

"Sure. She bought a leg for a black man. So we should let her go."

The director's eye twitch told her to get on with it already.

"Several years ago, her next-door neighbor, a black man named Clayton, was attacked by skinheads," she said, consulting her notes. "They crushed his leg with a pipe. Doctors had to amputate. The replacement was clunky and stiff, but he couldn't afford better. Davis bought him one that was state-of-the-art. He nicknamed it 'Kilroy.'"

"Why?"

"'Kilroy Was Here.'" She mimed writing. "During World War Two, GIs scribbled that phrase on buildings and fences to prove they'd once been there—"

"Why did she buy Clayton a new leg?" the director interrupted.

"Because he's her friend," Deb said. "Because skinheads piss her off. Because she'd recently gotten an inheritance from an aunt, so she had the money." She held up a corrective finger. "They, I mean. She and her husband, Derek. They thought it was the right thing to do." She sipped her Starbucks mocha latte. "Damn, they never put in enough sugar."

"Take it from the top," he said, leaning back in his Aeron chair to take the strain off his bad back. She talked without interruption for a half hour. "Bottom line, Mr. Director," she concluded, "there's no case against Sue."

Sue. The director steepled his fingers. "You like her."

Williams nodded as she drained her cup. "She's a straight shooter."

"So to speak."

"Uh, yeah," she said, grinning at the unintended pun. "Pretty fearless, taking on three psychos with a gun she wasn't sure worked." She explained. "She wasn't impressed by the full weight and majesty of the Bureau, either."

"I hate people we can't intimidate."

"They grow 'em tough in the Chi, boss," she chided. "Hog butcher for the world, tool maker, stacker of wheat—"

"City of broad shoulders, yeah, yeah, I read Carl Sandburg in college too," the director said.

"I wouldn't know. I was in diapers then."

The director snorted to hide a smile. He liked agents who could keep up with him. He opened his credenza and removed a royal blue mug, its FBI logo embossed in gold. He filled it with high-test, poured ten full seconds of sugar, and slid it across the desk. "Would you partner with her, Deb?" he said.

It was the ultimate measure of a cop: *Would you trust her to watch your back?*

Williams sipped her sorta-mocha, considering. "I didn't spend enough time to know for sure," she said. "But I think so, yes. Her street work is impressive. She handles herself well, and her fellow officers trust her completely."

"Guy cops too?"

"Even them." Which was saying something, as still too many men would rather suffer herpes than work with a Dickless Tracy. "Every guy I talked to swore he'd run into a dark alley with her. Women, ditto—not one catty remark disguised as praise. Apparently, to know her is to love her."

The director considered all she'd said. "So we shouldn't charge Sue with civil rights violations. Not for 'blackie' or 'black-eyed son of a bitch' or shooting the man in the back."

"No. We shouldn't."

He nodded slowly. Shuffled his papers. Refilled his cup. "Well, we are."

"Huh?" Williams said, dumbfounded.

"We're going to put her in prison. And when we're done, she'll thank us."

Williams blinked, still confused. "Why on Earth would she thank us for a jolt in a federal penitentiary?"

He explained, and Williams nodded, intrigued. "You think it'll work?" she said.

"It has to," he said, wincing as he shifted. His back was lousy, not because he took a bullet or saved a child from a burning building, but because he'd slipped on the freshly waxed floor of a Bureau bathroom, cracking two vertebrae on a toilet rim. An ignominy his friends still liked to jab him about—"Flush with success!" one crowed when he got the nod to run the elite counterterrorism division. He got to his feet and slowly roamed the office, rubbing his hips.

"Jimmy Garcia is why I got into this business, Deb. Not for the glory. Not for the money. Not for the promotions. I do this work to get monsters off the street. Monsters like Garcia. I'm going to cut off his head and stick it on a pike, and Superstition Davis is going to help me do it."

"Us," she said.

"Us?" he said.

"You said help 'me' do it. I want in."

He grinned. "I wouldn't dream of doing it without you."

"So what's next?" she said, holding up her cup in salute.

"Dry out your laptop, you're going hunting."

CHICAGO

"Didja ever have a booger you can't flick off?" Hanrahan growled, looking her up and down. "No matter how hard you try, it just sticks to your finger?"

"Nice to see you again, too," Williams said. "I couldn't stand even a day away."

"Yeah, yeah. Why are you here—"

"Gosh, thanks, I'd love to come in," she said, yanking his screen door and waltzing past him into the aluminum-sided raised ranch.

"Sure, hell, make yourself at home," he said, sarcasm dripping. "I was just sitting around relaxing, counting my blessings you were finally gone. Yet here you are again, aggravating the hernia that is my life."

"And they say cops aren't poets," she said.

They walked into his living room. It was neat as a pin, which surprised her. The furniture was Naugahyde, which didn't. He eased onto a three-cushion sofa but perched on the edge, knotty forearms on muscled thighs. His stare wasn't hostile, but neither was it welcoming. More like contemplating a root canal. She took the recliner, braced for the explosion.

"Your detective is going to prison," she said without Vaseline.

Hanrahan sprung off the cushions, eyes flashing daggers. "You got some fucking nerve, invading my home to issue threats, you arrogant piece of—"

"Listen to the rest," Williams said, "before you cuss me into a radioactive pile of Feeby sludge, all right?"

He put his hands on his hips. "You got five minutes," he growled. "Begin."

At three and a half, he held up a hand.

"You're willing to do that? You, your very own self?"

"Yes."

She was pleased to find she'd been right—when Hanrahan smiled, the room filled with light. "All right, then, Deb. Lay it out top to bottom."

She did.

"You're completely serious?" he said, retaking his seat. "This isn't a wet dream from some Mighty Mouse who's gonna abandon her midstream 'cause of budget or politics?"

"I'm serious as a heart attack," she said. "And the director of counterterrorism doesn't say anything unless he means it." She grinned. "Wet dreams, you'll have to find out for yourself, Ace. They don't pay me enough."

"Huh," Hanrahan said, intrigued. "Much as I hate to admit it, you might be onto something there. Want a drink?"

"Sure," she said, knowing she had him. "Do you have a nice Chardonnay?"

"I got Old Style," he said. "In pop-top cans."

"When in Rome . . .," she said.

Chapter 21

SUPERSTITION'S HOUSE
CHICAGO

Her cell phone sounded like a dental drill.

"Hello?" she mumbled, the word sending sparks through her hungover brain.

"Hi, Mrs. Davis, it's Brian Charvat," the Border Patrol chief said. "Calling from Arizona."

"Please, call me Superstition," she said, struggling to clear her head. "Or Sue. How are you, Brian?"

"Mending," he said. "Sad. Angry."

Superstition sighed. "I know. All I do is cry, yell at myself for being weak, then start all over again."

"Every cop's dilemma," he said. "Suck it up or let it out."

"I'm doing both." She touched her throbbing temple. "With alcohol chases."

"Me, too," he said, meaning it. "Tough" didn't mean "emotionless." "Listen, I'm calling to say how sorry I was to miss Derek's funeral. I wanted to attend, but the doctors banned me from traveling. They thought something might come unplugged in the air."

"Don't worry, you were here in spirit," she said. "And the note you sent"—her throat thickened as she recalled his spidery handwriting—"was just wonderful."

"I meant every word. He struck me as an exceptional young man."

Superstition eased into the leather sofa. Morning light streamed through the picture window, painting the floor with sundust. "He liked you too, Brian. I could tell from his calls."

They shared Derek stories, then he cleared his throat. "I don't know if you'd be up for this," he said. "But would you like to see the canyon where your husband died?"

She was so shocked, she couldn't form words.

"I'm sorry, I shouldn't have hit you with this so soon," he said. "It's too—"

"No! I mean, yes, I think so, um, yes," Superstition said, squeezing the phone so hard that it trembled. "I'd like that very much."

"I'll take you to the same cantinas, introduce you to the folks he met. Then we'll take the Jeeps out to Peck Canyon. We'll spend as much time as you want, do a little memorial thing, maybe." More throat-clearing. "It won't bring him back, Sue. But maybe it would be of some comfort to you, seeing things as he did that night. I'll arrange a Border Patrol jet to pick you up and return you home and—ah, hell—"

"Are you all right?" she said, alarmed at the industrial-grade hacking.

"I sucked . . . a bushel of rock dust . . . from the grenade blasts. It's still causing problems," Charvat said, his voice scraped. "But I'm better than I have any right to be, blessed be your husband." Another series of hacks, then a deep, cleansing breath. "What works for your schedule?"

She thought of her cramped little work dungeon, and decided City Hall wouldn't mind if she disappeared for a few days. "How about tomorrow?"

"Really?" he said, surprised. "Are you sure you don't want to rest some more? You've had a rough go between your bar shootings and Derek's murder."

She shook her head as if he could see. "Everyone's been terrific," she said. "Checking in every hour to make sure I'm all right. I've got so many meals in the freezer I can eat for a year, and I appreciate every bit of it. I really do." She blew out her breath. "But it's driving me nuts."

"And if you don't get away from it," he said, "you'll eat your gun."

She blinked rapidly. She'd walked into the icy Tucson morgue and saw Derek's blue, deflated body. She let out a cry and hugged him. He squished like rotten grapes. She pulled herself together and made the formal identification. On the way back to Chicago, she pulled her Glock 19 from her purse. Stroked it awhile. Thought how one bullet, just one, would let her be with Derek and the kids. "How did you—"

"My oldest was killed by an SUV," he said. "Whose driver was so cranked on meth he thought he was Captain Kirk smashing Klingons."

"Oh, my God, Brian, I'm so sorry—"

"Which we can talk about on the way to Nogales."

"You're coming with the plane? What about—"

"Hell with doctors," he said. "You need to talk, and I'm pretty good at listening. Lemme go scare up a jet, and I'll see you at O'Hare. Say, high noon?"

"Fitting," she said. "See you then."

Chapter 22

CATTLE RANCH
EIGHTY MILES EAST OF NOGALES, MEXICO

"Praise Allah, I love this soil," the engineer enthused over the quiet whir of the excavator he'd found on eBay. "Soft enough to chew through quickly, yet stiff enough to not collapse."

"Finish as fast as possible," Javier said. "We lost three tunnels this week alone." One to his boss's narrow escape, two to Border Patrol listening devices.

"No chance of that here," the engineer said, stepping aside to let the wheelbarrow men haul out the debris. "*Americanos* never venture this far east. Which is why we can use this." He patted the borer's steel rump. "Thousand times faster than picks and shovels."

"When you're done," Javier said, handing over the map, "dig here, here, and here."

"I can do that, but I'll need more strong backs," the engineer said, impressed at the scope of the expansion. Job security was a wonderful thing. "Is that a problem?"

"We're the only work around," Javier said. Unemployment among young men in Mexico was over fifty percent. "Donkeys are easy to find."

A barrow man scowled.

"No disrespect," Javier said, showing off his scars. "I'm a donkey too."

"Ee-haw, ee-haw, ee-haw," the barrow man brayed.

THE FURY

SEPTEMBER 27 SAFE HOUSE, NOGALES, MEXICO

Delgado flicked dandruff from his collar. He was plagued with such bad psoriasis that his scalp glowed like a stoplight. The last man to mention it found himself without one. "I'm delighted to not be delivering the eulogy at your funeral, *mi amigo*," he said. "But now you're stuck here in Mexico."

"I can't make deliveries for a while," Garcia admitted, touching his bandaged wounds. "But I can handle things from this side." He described the new tunnels he'd ordered dug and confirmed the Taliban's latest load of Afghan heroin had landed on a deserted beach in Honduras, awaiting transfer to September 27 trucks.

"Excellent," Delgado said, tipping his *cerveza*. "Any news on your sister?"

"The boyfriend confessed to the U.S. attorney in Phoenix. He handed over the video. But . . . nothing."

"The *gringos* don't believe him?"

Garcia grimaced. "It's not that. He's quite credible. They refuse to release her for the same reason they sent her to North Dakota: to punish me."

"I suspect you're right," Delgado said, pulling at his chin. "But how long can they keep up that ruse, given her proof of innocence?"

"Months, her lawyer says. Even years. U.S. attorneys are devious."

Delgado noted the steam in the measured responses. "That's a shame," he said. "But I have a way to make you feel better. It seems the CIA is paying Mexico a visit tomorrow."

That startled Garcia. "The Central Intelligence Agency? Why?"

"My sources don't know," Delgado said. "Only that they'll enter Mexico through Nogales, then drive for parts unknown."

"What does it have to do with us?"

"Nothing I know of," Delgado said. "The American CIA spies on politicians and industrialists, not the cartels. But Mexico City, they don't like it. They prefer to do business without foreign interference. Problem is, they can't do anything about it officially without getting a drone strike from Uncle Sam." He cocked an eyebrow as he drained his beer.

Garcia saw what he was getting at. "But if these agents never arrived at their destination," he said, "Mexico City can legitimately claim ignorance, and would be, mmm, grateful to whoever managed to solve that particular problem."

"Good to see tunnel dust doesn't affect your brain."

Garcia grinned. Refilled the *jefe's* glass. Made some calls.

Chapter 23

UNITED STATES PENITENTIARY
FARGO, NORTH DAKOTA

The scar-faced Chicana wagged her split tongue as she stared from the other side of the gray room. Isabel shivered, feeling the girl's sliminess down to her core. "You've got to get me out of here," she muttered. "This place is filled with jackals."

Her lawyer looked over his turquoise horn rims.

"I'm calling in every favor I know, Izzy. Just sit tight. And be aware they'll approach you with a deal," he said, keeping his voice down because the prison's visiting area was communal. "Immunity in exchange for telling them about cartel operations."

She jerked like she'd been branded. "In other words, if I rat out my brother?"

"Aren't any other words," the attorney said. "That's exactly what they'll want you to do."

"Not happening," she said.

"Don't be hasty," the attorney said, probing for weakness. He was her lawyer, technically, but September 27 paid the bills, including the one for the executive jet he'd taken to this godforsaken outpost of planet Earth. "Tell them some minor things. Nothing to get anyone in big trouble: small time for small fry. Meanwhile, you'd be free."

"I won't sell out!" she shouted, pounding the table.

"Calm down, calm down—"

A guard started over. She waved him off. "I'll rot before I hurt my family."
The attorney sat back.
Nodded.
"I believe you would at that," he said.
"Plus I don't know anything anyway," she said.
"That, my dear," the attorney said, "is entirely beside the point."

Chapter 24

BORDER CROSSING
NOGALES, ARIZONA

A tiny man with a long, black ponytail looked inside the dusty Explorer, shaking his head in profound sorrow. "I ask for pros," he moaned, "and they send me Polacks."

"Funny," Kowalski snickered from behind the wheel. "But how do you know it's an Italian helicopter?"

"I dunno," the tiny man said. "How?"

Kowalski whirled both index fingers. "The rotor goes *wop-wop-wop* and the tail goes *dago-dago-dago*."

The tiny man, whose name was Lombardo, laughed, dog-sniffing complete. He climbed in back, bumped fists all around, and accepted coffee from Nowak and doughnuts from Zielinski, whose scarred chin was shiny with frosting. "We breathed on 'em, you know," Nowak warned.

"No worries," Lombardo said, biting through the dark chocolate frosting. He'd assured his wife he'd watch his diet while in Mexico. Then again, he lied for a living. "It's a well-known fact that fat neutralizes Polack germs . . ."

They traded more insults between munches and sips, then got down to business. "We're rock hoppers for this assignment?" Lombardo said.

Kowalski nodded as he accelerated. "Texaco geologists, looking for new oil fields."

"Cover legend?"

Zielinski passed over two documents. The first was a Texaco photo ID. The other was a letter of introduction from the president of Pemex, the Mexican state-owned oil company, which allowed four "Texaco petro-geologists" to explore northern Mexico to their hearts' content. Both were fakes from the friendly forgers at Langley.

"Onward," Kowalski said, nosing Explorer, doughnuts, and CIA across the border.

The lookout adjusted his Zeiss binoculars, then dialed his satellite phone. "Four inbound," he said, tracking the rooster tail of dust.

"Very good," Jimmy Garcia said, sipping his long-neck *cerveza*. His boss's moles in American law enforcement were worth their weight in Afghan heroin.

He told his driver to move out, then called the roadblock.

"Any intelligence?" Kowalski said.

"Not in this car," Nowak said.

Lombardo played his PDA. "Garcia's leaving the tavern," he reported, the result of a micro-drone flying high overhead. CIA informants spotted the drug chieftain yesterday, and the drone was dispatched to keep track. "Two SUVs flanking his."

"Security," Nowak said.

"Nothing we can't handle," Zielinski said, patting the bag at his feet. Their weapons had been confiscated from Mexican narcotics gangs. Lombardo thought it fine irony that a CIA assassination team would kill *narcos* with the *narcos'* own guns. That fact would also convince *policía* that the bloody hit was just more gang warfare and not to be investigated seriously.

Kowalski took the next right and checked his watch. "Twenty minutes to intercept," he said. "They're armed, so hit them hard and fast."

"Thanks, Mom," the other three hit men chorused.

"Yeah, yeah, just making sure," Kowalski said, grinning. "Eye-talian on board, you gotta make allowances."

"Fuck you very much," Lombardo said.

"I would, but your mother beat me to it . . ."

"There's. The. Explorer," a spotter coughed through cigarette smoke as the Americans crested the hill on the rural highway.

"Stay calm," the roadblock leader reminded. "American spies are smarter than their Hollywood films suggest. I'll check their papers, accept their money, then let them on their way. Soon as they're moving, take them out hard and fast. Until then, look bored like real cops . . ."

"Ah, hell, now what?" Kowalski groaned as he spotted the flashing lights. It was a sucky morning already, with a balky GPS, a flat tire, and brakes that howled at the slightest pump.

Nowak put up binoculars. "Police roadblock," he said. "Checking papers."

Kowalski nodded. "No worries," he said, patting the shirt pocket where he kept the cash.

"What's the bribe down here?" Lombardo said. He hadn't worked the Americas in years, having recently transferred back to the States from Pakistan.

"Twenty bucks," Zielinski said.

"Cheaper than the Taliban," Lombardo marveled. "They wanted a hundred."

"Our people are more easily bought," said Nowak, who was Mexican despite his name.

"They'll learn," Lombardo said.

The roadblock leader let the pickup truck of farm workers go through the swing gate, then held up the stop sign. "Remember, look bored," he reminded everyone. "They get an inkling we're not real *policía*, they'll ruin your day."

Kowalski pumped the brakes. The Explorer shuddered to a halt. "Good morning," he said.

"Hello to you, too," the roadblock leader replied, bending to the open window. "Your Spanish is excellent."

"Rosetta Stone," Kowalski said.

"I used that to learn English," the leader said. "It works very well. Unlike your truck, which squeals like a pig. Brake problems?"

Kowalski nodded. Small talk always preceded the payoff. Nobody, even bribe-takers, liked to think of themselves as extortionists. "Unfortunately, yes," he said.

The leader peered into the car. "You are tourists?"

"Nah, we're petro-geologists," Kowalski said, handing over his papers. "We work for Texaco. Your Pemex oil company hired us to find new places to drill for oil. So here we are."

The leader nodded. "What does a geologist have to do with finding oil?"

Lombardo's antennae flickered. Even the Taliban, who were paranoid, weren't this chatty at roadblocks. They wanted a pleasantry, money, and get on with it already. The other cops seemed a shade too disinterested. Nothing he could put a finger on, but he'd learned in Pakistan to trust his instincts. So he cleared his throat.

Nowak caught it and eased his hand toward the gym bag of grenades.

"We study land formations," Kowalski explained. "Some types of rocks indicate the possibility of oil underneath. Enough of those rocks in one place, it's worth digging a test well."

The leader smiled. "Sounds interesting," he said, handing back the papers. "These look in order, *Señor*. May I see your . . . driver's license? It's the last thing before you go."

Lombardo's suspicion eased a fraction as Kowalski handed over the license, around which was folded not just one Jackson but a pair of Franklins. The leader's smile broadened to silver fillings. "You are quite in order, my friend," he said.

"You have many officers," Kowalski said, nodding at the milling cops. "They look thirsty."

"They are indeed," the leader said, motioning the gate open. "Please have those brakes examined in the next town." He named a garage. "My cousin owns it. He'll fix them in no time and for much less money than your American bandits would charge."

"I see you've met my mechanic," Kowalski said drily. He'd just dropped two grand for engine work on his wife's Chrysler.

THE FURY

The leader laughed. "I'll call ahead and let him know you're coming. I'd feel terrible if you were in an accident and I hadn't provided a way to prevent it."

Another way to squeegee dollars from *gringos*, Lombardo knew. No problem. Garcia would be buzzard bait and the CIA team exfiltrated by the time the cousin reported their no-show.

"I'll do that, thanks," Kowalski said, dropping the selector into DRIVE. The gate closed behind him. The leader fell back. The "cops" swiveled and crouched.

"Gun, gun, gun!" Lombardo shouted, pulling his from under his shirt . . .

. . . as masked Mexicans poured from a truck . . .

. . . as Kowalski stomped the accelerator while firing through the window . . .

. . . as Lombardo and Nowak pitched hand grenades over the roof . . .

. . . as ersatz *policía* filled the cobalt sky with RPGs . . .

. . . as Kowalski died running over three shooters . . .

. . . as Lombardo's scalp disappeared as his short-barreled AK disintegrated . . .

. . . along with Nowak's chest and Zielinski's face . . .

. . . as Jimmy Garcia observed the slaughter from the top of the next hill . . .

. . . as a ponytail attached to a tiny head flew from a window and splatted against a cactus, dripping brains and maple frosting.

Garcia dialed the roadblock leader. "Take what you need," he ordered as his driver made a U-turn. "Then get the box to FedEx."

Chapter 25

DESERTED BEACH NORTH OF TAMPICO
GULF COAST OF MEXICO

Eleven bombs washed slowly out of the surf and parked on sun-dappled sand.

Goosing a pelican.

Which turned, squawked, and pecked angrily at the nose of the dull green beast.

Which exploded.

Killing the pelican.

A seagull.

Its flock mates.

A school of fish.

And a horseshoe crab.

Blackflies, alerted by the smell of death, turned from the rotted burro on which they'd been feasting and headed for the seafood buffet.

Circled.

Landed.

Slurped.

Died.

FORT DETRICK, MARYLAND

The colonel stalked her lab in utter disbelief. "How in the hell did nerve gas get on a raggedy-ass tuna boat?"

"No clue," her chief scientist said. "Coast Guard doesn't know either."

"What type?" the colonel said, knowing there were several, each more dangerous than a truckload of vipers.

The scientist sucked on a can of Red Bull. "VX," he said. "With an anthrax chaser."

The colonel shuddered. While her specialty was biological warfare—the raison d'être of Fort Detrick, which housed the U.S. Army Medical Research Institute for Infectious Diseases—everyone in the weapons community understood the horror of those two little letters. VX was the world's most lethal chemical. Anthrax wasn't much better. Together . . .

"Current manufacture?" she said.

The scientist shook his head. "Nobody makes this stuff anymore, Colonel. The last factory closed in the eighties."

"So, then, it's Cold War vintage. Whose? Ours?"

He shrugged. "Probably, since it was found in the Gulf, and we were the only ones in the Americas who possessed that technology." He chucked his drooping chin, thinking. "We used the oceans for disposal back then. One might have drifted to the surface and gotten snagged up in their fishing nets."

The colonel stared, horrified. She'd grown up in Biloxi, a mile from the beach.

"We dumped nerve gas in our water supply?"

"Easiest way to dispose of it then," the scientist said, his expression showing he hardly believed it either. "Out of sight, out of mind, the thinking went."

It amazed the colonel, and not for the first time, that the human race still existed.

"All right, I'll alert the Navy," she said. "They can dust off their maps, see if any of the dump sites have been disturbed."

"Can't."

She ground her teeth. She desperately wished her scientists were military, not civilian, so she could flog them into briefing succinctly. "Why. Not."

"The maps don't exist. Operation CHASE was top secret—"

"Chase? Never heard of it," she interrupted.

"It's a Cold War acronym," he explained. "For 'Cut Holes And Sink 'Em.' Basically, the Army filled old ships with discarded munitions—nerve gas included—towed them into the oceans, and sent them to the bottom. Only the barest of records were kept, and most of those have disappeared."

The colonel flung her hands to the sky. "How? Boris and Natasha?"

"Bureaucracy. Paperwork fell into the wrong filing drawer. Storage depots burned down—remember the Pentagon lost eighteen million personnel files in that warehouse fire in St. Louis in 1973?" The colonel did, because she'd tried to get her father's service papers for a birthday scrapbook and learned they were ashes. "Boxes were pitched during spring housekeeping. People retired and died, and their replacements didn't care because that disposal program was ancient history."

The colonel got it. "We beat the Nazis, then the Japanese, then the Russians. We didn't need that particular doomsday weapon anymore because we had nukes. So we dumped them in the oceans and forgot all about them."

"Until now," the scientist said.

"Till they burped up like bad guacamole," the colonel agreed, winding hair around her little finger. "And Johnny Jihad gets a WMD."

"I'm only speculating, Colonel," the scientist warned. "I could be wrong about everything."

"But on the slightest chance you aren't," the colonel said, "I need to wake up some generals."

Chapter 26

THE WHITE HOUSE
WASHINGTON, D.C.

"Jesus Christ on a bender," the president of the United States groaned. "You sent a hit team into our backyard?"

The CIA director's nod was unapologetic. "Garcia blew up a Chicago cop," he said. "He shot a Border Patrol chief so full of holes he whistles like a calliope. He did it with a smile, and he does it to sell poison to our kids. You ordered the agency to take out anyone who—"

"I know, I know," the president muttered, recalling his fiery directives on that subject. "No mercy, no safe haven."

"Yes, sir."

"How did we find out about their deaths?"

The director slid a folder across the polished steel desk. "Those are Texaco identification cards," he explained as the president looked inside. "Our agents were carrying them as 'official' cover. The IDs showed up at Langley, and our techs took a look. Each card held one man's fingerprints, along with blood spatter from all four."

The president winced. Every day he learned about another brave American dying for his country. He'd never get used to it. "Poor bastards," he muttered. "What's the status of their bodies?"

"Still missing," the director said.

"Hole in the desert."

The director agreed. "My case officer in Phoenix, who arranged the intercept, called me when they didn't reappear. A few days later, these IDs showed up at Langley, addressed to 'The Head *El Stupido*.' " He smiled without humor. "The box was FedExed from Brownsville, Texas. We tracked down the mope who shipped them."

"Anything?"

The director shook his head. "Lives in a doorway. Says a Mexican with sunglasses gave him ten bucks and a bottle of Mad Dog to drop off the package, which was prepaid."

"Smart, using a cutout," the president said. "Was there a warning or any other explanation in the box?"

"No. The IDs spoke for themselves, they figured."

They figured right, the president thought. "Who's the most likely killer?"

"Jimmy Garcia's top of the list," the director said. "He found out we were coming to kill him, so he struck preemptively."

"Can we confirm that?"

"No. The drone following him experienced a malfunction, so we had to ground it. There's no video of the actual attack or of where Jimmy is now."

The president tapped his desktop till the steel rang. "Is Garcia crazy enough to murder four CIA agents?"

"He's violent enough. But he's sane. His boss, not so much."

The president searched his memory banks. So many bad guys to remember. "Del something . . . Delgado, right?"

"Vincente Delgado," the director said, impressed. This president remembered real facts, not just political. "Who once turned a girlfriend into a vest."

"A . . . vest?"

"She annoyed him." The director mimed buttoning. "He skinned her and tanned her and used her finger bones for buttons. So yeah, the cartel is fully capable of this." The director sighed. "But it also could be Mexico's military, who's in bed with the *narcos*. Or local cops, who'd make five years' salary by killing—"

"I understand," the president said sourly. "Does Braveheart know?" That was his derisive term for the new president of Mexico, whom he detested for making an accommodation with the *narcos*. The deal wasn't to reduce bloodshed, as Braveheart piously claimed at his inaugural, but for the money and votes they controlled.

"Not officially," the director said. "But if September 27 did this, it would be with the expectation of approval and protection from Mexico City."

"Sucks to be them, then," the president said. "Find whoever's responsible. Money is no object, and I don't care how high up their political protection goes, including Braveheart. I want the killers."

The director grinned, appreciating the crystal-clear directive, which was rare in Byzantine Washington. Then his face clouded. "Before I do that, sir, I need to plug a leak," he said. "This was a tightly held operation. Yet the assassins knew the exact route and schedule of my team's entrance into Mexico."

"Damn," the president said, his face mottling with anger at the Benedict Arnold who'd thrown four brave patriots in a hole with beetles and snakes. "Find your traitor and make an example."

"How big an example do you want?"

"Hiroshima."

Understood. The director nodded and left.

As soon as the door closed, the president pounded the desk he'd had built from the melted-down guns of the *USS Abbot*, a destroyer that joined the first bombardment of Japan in World War II. The force of his blows rattled the revolving bookstand crafted by Thomas Jefferson, who'd gone to war with the Barbary pirates in the 1800s, and a smiley-face coffee mug found miraculously intact in the smoking ruins of the World Trade Center. He kept the relics in his office as reminders that terrorism wasn't a new problem but reinvented for each age.

And would be dealt with accordingly . . .

His executive secretary poked her head into the Oval Office. "Your eleven o'clock's here, Mr. President."

"Send him in, Mrs. Ehlebracht," the president said. "Along with more coffee. You know how that boy loves his caffeine . . ."

"Bev, you read my mind," the FBI director said as the pretty, petite blonde handed him a purple-and-red china cup made for Abraham

Lincoln's White House. He sipped, nodded thanks. "What's up, sir?" the director said as she departed.

"Nothing good," the president said, telling him about the Texaco IDs.

"Damn," the director said. He had a great affection for undercovers, no matter which agency signed their checks. "What can I do to help?"

"Bring me the head of Alfredo Garcia," the president growled.

The movie reference was rhetorical, but it prompted the director to grin at the prescience of the intriguing proposal he'd just received from his chief of counterterrorism.

"Matter of fact, sir," he said, "I might have a way to do that. But I have one question before I explain."

The president arched an eyebrow. "And that is?"

"Do you want it on a platter or a pike?"

Chapter 27

UNITED STATES PENITENTIARY
FARGO, NORTH DAKOTA

The electronic lock clicked open.

The steel door exhaled an inch.

The overnight lockdown was lifted, with inmates free to move around.

Izzy Garcia straightened her khaki shirt and stepped into the hallway. She looked around cautiously. No long knives waiting. No prisoners trying too hard to look casual.

Her heartbeat slowed to normal. *Silly to be afraid, right?* After the initial terror from sensory onslaught—chains, concrete, bad food, orifice searches from gimlet-eyed guards—prison was actually boring. In the movies, it was all dramatic shadows and sadistic yard bulls. The reality was, you ate, got counted, worked, got counted, slept, got counted, rinse, repeat. Day after day, week after week, year after . . .

Stop it! Jimmy's working hard to spring you! Then again, she couldn't afford to think of that—unfulfilled hope, her lawyer warned, would wear her down like rivers carved canyons.

"Hey, Syndor," she greeted a neighbor to distract herself.

"Izzy," the former hash-house waitress said with a tonsil-illuminating yawn. ICE had caught her in San Diego with a thousand Baggies of marijuana. Unlike Izzy, she'd known the drugs were in her van, because she moonlighted as a transfer driver for the motorcycle gangs that handled U.S. retail sales for the cartels. "Whaddaya want for breakfast today? Omelette with truffles and a nice cup of mangos?"

They cackled. Today being Tuesday, breakfast was grits, three slices of white bread, two pats of margarine, one pat of grape jelly, two cups of milk.

And an apple, for health.

"Gosh, who'd want truffles when there's Wonder Bread?" Izzy said. "We'll squish 'em down and pretend they're meatballs."

They high-fived, then Syndor's eyes narrowed. Izzy turned to see four women, three black, one a black-Asian mix. Their faces were scarred and their arms sleeved with gang tattoos.

They marched straight for her.

"Hey, fish," the lead banger cooed in a falsetto singsong. "Let's you and me get acquainted."

Izzy covered her trembling with a mean-eyed, chin-up stare. She couldn't show a microgram of fear. She was a "new fish," prison slang for a new inmate. For the predators who ran prison cell blocks, fish were the human equivalent of crippled fawns.

"Get lost, bitch," she spat.

"Oooh, a hard-ass," the banger said. "I like that in a ho." She chortled. "Which do you like better, fish, top or bottom? Since you're new, I'll let you choose."

Izzy rolled her shoulders loose. Get in the first blow and make it count, her brother had counseled. Blood and gore will make them fear you, and the best way to get that is to attack like you're insane. Claw out their eyeballs or crush their windpipes . . .

Movement to her left. She swiveled. Another gang, this one all-Mexican. "Back off. She's under our protection," its leader said.

"Says who?" the black leader snarled.

"Says us," the leader of a second Mexican gang said as she moved her crew behind the blacks. "Izzy is a friend of September 27."

The black gang suddenly looked uneasy.

"That's right, 'girlfriend,' she's one of ours," the second Mexican leader trilled. "Leave now and we won't make you kiss her ass."

The black leader backed slowly down the hallway. The others withdrew with her, flexing and growling for show. Izzy wanted to vomit. To think she'd found prison boring . . .

THE FURY

"Don't worry, sister," the second Mexican leader said as she punched Izzy's arm. "Somebody wants you, they gotta get through us."

"And nobody," the first leader said, "gets through us."

Izzy nodded, relief flooding her. They were Mexican Mafia, the toughest gangsters in any place with cages. "It's good to have friends."

"Even better, a brother like yours," the second Mexican leader said.

"He sent you?"

"He did."

"Is he single?" Syndor said hopefully.

Chapter 28

PECK CANYON
NOGALES, ARIZONA

"What a beautiful service," Superstition sighed as they bounced along a rutted trail east of Peck Canyon Road. Dust ribbons slipped through her window and swirled out the back.

"Padre does a fine job," Charvat said. "Gets lots of practice."

Superstition looked at the harsh, transfixing landscape and raised a questioning eyebrow.

"Illegals, mostly," Charvat explained. "Last year I found eight kids desiccating in a dry wash. They were drinking their urine when they died."

Her heart lurched. Englewood, her city's most violent and poverty-stricken neighborhood, was Camelot compared to that.

"Denny's pays its busboys more than Mexico pays most workers," Charvat said. "So to these folks, we're the Land of Oz, and they're trying to follow the yellow brick road." He bumped over the lizard sprawled flat across the path. Flies were making a meal. He vaguely remembered one lumbering around the night of the shooting. Maybe the same one. Felt a little bad. "Too much death," he muttered.

They picked their way through a narrow half-tunnel in the canyon walls. Emerged in a dusty clearing striped with cactus and red rock. Charvat nodded at two giant boulders spalled by fire char and violence.

"That's where we took cover," he said.

He pointed at the stony ridge overlooking the clearing.

"And that's where they got Derek."

Superstition hopped out of the Jeep. Border Patrol agents kept watch at a respectful distance, rifles at the ready. Neither *banditos* nor wild animals respected times of mourning. They trudged up the ridge, Superstition going slow to accommodate Charvat's pronounced limp.

"When I was a baby beep, I ran this without breaking a sweat," he said, panting quietly.

"You will again," she said.

"Isn't it pretty to think so?"

She smiled, recognizing the passage. "Hemingway," she said.

"Spenser for Hire," he countered. "I'm just a poor country boy, ma'am. I wouldn't know them fancy literatures if they bit me on the pork knobs."

She squeezed his arm, letting him know the bumpkin act didn't fool her. "Thank you for arranging this," she said. "You have no idea how much I appreciate it."

He showed her where Derek made his final stand. Where the gunmen hid. Where the Jeep exploded in flames, where Derek dashed through bullet clouds hauling Charvat to safety, where the getaway car drove in, where Derek cut down the *narco* army all by himself, where the rocket grenades splashed his cover to flinders.

Where Derek became dead man crawling.

She knelt to the path. Saw a faint, ragged stain and imagined it was her husband's blood. It wasn't possible, of course—on desert sand, blood soaks in moments after it lands, then the sun evaporates any remaining trace. But this wasn't about logic. She lowered her face and kissed the stain, thinking of him and their children, shrouded together in their coffins. Sand and dust motes stuck to her moist lips. She licked them and swallowed hard, coughing as the grit went down.

Together forever.

"Stupid, right?" she said, looking up.

"Consecrated ground," he said.

"I knew you'd get it," she said, getting to her feet and suppressing a shiver.

He put his arm around her shoulder and squeezed gently. They stood that way awhile, listening to the desert sounds in the shifting wind. Then they walked back the way they came. She climbed into the passenger seat, eyes brimming. He hung back, letting her have the moment.

"What was she looking for, all knelt down like that?" Connor said as he stowed his rifle in his own Jeep.

"A clue," Charvat said.

"Find any?"

"No."

He climbed in the driver's seat and bounced them back toward civilization. "Would you like to come to the house?" he said, turning onto the hardtop. "Some friends of mine are there and want to express their condolences."

She was touched. "Sure, I'd be honored."

"Cool beans. And my wife's making dinner. Proud to have you at our table."

Her stomach accepted by growling. That surprised her because until now she'd had no interest in food other than a way to keep her going. "I'd love that," she said, hanging her elbow out the window. "I haven't eaten much since your highway patrol called that night. But now, after seeing the actual spot where Derek . . . you know . . ."

"Yeah, I do," Charvat said, thinking of when he buried his son. Other than a couple forks of Whatever when he became light-headed, he didn't eat for six months. Then, one morning, he woke up ravenous. He shook his wife awake, ran both hands up her nightie—he hadn't wanted that in six months, either—drove them south of the border, and put away three orders of *huevos rancheros* with *chocolate con leche*.

And half a cinnamon pie.

Life goes on.

He made the turn, said they were headed for Canyon View Drive. "Is there a canyon," Superstition said, "on Canyon View Drive?"

"Sure," Charvat said, "Just like there's gold at the end of Rainbow."

"Truth in advertising is dead and buried," she said.

All of a sudden Killer Bee looked gloomy. She started to ask why. Instead, she decided to enjoy the spectacular scenery. Time enough for gloom when she went home.

They rolled up Charvat's driveway, the crushed stone going *cracka-ta-crackata* under their tires. The house was crafted from timber and red rock. It hugged the landscape as if sprouted from cracks in the salty soil. The yard was landscaped in desert—cactus and yucca, swales of river stone—with low fences. A privacy wall was made of the same red rock that decorated the house. A bleached cattle skull was centered above the garage door.

"I'm impressed," Superstition said. He'd mentioned on the flight that he'd built his own place, but she'd expected something more primitive, like her and Derek's basement bar, which, while handsome, wouldn't be mistaken for Thomasville.

"The kids and I drove every nail," Charvat said. "It gave them skills and a sense of purpose growing up. And kept 'em from yapping, 'Mommy, I'm bored.'"

"Speaking of mommy," she said, sniffing theatrically as they pulled into the garage.

"Don't know what she's cooking up," Charvat said. "But it's bound to be terrific."

They walked into the spacious kitchen, where Charvat made introductions. Their light, smiling banter told Superstition they'd been in love forever.

Forever . . .

Her eyes burned. She blinked it away.

"They're on the patio, Bee," Delores said, stirring a pot of *mole*, that heady combination of chilies and chocolate. "Fix this poor gal a drink and get out there."

"Yes, ma'am," Charvat said, saluting.

"You always do what your wife tells you?" Superstition said.

"You bet."

"Good boy," Superstition said, patting his arm. "Double lime in mine, please."

Armed with gins and tonics, they approached the sliding door. The blacksmith's-forge heat had faded, so the outside air was refreshing and, at five percent humidity, so bracingly dry that Superstition had to triple her water intake to stave off headaches. Charvat tugged the handle—a copper six-gun, green with patina—and motioned her through. Superstition nodded and stepped onto the flagstone.

Dropped her glass with a startled gasp.

"Sorry, Sue," Robert Hanrahan said, tipping his beer. "I was sworn to secrecy."

"Likewise," Deb Williams said from the sofa.

Superstition stepped back in disbelief. "What . . . who . . ."

"I asked them here," said the final person on the patio. "So we could all talk privately."

She glared at Charvat, who was already sweeping up gin-scented shards. He had the grace to look embarrassed. "Yes, it bothered me to mislead you," he said. "But that memorial was real. Your husband is a hero, and I was honored to know him."

Her anger dropped to simmer.

"Sit down," the final person directed. "We don't have time to waste."

It flared to boil-over. "Who the hell are you to tell me to do anything?"

"Jerome Jerome," he said, rising to offer his hand. He was five-eleven, thin as a fly rod, and comically overdressed for Arizona: black pinstripe suit, regimental tie, button vest, and brogues so heavy that Herman Munster would whistle in admiration. "Director of the counterterrorism division at the Federal Bureau of Investigation."

"Jerome Jerome, huh?" Superstition said. "Bargain day at the name store, or was Mommy drunk when she named you?"

Jerome withdrew his hand. "Perhaps," he said, "your charm has been overstated."

"Oh, no," Hanrahan said cheerfully. "She's even charmier when you get to know her."

"Sorry," she said to Jerome, deciding to reel in her snark till she got to know the lay of the land. "I just don't appreciate being ambushed." Williams winced. A moment later, so did Superstition. "Think I'll sit," she muttered. "And take my feet out of mouth."

"A good rule for all of us," Jerome said, motioning her to a shellacked rocker.

They drank silently. Finger-sized geckos scampered across the slider, leaving tiny sucker prints on the glass. Hawks rode the air eddies, scouting for dinner. Tires hissed on the distant interstate. Dust motes drifted west to east, kicked to a swirl by the occasional downdraft.

"I need your help," Jerome said.

"To what?" Superstition said.

"Catch a murderer," Jerome said.

"Who?" Superstition said.

"Jiménez Garcia," Jerome said.

"Don't know him," Superstition said.

"You will," Jerome said.

"Why?" Superstition said.

"He killed your husband," Jerome said.

Superstition felt fire ants crawl from her eyes. She jumped to her feet and shook out her arms, trying to release the tension carpet-bombing her system. "What the hell is he talking about, Robbie?" she demanded. "You must know, since they brought you here as the convincer."

Hanrahan's smile said, *I told you goofs she was smart*. "The Border Patrol learned that Derek was killed by Jimmy Garcia," he said. He nodded at Charvat, who laid out Mailman's report of seeing the cartel strongman in Peck Canyon that day.

"So why haven't you arrested him?" Superstition said.

"We tried," Charvat said, describing the wild chase through the tunnel into Mexico.

Superstition ground her teeth in frustration. "Will they extradite?"

Williams shook her head. "Mexico City won't touch the cartels. The only way we can arrest him is on American soil."

"He's smart enough to not cross the border again," Superstition said.

"Unless we lure him," Williams said.

"That's where you come in, Mrs. Davis," Jerome said.

She crossed her arms, resisting, as he laid out the plan. Then she became intrigued. "One more time, from the top," she said.

This time, Williams laid it out.

"Complicated," Superstition said, tugging at her lip.

"But doable," Williams said.

"Sure, if it's not your bahoola on the line," Superstition said.

"Bahoola?"

"It was my grandmother's made-up word for 'ass.'"

"Which we cops never say 'cause swearing makes us suboptimal," Hanrahan said. "A captain told me that, so I know it's true."

Superstition asked for a fresh drink. Charvat poured and passed. Delores brought out snacks. They chewed and crunched and licked salt from fingers. She thought some more. Accepted another drink. Felt cold condensation drip onto her palm. Sucked on a lime slice.

"I'm in," she said.

"I recommend you sleep on it before deciding," Jerome said. "It's a dangerous gambit, with no guarantee you'll survive."

"Gambit?" Hanrahan said.

"I'm in," Superstition said.

Jerome sighed as he straightened his tie. "I'm only trying to impress upon you the seriousness of your decision, Mrs. Davis."

Superstition shook her chocolate hair loose. "Have you ever been in love, Jerome?" she said. "Deep as an ocean with no holds barred?"

The director hesitated. Then nodded. Williams gawped.

"I work sixteen hours a day, Agent Williams," Jerome said dryly. "Not twenty-four."

"Then you know who I'm talking about," Superstition said. "That one special person. The one you live for. The one who makes you dance. Makes you laugh. Makes you better."

"Yes," Jerome said.

"Well, Derek was mine." She took a deep breath, blew it out. "Losing the twins was a horror. Now I have to grow old without my *husband?* Garcia's going to pay for that, and I'm the cashier." Her eyes burned violet. "So how 'bout it, Mister FBI Big Kahuna? Are we just talking here? Or do we go get this scumbag?"

Jerome looked at his shoelaces, considering. Then he looked up.

"Welcome to the jungle," he said. "It gets worse here every day."

Superstition laughed. *Guns N' Roses from a man in checkered socks?* "I wasn't always uncool," Jerome said, correctly guessing her thoughts. "And you can change your mind till the moment we take Garcia into custody."

She shook her head. "Couldn't escape," she said, "if I wanted to."

He raised an eyebrow.

"Abba," she said. "Waterloo."

Jerome tented his manicured fingers. "Let's hope not," he said. "It didn't work out all that well for Napoleon."

1944

JUNE 13
THE EAGLE'S NEST
BAVARIAN ALPS, SOUTHERN GERMANY

Footsteps echoing like taps on a snare drum, Adolf Hitler strolled the long, dank tunnel, which hundreds of laborers had carved into the heart of the granite mountain to protect him from Allied bombers. He nodded at the storm trooper guarding his personal elevator, which was a roomy, elegant cage clad in mahogany, green leather, and brass burnished to a golden gleam. The storm trooper *seig-heiled*, closed the gilded cage, and pulled the lever.

Four hundred feet straight up.

Hitler emerged, blinking at the bright sunlight streaming through the windows. Waving to his mountaintop troopers, he strode to the railed edge of the craggy peak. He looked around the vast alpine panorama, grinned, and shouted at the snowcapped mountains, listening for the echo on the piney breeze.

Adolf . . . Adolf . . . Adolf . . .

He clicked his boot heels.

Pirouetted.

Trotted into the Eagle's Nest, laughing with delight, not feeling the usual fear of heights that tended to keep him off this panoramic peak in favor of the Berghof, his residential chalet in the Third Reich command center that occupied the lower parts of the mountain.

"Why is he so happy?" Speer whispered.

"Our first V-1 just struck London," Himmler said. "It flew straight and true and blew up a Royal Army barracks. Our spies sent word just before you walked in."

Speer shook his head as Hitler's cackling continued.

"I can see why that would please him," he said. The V-1 was Germany's newest terror weapon, a flying bomb powered by a rocket motor and steered by an internal guidance system. What the scientists called a "missile," from the Latin verb *mittere*, "to send." Without the need for expensive and fragile human pilots, V-1s could be launched as fast as assembly lines could bolt them together. "But millions of Allied troops have stormed into Normandy. The Russian front has collapsed. How can he be so ecstatic when—"

"Wolf sees things," Himmler said, "the rest of us do not."

Speer blinked rapidly. These days, Adolf relied more on mysticism than facts to shape his decisions. Sometimes it worked out brilliantly. Other times, like insisting D-Day couldn't possibly have happened because he hadn't yet dreamed about it . . .

"Everything you say is true, Albert," Himmler said, polishing his glasses with a pale kerchief. "The Allies are in Europe, and the Russian bear lumbers our way. But we have the secret gas. It will turn the tide, if we can convince Wolf"—their affectionate nickname for Hitler—"to use it."

He slurped his coffee. Frowned at the bitterness and signaled an aide for a fresh cup.

"That's why he asked Ambros here today. To discuss loading the V-1s with nerve gas and turning them loose on invading troops. If they don't get the message and withdraw from our lands, we'll drop it on their children." Himmler's smile showed striated yellow teeth. "Millions of chemical deaths in London will show the world that even wounded, our Wolf still bites."

Speer shook his head. "I can't support you on using the special gas. You know why."

Himmler's look was a mixture of pity and disgust. Speer flared. His balls were beyond reproach! Unlike Himmler, who generally steered clear of the death camps he commanded as head of the SS, Speer had specifically driven to Sachsenhausen to watch prisoners expire in the gas tests. Their death throes filled him with pride, as well as excitement—as minister of armament and war production, he adored efficient weapons.

His objection was practical. If the Allies had their own nerve gas—and the American ship explosion in Bari, Italy, last December strongly suggested they did—they would retaliate in kind. With America's industrial might—Liberty ships filled with war goods crisscrossed the Seven Seas every minute of every day—their beloved Fatherland would cease to exist—

"*Herr* Speer!" Hitler said, rushing over to pump his hand. "Your trip went well?"

"Very smoothly, thank you, Führer," Speer said, not mentioning the bullets dinging off his fenders as he navigated the highways from Berlin. People had sensed Germany's vulnerability in the wake of D-Day and were shifting allegiances. "Despite the rabble pouring onto the beaches in France."

"We'll make quick work of them," Hitler said dismissively, motioning everyone to the table. Teenage stewards served refreshments as everyone admired the crystalline views of Germany and Austria from the panoramic windows, a treat they didn't have in the dank bomb bunkers carved throughout the mountain below their feet. Martin Bormann built this retreat as Hitler's fiftieth birthday present. Hitler, delighted, called it the "top hat" of the Nazi headquarters complex that dominated Kehlstein Mountain and used it to entertain diplomatic visitors.

"The war is going splendidly," Hitler said. "Yes, the English and Americans have established beachheads in France. But our Panzers and Luftwaffe will obliterate them. And today we unleashed the flying bomb, built by our genius scientists at Peenemünde. Death will rain on the invaders without us risking a single pilot!"

His ministers and generals leapt to their feet, applauding fervently.

"But we'll discuss all that later," Hitler said, motioning for quiet. "Now, I want to hear from our honored guest."

Dr. Otto Ambros began sweating as dozens of blue eyes shifted his way. He was a dedicated Nazi, an intimate on Third Reich war committees, and the director of IG Farben's chemical weapons program. He had personally tested Zyklon-B and nerve gas on concentration camp prisoners. But he was not accustomed to being the star of the show, particularly one with so many luminaries in the audience.

"Thank you, Führer," Ambros said, running his fingers through his thinning brown hair. "It's an honor serving you."

Hitler sipped his drink. Steam dampened his pallid face. "What are the Allies doing about poison gas?" he said. "Do they have it? Can they deploy it effectively? Enlighten us, please."

Ambros adjusted his tie. "We know they have mustard gas," he began. "We learned that when the ship in Bari exploded—"

Hitler smacked his palms in delight. "Little Pearl Harbor!" he crowed, tossing his hair from his eyes. "Twenty-eight ships blown to the ocean bottom, thanks to our glorious bomber crews!" He'd personally decorated every pilot afterward. "I only wish I'd been there to see it."

"I'm glad you weren't, Führer," Ambros said. "The mustard blisters horrifically."

"An excellent point," Hitler said, who as a young corporal in World War One had been temporarily blinded by a British gas shell.

Ambros dabbed his forehead. "The problem is, the Allies can produce mustard in huge quantities because they have far greater access to petroleum than we—"

Hitler stopped him with a quietly raised hand.

"I don't care about mustard, phosgene, and the other traditional gases," he said, leaning conspiratorially. "Tell us about the special one. The one that swats men like mosquitoes. The one Germany monopolizes because we invented it."

"The nerve gas."

"The nerve gas," Hitler echoed.

Ambros nodded. He'd worked closely with its inventor, Dr. Gerhard Schrader, to bring Nazi nerve gas factories on line. They'd been spectacularly successful: IG Farben was producing hundreds of kilograms a day, in addition to the Zyklon-B that exterminated the Jews in the camp "showers" prior to their incineration in the ovens. "What do you wish to know?"

Hitler drank deeply, then belched. "Can we load your gas onto our new V-1s?"

"Yes," Ambros said. "Japan tested nerve gas rockets on Manchurian prisoners. They didn't work—the gas burned up in the explosions. But we engineered a solution. Our missiles can deliver the warheads with accuracy and spectacular effect."

"Predicted lethality?"

"One million dead per missile, if atmospheric conditions are right."

Hitler's eyebrows twitched. "What about artillery? Bombs? Mortars?"

"The same," Ambros said. "Lethality varying with warhead size."

"Of course. How quickly can you ship the gas to our missile men?"

"I can start tomorrow, if that's your wish."

Hitler's eyes glowed. "Some at this table insist I launch nerve gas immediately to break the Allied armies," he said. "Others say if I do, they will retaliate with their own nerve gas, which they developed while our backs were turned." He looked at Himmler, then Speer, then Ambros. "As the only true expert in this room, what do you say, *Herr Doktor*?"

Ambros put down his coffee. Speer held his breath. Everything rode on this answer.

"I cannot prove the Allies have nerve gas," Ambros said. "But the evidence suggests they do."

Speer made a silent *whoosh* as Hitler's smile glaciated. "Explain," the Führer demanded.

"Dr. Schrader invented nerve gas in 1936 and improved it two years later. We published the patents in scientific journals."

"But that formula is top secret!" Hitler said incredulously.

"Now, yes, certainly," Ambros said hastily. "But before the war, it was a mere insecticide, invented to control crop pests. In order to patent it, we had to publish our findings. The world had access between the patent date and its reclassification as top secret."

Hitler drummed his fingers, scowling. "How much do the Allies know?"

"Not everything," Ambros said. "We kept the most sensitive data to ourselves to maximize control of the insecticide market. But enough. The United States in particular has top scientific minds in its universities. They surely would have read those publications."

"So we must assume they have their own nerve weapons?" Speer probed.

"It would be prudent to assume that, yes," Ambros said.

"Then why haven't they used them already?" Himmler challenged, his harsh tone indicating his dismay at victory slipping away.

"They're keeping them under wraps," Ambros said. "Just in case."

"In case what?" Hitler said.

"We launch first and they want to retaliate."

Dead silence.

"*Scheisse*," Hitler swore, pushing back angrily from the table. He kicked one of the stewards on his way out. The teen fell to the floor screeching, clutching his splintered shin. No one moved to help him. Sympathizing with someone who annoyed Hitler might get one sent to the Russian front as a rifleman.

"So what do we do?" a general said as the second steward dragged him away. "Use the gas?"

Speer shook his head. He knew Wolf's moods. The violent departure was a signal: He didn't want to deploy the gas for fear of retaliation—if the Americans had it, they had mountains of it, given their industrial might—but didn't want to look weak by saying so.

"I'm sure he wishes to study this matter further," he said, deciding not to rub Himmler's nose in it. The SS chief's enemies had a bad habit of dying unexpectedly. "Because of the myriad strategic advantages of this weapon, I suggest we keep producing and testing the gas. But we should not use it unless he orders so." He glanced at Himmler. "What do you think, Heinrich?"

"I'm sure that's what Wolf had in mind," Himmler agreed, sounding almost placated.

Speer nodded, relieved. One more bullet dodged.

Just a million more coming their way.

Chapter 29

PRESENT DAY
CHICAGO

Superstition slid on sky-blue panties, still thinking about her mother's obsession with Jesus-juicing—her nickname for the hours Mom spent praying for whatever it was she prayed for. They'd been close all their lives, more like cherished sisters than The Mother and the Daughter. The easy intimacy that all girlfriends admired and remarked upon over the years began to unravel after the twins were killed, with Theresa Kallas turning increasingly rigid, cool, and uninterested in views that conflicted with hers. It was a profoundly unsettling change for a woman so hip and self-confident that she could name her baby "Superstition," without apology, and who would start discussions with strangers in stores and restaurants solely to see if her opinions would hold up to scrutiny. —and if they didn't, freely change them.

Something was eating Mom alive, and it was more than the twins; she was sure of it now, after the "So what if he's dead, he's up with God" nonsense from Derek's funeral. Old Theresa would rather eat glass than act that callously. So something else was going on. Supersitition had tried asking, but got the brush each time: "Still sad about the babies." Dad shrugged, claiming nothing had changed, but his nonchalance was a hair too evasive. It was time to demand real answers from them both. If they continued to tap-dance, she'd put her cop skills to work, and do whatever it took to get her old Mom back. She'd lost most of her family. She would lose no more.

"But not right now," she said to her mirror, punching her arms through her T-shirt, then pulling up and snapping her jeans. "You've got a party to trash."

KINGSTON MINES BLUES CLUB

Twangin' Howlin' Screamin' Do-Me Blues . . .

Oh honey babe
(Oh honey babe!)
Oh girl it's true
(Oh girl it's true!)
Oh honey babe oh girl it's true I got a thaaaaang for you . . .

"Muddy Waters with a Stevie Ray chaser!" Superstition shouted over the guitar-driven thunder. "Not bad for a bunch of flatfoots," Hanrahan agreed, hoisting his Old Style.

The way you talk
(The way you talk!)
The way you glare
(The way you glare!)
The way you dazzle in your keezy sleazy underwear . . .

"Keezy sleazy underwear?" she said.
"For narcs, that's Gershwin," he said, shrugging.
She looked at her watch for the third time in sixty seconds. Hanrahan frowned. She planted her wrist in her lap and held it with her other hand. Robbie was right; she needed to stay natural. It was hard because she was anxious. She'd never been nervous working undercover, not even the first time, when she went on the stroll at Forty-seventh and Pulaski in a halter, do-me cutoffs, and very little else, attracting johns "like flies on a dead rat," as her boss so colorfully put it. She wasn't even nervous the night she bought guns and meth from a biker gang, they smelled cop,

and she fought for her life as her partners thundered in like fullbacks. But tonight wasn't just another day at the office. It was the end of a life she'd liked a whole bunch.

So wiggle on in the bedroom, girl
I'll sing it loud and true
It's time to show you why I got
A rompin' stompin' twangin' howlin' screamin' punchin' crunchin' do-me thaaaaang...
For you!

"Great racket!" a drunken assistant state's attorney screamed in her ear. "Thanks for inviting me!"

"Sure, Donny," she said, chugging her beer. "Glad you could make it—"

She felt his hand sneaking into the gap between her jeans and polo. Disengaged it gently.

"Too early?" the ASA said.

"Too never," she said, patting him on the cheek.

"Nothing ventured, nothing gained," he said cheerfully, turning away.

"Maybe if he'd bought you dinner first," Hanrahan said.

She rolled her eyes.

As far as everyone was concerned, Hanrahan was throwing this racket to celebrate Sue's victory over not just three armed robbers but the grand jury, civilian shooting board, and U.S. attorney for northern Illinois, all of whom declined to press charges. He'd asked the manager of Kingston Mines, a North Side blues club that never bothered dyeing its sixties' roots—vinyl bar stools, bare concrete floors, country-kitchen lights with orange bulbs, faux-log-cabin main stage—to go private for the night. Hanrahan invited hundreds of officers to join the fun. "Uncle Otto and the Chicken Shack Ramblers," an electric-blues band fronted by narcotics sergeant Michael Ungethuem, provided the jams. It was a terrific party, so fun and forget-the-world she wished she could enjoy it.

"Come on up and say a few words, Sue!" Ungethuem bellowed, mopping his face with a shirttail. "They're here to see you, not me!"

Superstition grabbed a grocery bag and her bottle of Goose Island Matilda and bounded onto the stage, drawing wolf whistles as much for her I ♥ DONUTS polo shirt as her tight Secret Circus jeans. "Thanks so much for coming tonight," she said. The microphone screeched like a Skilsaw hitting a knot. Ungetheum tweaked the dials. "My husband would have loved this."

"Three cheers for Derek!" a traffic cop cheered.

"But he's not here, because some assholes murdered him," Superstition said. "The same kind of assholes we face on the streets every day." She took a deep breath and released it, noting how many cops were holding phone cameras. "Derek and me, we love you. Our precious babies love you, too. Your blood runs blue just like ours." The room hushed as more than one eye filled with tears. She wiped hers away, embarrassed.

"Another thing you might have heard is that I, uh, dig my husband." The whistles and cheers confirmed the story had indeed gotten around. The morning after the open house, she went to visit Derek's grave. She told him about the funeral and the open house, asked him how the twins were feeling, wondered if lying in the cold clay was aggravating his back . . . then dropped to her knees and started digging, her calloused hands going like steam shovels because it was time for her family to come home. A passing gravedigger gently suggested she stop before she hurt herself, and she snapped out of her weird little trance, horrified and embarrassed at the dirt chunks littering the perfectly manicured grass. "What you don't know is that Derek asked me to share something tonight," she continued. "Something he loved, something he couldn't live without. He wanted you to have it, and I'm honored to grant his final wish." She opened the bag and pulled out handfuls of doughnuts. She flung them into the air, a fleet of sugar Frisbees sailing over Cop Land. Powdered sugar, coconut shreds, and red, white, and blue sprinkles rained down on stomping and cheering so loud that the lights vibrated. "All right!" she screamed into the mike. "Let's get back to this celebration thang!"

The Chicken Shack Ramblers swung into a bluesy rendition of "Cops"—*Bad boys, bad boys, whatcha gonna do when they come for you?* —and Superstition headed back to her bar stool, nearly vibrating with anticipation.

"Nice touch," Hanrahan said, leaning against the Dew Drop Inn poster on the wall.

"What says love better than doughnuts?" she said, chomping the cruller she'd kept for herself.

Hanrahan tipped his bottle in agreement. A detective slammed through Kingston's front door, a grim scowl slashing his face. Hanrahan smiled faintly. "You ready, kiddo?" he said. Superstition nodded, feeling the fuzz-buzz from every corner of the room. "Yeah," she said. "I'm ready for anything—"

"Loot!" the detective shouted, running broken-field across the cavernous club. "Feebmobiles are pulling up outside—"

The door slammed open. A sturdy woman flanked by FBI agents in raid jackets rushed inside. The woman looked around, spotted Superstition, and waved a sheaf of papers.

"Superstition Kimberley Jones Kallas Davis!" Special Agent Deb Williams thundered. "This is a federal subpoena, and you are hereby served!"

Chicago cops slammed down their drinks, sloshing beer, bourbon, and gin across tabletops and floors. The FBI agents glanced at one another, wondering if they'd be attacked, then puffed out their chests to ensure they weren't. Cops stood up. Scowling agents pawed the floor. Cops began swearing, and an agent radioed for backup. "What are you talking about?" Superstition demanded, deploying every acting lesson she'd taken from suspects wheedling to escape their fates. "The U.S. attorney cleared me one hundred per—"

"This comes from Washington. The Justice Department has convened a grand jury to investigate your civil rights abuse of three African American robbery suspects, along with myriad other Chicago Police felonies," Williams said. "This is your subpoena to appear and testify. If you fail to comply, a warrant will be issued for your arrest."

"What the hell?" Hanrahan said as he jumped to his feet, astonishment spreading across his face. "If you'd called, she would have come to your office—"

"Sit down, Lieutenant," Williams snapped. "Or I'll bust you for interference." She rattled the hot-pink cuffs, which glowed in the overhead lights.

"This is my party, for my murdered husband," Superstition snarled, coiling into a martial arts stance. "If you don't leave immediately, I'll show you some interferes."

Williams stared. "Seriously? You're threatening an FBI agent?"

"You must be a college graduate," Superstition said, unleashing a kick at Williams's head.

The agent dodged it and moved in, locking Superstition in a painful arm bar. Superstition broke the hold and clopped Williams in the side of the head. Williams stumbled sideways as the crowd roared its delight, wrapping up the FBI detail so it couldn't interfere. "I should have done this at the funeral," Superstition shouted, throwing a punch that connected mid-ribs. "I was stupid to think you came just to pay respects." Williams regained her balance and charged, her face suffused with anger. They exchanged punches, kicks, slaps, finger-rakes, and elbow strikes, each drawing a mist of blood or setting a bruise. "You're a cop!" Williams panted. "You know how this goes! The more you resist, the more charges I pile on!"

"Pile on this, Feeby!" Superstition snapped, her foot rocketing for Williams's midsection. She'd gentle the bunker-buster at the last second, allowing Deb to escape with only a love tap instead of broken ribs—this kick was as staged as the entire fight, which they'd choreographed for the benefit of the camera phones that Hanrahan made sure would be in the audience.

But a burly agent wrenched free of his human chains and lunged, a murderous expression on his face. He slipped on a slop of Miller Lite and plowed sideways into Williams, who flew forward to take the kick not at love but full power.

Craaack!

"Gaaaah," Williams gasped, clutching her ribs. She staggered backwards in white-faced agony, seriously injured. Superstition ached to help her but couldn't break cover. Instead, she jeered, "Plenty more where that came from, Cupcake—"

FBI backups flooded into the club, brandishing rifles. Chicago cops bristled but one by one backed off, unwilling to chance a bullet. Williams, lumbering like Frankenstein's monster, pointed at Superstition. Her posse, freed from Chicago's embrace as Hanrahan ordered his cops to stand down, slammed their sweating, bloody prisoner over a scarred bar table.

"Superstition . . . Davis," Williams gasped as she cradled her screaming ribs. "You are under . . . arrest for assaulting a . . . federal officer." IPhones waved like dandelions, recording every moment. "If you and your . . . friends continue . . . to resist, my agents will subdue . . . you with all appropriate force . . . including lethal."

Exactly as they'd planned on Brian Charvat's patio.

"Hey, Roger, is your offer still good?" Superstition shouted at an assistant state's attorney. Not five minutes after she'd walked in, Roger was at her table, bussing her cheek, offering heartiest congratulations and saying he'd have defended her for free, dammit, he just wished he'd gotten the chance. "You're gonna be my lawyer for this, right?"

He pointed at his ears, pretending he couldn't hear.

Jerome Jerome was right, she realized. *Now that I'm under arrest, they're gonna drop me like a bad habit.*

Williams, growing paler by the second, ordered Superstition frog-marched through the police mob, the frost-faced FBI agents forming a Praetorian Guard to absorb the spittle and beer. They went out the door and onto the sidewalk. The harsh lights of videocams snapped on. TV reporter Marcella Raymond shouted questions from under a Hermès blazer that matched her hair. Radio reporter Doug Cummings elbowed her aside to push his microphone closer. Her cameraman shoved him away. Cummings shoved back. Raymond kicked Cummings in the shin and re-took her spot. Superstition bit back her amusement; media events here were rugby scrums.

"A perp walk?" one of Superstition's squad mates shouted, showering Williams with warm Budweiser. "What kind of asshole perp-walks a hero?"

"The kind who enforces the law!" Williams retorted, hands on hips, chin up, eyes glowing brown and green, refusing to wince despite her clear agony, drawing enough grudging admiration to stop the beer bombs. "If the city of Chicago won't deliver justice to its citizens, the federal government will!"

"This is bullshit!" Superstition screamed at the nearest camera, twisting her face into a gargoyle's. "My husband was murdered working for you people. He was shot in the brain, and this is how you repay him? You goddamn bunch of Nazis!"

Agents shoved her into the back of a black Suburban. Williams slid in from the other side. The shotgun rider held up a Taser and warned Superstition that if she moved one inch toward Williams, "you'll ride the lightning till your eyeballs smoke." "Don't worry, I'm done," Superstition said. "She fights like a girl anyway."

"MCC," Williams spat at the driver, who ran every red light between Kingston Mines and the federal Metropolitan Correctional Center, the slit-windowed prison skyscraper at Clark and Van Buren.

Sorry about your ribs, Superstition mouthed.

Fights like a girl??? Deb mouthed back.

Then she groaned so loud that the driver nearly swerved into oncoming traffic.

"Holy shit, Deb," the Taser man said over the angry chorus of horns. "You want to stop at a hospital before we put her in the can?"

"No," Williams said, pain tears rolling down her cheeks. "Her first, then me."

Superstition felt terrible.

But all she could do was sneer.

Chapter 30

A BAR ON THE OUTSKIRTS
NOGALES, MEXICO

Delgado laughed so hard that *cerveza* honked out his nose.

"What's so funny?" Garcia said, tossing his boss a napkin.

"This," Delgado said, passing over his iPad. Garcia watched the video of the blues club fight and whistled. "Some balls she got," he said with admiration. "Kicking the snot out of an FBI agent."

"You don't see that fire in *Americano* cops," Delgado said. "They're too busy stroking their pensions."

The waitress dropped off more beer. Foam sloshed over the rims. She bent to wipe it. Delgado patted her round behind. She sashayed away, accentuating the wiggle.

"Another true joy of my life," the cartel chief said as he rose from his chair.

They disappeared into the bathroom. His bodyguards sidled over to cover the door. Garcia clicked on a TMZ story about the hot policewoman who'd become an Internet sensation first by shooting three armed killers, then by clobbering the FBI agent who accused her of violating the killers' precious civil rights. *Only in America.* He switched to YouTube for the referenced gunfight at the oddly named Bubbles Lounge. Impressed by the officer's bravery and combat skills—she slid around bullets like a panther dipped in grease—he clicked on her photograph. Felt his pulse quicken. Superstition Davis was stunning, even in the unflattering uniform they made their *policía* wear. Those big violet eyes grabbed a man like a starving bear. And the cascades of chocolate hair stirred him like—

"Woooooo!" Delgado whooped from the bathroom as his bodyguards high-fived. "Ride 'em, cowgirl!"

Garcia laughed, clicked away from Superstition, and scanned the international news services for whatever might affect their business. It was quiet along the border, from Pacific to Gulf. No politicians vying for TV time in the insipid "war on drugs," nothing brewing in his American distribution centers. That suited him fine because he wasn't in the mood for problems. He had enough of his own, with the tunnel expansions, his exile from his biggest market, the massive drug shipment coming his way from the Taliban, upping the bribes to Mexican Mafia to ensure Izzy's continued safety in Fargo . . .

Ten minutes later, Delgado was back.

"That didn't take long," Garcia said.

"Foreplay is overrated," Delgado said, air-humping his chair. "How's your sister doing?"

Speaking of no foreplay. "Rotting in a cage as she awaits her fate," Garcia said. "How would you feel?"

"You know what's worse than Fargo?" Delgado said, blowing the head off his beer. "Punishing a young woman for the crimes of her brother. That U.S. attorney knows she's innocent—he has the confession of her ex along with the video proof—yet he refuses to drop the charges. He's a rodent, not a man."

"He'll pay," Garcia muttered. Mind-movies of him and Izzy—playing tag and soccer in the overheated slums of Mexico City, laughing and singing, turning refrigerator cartons into castles, talking feverishly about how they'd escape their poverty someday, him protecting her innocence with fists, pipes, and switchblades. They looped every waking moment, making him so furious that he itched to kill everything in sight. "I don't know how yet, or when, but he'll pay. They all will."

"I'll help when the time is ripe," Delgado said. "Even if it brings some heat."

"Thank you, *Jefe*," Garcia said, surprised. Delgado normally forbade attacks on Americans because it drove their media berserk, which inflamed their politicians, which forced Mexico City to make show arrests, disrupting business. "You're most kind."

"It's my pleasure. Did you remind the prison gangs she's under my protection?"

"Of course."

"Most important, did the lawyer confirm she's keeping her mouth shut?"

"Like I said before, Isabel doesn't know a thing about our operations. Even if she wanted to talk, which she doesn't, she has nothing to say."

"You did say that before," Delgado said. "Is it still true?"

"*Sí.*"

Delgado refilled their glasses. "Good. What about the man who put her there?"

Garcia had spent more than one sleepless night envisioning how he'd handle that sack of wormy potatoes. "I'm going to wait long enough for him to think I've forgotten. And then . . ."

Delgado's smile was wicked. "Make it creative, *amigo*."

Chapter 31

PRISON WARDEN'S OFFICE
UNITED STATES PENITENTIARY
FARGO, NORTH DAKOTA

"Officially," said the walrus-faced man who managed this for-profit detention facility on the far western outskirts of Fargo, "I have to condemn you for assaulting a federal officer in the commission of her duties."

"I understand," Superstition said.

He leaned over his desk, his poly-cotton shirt brushing the gray steel. "But unofficially," he whispered, "good for you."

Superstition raised an eyebrow, surprised he wasn't parroting the company line that convicts were always wrong. "Thank you, sir," she said. "I appreciate it."

"Showing up at your party was an unnecessary provocation," he said as he settled back in his chair. "It shows an arrogance that's carried by too many in law enforcement, particularly federal. But it's also ancient history. We need to focus on the here and now. We do a pretty good job protecting our inmates. But . . ."

"A cop behind bars is problematic."

The warden nodded. "It's hard enough keeping you safe in ad seg," he said. Administrative segregation—i.e., single-cell housing in a separate part of the facility—was standard practice for imprisoned law-enforcement officers because cons would attack them given the smallest opportunity. "In general population, you might as well have a sign on your back that says, SHIV ME."

She sighed. "I understand the risks, Warden, and I appreciate your offer. But I need to be around people. When I'm by myself more than a few hours, I think too much about my losses, and I start having really bad nightmares."

He reached for his Diet Coke. "Nailing Jimmy Garcia," he said, "will make those go away."

She stared, shocked. If that secret had leaked to the point that a prison warden knew the score, the gangs would know too, and she'd be dead by dawn.

"Who's Jimmy Garcia, sir?" she said cautiously.

The warden grinned. "Killer Bee says hello."

Her heart quit pounding in her gums. "Part of the Bee hive?" she said, vastly relieved.

"We started our careers together in the Border Patrol. He stayed law and I went order, but we always remained friends. Brian asked me to keep an eye on you." He took a sip. "Not much I can do day to day. I show any particular interest, people get suspicious. But if something goes seriously awry, I can maybe get you out of here in time."

"Good to know."

"So head on down to your cell," he said, "and get to know Izzy. Nice girl, for a drug queen."

Superstition shook her head, thinking about how otherworldly Fargo must seem to someone from the mountains of Mexico. "Why did the U.S. attorney send her all the way up here?" she said. "There's a women's wing at the federal pen in Tucson."

"The same politics that put you here instead of closer to Chicago: 'Mess with our family, we mess with yours.'"

Cops were that way too, so Superstition got it, even if she didn't like it. "But she's innocent of the crime," she said, having studied Isabel's file. "The U.S. attorney knows it."

The warden smiled. "Brian predicts Miss Garcia's terrible injustice will be resolved at just the right time, and she'll be set free to return home to her adoring brother."

"Funny how things work out," she said.

They stood and shook hands. "Go with God," he said.

"What my mother says," Superstition said.

The warden looked pleased. She noticed the dime-store crucifix on the wall behind him. "Has it worked for her?" he said.

"Not yet," Superstition said. "But she keeps hoping."

A HOUSE IN THE SLUMS, MEXICO CITY

"She hasn't said a word."

"But what if she does?"

"Why would she do that?"

"To gain early release."

"She won't."

"Why not?"

"Jimmy gave you his personal assurance."

Delgado grinned. "That's because he believes it. I'd believe it of my sister, too."

"Then what's the problem?"

"She's not my sister."

He let that sink in.

"I understand," said the supreme commander of the Mexican Mafia.

"Make it painless," Delgado said. "She's family."

SUPERSTITION'S CELL, FARGO

Superstition tossed her blanket on the top bunk. Noticed the body-shaped stain in the center of the mattress. Shook her head. The warden had promised no special treatment. He was a man of his word. She added her sheets and pillowcase, which, albeit laundered, were yellow from body oil. Khaki shirt and trousers. A bra so stiff that it could shape steel. Crew socks, grandma panties with limp elastic, and canvas shoes. She sighed. This was going to suck.

"Who the hell are you?" she heard from behind.

She turned to see Isabel scowling as she leaned against the bars of the cell door.

"Name's Davis," Superstition said, putting out her hand. "They assigned me to this cell."

Isabel didn't take it, choosing to study her from a distance.

"I don't bite, honest," Superstition tried.

Isabel relaxed a fraction. She walked forward and shook. "Nobody told me you were coming," she said. "All I knew, you were a banger planting contraband."

"That happen a lot?" Superstition said.

"More than you think," Isabel said.

Superstition nodded. "And you are?"

"Oh. Right," Isabel said. "I'm Isabel Garcia."

"I'm Superstition."

"Really? Why?"

"Long story," Superstition said. "I'll tell you when I know you better. Use 'Sue' if you like."

"Izzy for me." She looked at the jumble on the top bunk. "I'll teach you how to fix this, Sue," she said, patting the welded frame.

Superstition sneered. "I know how to make a damn bed."

"Not the way the guards want," Isabel said, standing her ground. "You mess it up, we both get in trouble."

Superstition's shrug said, *Knock yourself out.* Isabel wrapped the mattress so tight that she could bounce quarters off the sheets. She tucked the blankets, slap-tested with her palms, and stepped back.

"Pretty good," Superstition said grudgingly. The lights flickered. The cons began howling and whistling. She looked out the slit window. Thunderheads in the distance. She hoped this wasn't an omen.

"There's a way to do everything here," Isabel said. "It might be stupid, and it might be inefficient. But it's their way or the hole."

AKA, solitary confinement. "Toto, we're not in Kansas anymore," Superstition said, folding her clothes. The six-by-nine cell contained two bunks, stainless steel toilet and sink, shelves, desk, chair, hooks for coats and towels, and a window with a steel bar through the center. The door was a latticework of steel through which anybody could peer. *It's the monkey house at Brookfield,* she thought. *I'll never set foot in a zoo again.*

"Forget it, Jake. It's Fargotown," Isabel said.

Superstition grinned at the dueling film references. She scraped out the chair, sat hard. She raised her shoulders as if to say, *What now?*

"There's a million rules," Isabel said. "Violate any, and they write you up. Most of the guards are okay and don't overly hassle you. Some are whack jobs that nail you for sneezing too loud. Enough write-ups and the warden sticks you in solitary."

"Not fun."

"Unless you like things cold, grim, and lonely, no." She cleared her throat, plucked a cobweb with finger and thumb. "We wash the cell every Sunday, floor to ceiling."

Superstition saw no rags, broom, or bucket. "How?"

"Sanitary napkins make excellent scrub brushes. Water's from the sink." Superstition looked for the telltale smile. None. Izzy wasn't kidding. "We scrub the toilet and sink every day," Isabel continued. "If you take a dump that sticks—and you will, with all the starchy food they serve—you clean it right then and there."

"That a prison rule too?"

Isabel snorted. "That's my rule," she said. "Bad enough sleeping next to a toilet. I refuse to live in one."

Superstition smiled. She liked Garcia already. "Never let 'em see you sweat."

Isabel looked confused at the idiom.

"Something my lieutenant used to say," Superstition explained. "It means, Don't let the people who control you think they're getting under your skin. It only encourages their meanness."

Isabel nodded warily. "Lieutenant. Were you in the army?"

"Cops."

Isabel recoiled. "Why did they put a policeman in my cell?" she demanded.

"Ex-police," Superstition said. "I got fired after my conviction."

"Conviction for what?"

"I punched an FBI agent in the nose."

Isabel stared, contemplated, then relaxed. "I'd like to do that."

"It felt good," Superstition said. "But it landed me here, didn't it?"

Isabel offered her a Frito.

"Name-brand snacks?" Superstition said, surprised. Prisons always went low-bidder.

"You can buy real food from the commissary because the prison makes money on every sale," Isabel said. "Have someone put money in your account. You'll eat better and you can get fresh fruit and veggies. The meals here are vile."

Superstition recalled the food in Chicago's federal lockup. It was starchy and stale and occasionally flecked with maggots, normally dead, but sometimes not. "Extra protein!" her first cellmate squealed when she spotted the little wigglers. Superstition thought she was kidding, but the woman chewed them with gusto, saying they were fresher than the chicken in the mess hall warmers. Of course, she also plugged her ears with toilet paper, claiming that "Planet Kalgon—with a *K*, not *C*, there's two, you know—is trying to eat my brains." It was the first time, and surely not the last, Superstition realized how utterly insane this quest was going to get.

"Good to know, thanks," Superstition said. "So, what are you in for?"

"Drugs," Isabel said. "But I was framed."

"Everyone I've met so far says that."

Isabel flared. "You calling me a liar?" she said, cocking her petite fists.

"No, no," Superstition said. "Just that everyone has their story, like I got mine."

"Which is?"

Superstition told her. Isabel softened. "That's terrible, hounding you like that after you lost your husband."

"Why I popped her in the beezer." Actually, she'd broken three of Deb's ribs with the runaway kick. But a punch in the nose sounded cooler. It also let her say "beezer," one of her favorite old-timey words.

Isabel offered Fritos. Superstition declined. "Don't want to eat all your food."

"Plenty where that came from," Isabel said. "Even with the extortionist prices the prison charges, my lawyer keeps my account filled."

So Superstition, hungry, devoured the bag. Went to the sink to wash her salt-crusted hands. The pipes coughed like they had pneumonia. A bit of brown water dribbled out.

"Maybe we should call Roto-Rooter," she said, wiping her hands on her khakis.

"Wait till you flush the toilet," Isabel said. "It bangs like a kettle drum—"

They whirled as two stocky women sauntered into their cell.

"What's wrong with you? Get out of here," Isabel commanded.

"We ain't here for you, *mamacita*," said the mixed-race gangbanger, who Isabel recognized from the attack aborted by the Mexican Mafia. "Her."

"Me?" Superstition said. "Why?"

The banger grinned. "Heard you was a cop," she said. "Who sent three handsome brothers to the pearly gates."

News travels fast. "Some people need killing," Superstition said.

"So do you," the second banger said.

"Guard!" Isabel shouted.

"They off eating dark meat," the leader said, moving in on Superstition. "Don't worry, Garcia, you're off-limits. Just gonna show your homie a little love—*ahhgh!*" She collapsed as Superstition completed the kick to her right temple.

"You want some too?" Superstition said, baring her teeth.

The second banger picked up her dazed companion and backed away. "We'll see you in the showers, cooze," she hissed.

"Bring more than your good looks," Superstition said. "Or you'll leave in a body bag."

They disappeared, and Superstition blew out her breath. "So that's how it is?"

"Welcome to hell," Isabel said.

1945

SEPTEMBER 4
UNIT 731 HUMAN EXPERIMENTATION CAMP
HARBIN, OCCUPIED MANCHURIA

Sakamora gawped in astonished silence.

"The United States dropped an atomic bomb on Hiroshima," Ishii said. "Two days later, it dropped another on Nagasaki. Both cities were annihilated from blast and fire, and radiation has poisoned everything. One million people are dead."

Shame flooded Sakamora. If only he'd worked harder! His nerve gas performed perfectly when sprayed from airplanes. He'd proved that by annihilating an entire Chinese city with the military equivalent of crop dusters. But putting the gas into weapons Japanese troops could use in the field—bombs, artillery, rockets, mortars, grenades—had proved maddeningly elusive: the heat from warhead detonations destroyed the gas. He'd spent night after sleepless night crafting solutions, with the result that he fell asleep in the middle of meals, plunging face-first into whatever was in front of him. It earned him the nickname "Soup Nose." It was funny then . . .

"To spare the rest of our population, the emperor has surrendered unconditionally to Allied forces."

"The war is over?" a munitions sergeant asked incredulously.

"The War of Western Aggression is over," Ishii confirmed.

The silence lasted seemingly forever.

"What do we do now, General?" Sakamora said.

"Kill the logs," Ishii said. "And bury the bodies in the forest."

"Why bother?" the munitions sergeant said, his eyes blank and glassy. Sakamora recalled he'd moved his wife and children out of Tokyo last summer to spare them the Allied attacks everyone assumed were coming. He'd found them an apartment in downown Nagasaki . . .

"They will hunt for evidence of war crimes," Ishii said. "So we'll leave no trace of what we did here." He shook his head mournfully. "That's all. Get to work."

Soldiers and scientists shuffled out of the lamb-scented dining hall, shaking their heads. Japan had lost. The emperor had surrendered. The Empire of the Sun had been raped by the devil. No one could believe it.

Sakamora heard gunfire in the compound, followed by screaming in Russian and Chinese. The cleanup was already under way. Ishii strode past, seemingly lost in thought. Sakamora touched his sleeve. "I'm sorry, General," he said, eyes downcast, guilt pulsing through his trembling limbs. "If I'd only been able to perfect the nerve weapon, perhaps this would have ended differently."

"Fortunes of war," Ishii said. "We create weapons. The enemy creates better ones."

Sakamora nodded. "What will become of us?"

Ishii smiled and patted his young protégé's shoulder. "Go back to Tokyo," he said softly. "Find your family. You've done well here, Sakamora. That it didn't work out is immaterial—what you invented will live forever. Hold your head high and take pride in your contribution to the world." He made a waving motion. "Now go help the soldiers with their final task. Once the logs are buried, we'll board the trains and leave."

"Where will you go, sir?"

Ishii smiled mysteriously but said nothing.

"Good-bye, General," Sakamora said.

"Good-bye, Sakamora," Ishii said.

Chapter 32

FORTY MILES OFF THE FLORIDA KEYS
GULF OF MEXICO

The vacuum whirred. The gold coins jangled up the suction pipe. "Life is good," Denton chirped as the cache filled the submersible's collection tank.

Raider nodded. After fixing BP's broken well cap, they'd sailed to Guam to video the Marianas Trench, the world's deepest hole in the ocean floor, for filmmaker James Cameron, who needed fresh footage for a movie. They'd finished up three weeks ago and now were back in the Gulf, sucking doubloons from a Spanish galleon that sailed out of Havana in 1733 and crashed to the bottom in a monstrous storm. Raider found it playing with Google Earth one night over a six-pack of Abita beer. He'd spotted a faint anomaly east of Key Largo, played a hunch, brought his salvage ship *Stirred* to X-marks-the-spot, and launched his deepwater submersible *Shaken*. Three days later, he and his crew were doing their happy dance—there was, conservatively estimated, twenty million dollars in gold, silver, and artifacts aboard the splintered ship. He'd just started the harvest when the CEO of British Petroleum begged him to plug the fresh leak. Raider left armed security to protect his gold mine, welded the cap onto the well, brought home the human skeleton, dove the trench, then headed here.

"Damn skippy it's good," he said.

Denton heard the hidden *but*. "You're bored, aren't you?"

Raider nodded glumly. "If I wanted to vacuum, I'd be a Merry Maid."

Denton tipped his coffee cup, understanding; his friend had chronic ants-in-the-pants. "We've got Internet," he said. "Why don't you look up those cylinders?"

Raider cocked his head, not making the connection.

"The ones that floated away during the oil well job, Mr. Memory," Denton reminded.

Raider slapped his forehead. "Yeah, yeah, right. The ones inside the rusty net. I only forgot because my brain's so full of other important things."

"Full of something, anyway," Denton said.

Raider logged into their storage server and pulled up the video, which had been captured by the submersible's camera system. They laughed at the sea creature that sped by the viewing port like a flying saucer with hair. Shook their heads at the graveyard of oil rig parts surrounding the steel net, nodded soberly at the pecked-clean skeleton of Orlando Kemper, the chain-wrapped derrick man kicked into the sea when the *Deepwater Horizon* exploded. Raider and Denton delivered his remains to authorities in New Orleans, and a few weeks later, Kemper's family sent a thank-you note so thoughtful that Raider taped it to his cabin wall. With Kemper returned, that left ten souls still missing. Maybe when they were done vacuuming, they'd search the metal graveyard inch by inch, see if anyone else could be returned to their loved ones . . .

The first cigar-shaped cylinder emerged from the ripped netting. Raider fed a still shot into Google Images. "No match," he said. "Huh."

"Maybe you're confusing it with something else you saw," Denton said.

"No. It was years ago, but I saw these cylinders on some Web site. I'll try another engine." He fed the image into everything on his master list, from Bing and Yahoo! to Harvard and Oxford.

Nothing.

"Spooky," Raider said, beginning to wonder if he was getting senile. "Could the photos have been purged net-wide?"

"That's easier said than done, Hollywood notwithstanding," Denton said. "But the boys at the Pentagon could do it if they wanted. Try the Dark Net."

"I knew there was a reason I hired you," Raider said, tapping in the Level Nine password for the program that hacked military and government databases worldwide but left no digital traces of the visit. He'd gotten the NSA software from a boyhood chum who grew up to be an admiral, and contracted Raider for top secret snoops on behalf of Uncle Sam. In exchange for Raider's gratis efforts, which had stopped more than one terrorist attack on the United States, the admiral allowed him to use the black package to hunt down treasure ships reported by American military personnel in the course of their worldwide adventures. Dark Net contained everything ever loaded onto—or deleted from—the World Wide Web.

He fed in the image. Sipped a can of Red Bull, yawned, scratched his butt, increased the suction to make quicker work of the doubloons. The program beeped. There was a match.

"Holy shit," Denton muttered as his face whitened to candle wax.

Raider nodded, so disturbed that he couldn't stop trembling. He plugged his phone into the communications cable and chose an encryption level so high that it would take even the mighty NSA a year to decode, assuming it could trace the call, which, the admiral assured, it could not. He dialed the secret number from memory.

"Admiral?" he said, clutching the arms of his own chair. "It's Raider. I hope you're sitting down . . ."

Chapter 33

DESERTED BEACH NORTH OF TAMPICO
GULF COAST OF MEXICO

Ten bombs expanded as the sun baked their dull green scales, then contracted as high tides wetted them like sea otters. A pelican circled the pointed nose cone of the closest. Decided it was food. Tucked its wings, lowered its head, and dive-bombed the lunch buffet. At the last second it sensed the doom within.

It veered away squawking.

"Your ride's seen better days, *amigo*," Juan observed as their pickup truck rattled and belched along the coastal road.

"It'll last longer than both of us," Tomas said, wiping dust from the cracked windshield.

"I hope so. It's a long walk back home."

A pelican sailed past their windshield. It made a lazy turn, then flew with them awhile. Juan grinned and waved. The pelican seemed to wave back but of course was only trimming its wings. It squawked once, then cut back toward the water.

They laughed at the antics and kept rolling north. Remarked on the unusually heavy surf. Scanned the primer-colored undulate of the beaches to their right. "There," Juan said, pointing to a lump near the tree line.

They parked and hustled across the sand. "A truck engine," Tomas said happily, kicking a shredded fan belt. "That's worth a few pesos."

They lugged the grimy hulk to the pickup's cargo bed and threw it in. Shock absorbers groaned in protest. "Quiet," Tomas said, wagging his finger at the truck. "Weight lifting is good for you."

Juan laughed. "How much have we collected?"

Tomas ran a practiced eye over the jagged mound. "Two hundred kilos."

"Good haul."

"And the day is young," Tomas said.

"But ohhhh my back is weak," Juan said, rubbing himself gingerly. Scrapping was hard on even young bodies, and his was middle-aged.

"We'll stop for *cerveza* when we're done," Tomas said. "It cures everything."

They climbed into the ramshackle Chevrolet and resumed their search. They were scouting deserted beaches for sea junk. With metal prices so high on world markets, scrap picking beat tuna fishing hands down. Plus, you didn't get seasick. This was virgin territory, as far from Tampico as they'd ever ventured. There were more burros than people, so the jerry cans of gasoline they put in the back remained comforting.

"Any more news on Cousin Izzy?" Juan said as they rattled over a washout.

Tomas explained that she was waiting for the U.S. attorney to set a trial date. Her lawyer was optimistic he could spring her, but lawyers always said that. The family was hopeful at first, but that was fading as the months went by.

"Stinks," Juan sympathized.

"Yeah, it does. Izzy's a good girl, she got set up by . . . hey." Juan followed the point beyond the spindly copse of shore plants, and spotted the spread of glitter. They pulled to the side of the broken pavement and scampered down the hill. Slowed when they spotted a zoo of rotting animals surrounding what looked like giant metal cigars. Ten were intact. A blackened crater and crazily twisted metal marked where an eleventh had been. Juan wondered aloud what they were. Tomas picked up a pebble and wound up like the pitcher he'd been in *preparatoria*.

"Ha! Pus arm!" Juan teased as the pebble sailed wide.

Tomas, grinning, picked up a rock. He leaned back, judged the trajectory, adjusted an imaginary baseball cap, and hurled. It clanked off the tail of number four.

"Pretty good pitch," Juan allowed. "Let's check out our treasure."

They scampered to the cylinders. "Hmm," Tomas said, settling on his haunches. He patted the nearest with a palm hazed with metal cuts. No sound. He switched to his ring, which he'd hammered from a shard of scrap copper. It made a faint *clank-clank*. He ran his finger along a string of faded yellow stenciling. "*Americano* writing," he said.

Juan put his nose close, scrunched up his face, and sounded out the words. "Yew . . . Ess . . ."

"U.S. Army," Tomas said. "These cylinders are military. But what do those symbols mean?"

Juan looked at the chemical retorts crossed over a hexagon. He shrugged, having no idea. He should have paid more attention in English when he was a kid instead of throwing baseballs in hopes of making the New York Yankees. Maybe he'd be working in an office today, not hustling for scrap metal and stripping entrails from dead fish.

He kicked the cylinder angrily. "Doesn't matter," he said, puffing out his sun-tanned cheeks. "As long as it weighs a lot."

They trotted back to the truck, judging the sand stiff enough to hold its weight, which would save them the donkey work of dead-hauling ten large cylinders. Juan spotted a stone as round and smooth as a baseball. He picked it up, tossed it hand to hand.

"Hit one at this distance," Tomas urged, "and the beer's on me."

"Watch and learn, *niño*," Juan said.

The stone whanged off the sixth cigar, took a high bounce, and clipped the nose of the ninth.

"Wow!" Juan said, impressed. "I haven't thrown that straight since—"

They stiffened, hearing a low hiss from the sand. Snake? No. It was the ninth cylinder, the nose of which was misting from the rock-smack. A seagull swooped for the dead crab next to the cylinder. It flew into the dirty cloud. It stiffened and plunged to the ground in spasms.

"*Ay!* Let's get out of here!" Tomas shouted, shoving his friend toward the pickup. They struggled up the steep hill. Wave-weakened sand collapsed under his feet, and his right leg plunged into a suction hole. It wouldn't release. "Help!" he screamed, terrified.

The billowing poison cloud caught the wind and turned their way, engulfing a pack of terns, which plunged to the sand as if gut-shot.

Juan raced back and dropped to his knees.

"Go! Go! Save yourself!" Tomas begged.

"Pull as hard as you can," Juan ordered, shredding his fingernails as he dug. The cloud started up the hill.

Sweat poured off Tomas. He glanced over his shoulder at the onrushing monster. He slapped at Juan, urging him to save himself. No words formed, only grunts. Juan felt Tomas's shoe, grabbed it with both hands, and grunted like he'd torn a muscle. "Now run!" he said as Tomas's leg popped free.

They scrambled pell-mell for the truck. Hopped inside, shoved the key into the ignition. "Come on, please, come on," Tomas prayed as the starter ground and ground. He pumped the gas pedal, tried again. More grinding.

The dirty cloud shadowed their footsteps and crept over the edge of the pavement. "Get out, it's gonna kill us," Juan said, reaching for the door handle. "Run at right angles—"

Vroom! Tomas shoved the stick into DRIVE and shot down the broken highway, oily smoke billowing from his tailpipe.

"What . . . the . . ." Juan panted as the cloud grew small in the rear window.

"I've never seen anything die so fast," Tomas said, heart pounding in his gums. "Those cylinders must be a weapon."

"*Americano*," Juan said. "We have to tell someone. The police?"

Tomas made a gagging sound. "They'll arrest us for weapons possession."

"And confiscate your truck," Juan said. "You can't lose your truck."

They thought about whom they could trust with this secret. "My cousin," Tomas said, snapping his fingers. "He'll know what to do."

Juan wiped his brow with a badly shaking hand. "I think I'll take that beer now."

"It's on me, *Juanito*," Tomas said fervently. "For the rest of our lives, your beer is on me."

Chapter 34

UNITED STATES PENITENTIARY
FARGO, NORTH DAKOTA

"God, yes, down a little, girl, there, yes, right there, baby . . ."

"Hell of a . . . chess match they've got going," Isabel said.

Superstition smiled into the dark. Prison rules forbade sex between cellmates. But it wasn't unheard of, either. "Gay for the stay," they called it.

"I figured Parcheesi," she said.

"Hungry Hungry Hippos," Isabel countered, having seen them in the shower.

"Good one. Maybe it's—"

"Yes! Yes! Yessssssssss!"

"Bingo!" Superstition and Izzy shouted.

"Shut up!" the night guard carped from the end of the corridor.

Superstition chuckled. The conversation was refreshingly silly, the kind she used to have with her husband when they spooned up late at night.

"God, I miss sex," Izzy sighed.

Superstition thought about her own last time, on top of the bar and then again in their bed, the night before Derek flew to Arizona. Bagpipes and man-scent hummed in her brain. "Me, too," she said, squeezing her thighs together to feel the lonely ache. "How long has it been?"

"A year," Izzy said. "I was going to get laid on my birthday."

"Who was the lucky guy?"

"No idea. He was going to present himself at the bar, with a white rose and a gleam in his dangerous eyes." She snorted. "Instead, I got arrested."

"How'd that happen?" Superstition said. Despite their growing trust, they hadn't talked about their legal situations.

"I ran a bulldozer through my boyfriend's house," Izzy said.

"Really? Why?"

"He said he loved me. I caught him with another woman. Turns out he was sleeping all over town. So I borrowed a Caterpillar from a construction site."

Superstition burst out laughing.

"Final warning!" the guard yelled. "Shut the hell up, or I'll stick y'all in the hole."

Izzy and Superstition dropped to whispers. "That's awesome," Superstition said.

"No, it was dumb," Izzy said. "But I'd do it again."

"Me, too, if Derek ever did that to me."

"What you've said, he didn't sound the type."

"He wasn't. 'Run around like a dog, you catch fleas,' he said. He meant it."

"Nice to hear," Izzy said. "My dog, I smacked with a rolled-up newspaper."

"A ten-ton newspaper," Superstition said, punching the mattress with a soft thump.

"Yeah, but it backfired. He beat the hell out of me, then planted cocaine in my car. When I drove across the border, a drug dog sniffed it out."

"That bastard," Superstition said. "Sorry."

"He'll get his," Izzy said. "My brother will take care of it."

Superstition felt the *tug* . . . *tug-tug* of the bluegill hitting the baited hook. "You have a brother?" she said casually.

"Mm-hm."

"Is he cool?"

"Mm-hm."

"Is he cute?"

"Mm-hm!"

They snickered quietly. "Seriously, Sue," Izzy said. "My bro is great. You'd like him."

"Hope I get to meet him someday," Superstition said. "What's his name?"

"Jimmy."

"Has he ever come here to visit you?"

"No," Izzy said. "He's what you call, um, wanted."

"By who?"

"You policemen."

"*Those* policemen," Superstition said bitterly. "I'm not one anymore."

Silence.

"You want to talk about it?" Izzy said. "I'd be happy to listen. If, you know, you want."

Izzy had asked before about her situation, but Superstition had blown her off. Too many details delivered too soon led to suspicion. According to Deb Williams, Izzy and Jimmy were exceptionally close and had had each other's backs their entire lives. So Jimmy would hear every detail about Izzy's cellmate. Now was the time to start feeding her the lines.

"I was working undercover for the Chicago Police. As a decoy to catch men who hired prostitutes," she began. "My stage name was Fantasi—"

The prison lights flashed on, harsh and unblinking. "On yer feet!" the corridor guard shouted, raking his baton on a cell door. It rattled like a machine-gun burst. "Time for the count!"

"Oh, you weasel," Izzy groaned.

Prisoners were counted every four hours. Three a.m. was the most unpopular because everyone was asleep. Normally, the guards would pad silently through the cell block, using flashlights to ensure their charges were in bed. But the yakking had annoyed them, leading to this violent wake-up. Prison was bitchier than Cruella De Vil.

"Garcia and Davis, check," the guard said, leering at their sleep-wear—granny panties and wash-worn T's—till Superstition felt his greasiness drip down her spine. Rape by the guards was up there with homicide on the forbidden list. But like "gay for the stay," it happened more than the prison industrial complex would ever admit.

Twenty minutes later, the lights went off, and they were back in their bunks.

"So, then, Fantasi," Izzy prompted.

Superstition told her about the three gunmen she'd slain. About her oak tree of a husband, felled and buried. About the "racist" video, the open house, the first meeting with the FBI agent, then the fight at the blues club where she'd broken said agent's ribs, which led to her arrest, conviction, and imprisonment in Fargo. Finally, she told her about Timmy and Tommy.

"Oh, Sue, your twins," Izzy said, her heart breaking. She loved children and wanted lots of her own. To lose them so monstrously . . . "Your heart must have broken."

"It still is," Superstition grunted, her tone indicating that she didn't want to go any further.

"Why do they call you Superstition?" Izzy whispered instead. "It's such a different name."

Superstition punched up her pillow to ease the strain on her neck. The thinness of the mattress made the bunk an iron maiden, no matter how much she stretched and kneaded her muscles. "Mom wanted a family," she said. "So Dad got busy. Nothing worked. They tried and tried for years. A decade. Finally, they gave up. Then, out of the blue, I popped up. Mom was astonished. She'd finally accepted that, for her, babies would remain a superstition."

"So you became Superstition."

"Sue for short." She grinned into the darkness. "Or, if you like, Skeeter."

"Skeeter?" Izzy said. "As in . . . mosquito?"

"Yeah," Superstition said. "But only Dad calls me that. Mom thinks it's undignified."

"I can't imagine why," Izzy said. "Being nicknamed for an insect."

They giggled. "When I was a kid, he drove one of those fogger trucks," Superstition explained. "You know, for spraying mosquitoes?"

"They lay out a chemical fog," Izzy said, familiar with the government trucks that rolled mountains of poison through the slums twice a year to quell the vermin and disease spawned by too many bodies in too-close quarters.

"That's right. He was an exterminator. We drove around spraying mosquitoes. Like that TV commercial said, 'We killed bugs dead.'"

"Didn't you go to school?"

"During the week, sure. He took me with on weekends."

"Every girl's dream," Izzy teased, kicking the itchy blankets off her legs. "Walking barefoot in the sand. Dressing up for the prom. Poisoning mosquitoes."

"Time alone with Daddy," Superstition said, grinning. "My girlfriends were jealous." She thought about the potholes they'd bounced over in that ratty little truck. "His territory was the countryside south of Chicago, along the Lincoln Highway."

"Abraham Lincoln?" Izzy guessed.

"They named the highway in his honor, right. We sprayed Frankfort. Mokena. New Lenox. Lincoln Estates. Spencer."

"Those are cities?" Izzy said.

"Small rural towns," Superstition said. "Each alive with mosquitoes. The county hired Dad's company to do pest control. We drove along at thirty miles an hour, purple clouds rolling from the tanks. Kids used to run along behind us, playing in the clouds." She waved her hands. "It had this sweet smell, like cotton candy."

"Candy with a sledgehammer."

Superstition preferred not to think of all the brain-busting vapors she'd inhaled on all those trips. "He even built a mosquito for the roof."

"What roof?"

"The roof of the fogger truck. It was a big wooden mosquito that he carved from a log with a chain saw. It was four feet long, had wings and a stinger, the whole bit. He painted it neon colors so it would stand out. It was his signature—'Hey, everybody, Skeeter Man's coming.' Which is why his nickname for me was—"

"Skeeter," Izzy finished.

"Now you know," Superstition said. "How about you, Izzy? Where'd you grow up?"

"Mexico City," she said.

"I was there once," Superstition said, having visited with girlfriends during spring break her junior year of college. "Gorgeous city."

"Sure, if you're a tourist," Izzy said. "I grew up in an industrial slum on the outskirts. We were so poor even beggars spit on us."

"Ouch."

"It's all right. My family and I were very close. That helped. And when he got old enough, Jimmy figured out a way to make things better for all of us."

Superstition rolled off her bunk and padded to the toilet. Izzy turned to the wall. There was no privacy in such cramped quarters, so you created it artificially. *Flush.* Back to bed.

"How'd your brother do that?" Superstition prompted.

Silence.

"He joined the narcotics business," Izzy said.

"Lot of money in drugs," Superstition said neutrally.

"He tried to get honest work," Izzy said. "But there wasn't any. In Mexico, if you're not part of the ruling elite, you're worthless, and you get no opportunities. So he started as a mule, hauling marijuana into the United States. He was good at it and moved up in the organization."

"He became a *narco*?"

"He had no choice," Izzy said defensively.

"I'm not judging," Superstition said.

"Yes, you are," Izzy spat, her voice brimming with anger. "All Americans do. You believe *narcos* are monsters, bringing poison to your innocent children. But you're the ones who buy it! You make the narcotics trade possible because without buyers, there can be no sellers."

"I know," Superstition said. She'd tried marijuana in high school, then again in college, mostly at late-night parties. The buzz she got was so-so, and she eventually gave it up. But many of her friends liked the high and smoked their brains out. She'd never wondered where the dope came from or about the lives of the people who supplied it.

"In Mexico, people like us run narcotics or starve," Izzy said. "No second choice. I despise drugs. I hate what they've done to our nation, all the violence and corruption." She practically hissed with passion. "But I won't apologize for choosing life instead of dying in a gutter like my parents did, and I'm proud of my brother for supporting his family. He helped us when we couldn't help ourselves."

"I understand," Superstition said. "Really, I do."

"That's funny," Izzy said. "Because I don't."

More silence.

"It's why I became a police officer, I guess," Superstition said. "I didn't want to push people around. I just wanted to help folks who couldn't help themselves, and a badge allowed me do that. The world is full of evil, and I wanted to do something about it." She took a deep breath, remembering that fateful night in Bubbles Lounge. "I didn't want to kill those three men, Izzy, but it was necessary to protect a hundred innocents. And kicking that FBI agent was right, too. She spat on my husband and children by busting up my party."

"Would you do it again?" Izzy said. "Even knowing it would land you here?"

"Yes," Superstition said. "Some things are worth it no matter what the cost." *Like betraying a woman who's rapidly becoming a friend.* "So I get your brother. And you."

She saw Izzy's hand extend from the bunk. Squeezed it hard.

"You're all right, Fantasi," Izzy said, the humor back in her voice. "For a rich, coddled white *gringa* princess."

"Said the lazy, brown *narco*-sucking wetback," Superstition said.

"Uhhhhhh . . ." moaned the cellies.

"Shut up," said the guard.

"Amen," Superstition said.

1948

MARCH 13
ROOFTOP OF THE STATLER HOTEL
ST. LOUIS, MISSOURI

"Sandbox Leader to Sandbox One," the olive-drab radio crackled.

"This is One."

"Green light. Repeat, you have a green light. Release compound."

"Understood, Sandbox Leader," replied the U.S. Army Chemical Corps lieutenant. He licked his finger. The chill was on the nail side. Wind north to south, stiff but steady. Exactly what he wanted.

"Execute," he ordered.

Sergeants ran to their stations atop the Statler, the first hotel in the United States to offer that newfangled delight called "air conditioning." They cracked the lids of their casks, tipped them ass over teakettle, and watched zinc cadmium sulfide pour into the open air, catch the wind, and powder St. Louis like an aging movie queen.

Twenty stories below, canvas-topped trucks roamed the streets, soldiers working their foggers like the machine-gunners they'd been in Europe. In the humid sky, unmarked military planes coated the dull brown tide of the Mississippi River. One plane diverted briefly to Sportsman's Park, unleashing a double dose on the outfield grass. The pilot was a die-hard Boston Braves fan, Stan "The Man" Musial was swinging serious lumber for the St. Louis Cardinals, the only serious rival his beloved Boston Braves had for the NL pennant, and every little edge might help, go Braves . . .

"Look, Ma!" said the towheaded boy in the red Cardinals cap, pointing at the iridescent fog rolling from the bottom of the low-flying planes. "They're pissin' on us."

His mother twisted his ear. "Don't say 'piss,' Davey," she scolded. "It's not polite."

"What're they dropping, then?" he said.

The woman shrugged. "I don't know, honey," she said, feeling anxious. Even without their markings, those were U.S. Army planes—she'd been a civilian air raid warden and knew the silhouettes. But the war was over, the Nazis and Japs were smoked like spareribs, and America was at peace. Why would the Army bomb St. Louis?

She tightened her grip on her packages and hurried the boy toward the charcoal gray Packard her husband was idling in front of the downtown department store. "It's nothing, Davey," she muttered. "Just water."

"It can't be water, Ma, it smells funny," the boy persisted.

She sniffed as the nearly invisible dust swept across them. The odor was unusual, wasn't it? Metallic, laced with tar and mildew. "Maybe they're crop dusters, killing mosquitoes," she said, feeling a little faint.

"Skeeters?" the boy said, shaking his head. "In March? No way, Ma—"

"Don't talk back to me, young man!" she snapped.

"Quit sassing your mother, boy," his father said, revving the straight-eight till it shook like Jell-O. "And listen to how I tuned this engine."

"Neato torpedo!" the boy said, fog forgotten as the planes banked away. "It sounds great, Pops. What'd you do, hot-rod the carburetor with—uh-uh-uh—"

"Davey?" his mother gasped at the lung-wracking coughs suddenly enveloping her son.

"Can't . . . can't . . . breathe . . ." he gasped, clawing at his neck as his face tinged blue.

Pops leapt from the car. Pushed Davey's jaw down and fished around his mouth. The boy gagged so loudly that pigeons flew off their roosts. "No blockage," he said.

"What'll we do?" Mom wailed.

"Get in the car," Pops ordered, jacking open the back door and heaving Davey inside. Mom scrambled in next to the boy, cradling his head as he racked and heaved. Dad spotted a patrolman at the stop-and-go light. Waved his arms, blatted his horn. The prowl car motored over, and the cop rolled down his window. "What's up, Mac—"

"Our son's choking to death!" Mom shouted from the back.

The cop jumped as if horsewhipped. He had three boys of his own.

"Hospital's just a few blocks away. Follow me!" he ordered, laying twenty yards of Firestone as he toggled his siren and lights.

The chemical lieutenant rubbed his crew cut, pleased. The particles, as fine as his great-grandma's pie flour, were sticking to everything, and the ultraviolet detectors in the trucks and planes were charting the precise disbursement pattern. Soon as the results were collated, he'd transmit them to the War Department, per orders. Then, he'd treat his men to breakfast. No sense suffering Army hash back at base when big-city ham and eggs begged for inhalation.

"How's it looking down there?" he radioed.

"Wide coverage, Loot, and a nice, even spread," the lead detector man said over the roar of the truck. "Exactly what the slide-rule boys said."

The lieutenant nodded. Chemical soldiers were performing the same test in dozens of American cities today, from Minneapolis to Corpus Christi to Fort Wayne. Up in Canada, too, but he didn't know where. All to measure the dispersal patterns of zinc cadmium sulfide, a supposedly inert compound whose particles were the same mass and size as the powders and germs of chemical and biological warfare. The idea was to see how fast an Army biochem unit could clobber a major city. Like, say, Moscow or East Berlin . . .

WAR DEPARTMENT, WASHINGTON, D.C.

"Spectacular," the colonel said, thumping the hastily typed field reports. "Maximum spread on streets, sidewalks, roofs, and alleyways."

"Any complaints?" the general said. The tests were secret, so there shouldn't be any, but a local yokel might catch wise for some lucky reason and need to be handled.

"A few dozen people showed up at emergency rooms," the colonel said. "Coughing. Short breath. Respiratory distress."

The general frowned. "I thought this stuff wasn't poisonous."

"It isn't," the colonel assured. "These are lung spasms, apparently. Like you'd get from inhaling plain dirt."

"Ah, then. It'll go away," the general said, waving his hand dismissively. Even if it didn't, hell, a few civilian casualties was a small price to pay for the ability to obliterate the godless Bolsheviks, who, he knew with the certainty of the Baptist deacon he was Wednesdays and Sundays, cowered deep in their bunkers in Moscow, devouring uncooked cattle, steeling to attack the America he so deeply loved. "Water dispersal?"

"It's floating down that river like ol' Huck Finn," the colonel said.

The general planted a cheroot in his jaw. Punched his intercom. "I need you to send a cable," he ordered his secretary. "Flash priority."

"Right away, General," she said.

He leaned back in his chair, waiting for her to appear with her steno book. She took dictation like nobody's business. Her curvy legs were a bonus.

"All we need now is the poison," the colonel said. "And we're in like Flynn."

"That's up to Big Mac," the general said. "God bless 'im."

GENERAL MACARTHUR'S OFFICE, TOKYO

"The foregoing information warrants conclusion that Japanese Biological Warfare Group, headed by General Ishii, did violate rules of land warfare. This expression of opinion is not a recommendation that the Group be charged and tried as such."

General Douglas MacArthur reread the cable from the War Department. He saw the negatives of this crazy scheme because he was the one who suggested it, but then again, there were major upsides. He buzzed his adjutant. "Send him," MacArthur said.

The mustached man walked into the expansive, sunlit room—the Office of the Supreme Commander of Allied Forces in Japan—that looked down on the Imperial Palace. MacArthur waved him to a chair and took the one to the visitor's right. He planted his elbows on his thighs and leaned in like a hawk sizing up a rabbit.

"Here's the deal, plain and simple. You develop biological and chemical weapons for the United States," MacArthur said. "In return, I don't take you out back and put a bullet in your head."

Shiro Ishii looked amused.

"Don't be theatrical, General," he said, raking his fingers through his mustache. "You approached me, not the other way around."

"Washington's idea, not mine," MacArthur snapped, which wasn't true, but there was no reason for Ishii to know that. He tamped his corncob pipe and lit the tobacco. Fired a salvo of smoke at the commander of Japan's human experimentation program. "You sliced and diced American POWs in your chamber of horrors, in addition to thousands of other poor souls. I'd love to return the favor without anesthetic."

"But you can't, because you require my assistance."

MacArthur scowled. "Lousy Russians," he said. "Only thing that might stop 'em from taking up where Hitler left off is what you boys cooked up in Manchuria."

"Nerve gas."

"And germs."

Ishii nodded. The Americans, with their vast industrial know-how, would fix the problems he and Sakamora had with the delivery systems. But the gas and biological agents developed at Unit 731 were unique—not even Germany possessed everything Ishii had created at the cost of a mere two hundred thousand logs. America itched to get its hands on the formulas before Stalin because they believed as Ishii did: *The enemy of my enemy is my friend.*

"I receive complete and total immunity from war crimes," Ishii said. "Exactly like you granted the German rocket scientists."

"We bring you to the United States," MacArthur said, nodding agreement. "We provide housing, salary, and research facilities."

"Staffed by scientists of my choosing," Ishii said. "To replace the ones I lost." Including, unfortunately, Sakamora, his lamb chop–loving nerve gas chemist, who'd bitten a cyanide pill rather than endure the shame of

Japan's surrender. Poor Sakamora failed to see the bigger picture: that this new world order required ever more efficient ways of killing, and Americans would pay whatever it took to own them. Which is why Ishii was moving to a house in Maryland, and Sakamora was disintegrating in a cold, lonely grave.

"Yes, yes, that's the deal," MacArthur said irritably, handing over the amnesty documents. "The White House signed off. You have full immunity. I expect your files by the weekend."

Ishii smiled. The night of the day he got back from Manchuria, he hid five thousand pages of experimental notes in a secure location and leaked word to MacArthur's people. He knew the information was his passport from the gallows, and he was right.

He stood. Tented his hands as if praying, then bowed deeply.

MacArthur made one curt nod. Normally he'd respond with his own bow and a few minutes of stroking, in respect of Japan's social code and its soldiers' genuine bravery in battle. But this man, who'd doomed so many to deaths so piteous that a buzzard would choke . . .

"My guards will show you out," he said, buzzing for the soldiers who would put Ishii and his documents on a plane for Washington.

Ishii shrugged and left.

MacArthur pulled a bottle from his desk drawer and belted a double slug to kill the sour taste in his mouth. He hated making deals with the devil.

But he didn't have to like it.

He just had to do it.

Chapter 35

HUMBOLDT PARK
WEST SIDE OF CHICAGO

The house smelled like the urinals at Wrigley Field. But at least that blunted the stench of the mildew and rat droppings.

"Sold," Robert Hanrahan said.

The Realtor grinned. "This mook must be a real gem to merit a dump like this," he said, patting the cash that was his finder's fee. The broker was a softball buddy who stashed the occasional Hanrahan stoolie in an empty "downmarket"—"that's Realtor-speak for shithole," he'd said—and knew how to keep his mouth shut.

"You have no idea," Hanrahan said.

The Realtor tossed him the keys, saluted, and left.

Hanrahan got to work with buckets and bleach. As entertaining as Superstition's reaction to the filth would be—she was undoubtedly learning all kinds of new cuss words in prison—she might catch the plague, and then where would they be? *What a great line*, he thought. He'd lay it on her when they could talk freely . . .

His phone rang. He checked the number and answered.

"Yes, Mother, I'm cleaning, I'm cleaning," he said.

"If I were your mother," Deb Williams said, "I'd ask the doctor for my money back."

"I'm laughing on the inside," Hanrahan said. "Where are you?"

"Check your front door," she said.

He looked out the pigeon-splattered window. The FBI agent was standing on the concrete stoop, her body as stiff as electrical conduit. He nodded, impressed she was working rather than calling in sick. He opened the door and bade her in.

"Wow," Williams said as she looked around the living room. "I didn't think it'd be worse than Fargo."

"She needs to look ripe for the picking."

"This'll do it," Williams said, blowing her breath out slowly.

"How are you feeling?" he said.

She started to shrug. It brought a wince. "In the movies," she said, "cops handle cracked ribs with Black Label and wisecracks."

"Life ain't the funny pages," he said, sympathizing. A burglar broke one of Hanrahan's ribs in an alley brawl when he was back in patrol. It burned like napalm. On the way to the squad car, the burglar tripped and fell, then tripped and fell again. Burglars could be clumsy that way. "May I show you around?"

He took her into the kitchen, the bathroom, and finally, the bedroom, which contained a creaky-looking double bed, mismatched floor lamps, and a closet whose folding door was off its track. He noticed her staring at the mattress.

"Why don't you lay down awhile?" he said, concerned at how much pain she was really in, as opposed to what she claimed. "Take a load off those ribs."

Williams looked at him with an expression he couldn't read. "I'd love to take a nap. But you wouldn't be able to control your manly urges, and I'm too weak to fight you off."

"We could just cuddle," Hanrahan said, holding his hand in a Boy Scout salute. "I swear we'd never go any further."

They both burst out laughing at the cheesy pickup lines. He checked his watch. "You're heading to Fargo, right?"

"Yes, so I need to leave for the airport," she said. "It's the only flight today, so I miss it, I'm stuck till tomorrow."

The thought of an extra day with Deb didn't fill him with *agita*, as it would have just a week ago. Why his attitude toward her had changed so radically, he didn't really know. Probably volunteering to take that beating, which, while it wasn't supposed to have ended with broken ribs, there'd always been the chance, as undercover operations rarely go as planned. He liked how she was sharp and never backed down. He liked how she was pretty. He'd have liked to tell her all that, but there was no point—she spelled Hanrahan "B-U-T-T-H-E-A-D." Which, when he thought about how he'd treated her to date, wasn't all that far off the mark.

"Just take it easy, Deb," he said, walking her to the door. "Ribs are sturdy, so yours will heal fine. But jostling 'em hurts like a nail gun."

She patted his arm and headed out.

He watched her Franken-walk to the rental, then resumed scrubbing the walls. He worried about the constant gang attacks on Superstition. Yeah, she was tough, and she'd won every time. But granite shattered given enough dynamite. That he couldn't have her back was maddening. A commander's first job was looking out for his people.

Three hours later, he locked up and headed out, having left enough cruddy corners to give the house the grease-ring of realism. He gave the hairy eyeball to the corner knuckleheads eyeing his car with ill intent. Quick trip home, shower, change, armor up, then hit the mean streets. Tonight, he was breaking in the team's new "hooker," Yolanda. The officer was young, pretty, and hungry. She'd do well.

But his heart wasn't in it.

Chapter 36

DESERTED BEACH NORTH OF TAMPICO
GULF COAST OF MEXICO

Jimmy Garcia kicked one seagull, then ran his eyes over the rest. Deader'n disco.

"Does anyone else know about these weapons?" he said.

"No," Tomas assured him, puffing out his chest. "Just me and Juan."

"Nobody drove down this road?" Garcia pressed. "Beachcomber? Farmer? Police?"

Juan shook his head.

"Did you call anyone besides me?"

"You told us not to," Tomas said.

Garcia glared at them, looking for signs of deception. Finally, he grinned.

"You did well," he said, handing each an envelope.

Juan looked inside. His eyes bulged.

"This is a year's—"

"I appreciate smart men," Garcia said.

Tomas beamed. "I told you my cousin was king," he said, slapping Juan on the back.

Garcia squeezed Tomas's right triceps. Then made it brutal.

"We'll keep our mouths shut, I swear!" Tomas yelped, getting the message. "On this matter, we're dumb as rocks and ignorant as stumps."

"Very good," Jimmy said. "And your newfound money?"

"We found it on the side of the road."

"In what?"

"A can."

"What can?"

Tomas pointed to the empty pinto bean container, which Garcia had supplied.

"And if you tell *anyone* about the cylinders?" Garcia said, squeezing so hard now that his fingers trembled. "Your mother, your priest, or your girl after she takes your load?"

Juan pointed to the line of rotting birds. "You'll kill us as dead as them."

Garcia nodded. Smoothed Tomas's shirtsleeve. Barked orders.

The drivers backed trucks to the cylinders. Strapped steel muzzles over the nose cones to prevent the weapons from exploding. Tied lifting straps around the dull green bodies and began loading.

"Then enjoy your money, *mis amigos*," Garcia said. "Enjoy!"

They walked for Tomas's pickup, chattering with relief. Tossed the bean can into the cab and climbed inside. As they retreated, Garcia considered shooting them to ensure the secret remained so. Decided against it. Not because they were family—he'd executed more than one relative who'd gone against the cartel's interests—but because it would tell his people that no matter how smart and loyally they acted, their boss might kill them anyway. That was bad for business. And if Tomas and Juan did talk, bullets had no expiration date . . .

"Deliver these to our lab," he told Javier, the young tunnel man who'd become his unofficial right arm. "The weapons man will meet you there." The cartel kept experts on staff because *narco* was a dangerous business, and it paid to keep current with the technology. "He'll figure out how to use them to our advantage." He ran through his mental checklist. "Then get back to the truck tunnel and put a fire under the men."

"They're working sixteen hours a day," Javier objected.

"Double their pay and work them twenty-four," Garcia said. "Every day Taliban narcotics sit in our warehouse is a day we don't make money."

"*Sí, Jefe*," Javier said as he revved his engine. "I'll take care of it."

He followed the tire roosters of the loaded weapons trucks, choking from the dust.

Chapter 37

THE WHITE HOUSE
WASHINGTON, D.C.

The president mentally replayed the tense conversation with the admiral. He knew what nerve gas did to human beings. Syria killed thousands of rebelling citizens with it in the last civil war, and he'd seen the photographs. The CIA videos were even worse. The one of a boy whimpering for his mother as he retched and flailed hit him so hard that he'd wished he could bleach his eyeballs. That a flotilla of those devil bombs was loose in America's backyard . . .

"Get me the director," he told his secretary. "And the chairman."

Twenty minutes later, the door opened. "Yes, Mr. President?" the CIA director and the chairman of the military's Joint Chiefs of Staff said simultaneously.

"Grab a seat," the president said. "You're going to love this one." He explained what had been found.

"Good lord," the chairman murmured, removing his glasses and rubbing his eyes. The director tented his fingers and pressed his lips into a thin, flat line.

"Whatever you need," the president said. "Whatever it takes."

GULF OF MEXICO

"Flash traffic, sir," the executive officer said. "Your eyes only."

"I'll take it in my ready room," the captain said, spinning for his cabin in the rear of the command center. Four minutes later, he was reading the message and pursing his lips. He opened an encrypted link with the Pentagon and worked out a search pattern. He strode back to the command center, told the XO to get the cutter under way.

"What are we looking for?" the XO said as the *Bernard C. Webber* turned toward Mexico.

"Metal cylinders," the captain said. "They're old, green, and shaped like cigars."

"Filled with?"

"Can't say," the captain said.

The XO nodded and pushed the fast-response cutter full ahead.

The captain didn't like not being able to tell his crew. They were the ones who died if they touched that poison ungloved. It was noble to die for your country. It was stupid to die needlessly. He cleared his throat with great exaggeration. The crew hushed.

"Have we quality-checked our new NBCs?" he said.

The XO shook his head. Because the Coast Guard routinely interdicted drug boats filled with nasty chemicals, cutters carried military-grade nuclear-biological-chemical protection gear for the boarding teams. The *Webber* was due a new set after fishing the corpses from the tuna boat, and it arrived last night with other supplies. There hadn't been time to check the suits inch by inch.

"Might be good if we do," the captain said. "In case something . . . unusual turns up in the course of our travels."

The XO stroked his narrow chin. "Huh. Funny."

"What's that, XO?"

"I was just about to suggest that we make the suits fully operational and ensure everyone knows to operate them in an emergency."

"That's very efficient of you, XO."

"Thank you, sir. Would you mind if I tend to that right now?"

"Go ahead, make my day," the captain said.

Chapter 38

ONE MILE BELOW THE SURFACE
GULF OF MEXICO

"Let me get this straight," Denton said as he zigzagged through the graveyard. "The Navy has SEALs and nuclear submarines. But they're paying us to retrieve their nerve gas."

"No," Raider said.

"What'd I miss?"

"We're doing it for free."

Denton rolled his eyes.

"Look at the bright side," Raider said. "If we set one off, the water pressure will kill us before the gas gets its chance."

Denton released the exterior mechanical work arms from their locked position. "Yeah, I feel better already."

Raider turned the submersible six degrees to center it with the rusty steel net. "We watched the cylinders drift away," Denton said. "What makes the admiral think there's any left?"

Raider flipped on the spotlights. "Wishin' and hopin', I guess," he said. "One hundred yards to the net." Denton caressed the joystick and the work arms became erect. "I promise I'll be gentle, honey," he told the gap in the steel net.

"Always the romantic," Raider snorted.

Seventy yards. "No cylinders," Denton said. *Fifty yards.* "Maybe there?" Raider said, seeing a lump on his sensors. *Twenty yards.* "Nope," Denton said, turning up the gain on sonars and radars. *Eighteen. Seventeen. Sixteen.*

"There. At the far end of the netting," Raider said.

"Of course it is," Denton said, wiping sweat from his forehead.

"Nervous?" Raider said.

"Hell, no," Denton said.

"Yeah, me neither," Raider said, flicking his own sweat from his fingers.

Denton eased the arms under the net. Rust and barnacles popped off, spun away in the current. "I'll take the arms," Raider said. "You drive the truck."

Denton shook his joystick. Raider shook back to confirm he had control. He gently elevated the work arms, and the gap between net and ocean floor widened. Denton flipped on the tail lights and spotted a cylinder-shaped gleam.

"It's eleven-point-six yards from the end of the starboard claw," he reported.

"I see it," Raider confirmed.

"Don't touch that nose cone, man," Denton reminded. "Or we're sushi."

Raider manipulated the joystick. Hydraulics translated the movement to the steel hands at the end of the work arms. *Six yards. Four yards. Two yards. Two inches.* "I'm dead center of the device," Raider said. "Starting to clamp . . ."

A soft *shunk* confirmed contact.

"Good grip on both sides," Denton reported, examining the camera imagery.

"Reverse engines," Raider said. "Quarter speed."

Submersible and weapon moved as one.

"Ah, crap," Raider muttered as the tail hung up on a cluster of strands.

"Shake it a little," Denton suggested. "Maybe it'll work better."

"That's what she said," Raider said, moving the lobsters up and down. The weapon freed itself and resumed its emergence from the steel womb.

"Any other cylinders?" Raider said.

"Negative," Denton said, thumbing through instant replays. They circled the net twice to make sure. No more cylinders.

"All right. Let's get this bad boy upstairs, then search the route the Pentagon assumes the cylinders took toward Mexico."

Denton aimed for the surface, where a guided missile destroyer awaited. The media had asked why a U.S. Navy warship was in the Gulf. The Pentagon replied that it was testing how oil slicks affected the propulsion system of the new Zumwalt-class destroyers. The reporters bought it and went away. Raider figured they would. There were no cute kitties or missing white girls.

"Surface in three . . . two . . . one . . ." Denton said.

They popped through the waves and onto the giant hoist that would lift them out of the water. "Sixth floor, underwear and cosmetics," Denton quipped as the submersible inched upwards. Sailors in moon suits eased the dripping weapon off the lobsters, clamped a muzzle around the nose cone, dropped it into an armored blast tank, then signaled the hoist. The submersible sank into the waves and headed back to the ocean floor.

DESERTED BEACH NORTH OF TAMPICO
GULF COAST OF MEXICO

"They were here," the CIA weapons specialist reported via satellite link. "Now they're not."

"And you know this how?" the CIA director said.

"Minute traces of VX and anthrax," the specialist said, patting his portable detector. Pentagon geeks had analyzed Gulf currents, temperatures, wind speed, water density, cylinder weight, rust and barnacle load, and other variables, and predicted that the weapons would wash up on one of three beaches in this sector—if they didn't hit a cruise ship on the way. "Also, there are dead birds, shrapnel from a blast—the VX readings were higher in the crater than in the rest of the indentations, suggesting one went off—and tire ruts in the sand. They're shallow coming in and deep going out, indicating the addition of heavy loads. My opinion, someone took 'em."

"Who?"

"Don't know."

"Where?"

"No clue."

"Get one," the director said.

"No problem. All I need is time and money."

"The Bank of Sam is open for business," the director said. "No withdrawal limits."

"Good to know."

"As for time, I need this yesterday."

"Don't you always?" the specialist said.

Chapter 39

UNITED STATES PENITENTIARY
FARGO, NORTH DAKOTA

"Shower tiiime . . ." Superstition crooned into a flip-flop.

". . . and the living is easy," Izzy finished.

"Next stop, *American Idol*," Superstition said, stepping into her umber flips and grabbing her prison-issued soap, having chosen not to pay the commissary ten dollars for a bar of Ivory. They stepped from the cell into the corridor, listening to the Great Plains howl through the long, narrow cracks in the walls. Fargo, they'd learned from the convicts stacking more serious time, was a wind tunnel, the winter version of which, with its ice and snow and hard, leaden gloom, was a particular joy. They fervently hoped to avoid that fate by getting sprung.

But they weren't counting on it.

They greeted cell-block pals, warned off gang girls with chin-up stares, and wrinkled their noses at the breakfast stench wafting from the dining room: creamed beef on toast.

"Shit on a shingle," they said simultaneously.

Superstition snapped her towel, making Izzy yelp.

"You saw that, Doreen," Izzy kidded a thick-waisted ginger tucking sheets around her mattress. "Assault with a deadly weapon."

"Dint see nuffin bout no one," Doreen said, citing prison code chapter and verse as she opened a foil pack of Charlie the Tuna.

They laughed, waved, and flip-flopped into the communal shower, a windowless, low-ceilinged room with industrial water spigots poking from the flaking concrete walls. They kicked hairballs out of the welded floor grates to allow the sudsy gray water to drain. They shook their heads at the mildew tendrils that crept up the damp corners like Boston ivy, and looked enviously at the steam clouds caressing the room's sole occupant.

"You leave us any, D-Day?" Izzy demanded.

D'Nadia grinned. "A few drops," she said. "Catch you later." She wrapped herself in the terry robe she'd bought at the commissary—rich boyfriend—and skipped away.

"Ahhhh," Izzy said, stripping for the luxurious hot water.

"Hear ya clear," Superstition said, soaping and rinsing and soaping again, rubbing vigorously to raise fresh lather. She exercised feverishly in their cell—push-ups, planks, squats, handstands, hand and elbow chops to the concrete walls, hundreds in a row, hours at a stretch, and it felt good to remove the hardened sweat—

She felt, more than heard, slap-vibrations in the floor. Someone was running. More than one, coming hard.

She whirled as Izzy sang "It's the Hard Knock Life" from the Broadway show *Annie*, her face sudsy and her eyes closed, unaware. Six women charged through the door. They were Mexican, muscled, and mean. They wore blue-ink teardrops—prison-made gang tattoos—on their adrenaline-flushed cheeks, indicating that they'd killed before. Five carried soap bars in long socks, whirling them like medieval war flails. One wielded a shank—a toothbrush whose handle had been rubbed against rough concrete till it was sharp enough to pierce flesh.

"*Ssssss!*" the assassin hissed, cocking her arm as she drove for the kill.

But this time the target wasn't Superstition.

"Izzy!" Superstition yelped as she dove for the attacker's arm. If she timed it just right, she'd redirect the shank into the assassin's abdomen. She'd done it thousands of times in training and several times on the street. But the drain cover snagged one of her flip-flops, slowing her for the microsecond that separated life from murder.

Go for it.

She threw her body between weapon and target. "Ahhhhh!" she gasped as the tip pierced the flesh over her belly. She twisted violently to redirect the shank's thrust, keep it from stabbing deep into her organs. The sharpened plastic skidded off her lower rib and punched an exit hole, the assassin's momentum ripping out the flesh in between. Superstition didn't feel the pain. She didn't feel anything. She was gassed up with fully leaded fury.

"Die, die, die," she snarled, slamming the assassin's face against a pipe stub. She heard the crunch of cartilage and bone, grinned at the surprised mewl of a predator shocked that prey could bite back.

The second banger lunged for Izzy, who'd backed into a corner, eyes darting, looking for an escape route. Superstition moved sideways, locked up the banger in an elbow-cracking arm bar, and slammed her into a wall. The banger's skull bounced with a meaty *thunk*, and she spun to the floor bleeding.

"Behind you!" Izzy cried. Superstition unleashed a rearward mule kick that would break the spine of anyone in its path. The third banger twisted and took it in the upper thigh. With the power of the kick she went down anyway, mashing her nose on the floor.

A soap flail banged off Superstition's head, making her see stars. She kicked at the charging attacker. Missed by an inch as the fourth banger snatched the toothbrush from the drain and started to attack. Izzy swung a soap-sock directly into her face, connecting for a major-league triple. The banger tripped backward and slid along the blood-streaked floor. Superstition kicked her in the temple as she passed. The banger began retching.

An arm snaked around her throat as her kidneys absorbed rabbit punches. Every blow felt like a blackjack. Gasping for breath, she grabbed the tattooed arm with both hands, digging her fingernails in deep. No relief. She tucked down her mouth and bit so deep that she severed a pair of veins. Her attacker shrieked as blood geysered. Hanging onto the arm, Superstition drove them both backward, her steps a locomotive gaining steam, and slammed her attacker into the iron spigots, cracking the woman's tendons and bones, then whirling to crush her throat. The woman darted like a scalded cat and Superstition's hand bounced off the wall, her own bones cracking. The woman hooked her fingers into the wound in Superstition's belly and pried.

"Dammit!" Superstition gasped as flesh ripped, not in pain but annoyance that she'd missed the throat shot. She wanted these people dead. She wanted them dead now.

She yanked the fingers out of her wound and launched a flurry of body blows. No effect on the banger, who was built like a refrigerator. She took a fist in her eye socket, shook it off, and thrust the callused point of her elbow into the side of the banger's neck. The stocky woman collapsed like her strings were cut, then tried to get up. Superstition stomped her larynx. Heard the gurgle that said she was down for the count.

Superstition felt saliva flow down her chin. It wasn't fear, and it wasn't drool. It was hunger. *I'm gonna tear off your face for breakfast and suck your bones for lunch,* the saliva said. *I'm going to eat you alive, then shit you into a sewer.*

Five and Six stiffened with the fear of a plant eater meeting T. rex.

Superstition kicked off her flips for traction. Blood poured from her belly holes, broken nose, and macerated hand. It ran down her legs, onto the floor, into the drain. She laughed, flipping her long hair from one side to the other, blood and soap flying like semen spurts. She spit the remains of the banger's flesh at her attackers' feet, the veins wiggling like blue worms.

"*Monstruo,*" Six muttered.

Monster.

They ran from the room as the riot alarm finally started screeching.

Superstition collapsed onto the pink-washed floor as Izzy staggered drunkenly to help.

Chapter 40

BRISAS DEL MAR HOTEL
TAMPICO, MEXICO

Jimmy gripped his cell so tightly its metal casing bent. "What did you say?" he hissed.

"A prison gang attacked Isabel this morning," her lawyer said. "Mexican Mafia. Five carried bludgeons, one a sharpened toothbrush."

Garcia sagged against the balcony door, finding solace in the cool glass. He forced himself upright. Emotion was for weaklings. "Is she—"

"No, she's fine, she's safe," the lawyer assured. "Bruises and cuts, that's all. The woman who saved her life wasn't as lucky."

"Someone . . . protected Izzy?"

"Yes. Her cellmate. Her name is—"

"Superstition Davis," Garcia said, stalking the hotel suite. "I know who she is. Go on."

"They were in the communal showers when a wolf pack struck. Your sister fought bravely, but she was outmatched."

"She's a scholar, not a warrior," Garcia said.

"Fortunately, the Davis woman is. She took them all out."

Garcia stared at the phone. "She beat six rabid bats?" he said. The Mexican Mafia was so vicious that even the Aryan Brotherhood, the Nazi gang that ran the American prison system, steered a wide berth. "Impossible."

"I didn't believe it either, so I called the warden. It's true. One's in a coma from being slammed into a water pipe. Another's in critical condition with a fractured throat. Two are hospitalized with broken bones, concussions, and other serious injuries. As is Mrs. Davis."

"What happened to her?"

"The lead assassin was about to stab Izzy. Davis jumped between. The shank entered her belly and came out her appendix, tearing out the flesh in between."

Garcia winced, imagining the pain. He'd been shot, stabbed, scalded, and beaten over the years but had never had a toothbrush rip his flesh. "Get my sister out of that hellhole," he said. "I pay you millions, and it's time to earn your *dinero*."

"This isn't Mexico, Jimmy," the lawyer protested. "It's not even Arizona, where I have some clout. These are feds. They don't take bribes, and they don't scare."

"Then cut off their fucking heads. They'll get the message."

"Sure, if you want Special Forces up your ass," the lawyer said. "Put out a hit on a United States Attorney, and that's exactly what you'll get."

"Get. Her. Out."

"I already raised hell with him. He sounded sympathetic. But he's still, quote, 'reviewing the allegations of the boyfriend.' He promises a decision soon."

"What about that video?" Garcia said, his mind racing to find pressure points. "It's incriminating as hell."

"I can leak it to CNN if you want. But if they're going to cave soon, I don't want to risk changing their minds because I pissed them off. My recommendation is to wait while I—"

"You're gone!" Jimmy roared, his immense frustration bleeding from his ears. "Fired! Just like Donald the Trump!"

Silence.

"You can dismiss me anytime you want, Mr. Garcia. I serve at your pleasure. But no other lawyer will spring her faster. I'm pushing this twenty-four-seven, and I'm calling in favors from every congressman I ever met. But it'll take as long as it takes."

Garcia hated situations he couldn't bend to his will. This appeared to be one of them. "Shit."

"You're right. They're shit charges from a shitty prosecutor."

"Just do what you can, then," Garcia said. He paused. "Be sure you wipe afterwards, *amigo*."

"These assholes, I'll use extra paper," the lawyer said, relieved. Cartel legal work was the gift that kept on giving. He had no wish to lose it.

Garcia clicked off. Grabbed tequila from his nightstand. It was a thousand-dollar bottle with a worm wrapped in gold leaf, a gift from his boss. He swallowed four fingers. Four more.

And a couple extra for luck.

He sat on the bed, wondering why the Mexican Mafia, which earned top dollar protecting his sister, would renege on the deal. Rogue element in the prison? Palace coup at headquarters?

Altered contract?

He thought about the questions Delgado kept asking about Izzy giving evidence to the *gringos*. Would the cartel boss assassinate his chief enforcer's kid sister as insurance, knowing that if Jimmy found out, his intestines would squirm on a tabletop as his skin peeled off in strips? Was Jimmy himself in Delgado's gun sights because paranoia didn't need logic, just permission?

No!

Impossible!

Maybe . . .

He shuddered. Decided to quit thinking about it. He'd taken this fancy hotel room to relax, to get away from drugs and tunnels and brutality for just one night. Let the facts sit and percolate, and he'd draw the proper conclusions when it was time. So he pulled out his iPad and looked up Superstition Davis, who'd been on his mind. He studied her chocolate hair and violet eyes and her taut, muscled body. Felt himself stir. Watched the videos of the bar shooting, her bloody and defiant arrest at the blues club. This woman was a dynamo—strength and passion with beauty and poise, no matter how dire the circumstance. *My kind of woman* . . .

Even though she's a cop.

Was a cop, he corrected. The sackless wonders in Chicago had fired her ass for the crime of doing her job.

He admired how she'd kept her cool in the lounge, running and diving and shooting, then kicking that *puta* in the head. He zoomed on the dead black face and replayed the kick, laughing out loud at the ejaculation of blood and spittle. "What you get, pal, picking a fight with Scissorhands!" he crowed, wishing that was him and the U.S. attorney in Phoenix. Tequila clawed and thrashed in his brain. He crunched the gold worm, drained the bottle, and opened another. He read all the news articles and read them again. Figured out where he'd seen Superstition's name originally—in her husband's obituary. He howled at the delicious irony that she'd just saved the family of the man who'd killed hers. He wondered if she knew.

He put on a pay-per-porn and chortled at the fake tits and passion. Called a hooker and ordered her to bring a friend. He wondered if Superstition was good in bed. Decided she was, and even strong enough to hold those weird porno positions that would melt the legs of normal women. He sang *narcocorridos* loud and off-key, glorying in the way the Mexican folk ballads expressed adoration for the *narco* way of life. The songs that featured him he sang top-lung, since he knew the words by heart. The front desk called to say there'd been noise complaints and could he please hold it down. He said sure, no problem. Made a mental note to have the hotel firebombed after he checked out. Replayed the blues-club shooting, clapping each time flame spurted from Superstition's guns. No fake passion here, this is the real deal . . .

He drank more tequila and froze the video on the star of the show. Drank her in.

Chapter 41

UNITED STATES PENITENTIARY
FARGO, NORTH DAKOTA

Superstition groaned as the trusty jostled her intravenous drip.

"I'm sorry, baby," the Colombian murmured, patting her arm. "You all right?"

Superstition nodded, but she didn't mean it. She'd been stuck in the infirmary since her return from emergency surgery in Fargo. She'd saved Izzy's life, and she was proud of that. But she'd gone the max in Fight Club and had no idea if the bone-deep pain that came from that victory would ever disappear entirely.

"You have a visitor, Mrs. Davis," said the prison doctor, a bespectacled coot whose bulbous head rose from his shoulders like the Great Pumpkin.

"I don't want to see anyone," Superstition said.

"He insists," the doctor said. "The warden agreed. Just make it brief. You're out of the woods, but there's still a few trees in your way."

Superstition nodded and pulled the sheet over her breasts, which moved loosey-goosey under the threadbare gown. "Robbie?" she gasped theatrically as the large, familiar presence walked into the room.

Chicago Police Lieutenant Robert Hanrahan twiddled his fingers as they exchanged conspiratorial looks. "How ya doing?" he said.

She struggled to sit taller. Gave up as fresh pain washed her purple and green body. "I'm alive, no thanks to you," she snapped.

He brushed shiny raindrops off his jacket. They fell to the tile like bits of solder. "I called your parents the other day," he said. "They were unusually curt, and then they hung up on me. I gather they think I'm responsible for your being here?"

"You always were the smartest boy in class."

He ignored the snark-shot. "They also said you were attacked by a prison gang. So I flew here to see how you're doing."

"And so you have," she said, glaring. "Now leave."

Hanrahan sighed. "Listen, I know you blame me for—"

"I blame you because it's your fault," she interrupted, voice a pearl of anger. "You told the superintendent I shouldn't be a cop anymore. So here I am, alone in a psycho cage, beaten half to death and whacked out on morphine. That's on you."

Hanrahan folded his arms, tucking his thick hands under his armpits. "You're here because you assaulted an FBI agent. That's not on me—"

"I don't blame you for that. You sold me out with the department, Robbie. That's what hurts the most, and that's entirely your doing."

Hanrahan looked uneasy. "Maybe I should visit tomorrow, when you're feeling better—"

"I'm never going to feel better!" she shouted. "Don't you get it? Never! I have to sell my house. The house my dead husband—remember Derek? Died protecting his country?—and I turned into a home for our children, who are also dead thanks to me being a cop. I have to sell that house to pay my legal bills. My bank accounts are drained. My retirement savings are gone. I eat swill three times a day, and I can't take a crap without people watching."

"I'm sorry," he said.

She waved her hands. "I could have lived with that, you know," she said, forcing her voice to crack. "My home, my stuff, being here, I can deal. What I can't forgive is you. And the department." She shook her head, putting all she had into this performance of a lifetime. "We were family, Robbie. I had your back, you had mine. That's the deal when you put on the badge, right?" Her breathing became labored. "We grab our wounded and carry them to safety, like my husband did for Brian Charvat. Anybody gets in our way, we kick their ass into next Friday."

"Sue, let me—"

"But the minute Mayor No-Balls put the squeeze on to save his political ass from a federal grand jury investigation of his police department, you caved. You told them I shouldn't be a cop anymore. You told them to fire me." Her eyes glowed with tears, which were easy to generate because she hurt so much. "I was a great officer and a really close friend. Yet you treated me like a child molester. You screwed me to make points with the powers that be."

"I'm sorry you feel that way," he said.

The doctor waved his papery hands. "Lieutenant, you should leave."

"Go back to Chicago!" Superstition shouted. "Return to your cushy job and admiring sycophants. Don't ever come back. We were friends, and you stuck a knife in me. You and the department." She slapped her sheets till dust motes filled the air. "What the hell was I thinking, joining the cops? I wish I'd become a criminal. They don't kill their friends. They kill the assholes who hurt their friends." She threw a bandage at him. It bounced off his chest.

"Lieutenant," the doctor warned.

Hanrahan nodded curtly. "See ya, kid," he said, turning away.

"Kiss my ass, old man!" she raged at his back.

He disappeared. She collapsed, panting, into the pillows. "Take it easy, Mrs. Davis," the doctor said, worry bright on his face. "Your blood pressure's gone sky high."

"Wouldn't . . . yours?" she panted.

"If I were betrayed by a friend? You bet," the doctor said.

That surprised her. She'd expected a prison employee to take Hanrahan's side. Maybe this choreographed craziness was working. She'd believed it was going well enough, and the nearly fatal wound convinced her fellow inmates she'd had Izzy's back and was therefore no longer a cop or informant. Even the Mexican Mafia was giving her grudging respect for standing up, though they wouldn't miss the next chance to avenge their one-beats-six humiliation.

The trusty reappeared. Whispered in the doctor's ear. His cheeks and forehead crinkled. He excused himself, glancing back at Superstition as he headed out the door.

Hmmm...

He reappeared ten minutes later, accompanied by a face as stony as the doc's.

"Warden?" Superstition said, surprised, as the trusty cranked her bed to eye level.

"Mrs. Davis," the warden said, hands folded in front, as if delivering a eulogy. "I have some unfortunate news to share."

Superstition's heart began to race. "What?" she said.

The warden grimaced. "I'm sorry to be the one to tell you this, but your mother tried to commit suicide."

She stared. "Huh?" she said dumbly, the statement so bizarre she thought she was hallucinating. Maybe the morphine was playing tricks...

"Your father went out for his daily walk. When he returned home, he found your mother unconscious in their bed. She'd swallowed an entire bottle of pills."

Her throat clutched so tight she could barely breathe. "Jesus! Is she all right?"

"Your father believes so," the warden said. "Paramedics rushed her to emergency, where they pumped out her stomach. They kept her overnight, but she's back home now, resting. Your father called my office, asked me to inform you. He'll come visit you as soon as he can—"

She vomited like she'd guzzled a barrel of bathtub gin.

"Sorry about your moms," the trusty murmured, patting her arm as thunder rattled the walls. "But if she's already back home, she'll be all right. You will, too." The trusty's face radiated kindness. "You kicked ass in the showers, and you're gonna kick this too."

Superstition shook her head as misery enveloped her. She was pretty sure she knew what had prompted the suicide attempt: *Me. Being here.*

Which made her vomit again.

DEB WILLIAMS'S RENTAL HOUSE

The wind howled.

The gloom deepened.

The rain fell.

"How'd it go?" Williams said.

Hanrahan blew the foam off his beer. "Colonoscopy without anesthetic," he said.

"Think they bought it?"

Hanrahan nodded. "Warden says the trusty's a major-league gossip. What we said will spread the word like an oil slick."

Williams smiled. "Sue set the hook nicely."

"Line and sinker too," Hanrahan said.

Williams looked at him. "Yet you're glum."

Hanrahan finished the bottle. Asked for another.

"Hurt to hear it anyway."

"She was acting, Robbie," she reminded. "She thinks the world of you."

"I know," he said, recalling the "hate" on Superstition's bruised face. "Still . . ."

"You're all right, for a flatfoot," Deb said, patting his arm. She let her hand linger on his biceps a moment longer than merely comforting a colleague. She caught herself and took it away. Her feelings for Hanrahan had taken a one-eighty since their up-yours tango at Sue's open house, and she found herself attracted to him. He was smart, streetwise, and protected his blue flock with relentlessness rare in modern management. Not that it mattered, of course—he had little use for her, professionally or otherwise, so she might as well put her feelings on the train to Nowheresville. "Don't worry, we'll make it up to her."

"Gonna take a lot," Hanrahan said. "She was really beat to hell, Deb. Those bruises are the color of comic-book injuries."

"I know. I saw the hospital report." She pulled at her own beer. "We could call it off, you know," she said. "Go after Garcia another way. Director Jerome will approve."

Hanrahan shook his head. "To nail the man who killed her husband," he said, "Sue would eat twenty shivs."

Williams took a long drink. "Speaking of eating, are you interested in Chinese?"

He arched an eyebrow. "They got Chinese in Fargo?"

Williams thought about the HEART-HEALTH-Y wrap she'd eaten last night. She'd picked it up at a local diner and brought it to the house. She paired it with a salad and water from the fridge, sat at her table, and took a bite. It tasted . . . brown. She pitched the rest in the garbage and pulled out her emergency stash of Nutella, which she ate straight from the jar. It tasted so good she almost forgot her aching ribs.

"Sure they do. Macaroni in soy sauce," she said.

"Pass," he said, shuddering. "What else could we eat?"

She took a deep breath.

Slowly ran her index finger down his arm.

Hanrahan caught the meaning. Given their stormy history, he was astounded. Given it was her, he was transfixed. Even if she was a Feeb.

"J. Edgar approve of that sort of thing?" he said.

"Hoover did it in a dress," she said.

"But you're not wearing one," he said.

"We'll make do," she said, undoing the snap on her jeans.

"I thought you hated me," Hanrahan said as his racing heart finally began to calm.

"I do," Deb said.

He waved his hand at her gloriously nude body. "So?"

Deb grinned. "My boss is a fan of interagency cooperation. So I am, uh—"

"Cooperating?"

"And they said cops aren't smart," she said, stretching languidly.

Hanrahan admired the view, which radiated swamp heat so intense it could melt a Fargo winter. "Smart enough to like you," he murmured. Which astounded him even more than her courageous invitation. Deb was wholesome and sensible, not the high-wire acts he normally found himself chasing. She was intelligent, worked her ass off, and didn't give an inch when pushed. And, while not showgirl exotic, she was pretty in a way he liked. Maybe that's what he'd been looking for all along: a special kind of exotic.

He started for a cigarette, then repressed the urge, resettling in his pillow and hoping she hadn't noticed. He caught her knowing look and shrugged, kind of embarrassed, like a kid caught stealing rubbers. "Being an asshole earned me an ex," he said. "I thought I'd try something new. Surprised?"

Deb rested her cheek on his shoulder, which crawled with worm-scars from bullet holes. "Kinda," she admitted. "Considering you dig cover models, and I'm plain Jane."

He ran a hand across her breasts. She was warm. He was gentle. It was nice. "You're as plain as Helen of Troy," he said.

The face that launched a thousand ships? Williams thought, astonished. *That Helen?* The unexpected compliment made her brain fizz. She was single because she was scary smart, equally sarcastic, wore a gun, loved a bloody homicide scene, and radiated the exoticness of a gray bath towel. Men didn't mind that for romping, but took a powder when she hinted at her desire for something more lasting. "A literary reference?" she teased to cover her anxiety over getting in deeper with Hanrahan. "From a vice cop?"

"I read the classics when I'm not busting gash hounds," he said. "And believe it or not, I try not to be a dick all the time. Especially where certain people are involved."

" 'Certain?' " she said, wanting him to say it because no man ever had.

"Well, uh, you."

Deb wriggled closer to Hanrahan's body, which was finely sculpted, she noted, but more like Hercules than David. Or the Incredible Hulk. He smoked like a factory fire, one cigarette after the next, and he didn't care who objected. He was sarcastic and gruff, jumping at her from shadows, pushing himself into her comfort zone, spitting at her feet when she challenged his detective's honor. He hunted exotic prey, and it cost him his marriage.

But an hour ago, on the sofa, he'd made that nice return of her quip on J. Edgar's dress, and she'd shocked herself by unsnapping her jeans. He'd smiled, stood up, and kissed her, very gently, feathers on silk. She hadn't pulled away, and their kissis became more sensual. He finally broke off, saying he needed to use the bathroom. She'd pointed to the door, hand shaking with the adrenaline surge of the unknown. The lieutenant ambled inside, looked back at her, then closed the door and did, she presumed, his business. Then he'd turned on the faucet. A moment later, another sound left the bathroom, faint but familiar. Intrigued, she tiptoed to the door to listen.

He was brushing his teeth.

She kept a few spares in a glass on the sink—in addition to her mouth, she used toothbrushes to clean crud from her gun—so he must have unwrapped one and started in. That was such an unexpected thoughtfulness—freshening his breath in case she might permit him to take her all the way—that her heart went into overdrive.

The faucet went off, and she hurried back to the sofa. He ambled out, took his place, and continued their kisses, which led to caresses, which became teasing and silliness, then the removal of their clothing one button at a time, then kisses urgent and hot and sloppy, their skin shining with sweat and anticipation, his large, callused hands caressing through her gossamer underwear, her nipples popping like kernels on high heat, as they transferred from the sofa to the bed, careful not to bang her ribs. The sensation was so shivery joyous, she began to wonder: *Is this for real? Or an exhaustion-driven sleep fantasy . . .*

Deb bumped her hand down Robbie's abs, then crept farther south.

Nope, it's the real deal.

"I thought you didn't like me, either," she said.

"I guess you grew on me."

"You, uh, too," she said pointedly.

He looked down.

Grinned.

And kissed her, minty-fresh, all the way downtown . . .

"Oh, Jesus, not now," she moaned as her Bureau phone trilled.

"You'd better pick up, Agent Double-Oh-Wow," Hanrahan said. "It might be J. Edgar, wondering who stole his dress."

She groaned but knew she needed to answer. She pushed CONNECT and said, "This is Williams," as she tried to steady her breathing. That the lieutenant was taking the time and effort to pay attention to what her body wanted, as opposed to what his wanted, made her want him even more. Women appreciated romance, not *wham-bam*, though a little *wham* was cool, and even the occasional *bam*, but only if she liked the guy to begin with, and with Hanrahan, that hadn't been the case at all, or maybe it had, but she hadn't read the hidden signals until tonight. Maybe he was lonely just like her. Maybe they could be lonely together and see what happened.

"Jerome here. Anything new to report?"

Hanrahan moved away to give her space. She grabbed his hair and guided him back.

"Sue's been in more gang fights," she said, feeling Hanrahan grin at her tricky high-wire act. "She's still winning, but they're wearing her down."

"Worrisome," Jerome said. "Can she keep it up? Should I pull her out?"

Don't say pull out! "I don't think so," Deb said, her molecules doing a rhumba as Robbie worked his silent magic. "The lieutenant says she'll thrust ahead"—she felt him poke her down there and almost burst out laughing—"no matter how many shivs come her way."

"What I figured, too," Jerome said. "So we'll leave her in place." Pause. "I hear noises in the background. Is someone with you?"

"Uh, yes, the lieutenant stopped by. We're comparing notes," she said, letting out a small peep as Hanrahan found what she was looking for.

"What are you doing? Eating supper?" Jerome said, mistaking the sound for food.

She flushed. It had been a long time, and surely Mother Bureau could wait a few more hours before demanding more work from her daughter . . .

"That too," she said pointedly.

Silence.

Then a chuckle.

"Carry on, special agent," he said.

"Sir, yes sir," she said, disconnecting.

Hanrahan looked up.

"Jerome Jerome?"

"The one and only."

THE FURY

"What'd he say?"
 She ran her fingers through his dark, knotty hair.
"He said to carry on."
 Which they did.

Chapter 42

FEDERAL BUILDING
PHOENIX, ARIZONA

"It's a miracle Miss Garcia wasn't killed," the U.S. attorney said.

"The bigger miracle was another con protected her," the AUSA said. "That never happens."

"Well, she's an ex-cop," the U.S. attorney said. "Still got the ol' serve-and-protect thing going, I guess. What's she in for, anyway?"

The AUSA looked it up on his iPad. Chuckled. "She punched an FBI agent," he said.

They shook their heads in wonder, wishing they could punch FBI agents. They were so goddamned *smug*...

"We need to spring Izzy," the AUSA said. "Even under her brother's protection she made somebody's hit list. If she gets killed..."

"If she gets killed," the U.S. attorney said, picking up the thought, "her lawyer will leak the parking garage video, suggesting we were less than diligent in clearing an innocent woman. We'll wind up in Juneau, taking depositions from yaks."

"I thought it was North Dakota."

"Same difference."

They sighed.

"It was fun messing with Jimmy," the U.S. attorney said. "But all good things must come to an end. Get his sister out of Fargo."

The AUSA texted a friend in the Bureau of Prisons, getting the process started. "Should we reward Superstition for saving our ass?"

The U.S. attorney loosened his tie. "Maybe I've gotten soft, but that sounds like a good idea. You bird-dog Izzy's release. I'll call the judge who sentenced Superstition, get him to see things our way."

"Delay her release awhile, though, right?" the AUSA suggested. "So the press doesn't claim it's a quid pro quo?"

The U.S. attorney nodded, pleased at the man's initiative. "When I retire next year," he said, patting the arms of his chair, "I'm going to make sure they put you in this job."

"Hey, what'd I ever do to you?" the AUSA said.

Chapter 43

SUPERSTITION'S NEW HOME
CHICAGO

She locked the house and walked to her car, shaking her head. Robbie had warned her the new digs "needed some work," but that was like saying the *Titanic* needed fresh paint. It beat prison, she supposed. Not by much, but still . . .

She glared at the drug boys hooting their wares on the corners. She climbed into the rusted Fiesta she'd bought with money she'd squirreled away with a friend before incarceration and headed for what used to be her home in Edison Park.

"Man," she muttered, watching the commotion from down the street. A realtor hammered a SOLD! sign into the soft ground. Workers lugged her leather sofa, the "Derek dent" still visible, to an idling truck. Crates from her breakfront followed. The beloved basement bar they'd built from the distillery lumber rescued in Scotland inched unsteadily toward a U-Haul.

When they worked out the details of this operation on Killer Bee's patio in Arizona, Robbie suggested the FBI send in straw purchasers with federal money. "Feebs got more money than Scrooge McDuck," he'd said. "Spend a little buying her stuff so she gets it back after."

Jerome Jerome said he'd considered that, but with the cartels having their fingers in so many law-enforcement pies, the loss of Superstition's savings, home, and possessions would have to be genuine or Garcia might sniff it out. They'd argued heatedly, but Superstition agreed with Jerome. Reluctantly, because she really did love her home, but a fire sale was the right call . . .

"Eep!" she yelped at the knock on her window. It was her next-door neighbor, Clayton Brooks, smiling like he'd just seen Jesus in a 7-Eleven. She rolled down the window and twiddled her fingers. "Hey, neighbor," she said. "Long time no see."

"I was out walking Kilroy," Brooks said, patting his fake leg. "I saw you sitting here all lonesome and thought I'd welcome you home."

"Come sit with me," she said, patting the passenger seat. He climbed inside and grimaced. "Man, this stinks," he said.

"I know," she said. "But a rusted-out Fiesta's all I can afford—"

"No." Brooks waved his hand across the landscape. *"This."*

"Yeah," she said glumly. "I sold all my memories to feed the law shark."

"The Sacrifice of Isaac," Brooks mused. "With your lawyer holding the knife." He shook his head. "Are you moving in with your folks?"

"Nope. I found my own place, near Pulaski and Division."

He frowned. "Humboldt Park," he said. "Dangerous."

"Affordable," she countered.

"I got money," he said. "Happy to let you have some to find a nicer 'hood."

She was touched and said so. "But I can't depend on handouts."

"Friendship ain't charity," Brooks said. "Or so an angel told me after I lost my leg."

"I know, Clayton," Superstition said, remembering exactly what she'd argued in his hospital room. "You're so sweet to offer. But right now . . ."

"Just call me," he said, touching her arm. "Whenever. Whatever."

She kissed his cheek. A mover dropped his end of the bar with a loud curse. A corner broke, flinging shards of malted wood into the gutter.

"Like my life," she muttered, her heart breaking anew as the movers spit on their hands, rehefted, and pushed it into the U-Haul. It reminded her of a python stretching its jaws to swallow an antelope whole. "That's the one thing really killing me," she said, eyes brightening as the truck lumbered away. "That bar was me and Derek."

"You couldn't hide it from the wolves?"

"I tried," she said. "But my jerk of a lawyer snuck his PI inside and made a video inventory. The bar was the final payment to settle his bill."

"Cockroach," he said.

"Got those too," she said. "My place is fully furnished."

He laughed, then sobered. "Hey, how's your mother doing?" he said, touching her hand. "I saw the ambulance and went over to help your dad . . ."

"I don't know. I haven't told them I'm back."

"What?"

The warden had dropped by unannounced, saying the judge who'd convicted and sentenced her decided to reward her bravery with early release. The warden said she was entitled by company policy to one hundred dollars, a bus ticket anywhere in the continental United States, the clothes and money she'd surrendered during intake, and a lift to the Greyhound terminal in Fargo. The process was stark and unemotional; how prisons said good-bye. "I got back last week," she said. "Found the rental house yesterday and moved in."

"Where'd you stay meantime?" Brooks said.

"Sky King." A hot-sheet motel on Lincoln Avenue on the city's North Side. The booty-shrieks from neighboring rooms kept her up nights, but the price was right.

"Man," he said, shaking his head. "I would have given you my guest room."

"I know," she said. "But I couldn't see anyone I knew right away. Including my parents." She took a deep breath, released it. "I needed time to decompress, and I do that better alone."

"But now it's time to face the world?"

"Yeah."

He put up his fist. She bumped it.

"Our door is always open," he said, patting Kilroy. "My checkbook is too. Can I at least send you a housewarming gift?"

She laughed, thinking of her corner-boy "neighbors."

"Where I live, you'd better make it a shotgun," she said.

THE FURY

TAMPICO, GULF COAST OF MEXICO

"I can't believe it, *hombre*," Tomas crowed. "No matter how much I spend, the money bag doesn't shrink."

"Mine either," Juan agreed, raising his glass of Corona.

"I wonder what my cousin did with those bombs?" Tomas said.

Juan's eyes grew fearful. "Shhh," he hissed, looking around. "Jimmy has spies everywhere."

"Nobody can hear us," Tomas said, draining the pitcher. "My voice is soft as kittens."

"Except that you screech when you're drunk," Juan said.

"Said the kettle to the pan."

"Pot."

"No, thanks, I'll stick with beer," Tomas said, giggling from too much of it.

Juan laughed with him. "I suppose I'm too jumpy," he said. "Those weapons gave me the creeps, that's all."

"Birds took one whiff of that gas and *poom*, down for the count," Tomas agreed. "The U.S. Army takes its bombs seriously. Even if they do look like cigars."

"Cigars that explode in your mouth," Juan said.

They pounded the table, laughing. "Oh, man," Juan said. "I hope Jimmy didn't touch a nose cone when he carted them to his mountain ranch."

"I would have heard if he did, believe me," Tomas said. "I'm sure he arrived safely."

"He's a brave man," Juan said.

"The bravest," Tomas agreed. "*Narcos* are tougher than generals and kings. They even have ballads written about them!" He grew quiet, then tugged on his lower lip, looking ashamed. "Did I tell you I wet my pants when my leg fell in that hole?"

"No!"

"Well, I did."

"Huh. I thought I smelled a wet skunk but figured it was just your normal B.O. . . ."

They rabbit-punched each other's arms, giggling. The busboy picked up their empty pitcher and replaced it with fresh Corona. He moved to the adjoining table, wiping up peanuts and spills, then went back to the bar. "Take your break," his boss said.

The busboy nodded and walked outside. Looked around to ensure he was alone. Fired up a Lucky Strike and sucked it down to his toes.

Made a call.

WASHINGTON, D.C.

"Got. You," the CIA director crowed as he disconnected from the station chief in Mexico City.

"Got. Who?" the deputy director said, looking up from the budget spreadsheets they were rewriting to fund additional black operations in Pakistan, where terrorism had flared anew.

"Jimmy Garcia, the man with the nerve gas bombs," the director said.

"Garcia? I thought he was a *narco*."

"He is," the director said. "But now he's a terrorist. A busboy in Mexico just overheard two men talking about poisoned birds, cigar-shaped bombs, and their *narco* cousin who grabbed them off that beach. Busboy knows for certain the cousin is Jimmy, and he heard there's a serious reward for selling him to us."

"Does he know where Jimmy took the bombs?"

"Does the pope wear holy underwear?"

The deputy poured Blue Label as his boss punched up the White House.

A RESTAURANT IN NOGALES, MEXICO

"So these are the real deal," Jimmy said between bites of *camarones a la diabla*.

"*Sí, Jefe,*" his weapons expert confirmed. "They're VX nerve gas, manufactured by the United States Army during the Cold War."

"VX. That's the worst, right?"

The weapons man nodded. "A German scientist invented the first nerve agents, tabun and sarin, in the 1930s," he said. "Over the years, more potent versions were created, till finally, the British created VX. It remains the most deadly and fast-acting of all nerve agents." He pulled a green tomato from his sandwich, dipped it in mayonnaise, and ate it separately. "But your bombs are even worse."

Jimmy raised an eyebrow. "What can be worse than 'worst'?"

"The Americans sprinkled anthrax into the batter."

Jimmy whistled. "And they say *narcos* are ruthless."

"It was the height of the Cold War," the weapons man said. "The Americans were paranoid that Soviet armored divisions would invade Western Europe but were equally afraid that dropping atomic bombs to stop them would launch World War Three."

"So they went with VX, anthrax, and Ronnie the Reagan."

The weapons man crunched a fried plantain. "Eventually, the Soviet empire crumbled. America cornered the market on thermonuclear weapons and didn't need VX anymore. They dumped all their nerve bombs in the oceans, never to be seen again."

"Till now," Jimmy said.

"That's the thing about 'never,' " the weapons man said, using air quotes.

Jimmy snapped his fingers at the waiter. "Dessert menus, if you please," he said, adding the last to appear pleasant. The waiter ran for them, knowing better. "On the beach, they'd explode if you looked at them funny," Jimmy said. "That still the case?"

"No," the weapons man said, pushing his Harry Potter glasses up his needle nose. "I replaced the detonators with a modern design, then fitted them with remote controls. They won't go off unless you say so." He handed his boss an iPhone, along with a list of telephone numbers. "Each bomb has its own number. Dial it. A window will appear, asking for your passcode. Enter that. A second window appears. Enter the second passcode."

"Then?"

"Hold your ears."

"It's just like a spy movie," Jimmy said, intrigued.

"I did get the idea from the new Bourne," he said, merriment in his droopy eyes.

Jimmy laughed. "I knew Hollywood was good for something besides date nights. Are these remotes the only way to trigger the bombs?"

"Yes. That's what you asked for—"

"I know, I'm just thinking about further possibilities," Jimmy said. "For instance, can they be launched from drones? Dropped from airplanes? Put in the warheads of missiles?"

The weapons man pulled out a sketchbook, made some doodles, and surrounded them with equations. "Yes," he said, looking up. "Missiles would be the fastest to bring on line, since you gave me some to play with."

Jimmy nodded. A handful of tactical missiles came with the drug shipment from the Taliban. Payment for some favor Delgado granted their ayatollah or mullah or gonad or whatever the sand-sniffers called their fearless leader these days.

"Experiment to your heart's content," Jimmy said. "Just make it fast. Meantime, load two nerve bombs in my truck and move the rest to the storage site."

"Done," the weapons man said.

"Here are your menus," the nervous waiter said.

"Bring us a bottle of your finest tequila," Jimmy said. "And two orders of whatever my friend is having for dessert . . ."

Chapter 44

NOGALES, ARIZONA

"Howzit going?" Brian Charvat said, hopping out of his dusty Jeep. He'd noticed the flashing lights and stopped to offer assistance.

The cop pointed to the blood-spattered U.S. Postal Service truck. "It flattened a citizen."

"Dead?"

"As my dick."

Charvat laughed. "Mind if I take a peek?"

The cop wagged his eyebrows.

"No, thanks," Charvat said, playing along. "That's so massive I'd faint and hit my head, and I don't need that shit again. I wanna see your crime scene."

"Be my guest," the cop said, laughing. He didn't insult the Border Patrol chief with reminders to stay outside the yellow tape. The man was highly respected before he was shot. Now he was a legend. He even liked dick jokes.

Charvat wandered over, greeting cops, paramedics, and coroners. Law enforcement was a ball game, and he knew all the players—

He stopped like he'd been smacked with a bat. "Jesus H. Christ in a scoop-neck dress," he swore, hustling to the cops interviewing the driver.

"He fell off the curb!" the driver was shouting. "Right in front of me! I couldn't stop in time, Officer, I couldn't hit the brakes fast enough—"

"S'okay, it's all right," the interviewer assured. "It's not your fault, buddy, it's just bad luck—oh, hey, Bee."

Charvat gave him a head waggle. The cop finished up, walked over, stuck out his hand.

"What's new, Magoo?" he said.

"I know the deceased," Charvat said, shaking back. "Joseph Stancato."

"Joey the Mailman?" the cop said, surprised. "Cripes, I didn't recognize him." *Reck-a-nize.*

Charvat took a long look at his snitch, who was facedown on the sticky pavement. His bloody head was flat as a minute steak. His legs were straight and his toes pointed, as if executing a high dive. His arms angled out like tree branches. One hand was empty. The other clutched a Priority Mail carton. Plastic bags of marijuana spilled from the torn edge.

"No wonder. His own mother wouldn't recognize him," Charvat said. "What happened?"

The cop flipped through his notes. "Driver says Joey was fidgeting on the sidewalk. Looking around, stepping back and forth, glancing at his watch—you know."

"Doing the dope-head boogie," Charvat said.

The cop nodded. "Mail truck slowed in case he was going to jaywalk, but Joey waved him on. Driver got up to speed. Joey turned around to cross the street, but he was too close to the curb. He lost his footing and fell into the path of the truck. Brain soufflé."

Charvat appreciated black humor, but "brain soufflé" was pushing it. "Anyone think it was deliberate?" he said. "Like Joey was offing himself?"

"Driver says no. It appears to be an honest accident." The cop grinned, then fished again for a riff. "Stamp him special delivery?"

Charvat blew air out his nose. Joey the Mailman wasn't the salt of the earth, but he didn't steal, cheat his employees, abuse his women, or lie without a good reason. He supplied what the market demanded—pot and information—which helped Charvat drag some truly vile characters off the street. He wasn't Father Flanagan, no. But he deserved a better end than this.

Charvat looked at the slender, cooling corpse.

Then up at the sky.

"Return to sender," he said. "I hope."

JIMMY GARCIA'S RANCH, SIERRA MADRE MOUNTAINS

"God, it's wonderful to be home," Isabel Garcia said, drinking in the mountains like she'd never seen them before. "You have no idea how awful it was in there."

Jimmy did have an idea, actually, having been clapped into hard-core Mexican lockups—moldy food, scorpions, drunk and sadistic guards—till he paid the "bail." But hell, this was Izzy's nightmare; let her tell it her way. "I felt awful, not being able to spring you."

"You tried, big brother," she said, patting his face the way their father did when they were young. "That's all that matters to me—you tried."

He shook his head, still angry with himself. "I failed, little sister," he said. "You suffered the price. But I'll deliver payback to the bastard who put you there." He smiled at how he'd decided to exact that particular pound of flesh.

Her eyes darkened. "Not by yourself, you won't."

He cocked his head. Before prison, she wanted nothing to do with violence. Then again, prison left its heaviest scars on the innocent. "You want in on punishing your ex?"

"All the way." She sipped her margarita, which her brother had thoughtfully rechilled while she was napping. A cartel security truck rolled by, rooster tail of dust spinning lazily into the sunshine. "You know what else I want even more than watching him suffer, though? More than anything else in the world?"

"Name it."

"I want you to meet Sue."

He raised an eyebrow. "I'm wanted from Nome to Newark, Sis," he said.

Izzy sighed. "I know, I know," she said, fluttering her hands. "It's just a silly dream. I think of her as a sister now, and I miss her, that's all."

"Not surprising," he said. "She kept you going day to day, and then she saved your life."

Izzy teared up. "She wasn't friends with me to get something from you. She liked me just for me." Fat shining sorrow ran down her high-boned cheeks. "That assassin opened her belly like a can of stew, and all her blood jumped out. It was supposed to be me lying on that floor, Jimmy, not her. She took that shank for me."

He embraced her as she wept.

"I'm going to lie down again," she finally said, wiping the tears from her face.

"That's your third nap today," Jimmy said, concerned. "Do you feel all right?"

"Physically, yes, I'm fine. Emotionally, not so much." She shrugged, looking glum. "Since I got out, all I want to do is sleep."

"If it helps you cope, then sweet dreams, Sis," he said, pinching her cheek.

She stumbled off.

He considered what she'd asked.

He pulled out his phone.

Issued orders.

Chapter 45

SUPERSTITION'S PARENTS' HOUSE
CHICAGO

The front door creaked like an opening coffin. It reminded Superstition of the low-budget Svengoolie films she and her dad watched on the family Zenith when she was a kid.

"George?" her mother yelled. "Is that you?"

"No," Superstition said, pushing inside the house to the sound of running feet.

"My God," Theresa Kallas choked, clutching her chest. "You're... you're..."

"The judge said I was rehabilitated," Superstition said. "So here I am."

Theresa began to sob. Reached for her daughter. Superstition took a step back, still angry that her mother wouldn't talk to her after the suicide attempt, refusing to get on the phone the few times Superstition was able to call home from prison. But Mom looked so pathetic, arms hanging midair, face sliding like butter out of the fridge too long.

"Aw, geez, Mom, why'd you go and do it?" she muttered. "You scared me half to death."

They embraced. Theresa cried so hard that she began to hiccup.

"Hello?" her father shouted from the kitchen.

"In here!"

Quick heavy thumps.

"Skeeter, as I live and breathe," George Kallas said, grinning so widely that his eyes disappeared.

"The judge ordered an early release," she said. "I took the Greyhound home."

George grimaced. "The bus? You should have called. We would have driven to Fargo."

She embraced him, three becoming one. Then she pushed him away. "I want to talk to Mom," she said.

"Yes, I imagine you do," he said, nodding. "I've got things to do in the garage—"

"No!" Theresa said, panicking. "George, you stay, I'll put up some coffee and we'll all—"

"No, Mom," Superstition said. "We have to clear the air."

"No, really, I can't—"

"Now." Pause. "Or I won't be back."

Theresa sagged, defeated.

Superstition was shocked at how deeply the woman had shrunken into herself. Her hair, always perfectly dyed and coiffed, was shot with gray split ends. Her clothes were damp and formless, and by their aroma, hadn't been changed in days.

George disappeared. Superstition led them into the living room, Mom shuffling like the undead. They sat on the paisley divan. Theresa made sounds in her throat. Superstition put her arm around her shoulders, which shook like DT tremors.

"Why did you try to kill yourself, Mom?" she said gently.

Theresa huffed but didn't answer. Superstition tightened her grip.

"You abandoned me in there," she said. "You quit writing letters. I called, and you wouldn't get on the phone. Tell me why."

More trembling but still no explanation. Superstition shook her mother like a rag doll, her suppressed anger finally spilling over. "Dammit, Mother, you owe me an explanation!" she shouted. "Do you know how hard it was on me, hearing that you'd swallowed those pills? A lethal fucking dose?" She fought her own emotions in order to stay on point. "Do you know how guilty I feel, knowing I was the cause—"

"You aren't!" Theresa cried, leaping to her feet. "I am! I swallowed those pills because I sent you to that hellhole! Me! Not you! Me!"

Superstition shook her head. "No, Mom. Prison was my fault."

"I'm the murderer, not you," Theresa said. "It should have been me, not you, in that cell."

"Come on, how can you possibly believe that?" Superstition said, astonished at how delusional her mother had become in the time she'd been away. "I shot those three men, not you. I called them black-eyed sons of bitches, not you. You didn't kill anyone, Mom. You didn't do anything wrong. You never do. You're the most moral person I know—"

Theresa swept her arm down the fireplace mantel. Delicate jade and china figurines, which she'd collected on vacation cruises with her husband, arched through the air and shattered on impact, their shards jumping around like crickets.

"Mom!" Superstition gasped, shocked at her unexpected violence. "What are you—"

Theresa deflated as quickly as she'd ignited and curled her hands into tight little balls. "Oh, honey, I never wanted to tell you this," she said. "But I guess there's no longer any choice." She took a deep breath and let it out with a pursed-lips *ffffffff*. "I'm an assassin."

"Assassin? Really?" Superstition said carefully. This level of delusion was beyond her skills; Mom needed professional help. "How do you figure—"

"I killed the man who murdered your babies."

"Uh," Superstition said, blinking rapidly as her wounds started the anvil chorus.

"I know you don't believe me, but it's true: I hired a hit man to stab Maurice Bishop in jail. And when that bastard was dead, I danced a jig. A happy, lovely, loud Irish jig, at the foot of the bed where you were conceived." Her bottled emotions poured out, hot as lava. "I thought it would give me peace, killing that bastard. But all it did was put you in prison. Knowing you were there, being attacked by gang after gang, made me so insane I swallowed those pills." She wept. "Forgive me for doing this to you, Sue. God forgive me."

Superstition sat back, stunned.

"It was a month after you buried Timmy and Tommy. I had gone back at work at the Teamsters office," Theresa explained. "I was sitting at my desk, typing reports, and Jerzy noticed me sobbing. You remember Jerzy?"

Superstition nodded. Jerzy Petrovic was a Croatian slab of beef that enforced union rules for the International Brotherhood of Teamsters. Back in the day, he broke kneecaps, firebombed the cars of strikebreakers, and scared up votes for politicians who supported "da working men and womens of America." When bodily harm became politically unacceptable as a means of intimidation, he turned to more elegant methods—computer viruses, threats on Twitter—but the result was the same: *Cross us at your peril.*

"But Dad was a Teamster enforcer too," she said. "He never killed anyone."

"That's because of you, honey. Early on, your father cracked heads just like Jerzy. But after you were born he moved to the financial side—delivering money to strikers, arranging insurance for widows, untangling pension disputes, all that. After a while he even gave that up, and chose to drive the mosquito truck."

"Why?"

"If he'd stayed in enforcement, even financial, he knew he might wind up in prison. That wasn't an acceptable risk, not with you wrapping him around your pretty little finger. So he climbed in his truck and never looked back."

Superstition smiled, recalling the graveled potholes they'd bounced across, seeing if they could smack their heads on the roof. He'd chosen to do that for her . . .

Theresa wiped her eyes. "Anyway, Jerzy asked why I was crying."

"He didn't already know?"

Theresa shook her head. "He'd been traveling, setting up union outreach centers overseas. He'd just returned. I told him a gang member named Maurice Bishop kicked my grandchildren to death and put you in a hospital. He nodded and left. The next day, he took me out for coffee and asked if I wanted to do something about it. I asked what. He said, and I quote, 'Ace the spade. Courts don't got the balls.'"

"And?"

"I said yes."

Superstition was horrified and fascinated. She took her mother's trembling hands, asked her to continue.

"One of Jerzy's pals was doing a burglary bid in Cook County Jail. The friend had bone cancer, and it was untreatable. Jerzy promised the Teamster pension fund would take care of his family if the friend took care of a problem."

"The problem being Maurice Bishop."

"Momo was breathing, and my grandsons weren't," Theresa snapped, using Bishop's street name. "Jerzy's pal sliced Momo's throat on the way to the showers. Cut out his tongue for good measure and put out the word that Momo was a snitch."

"Which kept anyone from giving a damn," Superstition said.

"Cops *or* cons," Theresa agreed. "The friend died of cancer four months later."

"And Jerzy?"

"He retired to Costa Rica, where he runs a beachside bar. He sends us a Christmas card every year, hoping you're doing all right."

Superstition nodded. "Does Dad know?"

Theresa shook her head. "He was over the moon someone killed Bishop. I saw no reason to tell him it was me. He'd worry. I didn't want him to worry. So I kept it to myself. I just didn't realize how enormous a burden it would become, keeping secrets from everyone I loved."

Superstition nodded and tried to match all she'd said with Fargo. Couldn't.

"But why would *your* killing Bishop put *me* in prison?"

Theresa fluttered her hands. "If you weren't a police officer, you wouldn't have worn a badge at the car wash that day . . ."

Superstition shuddered, remembering.

Sun glittering. Air chilling. Clean tires dripping. Tattooed man drying. Blue puddle shimmering under high-top boots. Him waving a rag that said he was finished. Me pulling back jacket to fish out his tip. Him seeing the star on my belt, growing pale, tightening his lips. Me asking if he was all right. Him pulling back and kicking me deep in my pregnant belly, deep into the brains of my twins. Me tumbling to the asphalt, shrieking and paralyzed, unable to go for the gun in my pocket. Him kicking my belly again, driving his boot, flashing gang signs, rolling me over, stomping now, heel-heavy, rupturing me, dismembering my children, screaming that cops killed his brother so he'd kill me in revenge, Timmy and Tommy dead and me going fast, saved only by the rack of a shotgun by the manager of the car wash. Me whisked to Lutheran General for the first of nine surgeries. Him "subdued" by a hornet's nest of cops. Him booked in Cook County Jail, with word going out that he'd murdered a cop's children . . .

She opened her eyes as Mom continued. "If you didn't have that badge, Bishop wouldn't have kicked you. If Bishop didn't kick you, your babies would be alive. If your babies were alive, I wouldn't have killed Bishop, and Derek wouldn't have gone to Arizona, because he'd rather be home with you and the boys." She wrung her hands white. "If he hadn't gone to Arizona, he wouldn't have been murdered. If he hadn't been murdered, you wouldn't have had that party at Kingston Mines, that FBI woman wouldn't have shown up, and you wouldn't have broken her ribs."

"And if I hadn't broken her ribs," Superstition said, bringing it full circle, "I wouldn't have been sent to Fargo, and you wouldn't have become so unhinged with guilt that you tried to end your misery with a bottle of pills."

A long silence as they both chased down the bouncing ball.

"Mom," Superstition said. "That's crazy."

Theresa smiled for the first time since her daughter walked through the door.

"Now you tell me?"

Chapter 46

A SMALL PRIVATE AIRPORT IN MEXICO

"It's true?" Vincente Delgado whispered with shocked disbelief. "You got me a weapon of mass destruction?"

"More than one, *Jefe*," Jimmy said. "They're nerve gas, mixed with anthrax." He explained the find on the beach. "One whiff and your enemies go down for the count."

"How lethal is this VX?"

"Like nothing you've ever seen," Jimmy said. "One drop kills a full-grown adult. Every bomb contains a million drops. Do you want to see them?"

"Of course," Delgado said, wheeling his chair the length of his balcony. He'd taken a bad tumble the other day and broken his leg in four places. "But I'm stuck here."

"Got that covered," Jimmy said. "Javier is bringing you one as we speak."

"Javier? Why not you?"

"The truck tunnel is still behind schedule. I'm heading there to kick ass."

"I thought your boy was handling that," Delgado said.

"He's young and therefore unsure about how hard to squeeze men who are older than himself." Jimmy breathed as evenly as he knew how. "I told him to bring one of the weapons to your place while I give the tunnel men the proper, uh, motivation to perform a hard day's work."

Delgado's eyes gleamed at the prospect of violence unleashed. "All right, then, Javier it is," he said. "I appreciate your thoughtfulness."

"It's my pleasure, *Jefe*," Jimmy said.

"It won't blow up in my face, right?" Delgado kidded.

"Not unless you punch in the passcodes," Jimmy said, explaining how the remote detonator worked. "Which Javier will turn over when he arrives."

"You said more than one weapon. Where are the rest?"

"I locked them in our secure facility," Jimmy said. "But I thought you should have one for your trophy room. As a symbol of what you are capable of."

"You thought well," Delgado said. "Come to the house when you're done kicking ass. We'll roast a lamb to celebrate."

"The moment I'm free, I'll head your way," Jimmy assured him, looking at his watch. "Meantime, Javier is nearing your driveway. Warn your security team he's coming. I'd hate to lose such a promising employee because of a guard's itchy trigger finger."

"I'll take care of it, *amigo*," Delgado said. "Oh, and if I didn't mention it before, I'm delighted your sister is back home. Is she recovering?"

"She sleeps a lot," Jimmy said. "It lets the brain forget the horrors it has witnessed. Otherwise, she's doing well."

"Glad to hear that, she's a good girl. Did she get my flowers?"

"She did, *Jefe*, and she's writing a note to thank you properly," Jimmy said. "Did our friend in Mexican Mafia explain how the attack happened?"

"Rogue element inside the prison, apparently," Delgado lied. "Their *jefe* promises he will burn all six most cruelly."

"He also repaid the protection money?"

"He knows how things work," Delgado said. "Your money's in my safe. Be sure to pick it up when you arrive." He sighed theatrically. "It's tragic what happened to Isabel in Fargo, but traitorous elements pop up time to time in our business."

"Don't I know it," Jimmy murmured.

"What? I can't hear you."

Jimmy slapped the phone on his chest. "Looks like . . . breaking up," he said, wheezing to heighten the illusion. "A dead zone . . . I . . . call . . . when . . . way."

"Hurry. We'll christen my bomb with the '88 Krug in my cellar—"

Jimmy disconnected and called Javier. "Any problems?"

"None," Javier said, turning onto the long gravel road to the supreme commander's fortress. "I see the house now."

"Thank you for handling this," Jimmy said. "You really stepped up to the plate, and I won't forget."

"I appreciate your trust, *Jefe*," Javier said, over the moon to be entrusted with such an important job. "You're meeting us here, right?"

"As soon as I can," Jimmy said.

He disconnected, then walked out of the airport's waiting room, which he'd ordered cleared for privacy. He walked onto the runway apron, squinting against the brightness. He slipped on his Ray-Bans, frowned, and wiped off the smudges with a shirttail.

"Come on, Jimmy!" Izzy cried from the stairs of the executive jet. "If we leave right now, we can avoid the thunderstorms moving in from the Gulf!"

Jimmy laughed to himself. The real storm was in his pocket.

He slipped into his leather seat as the cabin door closed for takeoff. The attendant handed him tequila on ice. "Hello, Mr. Garcia," the pilot said from the cockpit. "Nice to see you again."

"You too, Stan," Jimmy said to the retired fighter pilot. "It's been awhile. Will the coordinates I provided work out?"

"Yes, sir, and if we leave now—"

"We avoid the storms," Jimmy said, grinning. "I heard. Let's rock and roll."

The pilot saluted, then turned to his flaps and ailerons.

DELGADO'S FORTRESS

The September 27 boss slapped the sea-pocked steel, making Javier cringe.

"Don't worry, my young friend," Delgado said jovially. "Jimmy swears it won't explode unless I want it to, and when he assures you of something, it's money in the bank."

"Yes, *Jefe*," Javier said, still worried. After delivering the bombs to the storage vault, he'd looked up VX on Wikipedia. He'd gotten so nauseous that he couldn't eat the rest of the day. To stand inches from one of these wild beasts . . .

"Would a drink settle your stomach?" Delgado said.

Javier's head bobbed. Delgado snapped his fingers at a white-coated waiter. "So what do you think of my little shack?" he said, twisting around in his wheelchair.

Javier drank it in. This room was bigger than any ten houses in the slum in which he'd been raised, and it was only the garage. It contained Jaguars, Rolls-Royces, Bugattis, and Pierce-Arrows, each in its own silk-draped berth. Propeller-driven warplanes hung from the ceiling; an armored battle tank—which army, he couldn't tell, since he couldn't read the markings—stood hulking by the door. Between them lay Colts and Winchesters and Deringers and Sharps, paintings and sculptures and mosaics, each lit by its own diamond-crusted lamp. The half-barrel ceiling was a duplicate of the Sistine Chapel's.

"It . . . it's beautiful," he said, meaning it. Delgado's house was the most exquisite he'd ever seen. "I've never seen so much artwork."

"I collect pretty things," Delgado said. "Monet, Rembrandt, Degas, Klimt, I buy 'em all. Originals only, naturally. When you get to where I am, Javier, you'll collect them too. Cars. Guns. Women. Antiquities. War goods. Rare masterpieces."

"But I know nothing about art," Javier protested.

"Neither do I," Delgado said, waving his hand in dismissal. "But they're worth millions, and that's good enough for me—ah, our drinks." He accepted the frosted glasses, handed one to Javier. "To your health."

"And to yours, Mr. Delgado," Javier said as the alcoholic fire slid down his throat.

FIVE THOUSAND FEET OVER DELGADO'S FORTRESS

Jimmy smelled the T-bones frying in the galley. His stomach growled, and he realized he was hungrier than he'd thought. But first . . .

He pulled out his cell phone and punched the video app. The spy cameras his weapons man hid in the bomb circuitry showed Delgado and Javier sipping frosted drinks. They were in the titanic "garage" with the cars and the tank and the jewels and the paintings. They stood ten feet from the warhead. They were laughing.

He switched to CALL. Waited for the signal to sink through a mile of air.

"*Amigo!* Are you on your way?" Delgado said jovially.

"I'm here already," Jimmy said.

"What?" Delgado said, looking around, appearing confused. "No one informed me—"

"I'm in my jet, directly over your house."

Silence.

"Jimmy, what kind of foolishness are you—"

"Did you really think you could assassinate Izzy," Jimmy hissed, pulling out the red phone and punching in the passcodes, "and I wouldn't do something about it?"

He watched Delgado grow pale.

"Kill your sister? Are you mad? I'd never do that, not to family," the crime boss pleaded, backing away from the bomb as Javier, looking panicked, dropped his drink, glass shattering on the marble inlays. "Land your plane, and we'll talk this through—"

Jimmy pressed the final number. Watched Rembrandts and Bugattis and Delgado explode till the video link shorted out.

"*El Norte,*" he said to the intercom.

The plane banked north. Izzy walked into the cabin. "Whatever you're working on, big brother, it's time to stop," she chided, kissing him on the forehead. "You're on vacation."

Jimmy smiled as he slipped both phones in his pocket. "I am now," he said as the attendant brought their meals on silver trays.

He felt a little bad about Javier as he chewed his bright red meat.

But he'd get over it.

U.S. BIOWATCH CENTER, WEST OF NOGALES, ARIZONA

"Who'd'ya wind up picking for Sunday's game?" the corporal said, stifling a yawn.

"I put twenty on the Cardinals," the sergeant said.

"Man, are you kidding?" the corporal protested. "You think the Arizona Cardinals are actually gonna beat the St. Louis Rams?"

"Yup."

The corporal shook his quarter-inch hair. "You've been in the desert too long, Sarge," he chided. "The Rams keep scoring like a frat in heat."

"Yeah, yeah, I read the sports section. But I got a good feeling," the sergeant said.

"Me too, that you're gonna lose that big investment—"

Zowt, zowt, zowt, zowt . . .

They spun to their flat-panel screens. Reds and yellows bloomed like roses. "What do you see?" the sergeant said for confirmation.

"Anthrax," the corporal sighed. "For the fourth damn time this shift." The BioWatch detection system routinely mistook bird shit and pollution for airborne biological warfare agents, setting off the alarm. As far as he knew, BioWatch had never once correctly detected a hostile germ. Which made this posting tedious, even for the military, which was saying something. But what the hell, it had kept him out of the infantry . . .

"Wind?" the sergeant said.

The corporal checked the weather center. "South to north, blowing twenty," he said. "Whatever we're detecting, it's straight outta Mexico."

"All right. Confirm the data and send it up the food chain. Tell the base to send a runner to deliver the air samples. Then call to confirm everything got where it's supposed to be."

The corporal raised an eyebrow at the belt-and-suspenders routine.

"Way I figure," the sergeant said, his hooded eyes dancing with mischief, "if we bother them enough with these false sightings, maybe they'll fix this goddamn system. So we can actually, you know, detect something besides our weenies."

"Huh. Think that'll actually work?"

The sergeant laughed. "Hell, no. But every time we call, a certain fulla-shit major has to get off his lazy ass, test the air samples, write a report, and send it to Washington. If you and me gotta sit in this tin can for hours at a time"—minus the fancy electronics, the mobile detection center was an overripe Winnebago—"he should suffer too."

"Works for me," the corporal said, hitting ENTER.

1954

MARCH 13
DUGWAY PROVING GROUND
SKULL VALLEY, UTAH

"Gonna hit a slam grand today," the rocket man said, rubbing his hands in glee.

Shiro Ishii nodded, pleased himself. He'd worked out the remaining problems with bundling anthrax with VX nerve gas and was ready for this final test sequence. If all four passed, America would add Ishii's poison arsenal to its fight with the godless Commies. If not, he and the rocket man would hop the next flight back to Maryland and keep tinkering. But he had a good feeling . . .

"Yew boys ready?" drawled the U.S. Army man who ran this open-air test facility.

"Yes, Colonel," Ishii said.

"Then let's get this show on the road."

The rocket man raised a questioning eyebrow. "It's a reference to New York theater," Ishii explained as they jumped into the truck. "When actors take their Broadway productions to other cities, it's called 'getting the show on the road.'"

The rocket man pulled his notebook and scribbled down the Americanism. He was trying to learn them all, to fit in better with the country that freed him to build bigger and better weapons for the new master race. Ten minutes later, they were on the observation platform, accepting coffee and doughnuts from mess-hall privates.

"Arty, go-go, swoop, and burn," the colonel said, ticking off the planned tests on his fingers.

"Artillery, missile, airplane, and . . . open-air burning?" the rocket man guessed.

"You got it, son," the colonel said. He radioed the sergeants supervising each test. A Klaxon blared, followed by a loudspeaker warning that live firing was about to commence.

"Woo-hoo!" the rocket man cheered as the arrowhead-shaped Nike missile roared over their heads to explode on a distant target . . .

. . . while artillery shells burst from squat gray howitzers . . .

. . . as two hundred gallons of nerve agent crackled in an open fire pit . . .

. . . and a fast-moving jet sprayed the mixture across a long, wide patch of dirt.

Ishii jotted notes as dirty tears drifted over the lonely desertscape. "The dispersal pattern appears excellent," he said. "What do you think, sir?"

The colonel looked through binoculars. Grinned. "We've got us a winner," he said. "Though them sheep might wish otherwise."

Ishii studied the six thousand test sheep that bleated helplessly as their lungs turned to Elmer's Glue-All.

"Damn shame we can't test on people like you fellas used to do," the colonel said, whacking desert dust off his cap. "Convicts, queers, that sort of thing."

"Yes," Ishii said, recalling the thousands of logs—Koreans and Chinese, Britons and Americans—he'd gassed, poisoned, frozen, vivisected, injected, burned, crushed, blinded, and felled at Unit 731. "But in this country that would be a . . . what do you call it . . . a foul ball."

The rocket man wrote it down.

Chapter 47

PRESENT DAY
SUPERSTITION'S NEW HOUSE
CHICAGO

"I have no intention of arresting Jimmy Garcia," Superstition said. "I'm going to kill him first chance."

The silence stretched.

"Aren't you going to talk me out of it?" she said.

Charvat ran his fingers over his wormy scars.

"Like I said," he said. "Some people need killing."

Relief flooded her. While she would have done it without Charvat's blessing, it would have been harder psychologically because she valued his opinion. "Thanks, Killer Bee," she said. "You're a real *mensch*—oh, wait, my public cell's ringing."

"Welcome Wagon, no doubt," he said.

"With a basket of fruit and meth," she said, reaching for the cell. "Never mind, they hung up." She checked the display. UNKNOWN CALLER. Probably Comcast, hawking the deal of the day. She grinned at the thought of Larry the Cable Guy coming to this neck of the woods.

"Back to Izzy for a minute. You gave her your cell number, right?" Charvat said.

"Sure, and my new street address. She texted me after she got home, and we've been writing back and forth. Girl stuff. Some prison gossip. It's been fun. We really did become friends in Fargo."

"That complicates matters."

"I know," she sighed. "I hate playing Judas 'cause I genuinely like her. But in a contest between Izzy and my husband . . ." She finger-combed her hair. "The problem is, I don't think she'll set foot in the U.S. again, even if I ask her to visit. Do you?"

"Given the wood chipper the U.S. attorney ran her through, do you blame her?"

"No. I'd avoid us like the plague. Jerome, Deb, and Robbie concur. So, next week I'm going to ask if she'd like me to drive down to Mexico and visit—"

The public cell rang again. "Don't hang up. I shall return," Superstition said.

"You and MacArthur," Charvat said.

Who? she thought, picking up the other. "Hello?" she said.

"Skeeter," Isabel Garcia said. "It's me."

Excitement dripped down Superstition's spine. "Hey, how are you, Izzy?" she said, loud enough for Charvat to overhear. "How's life treating you in Mexico?"

"Beats the heck out of prison," Izzy said.

"So do hemorrhoids," Superstition said.

"True dat," Izzy said. "But that's not why I'm calling."

Superstition plucked a water bottle from her nightstand. Unscrewed the cap with her teeth and spit it on the bedspread. "Go ahead, I'm all ears—"

"Surprise! I'm on your front porch!" Izzy cried.

Superstition did a spit-take.

"You're here? At my house?" she said.

"She's there? At your house?" Charvat said.

"And I brought Jimmy with me," Izzy said.

"You brought your brother?" Superstition said.

"Holy mother," Charvat said.

"Let us in," Izzy said.

"Calling in," Charvat said.

"In a minute," Superstition said. "I'm in the bathroom . . ."

She snuck into the kitchen. Grabbed two knives from a drawer. Slipped them into her waistband, under her shirt, one on each hip, like six-guns in a Western. The moment she got close enough, *Señor* Garcia would sport a crooked red smile across his throat.

"They're at my front door," she whispered. "I can't believe this."

"Listen, Sue, don't kill him," Charvat warned. "Forget what I said."

"I want to carve him like a Thanksgiving turkey."

"I know. But don't. I'll call Deb and Robbie, get you backup. Do the right thing and take him alive, so we can squeeze him for information on the cartels—"

"Gotta go," Superstition said, clicking off. She ducked back into the bathroom and flushed the toilet. Stashed the secret phone in the cutout behind the toilet paper dispenser. Patted her hair into place, made sure the knives were in reach, and walked to the door, grabbing the flaking chrome handle.

FBI SAFE HOUSE, CHICAGO

"Go-go-go!" Deb Williams radioed as she screeched away from her parking spot, tingling at the prospect of battle. Civil rights was a righteous gig, but takedowns stirred her blood. "And don't forget we need the target alive."

"If I can," the FBI SWAT commander replied, firing up his black SUV as shooters and door-crashers piled inside.

" 'If' doesn't cut it, Dukey," Williams said, jinking through the heavy traffic. "He's intimate with the Taliban, Hezbollah, and Islamic State. He knows all the players in global narcotics. Counterterrorism's gonna juice him like an orange."

CRIMINAL COURTHOUSE, CHICAGO

"Damn-damn-damn!" Robert Hanrahan spat, his frustration making his ears ring as cops, cons, and lawyers jostled for supremacy in the stuffy corridor outside the courtrooms. "I'm just about to testify in a case . . .

Deb's rolling, good, good . . . I'll shake free soon as I can, Bee, and meet her there . . . goddammit all to hell . . ."

J. EDGAR HOOVER BUILDING, WASHINGTON, D.C.

"Jimmy's at her house?" Jerome Jerome said, banging his chair against the wall as he bolted upright. His back seized up in cramps. He slumped across his desk, panting as the pain struck deep. "Right now? Hot damn! Keep him alive!"

SUPERSTITION'S NEW HOUSE, CHICAGO

Isabel danced onto the mottled pink linoleum, throwing her arms around her friend. "It's so good to see you!" she choked, eyes watering.

"You too, honey, you too," Superstition said, hugging fiercely, genuinely delighted to see the woman with whom she'd gotten close in prison. She looked past her shoulder to the rangy bundle of tattoos on the cracked stoop. "This must be the brother you kept talking about."

Jiménez Garcia bowed.

He walked into the house, drinking in his sister's "sister." Superstition's eyes glowed like crushed violets. Her hair was dark chocolate with strands of obsidian, tan, and cinnamon and hung nearly to her waist, brushing the cheeks of her finely sculpted ass. Her complexion was buttercream with a splash of whiskey, her nails short but manicured, her muscled arms unusually long, like an ape's, but not inelegant. Her stonewashed jeans—his favorite garment on a woman—caressed wide hips that promised great adventures for the man strong enough to attract her. Even her torn and rumpled shirt shouted "class," not "bag lady." He shook his head. The photographs and video were electrifying. The reality . . . well, he didn't have the words.

"Nice to meet you, *Señora*," he said, taking and kissing her hand.

The knife handles pressed into Superstition's abdominal scars. "I'm so glad you came, Mr. Garcia," she said, beaming. "What a wonderful surprise."

THE FURY

FORT DETRICK, MARYLAND

"Get me POTUS," the commanding colonel of America's biochem program ordered as she data-mined the anthrax report from BioWatch in Arizona. "Now."

THE WHITE HOUSE, WASHINGTON, D.C.

"Mother of God," the president of the United States whispered as he disconnected with Fort Detrick. "Garcia just set off a nerve gas bomb. Abort the takedown and alert Fort Bragg."

"On it," the FBI director said, reaching for his phone.

THREE BLOCKS AWAY

"Williams," she barked, skidding to avoid a Good Humor truck blowing the red.

"Abort, abort, abort," Jerome ordered.

"What?" Williams said, shocked. "We're nearly there, we're running hot—"

"Jimmy has VX nerve gas bombs, mixed with anthrax. He just set one off."

"Oh, dear God. Where?"

"In Mexico. Killed his boss. Anthrax drifted across the border, got snagged by BioWatch. Unique signature, it's one of ours from the Gulf of Mexico."

"All the more reason to grab Jimmy now," Williams argued.

"There's more bombs. Only Jimmy knows where they are. You need to get Sue into Mexico, so she can find and target them for Special Forces extraction."

"Right, geez, okay," Williams said, banging the wheel to blow off adrenaline. "I'll call off the troops—ah, wait one, it's Bee." She clicked over to Charvat. "What—"

"Sue's gonna whack Jimmy."

"Uhh . . ."

"We were on the phone when Jimmy and Izzy showed up. She told me she's going to kill him, not arrest. I gave her my blessing."

"Blessing? Are you insane?"

"Nope. The scumbag killed her husband, and I'm still in pain. Screw him."

"Aw, dammit, Brian—"

"But I changed my mind, told her to not do that, we need Garcia alive. As you might imagine, she doesn't agree with us."

Williams played geopolitical chess in her head. "I'll take care of it," she said, pulling out her iPad and composing a message with one hand. "I'm aborting the assault."

"Shit! Why?"

"Jimmy lit off an anthrax bomb," she said. "We need him alive to find the rest—"

"Oh, hell, go, go . . ."

"Blue Leader," she radioed.

"Blue Command, go," the SWAT commander said, his voice tight with adrenaline as he made the final turn to the target.

"Abort assault. Red light, I repeat, red, red, red."

Silence.

"Roger, Blue Command, we're standing down."

She felt his pain. *Assaultus interruptus* was worse than a man reaching for the towel while you were still building. Not that that was the case with Hanrahan, bless his nicotine-stained heart . . .

"Sorry, Blue Leader," she said, shelving the memory for a more opportune time. "New orders. I'm going in alone."

Chapter 48

SUPERSTITION'S HOUSE
CHICAGO

"Not to be impolite, Sue," Jimmy said, his eyes roving the mold-streaked walls. "But this place sucks *and* blows."

"Aw, Jimmy, how can you say that? My pets seem to like it," Superstition deadpanned, pointing to the cockroaches huddled in the corner. "Meet Keezy, Sleazy, Robbie, and Fargo . . ."

Jimmy laughed, genuinely amused. "I see why you like her, Sis," he said. Then, to Superstition: "Izzy says you're broke from legal bills. Your house here sort of agrees."

Superstition made an exaggerated shrug. "I drained my savings and sold my house. I can't touch my pension yet, and nobody will hire a felon, even one as pretty as me." She snorted. "So, yeah, you could say I'm hurting."

Jimmy dipped his head in acknowledgment. "You want a job?"

"Sure. You know somebody who's hiring?"

"Yeah. Me," Jimmy said, patting his broad chest. Superstition raised an eyebrow. "I know, cops and robbers," Jimmy said. "But I got work that needs doing, and I owe you for taking that shiv for my sister."

"I slipped on the soap, that's all," Superstition said.

"Bull," Izzy spat, slapping the sofa, which raised a mushroom cloud of dust. "You jumped between us and took that hit for me."

Superstition smiled. "Of course I did. If you were dead, they would have assigned me a bunkmate who smelled," she said. "Besides, who else would buy me Fritos?"

They high-fived.

"You're one hell of a fighter, you know," Jimmy said. "I couldn't take out six Mexican Mafia, and I'm pretty good. What'd you use, karate?"

"Krav maga," Superstition said. It was a brutally efficient hand-to-hand system invented by the Israelis. She'd broken her collarbone and both legs to attain a level nine black belt in what her guru affectionately called "Jew-jitsu." There was no level ten. She snapped her fingers as if another thought had occurred. "Say, you've got to be on the no-fly list, being a squinty-eyed terrorist and all. How'd you get here, hitchhike?"

Jimmy and Izzy laughed. "Why God invented the Gulfstream," he said. "Before heading to O'Hare to deliver legitimate cargo, my pilot did a touch-and-go on a rural airstrip south of Joliet. Chicago's one of my distribution hubs, so a car was waiting." He got up from the couch, stretching and coughing. "You got any beer, Sue?" he said. "My throat's a little scratchy from Sis imitating a dust mop."

Izzy stuck out her tongue and slapped harder, raising a bigger cloud.

"Sure," Superstition said, getting up and turning for the kitchen. This would be perfect. She'd hand him a drink with a razor-sharp chaser—

Bam-bam-bam-bam-bam!

"Superstition Davis!" a voice boomed. "Parole officer! Open up!"

Izzy clutched herself, frightened. Jimmy looked amused. "Got a place we can hide?" he said. "Wouldn't want your cop buddies to see you with a blinky-eyed terrorist—"

"Cops are not my friends," Superstition said, pointing them toward her bedroom. "Not since they threw me in the can."

They hustled inside. Superstition walked to the front door, opened it a fraction. "The hell you want?" she growled at Deb Williams.

"I'm from the Justice Department," Williams said, flashing a badge as she pulled her collar up and her hat down low to keep Garcia from recognizing her if he'd happened to see her on the fight video. "Parole division. I'm conducting a surprise inspection of your living arrangements."

Superstition put her hands on her hips. "Why?"

"Because I can," Williams snapped.

Superstition opened the door a little wider. "Make it quick, I got things to do."

"Like finding another FBI agent to cripple?" Williams said.

Superstition flared. "If I can't, you'll do just fine, bitch."

"Watch yourself, convict," Williams snarled back. "You're still on court supervision. If I report a threat, the Bureau of Prisons will remand you to a supermax. You'll be locked in a cell twenty-three hours a day with no one to talk to but your feces. They say you go nuts in a month, require a straitjacket in two—"

"I get the message," Superstition said, opening the door fully. "Come on in and search away." Williams walked onto the linoleum. Did a perfunctory look-around. "Are you associating with known criminals?" she said. "Taking illegal drugs?"

"No and no."

"Good," Williams said. "Is your bedroom back there?"

"Uh, yeah," Superstition said, crossing her eyes to send Williams a message.

"Say, convict, you look kind of nervous," Williams said. "Something in that room you don't want me to see?"

"No, no," Superstition said hastily. "It's empty. Just like the rest of the place."

"I should search it, make sure," Williams said, tapping her chin. "But I have appointments with a dozen other shitbirds today. Maybe if you convinced me I shouldn't waste my time . . ."

Superstition smiled. "Would twenty dollars help?"

"Fifty's a guarantee."

Superstition pulled five crumpled bills from her jeans and handed them over.

"Very good," Williams said. "Come up with this every visit, and you can do whatever you want."

"A cop on the take," Superstition said, *tsk*-ing. "Sad."

"Girl's gotta eat," Williams said. "Okay, I declare you clean, sober, and living up to the terms of your supervision. Sign this paperwork, and I'm outta here." She thrust out her iPad. Superstition didn't have to feign her confusion—*What do you want me to do, exactly?*

"Jesus, convict. They invented this thing called computers since you went away," Williams said, sarcasm dripping. "Just read the statement and sign the dotted line with your index finger." She held out the iPad, angling the screen away from the bedroom.

JIMMY SET OFF A NERVE GAS BOMB IN MEXICO. IT ALSO CONTAINS ANTHRAX. HE HAS MORE BOMBS, WHEREABOUTS UNKNOWN. YOU CANNOT KILL HIM. GO WITH HIM TO MEXICO AND LOCATE REMAINING BOMBS SO MILITARY CAN RECOVER.

Superstition scribbled her name, seething at not being able to deliver justice here and now but also nodding acceptance. Delay would just make the throat-slitting sweeter . . .

"Same time, same station, same fifty," Williams said, walking out the door. "*Ciao*, shitbird."

"*Ciao* this," Superstition said, slamming the door as she raised a middle finger.

Jimmy and Izzy emerged from the bedroom. "I'm not armed," he said, waving empty hands. "And Officer Friendly had a Glock on her hip."

"Which means?" Superstition said.

"You aren't a cop trying to win her bones by nailing a drug lord. You're as real as my sister says." He grinned easily. "You still got that beer in your fridge?"

"Sure," she said, turning her back to walk to the kitchen. She heard him spring from the couch, and before she could react, felt his arm snake around her neck.

"Jimmy!" Izzy said. "What are you—"

"She knows," Jimmy grunted, pulling tighter. "Doncha, copper?"

"Guh . . . guh," Superstition strangled as the light from the window turned spangly.

"And don't try that fancy judo shit. I'll snap your neck before your foot leaves the floor."

Superstition flopped her arms, trying to nod. She wasn't all that concerned . . . yet. Despite his warning, she'd gotten out of worse strangleholds in dark Chicago alleys, when suspects leapt from behind Dumpsters to take out their pursuers. She could easily break this strangle if she chose. But she wanted to know what Jimmy knew.

She slapped at his arm, feigning panic. He tightened his vise grip. "Tell me, Detective," he hissed. "Do. You. Know?"

He relaxed the grip just enough to let her reply. *"Hweee,"* she whistled, gulping in air.

"So?"

"Yes," she gargled. "I know."

"What do you know?"

"I know . . . you killed . . . my husband. In the . . . canyon."

"Ha!" Jimmy said, eyes flashing triumphantly. "I knew it. I can always tell when someone's hiding something from me. Always."

Izzy slumped into the sofa, raising a softer cloud. "That was you, Jimmy?" she gasped. "You gunned down Sue's husband and that Border Patrol man?"

"I had no choice, Sis. I was running a multimillion-dollar shipment," Jimmy said. "They discovered us in the canyon, and her boy wound up using us for target practice. It was him or me. I picked me. And Superduper here knows it."

"You knew he killed Derek?" Izzy said, astonished, not at her brother but at her new "sister." "Back when we were in Fargo?"

"Yes. I did," Superstition said. "And I'm glad the bastard's dead. I only hope it was painful—"

"Bullshit!" Izzy cried, scattering the cockroaches. "All that lovey-dovey about Derek Baby in our cell, that was real."

"I lied. I hated the son of a bitch," Superstition said.

"No way."

"Way," Superstition said. "Let me go, and I'll tell you why."

Instead, Jimmy tightened his grip. "Spill it now," he growled. "Or I'll snap your pretty neck."

Superstition whistled in a breath. "He used to beat me," she forced out. "When he got drunk. When the Bears lost. Whenever the mood was right."

"He beat you? Why?" Izzy said, her hostile expression softening a fraction.

"He should have made lieutenant. He should've been captain of the softball team. He should have won that commendation. Whatever it was, he took out his frustrations on me." She breathed deep, still whistling from her throat restriction. "He hit me with socks filled with BB's. He beat me till my ears rang but made sure it was nowhere people might see. Belly. Chest. Privates." She patted her crotch. "Before he was SWAT, he worked in the gang unit. He knew how to do me just like he did gangbangers who disrespected him—beat 'em quiet, beat 'em senseless. Keep it nice and . . . private." She pulled up her shirt, showing the flat pink scars on her chest wall, beneath her bra. "Remember seeing these in the cell?" She saw Izzy nod. "They came from darling Brian—"

"Brian? Who's Brian?" Jimmy barked.

"He's the guy you shot with my husband. I'm mixing them up because I don't think straight without oxygen," she snapped back, furious at her unintentional slip. "Derek didn't like the way I ironed his dress uniform, so he showed me how it was done, using me as the ironing board." In actuality, she'd gotten burned falling onto a fresh-welded truck frame during a raid on a chop shop. But they didn't have to know that.

Jimmy recalled his own tortures in the Tijuana lockup, the black and blue stripes on his belly, the ropy scars on his ass and thighs. He nodded. Izzy, though, was still angry at the deception. "Then why did you say all those nice things about Derek when we talked?"

Superstition forced tears to fall. It wasn't hard, because her throat was a hairball of pain. "I couldn't tell anyone," she sniffled. "I couldn't even admit to myself that I let my husband abuse me. My. Husband. The man I fell in love with, Iz. The man I let between my legs because he swore he loved me too." Knowing that would strike home with a woman so enraged with her lover that she'd bulldoze his house.

"Oh, girlfriend," Izzy murmured. "You should have told me."

"If he was such a louse, why didn't you divorce him?" Jimmy said, loosening his chokehold a little more.

"I couldn't," Superstition said. "Derek was political. He knew the judges because he collected their payoffs from people who wanted cases to go a certain way." She sucked in another deep breath. "If I'd filed for divorce, they'd have protected him. I'd wind up paying him alimony." She shook her head, despising her lies about Derek but having no choice if she wanted to find those bombs. "I wasn't going to let that happen, I had too much pride. So I stayed with him, but started martial arts training. I wanted to defend myself better on the street, sure. But mostly I wanted to protect myself from Derek Effing Davis. If he touched me again . . ."

"You'd kill him," Jimmy said.

"Like a rabid skunk," Superstition confirmed, straightening her back the best she could. "Hell, yes, I knew you shot him, Jimmy. The Border Patrol told my superintendent, who told my lieutenant, who told me. They gave him a hero's funeral. I didn't object because I'm glad he's down with the devil, getting his ass kicked. I was going to thank you if I met you someday." She shrugged. "But you never gave me the chance, did you? Showing up like this?"

Jimmy loosened even more, considering all she'd said.

"You wanna kill me, go ahead," Superstition said, going for broke. "You think I'm a cop trying to nail you, then go ahead and break my neck. Get it over with." Pause. "Otherwise, let me go. I'm not gonna stand here all day waiting for you to decide. Not in my own damn house."

The silence became so deep that she heard the wall clock ticking.

"Oh, Jimmy . . ." Izzy murmured.

"Yeah," Jimmy said, releasing her. Superstition stumbled away, retching. "Sorry," he said with a shrug. "But you befriended my sister. Most people who do that want something from me. I had to know for sure. A man in my position—"

"Can't be too careful, right," Superstition said, waving it off. "I get it. If you weren't careful, you'd have died years ago, and who would take care of your family?"

He nodded. "I had a feeling you'd understand—"

The reverse roundhouse kick caught him flat in the side of the head, bouncing him off the wall and across the dirty brown shag. The cockroaches scattered. "Jimmy!" Izzy yelped, running for her unconscious brother.

"Nobody does that to me, asshole," Superstition spat, hands on her hips. "Not anymore."

Ten seconds later Jimmy blinked awake, shaking the spiders from his brain. "Did anyone get the license of that truck?" he groaned. Superstition went to the kitchen and put the knives in a drawer. She returned with water and a towel. "Are you all right?" she said, handing them to Izzy, who wiped away Jimmy's blood and torn skin. He scowled, rubbing his temples. Then started laughing like the late show at Second City. "Pretty good move there, Sue," he said.

"Thanks."

He patted his own waist. "What'd you do with the pig-stickers?"

She arched an eyebrow, genuinely surprised. "You knew about the knives?"

"Felt 'em in your waist when I held you close. Even gave you a chance to use 'em."

She thought about that. "You left my arms and hands free."

"Mm-hm. But you didn't stick me. That sealed the deal."

"I also tap-dance and sing," she said.

"Don't have a need for entertainers. But other stuff . . ."

"You still offering me a job?"

"You still want to work for me?"

"I'm broke, and I like to eat. So, yeah. Where?"

"Mexico," he said. *Meh-he-co.*

"Doing what?"

"Do you care?"

She considered that. "Yes. I don't do windows."

Jimmy grinned. "How do you feel about tunnels?"

Chapter 49

PECK CANYON
NOGALES, ARIZONA

"Fifty-two pounds of Afghan gold, as promised," Superstition said.

The distributor frowned suspiciously. "Jimmy said fifty. This some kind of loyalty test?"

"Nope. The extra two's your bonus for a job well done."

The distributor showed gappy teeth and slapped the heavy backpack she'd hauled across the border. "Why's Jimmy being so generous?" he said, nodding to his associates to load the narcotics in the food truck.

"He likes being boss, I guess," Superstition said. Mexico City publicly declared the destruction of Vincente Delgado's palace "a tragic explosion from a gas leak," making further investigations unnecessary. Jiménez Garcia, the new commander of the September 27 narcotics cartel, told reporters it was a shame Delgado didn't lose his life in armed battle, as he'd wanted, and prayed he was worthy of filling his *jefe's* giant shoes. Everyone tried not to laugh. "You complaining?"

"Not me. Delgado was a cheapskate. Give Jimmy my regards."

She watched the food truck roll away, dust curling. "I'm inbound," she said into her cell.

"Any problems?" Jimmy said.

"Yeah. You didn't give me a bonus."

He laughed. "How 'bout I take you to lunch instead?"

"I'd rather have cash," she said. "But what the hell."

She rode her mountain bike to the border. Abandoned it to pull back the shrubbery covering the hole in the ground. Jumped in, dropped to her hands and knees, and crawled back to Mexico. "Ow," she muttered as she emerged on the other side.

"What?" Jimmy said.

"I forgot my knee pads," she said, slapping dirt off her Wranglers.

"Poor you."

She lifted her middle finger.

"What's that?" he said.

"Just sayin' you're Number One," she said. *"Jefe."*

He laughed and pointed at his car. They drove to a restaurant whose food was light-years better than its ramshackle appearance. "You did a great job, Sue," he said, tipping his glass of *cerveza*. "Again."

"Thanks," she said. It was her fourth trip into the United States, delivering narcotics to Garcia's stateside distributors. Her personal bank account—safety stashed in a Cayman Islands bank owned by associates of September 27—was fattening nicely. But she still had no clue where the bombs were, and Jerome Jerome was getting itchy.

"Ready to take the next big step?" Jimmy said between bites of *birria*, a stew of beef and pork with chili peppers and spices.

"Always," she said.

He handed her a small padded case. She looked inside and raised an eyebrow. "I want you to kill someone," he said.

Superstition flushed angrily. "You still don't trust me, do you?" she snapped. After the strangling in her living room, Jimmy received a phone call from Nogales. He spoke briefly, then disconnected. Said his boss was dead—explosion in the house, no survivors—and he was now supreme commander. "We gotta get back," he said, speed-dialing his pilot. "You coming?" She nodded, boarded the plane with them, landed in Mexico, slept in a September 27 safe house, and started delivering drugs after an intense round of training. She'd assumed they were beyond the "trust-me" dance.

"On the contrary," Jimmy said. "This is a critical mission I can't give to just anyone."

"Don't lie to me," she said. "You think I'm a cop, and this is another test."

He drained his beer, waved at the waiter for another. "Well, that too."

She rolled her eyes. "All right. You gave me a nine, so who do you want me to shoot?"

He grinned like a Halloween pumpkin. "You know the U.S. attorney in Phoenix?"

"Not personally, but I've heard the name."

"He's the asswipe that put Izzy in the slammer. I want him full of lead. You do that, no more bullshit and no more loyalty tests. You're one of us for real."

She stared at him. He stared back.

"But hey, Sue, if you don't have the stones, no hard feelings, I'd understand . . ."

"I'll do it," she said, setting her face with grit and determination.

Thinking, *Gulp.*

Chapter 50

FEDERAL BUILDING
PHOENIX, ARIZONA

Superstition leaned on her cane, feigning a slow walking limp, as the U.S. attorney emerged from the federal building. She checked her watch. Right on time. Jimmy's scouts had been monitoring the building since Izzy's arrest. They discovered that the U.S. attorney left for lunch at noon, each and every day. It was a serious breach in security—important people were supposed to vary their routines daily, sometimes hourly, to thwart kidnappers and assassins. But politicians, particularly American, often ignored the advice, figuring that their lofty titles immunized them from predators.

"Ouch!" she said as a plump woman in golf attire crashed into her, sending the cane flying one way and Superstition the other.

"Oh, honey, my bad!" the woman cried, waving her smartphone like absolution. "I was texting my brother and . . . never mind, let me help you up!" She retrieved the cane, then bent and grabbed Superstition's arm. "I'm so sorry!"

"No problem," Superstition said, rubbing her raw-scraped arm.

"Killer Bee says hello," the woman whispered.

Wonder of wonders, it worked. Deb Williams had provided a burst-transmitter from the FBI weapons labs. For ultimate camouflage, it was disguised as a tampon; "there isn't a tough guy on the planet that will frisk you that far," Deb assured her. To use it, she spoke her message into the tip soaked in polymer "blood"—further assurance of repelling deep frisks—then pulled the tampon "string" like a lamp chain. The encoded message was pulsed to a military satellite. The burst lasted only a microsecond to avoid discovery by cartel radio detection equipment. Between *birria* and dessert at the restaurant after her last tunnel job, she'd excused herself for the ladies' and messaged Jimmy's assassination plan. This woman was Charvat's way of confirming that the message had gotten through.

"I'm shooting him at noon tomorrow," Superstition murmured back to the woman. "Right here on the sidewalk. Tell Bee it's got to look real."

"Noon tomorrow, we'll be ready," the woman said. Then, louder: "Are you sure you don't want me to call you an ambulance? I'm happy to pay for it."

"No, no, I'm fine," Superstition said, dusting herself off.

"All right then, honey, thanks for understanding . . ."

Superstition fake-limped to her car and drove back to the Econo Lodge near Phoenix Sky Harbor Airport. She went to the pool, pulled the iPhone Jimmy provided, and surfed to a private Internet chat room. "TARGET CONFIRMED. TOMORROW NOON," she wrote.

Ten minutes later, his answer appeared:

"HOPE YOU CUSSED THAT FATTY LIKE YOU ALWAYS CUSS ME."

They're always watching, she thought with a cold shiver that belied the heat of the sun.

"Need a drink, miss?" a passing waiter said.

"Several," Superstition said. "But I'll stick with Diet Coke."

U.S. ATTORNEY'S HOUSE, SCOTTSDALE

"What are you doing for lunch tomorrow?" Charvat said.

"Dining with my wife, like always," the U.S. attorney said. "Why?"

"Wanna get shot instead?" Charvat said.

The U.S. attorney rolled his eyes, looking amused. "Awright, Bee, who put you up to this?" he said. "The defense bar?"

"No joke," Charvat said. "At noon tomorrow you're gonna be assassinated..."

FEDERAL BUILDING, PHOENIX

The *narco* driver slowed the dingy white Nissan and rolled down the windows. The wind caught his cigarette and flipped it onto the carpeting. He bent to retrieve it and drifted into oncoming traffic.

"Watch it!" Superstition barked as horns blared, as much for the attention drawn to the getaway car as fear of a disastrous *crunch*.

"Sorry, sorry," the driver said, yanking them straight. A few seconds later, he signaled and turned the corner. "Building in sight. You see the target?"

"Not yet," she said, shading her eyes.

"He better show," the driver said. "Or Jimmy'll be pissed."

"Not more than me," Superstition said. "Sitting in traffic with a *narco* and loaded weapons—ah, there."

The U.S. attorney was emerging from the entrance. Nodding to a pedestrian. Waving to a honking car. "Pull to the curb, nice and easy," she said, racking the long-barreled nine-millimeter handgun.

"I've done this before," the driver said. "You just do your part."

She thought about Derek and the kids to make the butterflies to go away. Amazingly, they did.

"Fifteen seconds," the driver said.

"He'll walk in the direction we're driving," she said. "As soon as we're even, I'll do him."

"Wish it was me," the driver said. "It's fun shootin' people."

He reduced his speed. She tightened her hold on the bulky black pistol, which was loaded with Federal hollow-points. One would do the job. She'd fire more, for insurance.

"Eight seconds," the driver said.

Superstition pushed her right elbow over the windowsill and wrapped her left hand over her right, which was already tight on the taped grips.

"Four seconds," the driver said.

She took a deep breath, blew it out, took another. Pulled the nylon mask over her face.

"Showtime," the driver said, pulling down his mask while bumping over the curb. "Hey, asshole!" Superstition bellowed to attract attention.

The U.S. attorney turned. Saw the masks. Saw the gun. He stumbled backward against the building, face twisting with fear, mahogany leather briefcase flying, holding out his palms like they'd stop supersonic lead.

Blam.

Kill shot.

Blam.

Insurance.

The U.S. attorney clutched the holes in his white shirt, over his heart. Buckled.

She emptied the magazine to scatter witnesses, bullets shattering glass and pocking concrete. "Rock and roll!" the driver sang, punching the gas pedal. She twisted around as they raced down the street. The U.S. attorney wasn't moving.

The *narco* drove another block and zipped into a garage. Hustled her to a waiting Honda and took off. They repeated the drill with a Dodge in a supermarket lot.

Superstition finally slumped, blowing out her breath.

"You okay?" the driver said, passing over a bottle as they drove south.

"Yes . . . yes, fine," she said between glugs of Evian.

"That asshole went down like a sack of beans." The men in the backseat laughed, bumping fists. One aimed his at hers. She bumped back over her head, knuckles to knuckles as the driver dialed his cell. "It's done," he said. "Yeah, two in the heart. Lady's a champ." He listened, then disconnected. "Border security's already going *loco*," he said.

"Good news travels fast," she marveled.

"Yeah. So we'll store you in Tucson tonight," he said. "Move you across tomorrow. But the best part?" He waggled his heavy brows. "Dinner at Jimmy's mountain ranch tomorrow night. All of us." His grin matched the happy murmurs from the backseat.

"What does that mean?" she said, heart thumping.

"He trusts you," the *narco* said. "Welcome to September 27."

NEWSROOM, THE ARIZONA REPUBLIC

"Put every reporter on live video," the publisher insisted.

"They're already live-Tweeting," the editor repeated. "And live-blogging."

"Faces go places," the publisher said. "Videocams. Now."

The editor sighed. Walked through the newsroom, reassigning writers to laptop live feeds like they were little anchorpeople. Came back.

"Who did you want at the federal building in case something else happens?" the editor said. "The photo staff?" He slapped his head. "Oh, wait. You laid them all off. Housewives with iPhones are as good as real photographers, you said."

"Just get it done," the publisher scowled. "And don't forget celebrity reaction to this tragic event." He stalked toward his office suite. "Madonna's in concert at the stadium tonight. Get a video team over there, try to get her on camera."

"Madonna?" the managing editor said.

"Unless you find a Kardashian for him to blow," the editor muttered.

"They give Pulitzers for that?" the managing editor said hopefully.

HICKORY CREEK RANCH, BETHEL, TEXAS

"You might have mentioned how bad that was gonna hurt," the U.S. attorney complained.

"And have you back out?" Killer Bee said, waggling his eyebrows. "Think Mrs. Charvat raised any stupid children?"

"One I know of."

"Yet I was smart enough not to volunteer," Charvat said. "You're gonna have bruises in addition to that cracked rib." The Point Blank ballistic vest in which he'd wrapped the U.S. attorney prevented death, not injuries.

The U.S. attorney grinned.

"What?" Charvat said.

"Make a nice campaign trailer," the U.S. attorney said fondly. "All these nasty blacks and purples. Can you get my video guy here before they fade?"

Charvat nodded. The man craved a Senate seat like squirrels craved nuts. "Voters do like a hero," he said.

"Especially one shot bravely in the line of duty," the U.S. attorney said, rubbing his chest with a wince. "Thank your agent for not hitting me in the pecker."

"She couldn't. Too small a target," Charvat said.

"Yeah, screw you too." He and Bee went back a ways.

Charvat put out his fist. "Seriously, man, you did a phenomenal job. It's tough standing still when you know a freight train's about to hit."

"Thanks," the U.S. attorney said, bumping back. "How long do I stay hidden?"

"Till we rake up those bombs," Charvat said. Jerome Jerome hadn't wanted to bring the U.S. attorney into the conspiracy, but Garcia had left no choice. "Your office told the press you're in a secure location till we catch your assassin."

"I'll practice holding up bravely while I wait," the U.S. attorney said.

Chapter 51

THE WHITE HOUSE
WASHINGTON, D.C.

"Couldn't she have shot him in the ass at least?" the president said.

The FBI director laughed. "You're still annoyed he outdunks you," he said. The commander in chief, who'd been good enough for European pro ball after college, invited people from both parties to play on the White House court. The U.S. attorney for Phoenix, a standout guard at Ohio State, had a standing invitation when he was in town; the president liked the competition. Like all presidents, he liked winning better.

"Wrong. I'm annoyed he trash-talks me when he does," the president said, grinning. "What's the latest from Superstition?"

"She believes the shooting was her final test because Jimmy knows that no American cop, not even a mile undercover, can assassinate a public official. We believe she's right."

"Then she'll find the bombs."

"Hopefully," the FBI director said. "Jimmy didn't get where he is by opening his heart to employees, no matter how pretty they are. Probably not going to share the location right away."

The president slammed the desk, rattling the relics. "Dammit," he thundered. "We need those things scooped up and destroyed. Push her."

"She knows what's at stake, and she'll do what she can. But cartel guys are paranoid. She pushes too hard, she winds up a crispy critter. It'll take what it takes."

"That's not what I want to hear."

"Oh, I'm sorry. How about, 'Aw, gee, Mr. President, my gal's gonna get that beady-eyed jasper by sundown, so how's about I scoop some ice cream on your apple pie?' "

The president rolled his eyes. "Yeah, yeah. So what else are we doing, in case she isn't able to deliver the goods?"

The FBI director pulled out his note pad. "Glad you asked . . ."

A ROOMING HOUSE IN TAMPICO
GULF COAST OF MEXICO

The busboy counted his money. Shook his head in frustration. The man from the CIA had handed over a bag of cash for informing on Jimmy Garcia. The busboy intended to use it to buy a boat. Unfortunately, he'd blown most it on booze, clothes, and women.

He scratched his greasy head, thinking.

If they gave me this much for saying Jimmy's got those bombs . . .

. . . they'd pay even more if I tell them where the bombs are hidden.

That he didn't actually know didn't figure into it. He knew the location of Jimmy's mountaintop ranch, and that was good enough. By the time the *Americanos* realized they'd been conned, he'd have his charter fishing service and his freedom.

He pulled his cell phone.

THE WHITE HOUSE

The map glowed yellow. The laser dot burned pink.

"This is Jimmy's ranch," said the CIA director. "Right at the top of the mountain."

"Just like the Eagle's Nest," said the commander of Delta Force, a World War II buff.

The CIA director switched to photographs of the buildings. They were detailed enough to see every mortar line in the stone and timbering.

"How reliable is this information?" the president said, wishing he had a waterfall as nice as Garcia's. Then again, narcotics paid better than public service.

"It came from the same busboy," the CIA director said.

"The one who called in the bombs?"

"Yes, sir. He says Garcia stores them at the ranch, in some kind of underground bunker. We've done a couple high-altitude fly-bys—that's where we got these photos—and spotted antiaircraft pods and other defensive weapons. It all fits."

"All right," the president said. "Where is this bunker, precisely? I'd hate to make your D-boys run up and down the mountain finding the door."

"We're still working on that," the CIA director said. "Our drones are up and running, and the Pentagon repositioned a military satellite to provide live feeds and data links for an assault."

"Speaking of which," the president said.

"We're training from maps and photographs provided by Christians in Action," the Delta commander said. "Give the word, we're happy to get sweaty."

The president nodded. "Superstition's out of the way, right?"

"She's in a safe house in Nogales," the FBI director assured. "Three hundred miles from the ranch."

"Can you warn her we're coming?"

"No. That burst-transmitter is one-way, her to us." The FBI director smiled. "I didn't think her lady parts should ring in the middle of dinner with Jimmy."

"Amen. That psycho doesn't touch Sue, she's suffered enough already."

"Are you sure you don't want to involve Mexico City?" the secretary of state said. "Give them a piece of this operation, so they have ownership? You don't, and they find out, it's gonna splash back in a very nasty way—"

"We can't, Mr. President," the Delta boss interjected. "Mexico's compromised. We tell anyone down there, Garcia hears ten minutes later. He moves the bombs, and we're screwed."

"What about their navy?" the president said. "Mexican SEALs know how to keep secrets."

"They did in the old days," the Delta boss said. "I worked with them on a dozen renditions and was highly impressed." He thumped the table. "But this new government is all about 'cooperation in hopes of easing the murder rate.'"

"Meaning, 'lining our pockets with cartel money,'" the CIA director spat.

"So, we go in unannounced," the president said.

1969

MAY 14
THE WHITE HOUSE
WASHINGTON, D.C.

"For Chrissakes, Henry, relax," Richard Nixon said. "The United States has more nukes than JFK got blowjobs."

"But dropping one, no matter how justified, starts World War Three," Henry Kissinger argued. "There's no such risk with deploying nerve gas. We should keep it in the arsenal."

"Communists respect power, not subtlety," the president said. "If they know we've eliminated softer weapons like VX and germs, they also understand we'll launch ICBMs if they invade Europe. If the only thing in our toolbox is a sledgehammer . . ."

"We have no choice but to swing it. Ergo, they dare not invade," Kissinger said.

Nixon slugged down a Tab. Burped softly. "Another thing. Except for the Soviets, only the good guys own nukes."

Kissinger nodded. The British and French made the same point when he secretly tested the water on eliminating chemical and biological weapons worldwide: Any nation advanced enough to develop nuclear weapons could be trusted not to deploy them, whereas any tin-pot dictator with enough money could get his hands on a chemical weapon.

"Which they can use against us anytime they like," Nixon said, popping another can. "But if I convince the entire world to get rid of these 'inhuman' poisons . . ."

"You guarantee your place in history, while reducing the odds we'll be attacked with germs or gas," Kissinger said. He cleaned his glasses, admiring the president's political genius. It was almost as finely tuned as his own. "So you'll urge the world to sign the Geneva accord banning CBWs?"

"Yes. And if they refuse, fuck 'em, I'll do it unilaterally and embarrass them into signing." He tossed a quarter at Kissinger. "You see George Washington?"

"I do."

"See his tiny little eye? Right there above his nose?"

"Um, yes . . ."

"A drop of VX that size will kill a full-grown man," Nixon said. "The average VX bomb contains a million." He shook his head. "I've decided, Henry. We're going to eliminate every poison bomb in our inventory. Every biological weapon. Close every arsenal that manufactures them and force every nation to go along."

" 'Cause it's good for mankind?" Kissinger said.

Nixon laughed.

" 'Cause the Kennedys will shit and go blind," Nixon said.

Chapter 52

**PRESENT DAY
JIMMY GARCIA'S RANCH
SIERRA MADRE MOUNTAINS, SOUTHEAST OF NOGALES**

"I've never tasted anything like this," Superstition marveled. "What's it called again?"

"*Cochinita pibil*," Isabel said, ladling another helping on her friend's plate. "Suckling pig with chilies and bitter oranges. You like?"

"Absolutely delicious." She blew the foam off her Tecate. "Of course, nothing compares to Spam loaf in Fargo."

Izzy punched Superstition's arm, laughing. Jimmy waved a caramelized pig cheek. Fat and *habanero*–infused butter ran down his arm. "Mama would have loved this," he said. "That woman could turn flattened armadillos into a first-class meal, swear to God. Imagine what she could do with these fresh ingredients."

Isabel lifted her wine in salute. Mama had died giving birth to her, but she'd heard all the affectionate stories. "She was a marvelous cook."

"Fortunately, so is our chef," Jimmy said. "Antonio! Bravo!"

The white-toqued beanpole turned from the fire pit. He'd been a September 27 accountant until Delgado found out he loved to cook. Impressed, the cartel boss apprenticed him to a Michelin-rated restaurant in New York, then made him a chef in Acapulco. A few years ago, he was moved into Delgado's mansion to cook full-time for September 27. "He's the finest work of art I ever acquired," Delgado liked to brag.

"Thank you, *Jefe*," Antonio said, bowing as family and *narcos* burst into applause. "It's an honor to prepare this feast for the return of your sister. But I have a serious question that only a supreme boss of bosses can answer."

Jimmy's expression turned grave. "Yes?"

"Are you ready for dessert?"

Jimmy burst out laughing. "Always, Antonio, bring it on," he crowed.

They dove into *flan* and *dulce de leche* like someone had banned sugar as dangerous. Superstition's assassination driver groaned. "One more bite, *Jefe*," he said, patting his belly, "and I won't fit through the escape hatch. So let's not have no invasions tonight!"

"Here-here!" Jimmy said, bumping fists.

"What escape hatch?" Superstition said.

"Behind the main house," Jimmy said, pointing with his silver fork. "A concealed door in the ground leads to a tunnel. It gets us off the mountain if we ever get overrun."

She looked at his ring of defenses, then at the steep topography. "Who could possibly overrun this?" she said.

Jimmy took another bite. "Whoever wants to be king."

His phone rang.

He answered, listened, and scowled.

AMERICAN AIRSPACE, EAST OF NOGALES

"Whatcha eatin', Nobes?" Karson said over the Shop-Vac howl of the helicopter engines.

"MRE pork chunks," Norobi said.

"Dayum!" Karson shuddered, remembering the snow leopard in the mountains of Afghanistan, the one bubbling with death-rot. He'd been forced to eat it because he'd gotten lost during a firefight, most of the flora was poisonous, and he was out of bugs and rodents. He spent four nights puking, and then a month in sick bay, riddled with fever and dysentery, after a search chopper locked onto his rescue beam. In his experience, the military's vacuum-packed Meals Ready to Eat didn't taste much better.

"It's good with hot sauce," Norobi said, dotting the chunk with Tabasco.

Karson shook his head. Norobi would eat a tree stump if there were enough sauce. Then again, so would Delaney. Karson smiled, wondering how his old comrade-in-arms was handling retirement. He'd meant to call him . . .

"Stow it, ladies, we just crossed into Mexico," the Delta Force raid commander told them. "Gear check, commo check . . ."

JIMMY GARCIA'S RANCH

"Bang, bang, two in the chest," Superstition sputtered, waving her hands. "He fell to the sidewalk like a bag of hammers. Everyone in the car saw it!" She saw the nods all around. "What do you mean, he's alive?"

A thin line of blue curled from Jimmy's Cohiba. His family had retired for the night, leaving the September 27 team to talk shop.

"Body armor, I'd guess," he said, slipping the fishing-fly lighter back into his pocket. "He must have been wearing it under his shirt. Tailored it, too, 'cause none of my watchers spotted it, and they know what to look for."

She slapped her forehead. "I knew I should have gone for the head shot."

"Then you mighta missed altogether," Jimmy said. "Don't worry about it. You delivered my message loud and clear."

"Which is?"

"Fuck with the best, die with the rest."

His henchmen chortled. Superstition didn't. "It's not funny. I blew it."

"No, you didn't," Jimmy said, patting her arm. "Shit happens in narcoville."

"Don't it ever," her driver agreed.

Jimmy leaned back in his chair, a memory washing over his face. "Years ago, I shot a guy a dozen times. Left him in the trunk of his car, on the side of a road. Two days later, he pops the lock, crawls to the next town, and checks into a hospital. He makes it."

"Geez," Superstition murmured, drawing from her beer. "Is he still alive?"

"Not only that, I gave him a job," Jimmy said. "Man that lucky, I want him on my side."

They all laughed this time. A waiter poured flutes of Dom Pérignon as an eight-wheel truck pulled into the compound. "All right, *amigos*," Jimmy said. "Time for show-and-tell."

"What's this, *Jefe*?" a mule driver said.

"My newest toy."

He led them to the truck and yanked back the canvas tail. "Ta-da!" he crowed.

Superstition looked at the long, stout missile, and chills dripped down her backbone. "Cool!" she squealed, feigning delight. "Where did you get this?"

"Taliban. It came with the drugs. A thank-you for some favor Delgado granted them." He told his weapons man, who was driving the truck, to extend the launch carriage. It whirred almost noiselessly, raising the gleaming metal into the moonlight. "My genius here figured out a way to arm the warhead with VX."

"What's VX?" Superstition said.

"Nerve gas," the weapons man answered. "One drop kills you dead. Oh, and there's anthrax, too, for extra bite."

Her driver yanked his hand off the nose cone. "This the shit that killed . . ."

Jimmy nodded soberly. "Not to speak ill of the dead, but Vincente was a fool," he said. "He played with the transmitter and set off the bomb, right inside his house."

"Sometimes you're the pigeon," Superstition said. "And sometimes you're the statue."

"Very good," Jimmy said, smacking her shoulder. "But ain't no pigeon gonna dump his load on me, no sir." He slapped his chest. "The transmitter's safely tucked away. So fondle this missile all you want."

Which they all did, followed with a shower of Dom.

"To us," Jimmy said. "The world's baddest *Meh-he-cans*."

"And their token *gringa* chick," Superstition added.

"No token about it," Jimmy said. "You one of us now."

They cheered. They drank. She crossed her legs theatrically.

"Mention my name, get a good seat," Jimmy said, pointing to the main house.

WEAPONS STORAGE DEPOT, SOUTH OF NOGALES

The *narco* poked his head out the truck cab. "Load a VX bomb," he ordered. "And hurry."

The guard's mouth dropped open. "My God, it's—no way, you were killed at—"

Javier winked. "That's what everyone's supposed to think."

"But . . . but I have no orders . . ."

"He wants VX, and he wants it now." Javier smiled without humor. "Or perhaps you'd like to call Jimmy and explain why you were unable to obey his commands?"

The guard flashed back to the *jefe's* barbecued cousin. "No problem, Javier," he said, snapping his fingers at his team. They wheeled out a VX bomb, loaded it, then closed the tailgate and stepped back, several of them crossing themselves.

"Thank you," Javier said. "I'll mention your efficiency to him."

And drove off into the night.

A grim smile crossed his fire-scarred face as he bounced to the rendezvous point. He was supposed to have died in that explosion. But he'd read up on those nerve gas bombs, and, freaked out about what even a tiny leak could do to a human body, obtained an auto-injector of antidote from a burglar who ripped off hospital supply warehouses. Just as the bomb went off, he dove behind the battle tank, sparing him the blast and shrapnel, then smashed through a damaged side door, avoiding most, but not all, of the flames and poison. Wheezing and shuddering, he crawled into a ditch, jammed the syringe into his thigh, and flooded himself with antidote. When he could walk again, he found a car that would start, and drove away unnoticed. Because so many in the mansion had been cremated by the inferno—the blast ignited the mansion's gas lines—Jimmy would assume he was dead too.

But living well is the best revenge, and for that, he needed cash.

Owl eyes flashed in the valley. He flashed his headlights in return and pulled up to the mud-chunked truck idling between two boulders.

"Nice night for a drive," the Taliban agent said from the passenger seat.

"Queen Victoria," Javier said.

"And her monkey's monkey's uncle," the Taliban said.

Two monkeys. Passwords confirmed.

The Taliban helped move the bomb from Javier's truck to his own, then handed over the backpack. "One hundred thousand dollars American, as promised," he said. "Want to count it?"

"No," Javier said.

The Taliban smiled at the show of respect. He looked at the expert going over the merchandise. The expert poked and prodded, then nodded.

"Splendid," the Taliban said. "You may transfer the balance from my bank to yours."

"Account number?" Javier said, pulling out his smartphone. The Taliban recited from memory, and Javier played the keyboard like a piano. TRANSFER CONFIRMED, the screen read. NINE HUNDRED THOUSAND USD.

"A million thanks, *Señor*," Javier said as he bowed his head.

"My pleasure. But if you'd taken all the bombs, you'd be floating in a sea of money."

"I could steal one without the guard alerting Jimmy," Javier said. "Taking more . . ."

"I like smart men," the Taliban said. "Are you in need of a job?"

"No, thanks."

"Even smarter. How do you know I won't shoot you and keep everything?"

"For the same reason my *amigo* listening to this conversation"—he nodded at the cell phone on the passenger seat—"won't press the spare transmitter and blow you to Allah's sweet embrace," Javier said. "It's business. What do you plan to do with it? Avenge *Señor* bin Laden?"

The moonlit face crinkled but said nothing.

They shook hands, then went their respective ways. Javier headed for the coast, where a boat would take him to the Cayman Islands, the bank account that matched his forged identity papers, and the house on a beach he'd already found on the Internet.

Where he'd disappear forever.

But first, one more *pinche pendejo* to the man he'd once regarded as a brother. He picked up the cell from the passenger seat—the "spotter with a transmitter" being as fake as Jimmy's pious regard for his people's welfare—and made the first of two calls.

Chapter 53

JIMMY GARCIA'S RANCH

"I'm at the mountain ranch," Superstition whispered into the burst-transmitter as she flushed the toilet for camouflage. "Jimmy's got one of the—"

"Skeeter! You in there?"

Superstition, startled, dropped the faux tampon. It rolled out of the stall. Cursing, she yanked up her jeans and hobbled toward it as the oaken door swung wide.

"You okay, honey?" Isabel said, face a picture of concern. "I went out to the table to see if you wanted to watch a movie with us, but Jimmy said you were in the toilet and hadn't come back yet. I hope the food isn't disagreeing—"

"Oh, no, I'm fine," Superstition said, heart pounding in her ears. If Izzy figured out the "tampon" was a radio, Jimmy would make her the next suckling pig. "Just, you know . . ."

Izzy saw the escaped "tampon" and crinkled her eyes. "Girl problems?" she said, kicking it Superstition's way.

"Yeah, and unexpected," Superstition said, bending and casually wrapping her hand around the slender white tube. "Prison messed up my cycle."

"Stress and lousy food," Izzy agreed.

"You got it. I was just about finished when she decided to make a run for it."

Izzy washed her hands. "You're getting along good with the crew."

"Nice guys," Superstition said, pitching the "tampon" into the trash, because if she didn't, Izzy would wonder why—no woman on Earth would use a tampon that had touched a bathroom floor. "For a bunch of stone killers."

Izzy laughed. "They're sweet, actually, if you ignore what they do for a living. I'm glad Jimmy put you to work. Help you rebuild your nest egg."

"Yeah, that's nice," Superstition said. "But the best part is getting to hang out with you."

Izzy dried her hands. Then she ran over and hugged Superstition, her eyes filling with tears of gratitude. "It means so much that you came home with me," she sobbed. "I love having a sister around."

"Likewise," Superstition said, patting Izzy's back. "But let's continue this later, huh? I gotta finish my—"

"Girl stuff," Izzy finished. "I think they're done fondling whatever it is Jimmy brought home, so I'll see you outside."

"Wanna know what it is? I'll tell you—"

"No," Isabel said, stomping her foot for emphasis. "I meant it when I said I'm not part of the family business. I'm going my own way in the world"—she pointed at the skylight—"and I'm going to burn as bright as those stars. Fargo made me realize it's time to fulfill my destiny, whatever that might be."

"Gotcha," Superstition said. "And I know you will, honey. I know it in my bones."

She waited till Izzy's footsteps faded. Turned on the faucets, plucked her tampon radio from the trash, and finished her transmission.

NIGHTCLUB, HOUSTON, TEXAS

"Did it hurt when you fell out of heaven?" the redhead purred as she caressed the blond man's arm.

Peter Lawrence grinned at the cheesy, but strangely alluring, line. He slicked back his forelock, pleased with himself. *Chicks just can't help themselves . . .*

"So what do you do for a living," he parried, "besides being sexy?"

The drunken head-turner giggled. "I'm an investment banker."

"For real?"

"*Sí.* I'm a vice president at Wells Fargo. I handle hot portfolios." She ran her tongue over her gleaming white teeth. "Want to check out mine?"

Lawrence grinned, enjoying the rod-hardening back-and-forth. He'd sworn off Mexicans after that crazy Garcia clan. But that was then, this was now, and he was horny . . .

"Let's go find your bottom line," he said.

She nodded, bright-eyed from rum and lust. They stumbled to his Benz at the dead-end of the street and groped each other awhile, her hands stroking the Promised Land through his pants.

"Ready to get happy?" Lawrence said, pawing at her micro-skirt.

"Oh, no, let me do you first, *Señor Mucho Gusto,*" she purred, unzipping his fly. "Then you can have all the bottom line you want."

She knelt. He tugged it out. She swallowed it tip to tail . . .

Then ripped it off with a single sharp bite.

"Gaaaah!" Lawrence howled as arterial blood gushed from his torn member. She followed with a razor slice across his femoral artery.

He knocked her away, frantically clamping hands on both wounds. "Oh, God, please, call nine-one-one, please, don't let me die," he begged.

"They can't help you, Mr. Lawrence," the suddenly un-drunk redhead said, dabbing her bloody mouth on a tissue. "You'll drain out in thirty seconds, and there's no way to stop it."

"What . . . why . . . who . . ." Lawrence gargled, head spinning as his life splashed onto the steaming Texas asphalt.

"Jimmy Garcia sends his regards," the redhead said, walking away.

Chapter 54

NOGALES, ARIZONA

Charvat did a spit-take as he read the real-time decryption of the "tampon" signal. "Dammit! Sue's at Jimmy's ranch!"

"What's she doing there?" Williams said, aghast.

"She didn't say, the transmission was interrupted . . . wait, she's starting again . . . oh, damn, get on the horn to the Pentagon . . ."

Williams, eyes wide, sent it flash priority.

MEXICAN AIRSPACE, SIXTY MILES FROM JIMMY'S RANCH

"Well, this just got more interesting," said the Delta Force raid commander.

"Yeah?" the assault pilot said, adjusting his altitude. He was a senior aviator in the Sixtieth Special Operations Aviation Regiment, the "Night Stalkers." He'd flown so many Delta and SEAL operators into battle zones that nothing much surprised him anymore.

The raid commander spoke the flash message aloud: "Friendly confirms VX missile is at ranch," he said. "Friendly confirms mobile launcher with truck. Missile and launcher are three hundred yards north of main building. Radar and heat-seeking capabilities undetermined. Friendly is still on site, repeat, still on site. Description follows . . ."

"So there *is* something new under the sun," the pilot said.

"Confirms our VX is there, anyway," the commander said.

"Should we assume that missile is surface-to-air and can therefore wax our ass?"

"We'd be dumb not to. Go in hot, I'll notify the others . . ."

JIMMY'S RANCH

Ah-ooh-ga! Ah-ooh-ga!

"What the hell?" Jimmy said, leaping to his feet as attack Klaxons brayed.

"Choppers, *Jefe*!" the chief of security screamed as he ran from the main house, chopping his arm to the north-northeast. "A fleet just popped up on my radar!"

"Someone begs to die tonight, *amigos*! Get to your battle stations!" Jimmy commanded. "Antiaircraft teams, fire the moment you confirm target lock!"

"What about the VX?" the weapons man shouted as helicopter rotors washed in and out of the stiff mountain wind.

"Prepare to launch. If ground troops are with the choppers, we'll annihilate—"

Sunbursts twinkled from the bottom of the lead chopper. A stream of depleted-uranium bullets—tank killers—slammed into the VX missile, rupturing it.

"Jimmy! Who are these people, what's happening?" Izzy screamed as she ran from the house.

"Get back, get away, that's poison gas!" Jimmy shouted, waving his arms like a madman. Izzy froze as the translucent cloud bent in her direction. "Move, Izzy, run!" Superstition screamed, breaking into a sprint as September 27 fire teams opened up.

LEAD CHOPPER, DELTA FORCE

"Ahhhh, shit!" Karson and Norobi chorused as an antiaircraft missile sheared the tail rotor and forced the chopper into a flat, lethal spin. "Brace for impact," the SOAR pilot said calmly, batting away a chunk of pork that sailed through the fuselage and splashed hot sauce on his windshield. "We're gonna land in that waterfall."

"All units, lay suppressive fire," the raid commander ordered.

JIMMY'S RANCH

Gunships rained fire and destruction. Uncles, aunts, and cousins disintegrated as their homes exploded, joined by the fuel tank on the missile truck, which kicked its launch machinery into a high, wide arc. The beast banged off a wall and tumbled down the steep terrain.

Straight onto Isabel.

"Help me!" she screamed as three tons of steel nailed her pelvis to the mountaintop.

"Kill them!" Jimmy bellowed to his *narcos*. "Kill them all!" He ran for Isabel, Superstition hard on his heels, as the VX grew like a thunderhead.

"Jimmy!" she shouted. "Are there any other bombs to worry about?"

"No," Jimmy said, panting as he got to the mangled launcher. "The rest are in storage."

Then I have to get you out of here, so I can find them. "We'll save you, Izzy!" she screamed, trying to push the launcher with her shoulder.

"Put your back into it!" Jimmy screeched as strain-sweat popped off his face. "We have to get her out!"

The dirty tears crept to thirty yards, then twenty yards. *Narcos* collapsed in the mist, vomiting, praying, and curling into commas. "Go . . . get away . . ." Izzy gargled as blood from internal injuries frothed over her lips. "Save yourselves."

"Forget it, Sis," Jimmy snarled, scraping dirt from under her shoulders. "You're gonna be fine and you're gonna have babies and Sue's gonna stay so you two can be friends forever."

Isabel locked her eyes on Superstition. "Too . . . late," she croaked. "This . . . my . . . destiny. Yours is save . . . my brother. Save . . . Jimmy."

Ten yards.

Nine yards.

"I will, I swear," Superstition said, nodding through her tears.

"I love you, Skeeter," Isabel said.

"Me too," Superstition choked, kissing each cheek. "Save me a nice soft cloud and don't forget the Fritos, little sister." She chopped Jimmy in the nerve bundle at the base of his neck. The cartel strongman collapsed, unconscious. She scooped him up and started running.

Six yards.
Five yards.
Her eyes burned. Her nose ran. She prayed it was adrenaline, not VX.
Four yards.
Three yards.
Four yards.
Six yards.
Nine yards.

Superstition whirled around as she kept running. Isabel was waving, her face bright pink, her eyes unblinking. The dirty tears engulfed her. She stiffened. Gasped. Curled like a comma.

Superstition sprinted behind the main house, the various fireballs scorching her flesh. She aimed for the rabbit hole Jimmy had mentioned at supper. The mile-long escape tunnel, blasted from solid granite, led to prepositioned weapons, food, water . . .

And a heavy-sprung, mountain-ready, Kevlar-armored Jeep.

THE WHITE HOUSE

"Any other nerve bombs?" the president said.

"No, sir, just the one on the missile," the Delta raid commander said on the encrypted video feed, his clothing drenched and bloody from pulling wounded men from the waterfall. "Maybe your busboy was dialing for dollars."

The CIA director looked away.

"What about Mrs. Davis?" the president said.

"No sign of her or Garcia," the commander said.

"Keep looking," the president ordered between gritted teeth.

ESCAPE FROM THE MOUNTAIN

"Wake up, Jimmy, I need your help," Superstition said, steering with one hand and slapping with the other. Only groans. She doused him with canteen water, drew back for another strike.

He caught her hand mid-swing. "Where . . . are we?"

"Escaping," she said.

He groaned as he struggled upright. "I remember now. Is my sister . . ."

"Yes," Superstition said, dodging a coyote as she raced down the rock-strewn goat path, the mountaintop hacienda a smudged, undulating glow in the rearview mirror. "Her final request was that I save you, Jimmy. She said it was her destiny to die so you could live. So I knocked you unconscious and carried you into the tunnel."

"You had no way to free her?"

"None. She was pinned too tightly. Even if we managed, she'd have bled out before we got ten yards." She blew out her breath. "I'm really sorry, Jimmy. I loved her too."

"She meant the world to me," Jimmy said, putting his hand on Superstition's arm. "Thanks for being her friend."

"I'm glad I was there. At the end. When she . . . passed."

His eyes widened. "You actually saw her die?" he said, his voice thick.

Superstition nodded. "Izzy was as brave as any ten *narcos*."

"Tell me. Every detail."

She did. He listened without interruption, rubbing his eyes.

"*Americanos* did this, you know," he said when she was finished.

"How do you figure that?" Superstition said, having no doubt but wanting to know what he knew. "The helicopters were unmarked."

"When you're wanted by the whole world, you recognize the things that can kill you. Those choppers were U.S. military. SEAL, Delta, Rangers, one of those special units. Or CIA hunter-killer teams, which use the same equipment."

"You can't be surprised," she said. "A bomb exploded at Delgado's. If the wind was blowing right, border detectors picked up the scent, and the Pentagon got scared—"

"They ain't seen nothing yet," Jimmy said, his voice raspy with anger and grief. "I have friends in your military, so I'll find the soldiers and pilots who killed my family." He punched his fist in his other palm, over and over, each wet smack a gunshot. "I'll hang them from ceiling pipes, rape their children, set their wives on fire, then torture everyone to death. Then I'll go to their graves, dig them up, and kill them all over again."

"I'll help you," Superstition lied, recalling the cold frenzy with which she'd tried to dig up Derek. She was perfectly sane, yet grief still made her that crazy. She couldn't imagine the volcanic eruptions going off in this psycho's brain. "The way Izzy died . . . the way I've been treated since my arrest . . . I'm ready for payback. Wanna use those other bombs to do it?"

Jimmy coughed up dirt and spit it out the window. "Hell yeah," he said. "And I got just the place to light one. Dallas."

"Why Dallas?"

His grin was as a shark's. "I'm sentimental that way."

THE WHITE HOUSE

"Still no sign of them?" the FBI director said.

"Sue or Jimmy, no," the CIA director said, shaking his head. "We found his little sister, though. She was pinned by shrapnel and caught a full boat of VX." The ghastly raid video captured by Delta helmet cams disturbed him greatly. While he loved sticking it to the man who'd killed his four agents—the sight of their crusty fingerprints on the Texaco ID cards still kept him awake at night—that didn't extend to innocent bystanders. And Isabel Garcia, despite her royal shafting by the Justice Department, was an innocent bystander.

"How many dead?" the president said.

"Sixty, give or take," the CIA director said. "Some *narcos*, most Jimmy's extended family, according to his chef." To the president's arched eyebrows, he explained: "He was lugging garbage to the incinerator when our choppers arrived. He kept running."

"Bright boy. Any way the chef knows it was us?"

"No, sir," said the chairman of the joint chiefs. "Several of the D-boys speak perfect Spanish, and they swagger like *narco* toughs. The chef swears on a stack it was a sneak attack by a rival cartel. Fortunately for our cover story, such raids are not uncommon among cartels."

"Crips and Bloods, writ large?" the president said.

"Something like that, Mr. President."

"Looks like our cover will hold, then. How many of our people are . . . gone?"

"Two, Mr. President, a SOAR pilot and a Delta operator. A missile clipped the tail of the lead craft and dumped it into that waterfall." He chugged his French roast, needing the jolt; it would be a long night. "The ranch was lousy with hidden antiaircraft. We were lucky to get out with as few casualties as we did."

The FBI director nodded, thinking about Superstition. He'd been shocked to learn she was at the ranch, and prayed she was still alive. "Any squawking from Mexico City?" he asked.

"A dozen phone messages from Braveheart," the president said. "I'm letting him stew awhile before I swear I know nothing about it."

"He's worried about the other *narcos*," the CIA director said. "If they think he didn't give his all to protect their interests, they'll give him a twenty-one-gun salute. Which would serve the bastard right, cozying up with those whacks."

They kicked that around for a while. "All right, let's call it a night," the president said, stretching as he yawned. "I've got an early flight tomorrow."

Shock crossed the FBI director's face. "You still going to Dallas?" he said.

"Why wouldn't I?" the president said.

"We just wiped out Jimmy's family, he's got VX, and Dallas ain't all that far from Mexico," the FBI director argued, ticking off the arguments on his fingers. "You should stay in Washington till we catch the creep."

"No can do," the president said. "It's my biggest fund-raiser this year."

The CIA director shook his head. "Kennedy flew to Dallas. They call him tragic."

"Bush avoided Manhattan. They call him yellow," the president said. "I leave at six."

1970

JULY 4
ABOARD THE SS LEE HOUSTON
GULF OF MEXICO

"Sucks to work holidays," the Army lieutenant griped over the bellow of diesel engines.

"My kids are with my ex in Memphis," the Navy captain said. "So I got nothing better to do than work." He waggled his eyebrows. "If you haven't heard, New Orleans throws a helluva party on the Fourth, and they love a man in uniform."

The lieutenant brightened. Offered the captain a Twinkie. They munched contentedly.

"Approaching disposal coordinates, Captain," his navigator sang out.

"Very well," the captain said. "Prepare for demolition."

The *Lee Houston* was born in 1942 as a United States Liberty ship. It hauled beef, bombs, and bullets to ports from Great Britain to Guadalcanal, fueling the ravenous war machine that bombed Hitler and Tojo back to the Stone Age. But Liberties were, by necessity, constructed quick and cheap, so they wore out fast. The *Lee Houston* was no exception, and after the Korean War ended, the ship was unceremoniously mothballed to drift at anchor in a backwater southern port, collecting barnacles, wharf rats, and rust.

Until this final run to the sea.

"Let's check the loading one more time," the lieutenant said.

"Belts and suspenders," the captain agreed.

They took the corrosion-pocked stairs into the main cargo hold. A dozen long metal cylinders, each painted a matte olive drab, stenciled with yellow symbols and letters, and wrapped together in a hair net made of welded steel wire, glowed from the light of the bare bulbs overhead. The cylinders were pointed at one end and flat on the other, looking to the captain like eight-foot cigars. "General Patton smoked stogies this big, right?" he said.

" 'Course he did," the lieutenant snorted. "Everything's bigger in the Army, including our cigars. Hell, the matches to light 'em are pine trees dipped in sulfur."

The captain grinned, enjoying the competitive banter that military folks had engaged in since, he supposed, Og threw rocks at Throg. "Since we're stubbing these 'stogies' out anyway, can you tell me what's in them?" he said. "Be fun to tell my grandkids someday how Grandpa won the Cold War all by himself."

The lieutenant hesitated. Nobody got told, for operational security. *But what the hell, Hitler's dead, Japan's radioactive, and I retire next month.*

"Nerve gas," the lieutenant said. "With a death-germ chaser."

The captain jerked like a bilge rat bit his ankle. "Are you kidding?"

"Nope, it's VX and anthrax," the lieutenant said. To him this was old hat, having served in the Chemical Corps most of his career. He forgot that civilians—which meant everyone not wearing Army khaki, in his humble opinion—got the vapors when they heard "chemicals" and "germs." "Don't worry, the bombs are harmless. Unless you kick the nose cones." His gummy grin showed Twinkie crumbs. "Do that, we'll have our own fireworks display right here."

The captain had regained his composure. "These look factory fresh."

"They should. They're straight off the production line at Edgewood Arsenal."

"So why the hell are we throwing them away?"

"Up to me, we wouldn't," the lieutenant said, shrugging. "It's a useful weapon to drop on the Commies if they invade Europe. But it's not up to me. Nixon decided—"

"President Nixon," the captain, a stickler for military courtesy, reminded.

"Right, President Nixon decided to ban chemical and biological weapons," the lieutenant said. "The world went along." He ran his fingers through his hair, repositioned his cap. "The technical problem is there's no good way to neutralize this stuff. So the Pentagon decided to dump it in the sea, let pressure and salt water do the rest." He waved his hand. "Congratulations, Captain. You're officially a soldier in Operation CHASE."

"Which is?"

" 'Cut Holes And Sink 'Em,' " the lieutenant said. The captain rolled his eyes, and the lieutenant snickered in sympathy. The military loved its acronyms, no matter how tortured—

"Sir, we're dead on target," the navigator hollered into the hold.

"Be right up," the captain responded. To the lieutenant: "Bourbon Street awaits, so let's get the show on the road."

They watched from the bow of the transfer boat as explosive ordinance demolition teams blew the seacocks of the bent-and-bowed Liberty ship. Seawater raced in unchecked, flooding cargo holds and crew berths and engine bays. Yeomen served coffee and fresh-fried doughnuts. The dented stern sank first. The rust-pocked bow joined next. When the radio mast disappeared, the crew saluted the bubbles. Twenty minutes later, timed charges blew the hull apart. The explosion came to the surface as a giant belch.

"Another brave soldier bites the dust," the lieutenant murmured as the transfer boat swung toward New Orleans. This was his seventh CHASE disposal. Most were loaded with conventional arms—bombs, torpedoes, mines, projectiles, fuzes, detonators, rocket motors, boosters, cannon barrels, and in one odd case, contaminated cake mix, which an Army court had ordered dumped at sea. The rest were biochem. All bothered him. Liberty ships like the *Lee Houston* were the workhorses of a noble crusade—without their nonpareil ability to get millions of tons of cargo into the hands of the Allied troops doing the fighting, the entire world would be speaking German and Japanese. He'd rather put these vessels in museums than drown them like unwanted kittens, but those decisions were above his pay grade.

"I hope this doesn't come back to bite us," the captain said, stroking his wide chin. "Dumping poison into our home waters, I mean."

The lieutenant scoffed. "No way that can happen. The bombs will settle on the floor of the Gulf of Mexico, five thousand feet below our feet." He stamped the steel deck for emphasis. "Where they'll be safe from prying eyes forever."

"You hope."

"The slide-rule boys ran simulations. Not even plankton can survive water pressure that immense, let alone a man or a submarine. Nothing's going to get to those bombs except salt and pressure. Over time, they'll corrode, implode, and explode—that's why we left the nose-cone detonators intact—and that's the end of 'em. Gone forever."

"Unless," the captain said.

"Unless what?"

The captain pointed toward the sea floor. "Davy Jones decides forever, ain't."

Chapter 55

PRESENT DAY
WEAPONS STORAGE DEPOT
SOUTH OF NOGALES, MEXICO

"Good evening, *Jefe*, it's nice to see you," the guard preened. "I hope he informed you of the excellent job I did."

"He who?" Jimmy said, yawning as he flicked a cigarette out the Jeep's window.

"Javier."

Jimmy jolted upright. "Javier?" he said. "Are you *loco*? The man was killed in—"

"No, *Jefe*," the guard insisted. "He was here a few hours ago, driving a cargo truck. He said you wanted the VX—"

Jimmy bounded from the Jeep and grabbed the guard by the shirt. "The bombs!" he shouted. "He took the bombs?"

"Just one. The rest are still here."

"Idiot! Why didn't you call me to confirm?"

The guard began sweating. "He said it was a secret plan! He said you ordered it! He said if I questioned you I would be put to death and my family—"

"All right, all right," Jimmy said, pushing the man away. "Let me think."

"You said the rest are here, right?" Superstition jumped in.

The guard glanced fearfully at Jimmy. "Answer her, fool, before I shoot you for ignorance," Jimmy growled.

"*S-s-sí, Señora,*" he stuttered, slapping the door. "The rest are behind this solid steel."

"Then go ahead and unlock it," she commanded. "Load one into the Jeep."

"Just one?" Jimmy said, raising an eyebrow.

"It contains a million bullets," Superstition said. "That's enough to handle one little president, don't you think?" *And it leaves only one bomb to track down after America destroys this depot.*

Jimmy grinned. "One million droplets, one million dead. If your countrymen ever learn of your traitorous heart—"

"Fuck them," she snarled. "And the choppers they rode in on."

"*Sí,*" Jimmy said, holding the passenger door as she hopped into the shotgun seat, wondering how she'd get between her legs without him noticing. She thought briefly of Derek, who did it all the time, and smiled to herself. Scotland the Horny . . .

The Jeep rocked as the bomb was loaded. The guard threw a worn painters' tarp over the top and slapped the roof twice. Jimmy laid rubber for Texas. She put her hands between her legs and pulled the chain four times—once, a three-second pause, then twice in quick succession, another three-second pause, and then the final pull. She prayed someone recognized Morse code, as it'd been out of fashion for years.

"What are you doing?" Jimmy said.

"I'm fixing my underwear creep," she explained, mentally inserting the comma.

"Or you're thinking about me," Jimmy said with a sly grin.

She choked down rising bile and forced out a laugh. "It's been awhile since I've done that," she said. "Derek and I weren't exactly, you know . . ."

"He didn't appreciate a strong woman."

"No. He didn't."

"Well, I do."

She noticed the bulge in his skinny jeans. Tried not to gag. "When this is over, *Jefe,*" she murmured, running a fingernail up his leg, "I'll give you something you'll never forget."

WASHINGTON, D.C.
J. EDGAR HOOVER BUILDING

"That's Superstition!" Jerome Jerome shouted, thumping the desk in the FBI's Operations Command Center. "That's her signal. Where's it coming from?"

The signals analyst pointed to the originating coordinates on the wall-sized digital map.

"Is a message attached to the signal?" Jerome said.

"None, sir, just the coordinates . . . there it is again. And again." He checked to ensure it wasn't a computer hiccup. "Same exact map location, but sent four separate times: flash, pause, flash-flash, pause, flash."

Jerome considered that. Transmission without a message meant someone was watching her. Without knowledge of where the bombs were hidden, she wouldn't risk capture and execution even once—let alone four times—without a compelling reason . . .

Dash-dot-dot-dash!

THE WHITE HOUSE

"Good work, J. J., outstanding!" the FBI director yelped into the phone. The president poked his head back inside the Situation Room, having just departed to get his shut-eye for the morning flight. "What's up, Doc?"

"Sue's alive. She flashed the same map coordinate four times. No message was attached."

"Four separate contacts *is* a message," said the commander of Delta Force.

"But what's it mean?" the defense secretary said.

"It's Morse code for the letter X," the FBI director said, concurring with Jerome Jerome's instincts. "As in, X marks the spot. She found the rest of the bombs, and this is the location."

"Hot damn," the defense secretary said, smacking one fist into another. "Where are your choppers, Eric?"

"Just entering Tucson air space," the Delta commander said. "They'll refuel at Davis-Monthan AFB and return to Fort Bragg."

"Can you turn 'em around?" the president said.

The commander rushed the logistics in his head. "If you give the order in the next sixty seconds. Otherwise, they've got to refuel."

"Invade a sovereign nation once, you'll get away with it," the secretary of state warned. "Twice is political suicide."

"How do we know that's what Sue means, anyway?" the CIA director said, still smarting from the unanticipated disaster at Jimmy's ranch. "Maybe she pulled the string by accident."

"Four times?" the FBI director said.

"I'm sold," the defense secretary said.

"I'm not," the CIA director said.

"Me neither," the secretary of state said.

"Gotta know now, Mr. President," the Delta commander warned, hand on the hotline to Raid Leader. He had his own opinion on what Davis was trying to say—*I found the bombs, guys, come get them*—but kept it to himself because it wasn't his call.

Everyone looked at the president.

NATIONAL PALACE, MEXICO CITY

"Jimmy Garcia just blew up his own ranch!" the defense minister shouted as he raced into the president's office, his hands trembling so hard that his portfolio shook like a paint mixer. "And the CIA is helping him flee the country!"

"What?" the president of Mexico said, blinking rapidly with confusion. "The CIA tried to assassinate him. Why would he cooperate with them now?"

"The cartels put out a hit on his sister when she was in prison in Fargo. Jimmy found out and contacted the CIA. He offered the location of every *narco* warehouse in Mexico in exchange for twenty million dollars and safe passage to the United States. CIA drones are heading for the warehouses as we speak!"

The president banged his kneecaps jumping out of his chair. "Have we confirmed the destruction of the ranch? If so, can we prove Jimmy ordered it, as opposed to an accident?"

"Yes and yes," the minister said. "A policeman patrolling that sector reported massive explosions at the top of the mountain. He's driving up now to confirm, but he's positive they were real, as he can still see the fires." He cleared his throat. "As to Jimmy ordering it, that was confirmed by a man who called our switchboard."

"Really? What is this man's name?" the president said, smelling a hoax.

"He wouldn't provide it."

"Of course not—"

"But he says he worked for September 27 and that he was inside Delgado's mansion when the nerve gas bomb exploded in the trophy room—"

"He used that term? He actually said 'nerve gas'?" the president gasped. His military scientists had confirmed the blast was VX and anthrax. But admitting tht publicly would cause a nationwide panic; worse, the cartels would blame him for the ensuing disruption in business. So the president released the cover story about a "natural gas explosion" and put out the word that whoever dared claim otherwise would be shot at sunrise. If this caller knew it was nerve gas and it happened in Delgado's "Sistine Chapel," this was no hoax. "How on Earth did he survive?"

The minister sat before he collapsed from fear. In a fight to the death with the combined cartels of Mexico, no one in government would survive, including him. "When the caller learned Jimmy had nerve gas, he got himself a syringe of antidote, just in case," the minister said. "He injected his thigh when the bomb went off, and it kept him alive. He knew only Jimmy could have pushed the button—remote detonator, he claims—so he called to rat him out."

"Thank God for revenge," the president said. "What else did this caller tell you?"

"That Jimmy blew up his ranch and family to make it look like one of the CIA strikes," the minister said. "That Jimmy and his handlers are heading for a tunnel east of Nogales. The caller says he personally supervised that tunnel dig, and he provided us the GPS coordinates." The minister shook his head. "As soon as the CIA gets him across the border, Jimmy will disappear into their federal witness protection program and—"

"You will not let that happen," the president said in a whisper so strangled that it hit like an iron pipe. "You will capture him alive, and you will see to his execution. And while you're doing that, you'll get your Marines in the air and kill that tunnel." He swallowed hard. *"Ándale!"*

TRUCK REPAIR FACILITY, MIRACLE VALLEY, ARIZONA

"Sí, Jefe!" the tunnel engineer yelped, the unexpected call from September 27's boss startling him from his post-meal drowse. "It'll be ready when you arrive." He barked at the *narcos* to shove back the rolling door from the truck-sized opening. Finished just yesterday, this tunnel was, in his opinion, so breathtakingly sculpted that Michelangelo would have wept in jealousy. "Jimmy needs a van with Texas plates," he said.

The *narco* grabbed a set from the fifty-state drawer. "Load?"

"Camping gear. Food and water. Two Uzis, two Glocks," the engineer said, ticking off the list. "A case of loaded magazines—no, two. Better to have and not need."

"Cell phones?"

"Burners," the engineer said. "And iPads with the latest U.S. maps."

The warehouse team scrambled to comply. "Is Jimmy going to war?" the *narco* said.

"So it seems," the engineer sighed. "I just hope he doesn't destroy my pretty new hole in the process."

BACK ROADS OF MEXICO, EN ROUTE TO MIRACLE VALLEY

"How do we cross the border without your jet?" Superstition said, rubbing her head from the thirtieth smack on the roof from the washboard highway. "Ride a magic carpet?"

"I have a brand-new tunnel," Jimmy said, not bothering to steer around the coyote in the middle of the road. The ragged gray animal smacked the bumper and flew over the roof, its broken teeth rattling off the windshield like hail. "I built it to bring my Taliban drugs into the United States. It's wide and high enough to run full supply trucks."

"An underground interstate," she said in genuine, if horrified, admiration. For a psychotic killer, he was pretty resourceful. "That's the height of efficiency."

"Hell, yeah. I'm the Henry Ford of *narco*." He grinned briefly. "I'm putting you in charge of the smuggling operations, if you're up for it."

"We're going to keep running drugs," Superstition said incredulously, "after assassinating the president of the United States?"

"We have no choice, Sue," Jimmy said. "We need money to build our empire."

We. Our.

"Fine by me," she said.

"Are you sure?" he said. "What you've done till now is small potatoes. Taking this next step is . . . well, it's murder and treason. There's no going back after this. If they catch you, Fargo will be the Four Seasons compared to where they'll stick your narrow white ass."

"They stole my life," Superstition said. "Now they killed Izzy, my best friend. I'm in if you are." She grinned. "And my ass ain't so narrow, as you'll find out soon enough."

"Attagirl," he said, pinching her left breast.

She considered killing him right now and sending another *X*; let Jerome Jerome clean up this mess. But the Jeep might swerve out of control and set off the bomb, endangering any town through which they passed. And shutting down a Taliban drug highway would be a nice bonus.

"Driving an air-conditioned truck sure beats climbing through those sewer pipes you call tunnels," she fake-complained.

"Hey, I gave you the easy routes," he said. "Shoulda seen some of the snake holes Delgado sent me through."

She shuddered. Not a fan of confined spaces in the best of circumstances, she'd bulled through her claustrophobia by remembering how Derek had squished like rotten grapes in the morgue. "How'd you dig this big a hole without being detected?"

Jimmy waved in the direction of the United States. "Border Patrol doesn't install listening devices that far east of Nogales. No budget. My engineer tested the soil, found it ideal for an oversized tunnel. My lawyer bought an abandoned factory on the American side for the exit and turned it into a truck repair facility."

"Fake, of course," she assumed.

"No, they fix trucks for real," he said. "Including U.S. government fleet contracts, which cracks me up. It's a good way to launder money, too, which you'll have to learn when you take over that part."

"What's on your side of the border?" she said.

Jimmy recalled the stubborn old cattle rancher. Recalled his proud refusal to accept September 27's money. Recalled the lumpy brain-spatter. He explained. "Javier was running this dig before he . . . well, didn't die, I guess." He explained that, too.

"How'd he escape?" she said, astonished that anyone could have survived such poisonous napalm. Jimmy's shrug said, *Who knows,* and that's all she got. He turned onto a wider, smoother road. "Next stop, Miracle Valley," he said.

"I've never heard of it," she said, trying to draw out details.

"It's on the border, south of Tombstone and west of Bisbee," he said. "Home of sun, scorpions, and most important, Rough River Road."

"Is there a rough river?" she said, recalling the back-and-forth with Killer Bee about the pot of gold at the end of Rainbow Street. "On Rough River Road?"

"Fuck if I know," he said. "It's where the facility is—Rough River Road."

Bingo. "I gotta pee," she said. "All that Champagne you forced me to drink."

He smirked. "Forced? You drank some of my best men under the table." He stopped the truck and swept his arm at the dry, high desertscape. "Take your pick of toilets."

She swung her legs out of the Jeep. Heard a thrum in the distant gray clouds. Looked up and around. It was a tight formation of Apache gunships and Little Bird helicopters, flying south at top speed. Both models were used by American Special Forces, though these particular choppers were unmarked. "How about it?" she said, pointing.

"Long as they aren't shooting at us," Jimmy said with a shrug, lighting a cigarette with the embers of the last, "who cares?" He flicked his hand impatiently. "G'wan, pee so we can go."

She ran for the rocks. Lifted her skirt and slipped out the transmitter. "Tunnel ends at truck repair facility in Paradise Valley, Arizona," she said in a low, steady voice. "Rough River Road, ETA ninety minutes, in Jeep with Garcia, one nerve bomb on board." She pulled the chain and started the second part. "The other bombs are stored at—"

"Hide! Now!" Jimmy screamed from not ten yards behind.

She jumped, heart pounding, adrenaline roaring. If he caught her, she would die without having confirmed the bomb depot coordinates—her "X marks the spot" gambit might not have been interpreted correctly. She started to slide the "tampon" back home, but the sand shifted under her weight, knocking her sideways. The radio fell into a hole like a wedding ring down a drain. "What? Why?" she gasped as much to herself as Jimmy, yanking up her pants and whirling to see an Uzi and a dark, mean expression.

"Mexican Marines," he warned, pointing to the sky as three pairs of Black Hawk attack helicopters, bristling with rockets and chain guns, roared north toward the border.

She flattened herself against the boulder. "Do they know we're here?"

"No," he said, crouching next to her. "No one knew where we were heading, so this has to be coincidence." He stroked his blood-scabbed chin. "Either that, or Mexico City heard about my fancy new tunnel and decided to take it for ransom."

"They use Marines as bagmen?" she said, raising an eyebrow.

"Politicians are addicted to money," he said. "Cartels got more than they do, so who better than armed troops to make us hand it over?" His breathing was deep but steady. "Either way, the tunnel's no good to us, 'cause that's where those choppers are heading."

And there's no way to tell anyone, she thought, glaring at the broken crust of sand.

The chopper noise faded, and they hustled to the Jeep. They pulled up maps and debated options. Too guarded, too far, too whatever. He pulled at his greasy neck. "This sucks," he said irritably. "There's gotta be somewhere we can cross—"

"There is!" Superstition said, snapping her fingers. The audacity of her plan was as frightening as it was compelling. She could only pray Killer

Bee was still enough on her wavelength to suss out her intentions. "It's the very last place they'd expect us . . ."

They turned west for the crossing at Nogales.

Chapter 56

J. EDGAR HOOVER BUILDING
WASHINGTON, D.C.

Jerome relayed the coordinates of the truck tunnel to his boss, the director. Then he called Williams. "The military wants the glory, but it's our damn case," he said. "So go get him."

NOGALES, ARIZONA

Williams explained what Jerome wanted. Charvat tossed her the keys to his Jeep. She raised an eyebrow. It was a Border Patrol ride, so he'd been driving the entire time, with her handling communications, navigation, and weapons.

"I'm starting to leak," he said, patting his wounds.

She looked at his shirt. Several spots were damp with blood. Likewise, his khaki slacks. "Where's the nearest hospital?" she said, alarmed at how wan the Border Patrol chief suddenly looked. "I'll drop you at Emergency, then head out myself—"

He gave her a withering look.

"Yeah, yeah, I know," she said. "Tough guy to the end." He held up Boy Scout fingers. "I won't bleed to death," he said. "But I can't drive safely, either."

"Who said anything about safe?" Williams said, punching the accelerator so hard that their skulls jammed into their headrests.

BOMB STORAGE DEPOT, SOUTH OF NOGALES

The depot guards saw the choppers. Saw the cannons and chain guns and rockets. Saw the troops rope down to the sand and turn their way.

They dropped their rifles and ran for the hills.

The Delta raid commander aimed his M4 at the closest back, then lowered the barrel. "You old softie," an operator gibed. "I only hunt big game," the raid commander said, figuring that the guys were too low-level to waste good bullets on. "Blow that door, Karson . . ."

The steel door crashed off its hinges. D-boys swirled in. "Clear!" they shouted.

"Bombs?" the raid commander said, striding inside.

"Right here!"

He counted. Sent the number up the food chain, along with live video. "Wire and fire," he ordered. D-boys wrapped each bomb with C4 plastic explosive. Attached detonators and signal receivers. Distributed canisters of "big hurt"—napalm, magnesium, and thermite.

They reattached the door and welded it shut. Moved the *narcos'* abandoned truck in front for extra mass. Scrambled to the choppers and flew back a half mile.

"Fire in the hole!" the commander sang, pushing TRANSMIT.

The C4 exploded, which triggered the VX bombs, which ignited the jellied gasoline, which fused the powdered magnesium, which burned at six thousand degrees Fahrenheit, which ignited the thermite, which burned even hotter, turning the bunker into an iron smelter.

Destroying the VX.

Frying the anthrax.

Fusing bomb casings, floors, walls, ceilings, doors, locks, rocks, dirt, pee bottles, straw hats, and scorpions into the D-boy equivalent of modern art . . .

Along with a hundred AKs and rocket grenades purchased from Uncle Sam.

The commander checked his various detectors as the bubbling mass congealed. Zero emissions. "Target destroyed," he radioed. "No leaks."

"Well done," the president said. "Head on back before you run out of gas." Pause. "Uh, make that fuel, Raid Leader. You just took care of the gas . . ."

JIMMY'S TUNNEL, MEXICO

"Why, yes, waiter, I do like my steaks well done," the Mexican Marine pilot quipped as he pickled the button marked MISSILES. Six high-explosive warheads slammed into the ranch house that covered the tunnel entrance. The thunderous blasts ignited the thermite packs his ground troops had wired to the tunnel walls and ceiling, right up to the invisible line in the sand that marked the border with the United States, and a little beyond for kicks.

KILLER BEE'S JEEP

Charvat waved Williams's smartphone. "Shit, they just nuked our tunnel!"

She skidded to a halt, the stink of burned rubber filling the Jeep. "Jimmy and Sue haven't arrived yet," she said, checking her watch. "Why'd we cut off their exit?"

Charvat read the rest of Jerome's long text. "We didn't. It was a Mexican military strike," he said. "They blew up the tunnel from their end, and the whole thing collapsed. Half of Miracle Valley's on fire."

She shook her head in mounting frustration as another opportunity slithered out of her grasp. This guy had more lives than nine cats. "Where else can they cross?"

Charvat pulled out his iPad and loaded his maps, scratching his head as he computed times and distances. "They have to truck the bomb across because it's too heavy to lift," he said. "But Mexican Marines just destroyed the only tunnel big enough to handle vehicles." He ran his fingers through his hair. "I hope it's the only truck tunnel. Hell, we didn't know about this one."

"Something that big is difficult and time-consuming to build, right?"

"Right," Charvat said.

"Then I'm guessing there's only one. Meaning, they'll need to cross out in the open," Williams said, frantically thinking of and rejecting possibilities. Visions of murders she was supposed to prevent whipped her like steel chains. "But where, Brian? Where will they come across? Arizona? Texas? New Mexico? Where? Just tell me, give me one little hint—"

"Jesus Christ, Feeby, I gotta do all the thinking?" Charvat roared as he slammed the dashboard with his fists. The unexpected outburst startled her so much that she nearly skidded off the road, which startled her even more as she overcorrected to get the Jeep back straight. It also did its intended job, she realized when her heart slowed—short-circuiting her panic.

"Meaning," she sighed, "you don't have a clue."

"No," he sighed back. "I don't. It's all conjecture now." He shifted in pain, tried not to show it. "And, Deb?"

"Yeah?"

"If a bomb does go off on American soil, that isn't on you. Or me, or any of us. That is solely on Jimmy Garcia." He winked. "But let's make sure that doesn't happen, huh? The paperwork would be substantial..."

They went back to the digital maps, batting around ideas, points, counterpoints, and his encyclopedic knowledge of the border landscape. Nothing rose to the level of tinfoil, let alone gold. Then Charvat snapped his fingers, eyes widening. "Here's where I'd go if I were Sue..."

Williams began objecting before he finished explaining. "It's one-in-a-million at best," she argued. "It only works if she thinks exactly the same way you do."

"She's bleeding, out of options, and sitting next to a maniac," Charvat said. "So, yeah, she's thinking exactly like me." He chuckled as Williams smacked his arm, then sobered. "Face it, Deb: This is our only shot. If we're right, we save the day. If we're wrong..."

She nodded and put the Jeep in a bootlegger one-eighty as Charvat called in orders to his agents, praying that he and Deb would make it to the final showdown. As she raced west, a thought occurred. "Do you keep a Taser in this vehicle?" she said, glancing around.

"Sure," Charvat said, pointing to the floor box where he stored extra gear. "Why?"

She told him as she pushed all the gauges into the red.

Chapter 57

BORDER CROSSING
NOGALES, ARIZONA

"Make sure you cover up everything," Jimmy said, flicking his lighter for luck as they inched to the head of the long line.

"This is insane," Superstition said, tugging the tent flaps to make sure camping gear shrouded every inch of the bomb.

"It was your idea, hiding in plain sight," Jimmy said. "Now behave, our company's here."

Border Patrol agents strolled up to the Jeep. Jimmy put his elbow out the window and blew a thin brown stream of Marlboro.

"Those things are worse than rattlesnakes," the agent said with a friendly smile. "I oughta know since I smoke 'em myself."

"I tried to quit," Jimmy said. "But nicotine patches are hard to light."

The agent laughed. "Mind if I bum one?"

Jimmy held out the pack, then fired the tip for him.

"My dad had one of those fishing-fly lighters," the agent enthused through rings of blue exhalation. "Back in the day."

"Papa left me this," Jimmy said. "When he died."

"Sorry to hear it. His death, I mean."

Jimmy felt no bad vibes. Excellent. A couple more yards, and they'd be free and clear for the fifteen-hour drive to Dallas, where he'd enter one passcode and then one more, and the bomb would turn their president into *mole*, just like John F. Kennedy in that motorcade.

"Mind if we sniff you for drugs?" the agent said.

"Be my guest," Jimmy said as Superstition nodded.

The German shepherd came around. Superstition wondered if it was the dog that nailed Izzy all those months ago. "They're clean," the handler announced.

"Welcome to the United States," the agent said. "Drive ahead for passport control."

Jimmy moved to the next line. More agents checked their passports. Hers was real. His was forged. Both were accepted. "Where you headed, folks?" the passport woman said.

"The Grand Canyon," Superstition chirped, fluttering her hands like a tourist, as they'd rehearsed. "We just got back from Copper Canyon."

"That's Mexico's version of Arizona's," Jimmy said. "We wanted to see which was bigger."

"Yours is," the passport woman said.

"Hey, thanks for noticing," Jimmy said, winking.

"Oh, honey, you're terrible!" Superstition said, playfully slapping "her man's" shoulder. "Never you mind this rascal, he's always saying things like that."

"Okay, handsome, you can go," the agent said with an easy smile. "Take that detour around the back of the building, and you'll find the entrance to the interstate. Enjoy your trip."

"We will," Jimmy said as he accelerated into the United States.

Superstition wondered what she could do if this bright idea fizzled. Brian and Deb were nowhere to be found. No strike teams were swinging from ropes like Batman and Wonder Woman. She'd have to crush Jimmy's throat at highway speed and pray the bomb didn't explode in the wreck. Once they were safely in the desert, away from civilization, she would do just that.

"Americans are such idiots," Jimmy said, smirking. "It's no wonder they're swirling down the toilet." He turned at the corner of the building . . .

. . . into a porcupine of gun barrels.

"This is the Border Patrol," Charvat graveled through the loudspeaker. "You are surrounded. Turn off your engine and put your hands in the air.

If you do not comply, you will be shot. This is your only warning—we will shoot to kill."

"It's . . . you!" Jimmy gasped, blinking rapidly. "The agent from Peck Canyon!"

Charvat grinned over the barrel of his submachine gun. "Yeah. Welcome back, asshole."

Agents rushed the doors. Slit their seat belts and yanked them out. Slammed them over the hood of the Jeep, frisked them hard enough to shear sheep.

"Transmitter!" an agent crowed, holding up Garcia's red phone.

"Don't touch the buttons," said the bomb squad commander, wheeling over a lead-lined safe that would cut off any signals from the device. "Rest of you, move the trailer in place . . ."

Williams raced up, raising her FBI badge with one hand and gun with the other. "Jiménez Garcia, you're under arrest," she announced. "You have the right to remain silent . . ."

Arrest??? "Oh hell no," Superstition murmured.

She grabbed a belt knife from an agent who'd drifted too close.

Wheeled for Jimmy's exposed throat.

Flopped to the ground as the Taser strike pulsed her like a radio fell in her bathtub.

"Guh, guh, guh, guh!" she slobbered, flopping like a gaffed tuna.

Which ignited all her wounds.

Which vapor-locked her brain with traumatic overload.

Which faded her world to black.

Chapter 58

THREE DAYS LATER
TUCSON MEDICAL CENTER

"I'm sorry I had to lie," Superstition murmured as the machines whirred and bleeped. "But millions of lives were at stake."

"We understand, honey, we do," Theresa said, squeezing her daughter's hand. "If you hadn't gone to prison, Jimmy would have murdered . . . well, everybody."

"We're in awe of you, Skeeter," George said, wiggling her toes from the end of the bed. "You're a national hero, and Derek would have been awfully proud. Timmy and Tommy, too."

Superstition nodded. Even as the Taser unhinged her molecules, her husband and children had been uppermost in her mind. She'd finally accepted that she'd have to go on without them, but it was nice to know Derek's emotional scent—as well as his real scent from the funky Chicago Bears jersey she rescued from the fire sale—would stay with her forever. She tried to shift. Winced.

"Careful," the doctor warned. "Open up those wounds again, I'll have to use duct tape. You used up all our sewing thread."

Superstition started to chuckle. But that hurt too. She sighed instead.

"You're still griping?" she heard a familiar voice say. "You just had two days off."

"Hey, Lieutenant," she said as her boss loped through the door. "How's tricks?"

"*So* not the same without you," Hanrahan said, waving the blindingly orange dress she'd worn the night this all began.

Theresa jumped up to hug him. "We're so delighted to have been wrong about you, Robbie," she choked. "Thank you, Jesus. Thank you, thank you, thank you."

"Ask Him to turn down the heat while you're at it, huh, Mrs. Kallas?" Deb Williams pleaded as she walked in with Jerome Jerome. "It's a hundred and nine out there, for pity's sake."

"Mom, Dad, meet Deb and Jerome," Superstition said. "My FBI handlers."

"Thank you for keeping her alive," George said, shaking their hands.

"Thank you for raising an exceptional woman," Jerome said.

Hanrahan rolled his eyes.

"What?" Jerome said.

"You never said that about me," Hanrahan said.

"Okay. You're an exceptional woman."

"That's not what I meant . . ."

"Hail, hail, the gang's all here," Brian Charvat said, sneaking in behind Williams and Jerome.

"Come on in, Killer Bee," Deb said, handing him a cup of Starbucks. "We're making fun of Robbie."

"That never gets old," Charvat said.

"But all good things must come to an end," Jerome said pointedly. "Mr. and Mrs. Kallas, can you give us some time with your daughter?" Theresa looked concerned. "Just wrapping up details, that's all," Jerome assured. "Then you can have her back, I promise."

"Every girl's dream," Superstition murmured, watching her parents stroll out hand in hand. When Dad saw the broken keepsakes in the living room, he demanded to know what was really going on. Mom confessed to the hit on Maurice Bishop. After recovering from his shock, he said he was proud as hell of her. He only wished she'd told him right away, so he could have helped her through the valley of the shadow of death . . .

Superstition moaned.

"Hit your pain button," Charvat said.

"That's not why I'm moaning," Superstition said.

"So?"

She blew out her breath. "I didn't get Jimmy. I wanted him so bad I could taste it. I wanted to cut his throat and watch him bleed out at my feet."

Williams nodded. "That's why I borrowed the Taser," she said. "As soon as the bomb was secure, I knew you'd go for the jugular. I couldn't let that happen."

Superstition understood: For Deb, law trumped justice. Most of the time, she agreed—without law, anarchy ruled and everyone suffered. But none of this was normal. Which is why she'd never tell anyone about the woman who killed the man who killed her babies.

"What happens to Jimmy?" she said, pressing the toggle to move up her head.

"That's classified," Jerome said.

"Yeah, I figured. But?"

His lips curled without humor. "Let's just say he's on a slow boat to the Caribbean."

Guantanamo.

That worked for her.

Well, sorta, anyway . . .

"Is he singing?" she said.

"Like a bird," Jerome said. "The minute I laid out his travel arrangements, he called his lawyer and begged for a deal."

"Freedom in exchange for everything he knows about the Taliban and cartels?"

"That's *really* classified," Jerome said, looking at the ceiling.

"Meaning," Hanrahan said with a yawn, "you bet your sweet Feeby ass."

Jerome frowned. "I'd never say something so crude. Come on, all of you, it's time to vacate the premises. I have something to say to Sue, alone." He shooed everyone to the door. "I'll meet you for dinner in an hour," he said. "Don't scarf *all* the ribs, Lieutenant."

Hanrahan shot a finger gun at Jerome, draped the orange dress over Superstition's feet, kissed her forehead, then fell in with Deb to leave.

Their body language suggested they'd buried the hatchet. Maybe even had grown to like each other. She hoped so.

Jerome moved a chair to her bedside. "I got you something," he said, pulling a long, irregularly shaped package from his briefcase. It was gift-wrapped in cartoon bagpipers.

She blinked with surprise. Jerome Jerome was many things, but touchy-feely-gift-y was not among them. She tore through the chanters and tartans with some effort, then cocked her head, unsure what to think. "You got me a chunk of wood?"

"Not just any old chunk. It's from your bar."

"From . . . my . . ."

Jerome smiled. "Your neighbor Clayton Brooks decided to rescue the piece that fell off when the movers got sloppy. This is it."

She nodded, remembering now. What she and Derek had built slipped out of the movers' hands while taking it to the U-Haul, breaking the bar and her heart. Excited, she put the jagged shard to her face. It still smelled of smoke and whiskey. "And Clayton called you?"

"Not me personally. Our Chicago field office. He asked them to relay a message to Agent Williams, see if she could give you back this piece of your life. That's what he called it, 'this piece of your life.' Deb told me, and I decided to play Santa."

Superstition's eyes watered with gratitude, and she touched Jerome's hand. "The wrapping paper, though, that was totally your idea, right?"

"Why they call me Mister Thoughtful at the office," he said.

"Do they really call you that?"

"Um, no," he said, horrified that she'd actually think so. He twisted gently in his chair, trying to ease the ache in his back. "So, Detective, what are you doing the rest of your life?"

She shrugged. "Getting well, first and foremost."

"Naturally. And then?"

"I've been cleared by the department," she said. "I can have my old job back."

"They'd be lucky to have you," Jerome said. "If that's what you really want."

Silence.

"Not anymore," she said.

"I'm glad you think that way," he said. "Would you like to work for me?"

She shook her head so hard that her hair jumped. "God no," she said. "You saw what happened the last time you offered me a job."

He looked crestfallen. "A bomb's still missing, you know," he said.

She put her hand to her mouth. "I thought we got them all," she said.

"So does everyone," he said. "Video from the submersible that first discovered the bombs, along with photographs taken by Delta operators inside the storage bunker, suggests that one remains at large. The president asked me to hunt it down, if it indeed exists. I'm putting together a team. I'd like you on board when you're ready."

She closed her eyes.

Thought of Derek.

Thought of Tommy and Timmy.

Thought of how dead she'd feel if there was a bomb and she hadn't tried to find it.

"When I can walk," she said, patting all her wounds, "I'll be ready."

Pleased, Jerome tapped her forehead with his index finger. He told her to call when she was up and around, and he'd send the FBI Gulfstream. And then he disappeared, argyles inside brogues under suit and tie and vest, tipped with a tri-color hanky.

She looked at the orange dress Robbie brought from the night this all began. Shook her head.

"Here we go again," she said.

Epilogue

FIVE MONTHS LATER
ST. MARTIN/SINT MAARTEN
LEEWARD ISLANDS

Jimmy Garcia brushed his teeth and combed his hair. He slipped on a Tommy Bahama shirt, white slacks, and penny loafers without socks.

Just the way she liked it.

He smiled in the mirror of the thousand-dollar suite. Enjoyed what looked back.

A free man.

Yeah, he'd spent a couple months at the U.S. military prison at Guantanamo. Big deal. The moment he'd started singing, they'd treated him like a pasha. Shade in the day, AC at night. Decent food and real coffee. Not like they gave the terrorist assholes, those sand monkeys who screeched and babbled in that psycho talk that gave him the shivers. He wasn't one of them.

Not by a long shot.

He left his suite and strolled through the lobby, giving the eye to anything with tits. One thing they didn't provide in Cuba was pussy. He was making up for that now.

The deal his lawyer cut was simple: Jimmy has information you'd kill your Aunt Bessie to learn. He knows the Taliban. He knows Hezbollah, al-Qaeda, Islamic State. He knows the cartels and their financiers, suppliers, weapons, routes, and banks. He'll even draw you a Google map to show how they all relate. All in exchange for . . .

Immunity.

Complete.

Which came last week in the form of a presidential pardon. Signed by The Man Himself and locked in a safe at his attorney's.

"Fuck 'em all!" he crowed to the dusking sky. A passerby frowned. He apologized and gave her a hundred-dollar bill. She actually curtsied. He got her phone number, too. Might have a need for dessert at midnight . . .

But the main course was Veronique.

He'd met her in Marigot, the nation's capital, on the white-powder beach at Princess Juliana Airport, where the jumbos thundered in just feet over sunbathers' heads. He found their power exhilarating, and the women who admired their beastly thrust, equally so. Veronique had been sunbathing in a green nano-kini. She was young. She was blond. She was toned, with big jugs, long legs, flaring hips, and an ass that could bounce a handful of quarters. Just the way he liked 'em. She'd smiled when he walked past. He'd said hello and bought her a drink. She'd said thanks and asked what he did. He'd said international man of mystery and how 'bout her? She'd said heiress and would he rub cream on her back? He'd said fine but there's no lotion. She'd said an international man of mystery could surely come up with a creamy substitute . . .

As night followed day followed day followed night.

Till now.

Twilight.

He was meeting her on a remote beach at the east end of the island. For a lovers' crescendo, she'd whispered. Just them, caviar, and Dom. Veronique was a shipping heiress from the south of France. She liked to spend, she said. She liked him, she said. She liked his unapologetic *macho*, she said. She liked his dick, she said. She was smitten, she said.

He was too.

But men did what men do, "desserts" included . . .

He flicked his see-through lighter, laughing.

He climbed into his Jeep and navigated the lonely, humping road along the coast. The island was bisexual, Veronique had kidded—the French half Saint Martin, the Dutch half Sint Maarten. They'd meet at the beach on the border, spread the blanket across the invisible line.

So they could, she'd said, suck in one country and fuck in the other.

He pulled into the deserted cove, fingering the silken Tommy Bahama, which flapped in the salt-laden breeze. Veronique gave it to him today, after eating him for lunch. The shirt was her favorite color, she said—orange—and long enough that it could double as a woman's dress. She thought it would look good against his tattooed chest and deep, piercing eyes. *Wear it to the picnic,* she'd urged. *When the sun slides into the water, I'll let you slide into me.*

He throbbed at the thought.

He walked off the parking gravel and onto the pie-flour sand. Kicked off his loafers, rolled up his slacks, and ambled for the sea, which everyone called the "Caribbean" but was really the far eastern end of the Gulf of *Meh-he-co.*

Veronique waved from its sapphire edge. Palms framed her. The setting sun burnished her. He waved back, his joy and lust swelling. Began to shout the dirty things that thrilled her . . .

Saw a twinkle.

Felt the impact.

Looked down in blinking disbelief to see a second bullet hit his second knee.

He collapsed into the sand, squawking and flapping, his blood attracting sand crabs and flies.

Veronique sprinted his way. "Help . . . me," he croaked, holding out a trembling hand. But she rushed past, replaced by a woman in Secret Circus jeans, who stepped from behind a jagged dune.

"You . . . you . . ." he gargled, struggling to stand on his shattered legs. He collapsed back to the beetles and crabs. He swallowed hard, mustered all his pride. Got up on a shoulder, which was, he considered, a miracle, as his knees had just been pulverized by a large-caliber weapon. He was amazed there wasn't any pain. But it would come. Pain always did . . .

"We didn't get a chance to say good-bye in Nogales," Superstition said, her eyes burning in violet anger. "So I thought I'd come over and fix that. Did you like Veronique?"

Jimmy's smile was a death's head. "Who is she? FBI? CIA?"

"Does it matter?" she said.

"I must have been in a fog," he acknowledged. "I never saw you coming."

"Then let me make things clear for you," she said, pulling a small pistol from her pocket.

"Bullets? You're not the first, sweetheart," he scoffed, pointing to the wormy holes dotting his body and the fresh ones in his knees. "I've survived plenty of lead."

She laid the sights on target. "But not teardrops," she said. "You've never survived a teardrop."

My knees must be affecting my hearing! "Teardrops?" Jimmy said. "What are you talking about? What kind of teardrops?"

"The one million drops I cried for my husband."

He stared as the implications of that number sunk in, and his linen crotch turned transparent. "What are you talking about?" he raged. "You despised Derek! He beat you! He didn't want your babies! You were happy I shot him dead."

"I lied," she said, pulling the trigger.

The air gun went *sput*. The VX-saturated pellet hit his chest in the orange V formed by the shirt's lapels and stayed put from the quick-acting glue. Jimmy's eyes widened in horror. He tried to grab her, tried to curse her. But his blood-laced vomit strangled word and deed.

"Say hi to Delgado," she said as he soiled the back of his white linen pants. "And the rest of your merry men."

"Whyyyy . . ." he managed to croak as his eyes went still and glassy, reflecting the orange of the setting sun as he began curling into a comma. "Whyyyy . . ."

"Because some people," she said, "just need killing."

She waited to make sure that was actually the case.

Then she injected herself with antidote and put on the special gloves. She pried the VX pellet off his mottled neck, sealed it and the gun in the special bag, and stuffed it in her pocket.

She smashed Jimmy's head with a handy rock and rifled his pockets to make it look like robbery. Then she walked into the waves to meet the rubber Zodiac purring noiselessly from the sea. She felt her stomach flip and paused to vomit. Sighing, she splashed seawater on her face and wiped it clean, rivulets of salt dripping off her chin. Poisoning Jiménez Garcia was the right thing to do. She'd have no regrets and lose no sleep. But she'd meant what she said to Deb in her basement rec room so many months ago: *I don't enjoy killing.*

The Zodiac pilot saluted. She waved and climbed aboard. It turned one-eighty, got zippy. Having spent hours on her father's fishing boats in Lake Michigan, she enjoyed the bouncy ride. The shimmering rainbow streaks from the latest leak in the *Deepwater Horizon* oil well saddened her, though. *Poor water,* she thought. *We don't deserve you . . .*

A power cruiser roared past, drop-kicking the Zodiac through its wake. "Hey, jerkoff!" the Zodiac pilot yelled, shaking his fist. "Slow down!"

"Sorry!" the captain yelled back as the big boat shuddered to a halt. "Stuck throttle."

"Oh, then no problem, sorry, mate," the pilot said. Superstition brightened. "Is that a submarine?" she said, pointing to the stern. The wind-burned captain gave a thumbs-up. "It's a deep-ocean submersible," he said. "*Stirred*'s the name. I'm Raider."

"Fantasi," she lied. "With an i."

"Nice to meet you, Fantasi," Raider said. "We're treasure hunters, sailing the briny deep for doubloons and plunder. What's your line? Yachting? Movies? Finance?"

She thought about that and thought about Jimmy.

"Pest control," she said. "I hope your seas are gentle, Captain . . ."

The Zodiac resumed course for the sleek white yacht on the horizon. Fifteen minutes later they were near enough to read the name on its stern:

TISIPHONE
ST. THOMAS, USVI

She shook her head, chuckling. Only Jerome Jerome could have found such a perfect boat, and only Jerome Jerome would wear a suit, tie, and brogues aboard her.

"Any problems?" he said as she climbed aboard.

"Yeah, Commodore," she smirked. "Yachts demand shorts and Topsiders."

"You have me confused with someone who approves of casual Friday," Jerome said, cocking his head at her proffered hand. "What's this?"

"Jimmy's cigarette lighter," Superstition said, shaking it till the Scripto Vu-Lighter's fishing fly and hook bobbed in the transparent base. "His favorite good luck charm. Don't say I never gave you anything."

Jerome flicked it alive. Watched the flame dance in the buffeting breeze. Seemed very pleased to receive it. "Thanks," he said, slipping it into his pocket. "Did he suffer?"

"Not near enough."

"They never do," the CIA rifleman said.

"Let's get back to port," Jerome said. "We've got planes to catch and bad guys to fillet."

"Amen," Superstition said, thinking of her mother.

As the great white yacht turned into the embers of the sun . . .

Painting them orange.

Real **FURY**

This is a work of fiction, hatched entirely by my overly caffeinated brain.

But many scenes, particularly the flashbacks to World War Two and the Cold War, were inspired by real events. Some were fun. Most would scare any sane person half to death. All were fascinating, so I thought you'd be interested, too.

So, here are the things I found while looking up other things:

Oil rig disappears: British Petroleum's *Deepwater Horizon* exploded in the Gulf of Mexico on April 10, 2010. Two hundred million gallons of crude oil and tons of methane gas were fire-hosed into the Gulf and its shorelines. The globby and highly toxic crude killed jobs, businesses, birds, fish, and animals. Complete recovery of the Gulf will take years.

Innocents lost: The drama of the spill overshadowed the fact that eleven workers died horribly that night. We remember the fireball and the whiny CEO and the oil-streaked pelicans but not the names of the dead. Here they are, for the record: Jason Anderson, Aaron Burkeen, Donald Clark, Stephen Curtis, Gordon Jones, Roy Kemp, Karl Kleppinger, Keith Manuel, Dewey Revette, Shane Roshto, and Adam Weise. Rest in peace, good people.

Gassing the deep blue sea: In the late 1960s, the United States military crammed a dozen mothballed freighters—the storied Liberty ships, which supplied Allied troops with everything from beans to bullets during World War Two—with obsolete munitions, including the world's deadliest chemical, VX nerve gas. The ships were towed several miles off our shores and then sent to the briny deep on the scientific theory of "out of sight, out of mind." The program even had a catchy name: Operation CHASE, for "Cut Holes And Sink 'Em."

Why'd we do it, then? The idea was noble enough: *Poison gas is barbaric (and besides, we've got nukes!) so let's get rid of it.* But dumping it into the global water supply was, in retrospect, ill-considered. Nowadays, we safely neutralize our industrial and military poisons. But that technology wasn't available when President Nixon convinced the world to abandon its chemical and biological weapons programs and deep-six its inventories. So into the sea it went.

View the Vu: On a lighter note, readers of a certain age—like me—may remember my bad guy's good luck charm: the Scripto Vu-Lighter. The flint-wheel cigarette lighter was an icon of the 1960s, with its body molded from transparent material to show off the fishing fly and hook, advertising logo, or pinup girl bobbing in the lighter fluid. While less ubiquitous than the Zippo, it was far more kitschy.

Hitler was a weenie: Yes, *der Führer* owned the famed Eagle's Nest, that gorgeous alpine chalet on the peak of the Kehlstein Mountain that housed the Third Reich in southern Germany. (It was a fiftieth birthday present from Nazi pal Martin Bormann.) But Adolf was deathly afraid of heights, so he rarely visited.

Crime *does* pay: During World War Two, General Shiro Ishii of the Imperial Japanese Army conducted live experiments on thousands of innocent civilians at his Unit 731 human experimentation laboratory in Harbin, Manchuria. An estimated quarter million people were kidnapped and killed for Ishii's ghastly "medical research"—primarily Russians and Chinese but also American and British prisoners of war. The camp was nicknamed the "Asian Auschwitz," but Ishii remains far less familiar than his Nazi doppelgänger, Dr. Josef Mengele.

Crime *does* pay, Part II: When the war ended, America wanted ever-more-exotic weapons to hurl at its newest archvillain, the Soviet Union. Ishii possessed thousands of pages of data from his experiments, so General Douglas "I Shall Return" MacArthur arranged a war crimes pardon in exchange for Ishii moving to Maryland to work for Uncle Sam. Being no fool, Ishii agreed. He died of throat cancer at age 67—whether in Maryland or back home in Tokyo is uncertain, as the records are not definitive—without being charged with a single crime. His victims still disintegrate in the cold, bitter soils of Manchuria.

I'm a lumberjack, and I'm okay: Ishii nicknamed his human guinea pigs "logs of wood." Why? Because the civilian leaders of nearby Harbin were told the sprawling, one-hundred-fifty-building laboratory was a "water purification research center" that contained a large lumber mill. (There is no record of whether they actually believed that, but at the time, if a Japanese general insisted that the moon was made of cantaloupes, you agreed.) When Ishii's scientists and doctors needed test subjects, his soldiers went out and "felled more logs."

Cream or Dream? Superstition Davis's undercover outfit—microdress and stiletto heels—is the neon orange of a Creamsicle. (Or a bottle of Orange Crush, for those who prefer maximum sugary goodness.) But what makes a Creamsicle different from a Dreamsicle? The insides. Creamsicles are ice cream, Dreamsicles are ice milk. (*Were* ice milk; sadly, Dreamsicles are no longer manufactured.) The shell is the same, though: a tasty orange sherbet.

Fast and Furious: In 2009, the U.S. Justice Department decided it would be a swell idea for American gun dealers to sell arms to Mexico's narcotics cartels. The deep-cover sting would allow the Bureau of Alcohol, Tobacco, Firearms, and Explosives—the vaunted ATF—to trace the weapons and, when the time was right, arrest truckloads of *narco* warlords, using the guns as evidence. Problem was, ATF lost track, and an estimated 1,400 assault weapons vanished into the hands of the world's most violent criminal gangs.

Deadly consequences: Some of those weapons turned up at the murder scenes of American law enforcement officers, including that of Border Patrol agent Brian Terry, who was shot to death in Peck Canyon, Arizona, in December 2010. Two weapons from the Fast and Furious sales were found at the site. Peck Canyon, by the way, is fifteen miles north of the border, nearer to Rio Rico than Nogales. In my book, I made all references to Nogales in order to minimize the number of locations the reader has to remember. For those who know their southern Arizona geography, my apologies. Ditto for any other real-life mountain, stream, or highway that got moved to serve the demands of fictional entertainment.

A tip o' the cap to Bill Page, who graciously fact-checked my research. For more Real Fury with photos, maps, graphics, and links, please visit furybook.com or shanegericke.com.

ACKNOWLEDGMENTS

No man is an island; no man writes alone.
Especially me.
So I'd like to thank the people who helped scrub and polish this story to the high gloss that readers deserve. Please join me in applauding:

My legion of fans: That I actually have a legion delights me. Without you, I'd be typing into a digital black hole, which would be no fun. So thanks for purchasing and reading my books, sending me thoughtful (and occasionally scandalous!) e-notes, and showing up at my events and social media pages. You guys are the best, and I mean that most sincerely.

My editor: John Paine of John Paine Editorial Services helped separate wheat from chaff and did it with expertise and professionalism. Every author should have an editor who can point out a story's miscues so courteously that you thank him afterwards.

My agent: Bob Diforio of the D4EO Literary Agency is the world's best navigator through the churning seas of publishing. Thanks, Bob, for your help and continued wisdom.

Tantor Media: While I made up the story and typed it into the computer, this remarkable publishing house led by Kevin and Laura Colebank wrapped it in a neat, colorful package and rushed it to you via print, eBook, and audiobook. I particularly appreciate the efforts of Dave Brackley, Abbey Kent, Mike Campbell, Hilary Eurich, Ron Formica, Allan Hoving, Cassandra McNeil, Suzanne Mitchell, and John Molish. The look, from eye-grabbing cover to info-drenched maps and interiors, came from Jessica Daigle.

Tantor Audio: The audiobook version of *The Fury* was narrated by Robertson Dean, whose sterling voice perfectly conveys Superstition Davis and her merry band of marauders. It takes a remarkable actor to juggle such a vast range of characters, places, plotlines, accents, and emotions, and in my opinion, Dean is the very best.

My artists: Abbie Miller of StoriesFramed Photography shot the author photos, and Paul Cowan of Iconix.Biz designed my Web sites. Their artistry shines through.

My first readers: The sharp-eyed friends who read my first draft and suggested improvements. Led by Bill Page, the man I call "The Manuscript Whisperer" because of his uncanny talent for checking facts and finding typos, my first readers are Joshua Corin, Doug M. Cummings, Millie Hast, Kimberley Howe, Jan Page, David Robinson, Terry Rodgers, and Marianne Gericke Taylor. If an error crept through their firewalls, blame me, because I put it there in the first place. Then again, this *is* a work of fiction, so perhaps I deliberately inserted those "errors" so you could catch them and entertainment be further charmed and entertained. That's my story, and I'm sticking to it, anyway.

Author, Author! Bestselling thriller authors Steve Berry and David Morrell suggested a change in style that supercharged the pacing of this book, and I thank them for that sound advice. Douglas Preston, Gayle Lynds, and Jon Land were early sounding boards for my plot, and Joshua Corin, Doug M. Cummings, and Rebecca Cantrell provided invaluable feedback later on. Deepest thanks for all your help, *mis amigos*.

And last, but first: Jerrle M. Gericke, my wife of nearly four decades and partner-in-crime in life and writing: I love you.
Which says it all.

Abbie Miller, StoriesFramed Photography

About Shane Gericke

Bestselling novelist Shane Gericke is the author of *Torn Apart*, which was short-listed for the prestigious Thriller Award and named a Book of the Year by *Suspense* magazine. *RT Book Reviews* named his *Blown Away* the best debut mystery of the year. A bestseller in both print and eBooks, Shane's thrillers have been translated into German, Chinese, Turkish, and Slovak, allowing him to correspond with readers around the world. Shane, whose last name is pronounced YER-kee, spent twenty-five years as a newspaper editor, most prominently at the *Chicago Sun-Times*, before jumping into fiction. He keeps his hand in nonfiction by writing for digital media and trade magazines. Shane lives in the Chicago suburb of Naperville. Visit him at shanegericke.com.